A Conspiracy of Ravens

MW

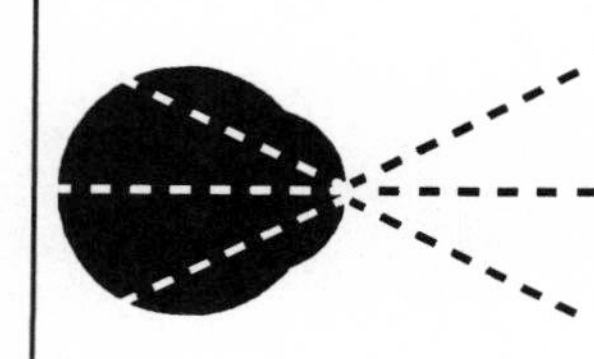

This Large Print Book carries the Seal of Approval of N.A.V.H.

A LADY TRENT MYSTERY, BOOK 2

A CONSPIRACY OF RAVENS

GILBERT MORRIS

THORNDIKE PRESS
A part of Gale, Cengage Learning

GALE
CENGAGE Learning™

Detroit • New York • San Francisco • New Haven, Conn • Waterville, Maine • London

Scripture quotations are from the King James Version of the Bible.
Thorndike Press, a part of Gale, Cengage Learning.

Thorndike Press® Large Print Christian Historical Fiction.
The text of this Large Print edition is unabridged.
Other aspects of the book may vary from the original edition.
Set in 16 pt. Plantin.
Printed on permanent paper.

LIBRARY OF CONGRESS CATALOGING-IN-PUBLICATION DATA

Morris, Gilbert.
A conspiracy of ravens / by Gilbert Morris.
p. cm. — (Thorndike Press large print Christian historical fiction) (A Lady Trent mystery ; bk. 2)
ISBN-13: 978-1-4104-1757-2 (alk. paper)
ISBN-10: 1-4104-1757-3 (alk. paper)
1. Aristocracy (Social class)—England—Fiction. 2. Women private investigators—England—Fiction. 3. Large type books. I. Title.
PS3563.O8742C58 2009
813'.54—dc22 2009011859

Published in 2009 by arrangement with Thomas Nelson, Inc.

Printed in the United States of America
1 2 3 4 5 6 7 13 12 11 10 09

A Conspiracy of Ravens

One

October, the harbinger of winter, had fallen upon England. A cold, blustery day swept across London and the many houses that bordered the city itself. Lady Serafina Trent stared out the window, and the gloom of the day dampened her spirit. The enormous oaks seemed to be spectres raising skeletal limbs toward the sky. She was a striking woman of twenty-seven with strawberry blonde hair and violet eyes. Her face was squarish, and her mouth had a sensuous softness. She was not a woman who paid a great deal of attention to her appearance, her beauty naturally elegant.

As she looked out over the grounds, a fleeting memory came to her as she thought of how she had come, as a young bride, to Trentwood House. She remembered the joy and the anticipation that had been hers when she had married Charles Trent, but then a trembling, not caused by the temperature, shook her. She thought of her husband now dead and buried in the family cemetery and then forced the thought away.

Serafina's eyes lingered on the grounds of Trentwood, the ancestral estate of the Trents, but now the grass was a leprous grey, the trees had dropped their leaves, and the death of summer took away the beauty of the world. Serafina suddenly turned and, with a quick movement, walked away from the window and toward the large table where her son, David, sat in a chair made especially for him. The blaze in the fireplace sent out its cheerful popping and cracking, and myriads of fiery sparks flew upward through the chimney in a magic dance.

The heat radiated throughout the room as Serafina took a seat beside her son. She glanced around, and once again old memories came — but this time more pleasant ones. This was the room that she had persuaded Charles to give her as a study, and it was lined with the artifacts of the anatomy trade. A grinning skeleton, wired together, stood at attention across the room. She and her father had built it when she was only thirteen, and after her marriage it had come with her to Trentwood. Charles had laughed at her, saying, "You love death more than life, Serafina."

Once again the bitter memory of her marriage to Charles Trent brought a gloom to Serafina. She quickly scanned the room, noting the familiar bookshelves stuffed with leather-bound books, the drawings of various parts of the human anatomy on the walls, the stuffed animals that she and her father had dissected and put back together again. A table stretched the length of one wall, covered with vials, glasses, and containers, and she remembered how she had labored in the world of chemistry during her early years at Trentwood.

"Mum, I can't do these fractions!"

Serafina smiled and put her arm around David. At the age of seven he had some of her looks — her fair hair complemented by dark blue eyes that had just a touch of aquamarine. He was small, but there was the hint of a tall frame to come.

"Of course you can, David."

"No, I can't," David complained, and as he turned to her, she admired the smooth planes of his face, thinking what a handsome young man he would be as he grew older. She saw also that instead of figures on the sheet of paper before him, he had drawn pictures of strange animals and birds. He had a gift for drawing, she knew, but now she shook her head saying, "You haven't been working on fractions. You've been drawing birds."

"I'd rather draw birds than do these old fractions, Mum."

Serafina had learnt from experience that David had inherited neither her passion for science nor the mathematical genes of his grandfather, Septimus. He was intrigued more by fanciful things than numbers and hard facts, which troubled Serafina.

"David, if you want to subtract a fraction from a whole number, you simply turn one of the whole numbers to a fraction. You change this number five to four, and that gives you a whole number. Now you want to subtract one-fourth from that. How many fourths are there in a whole number?"

"I dunno, Mum."

Serafina shook her head slowly and insisted, "You must learn fractions, David."

"I don't like them."

David suddenly gave her an odd, secretive look that she knew well. "What are you thinking, Son?"

"May I show you something I like?"

Serafina sighed. "Yes, I suppose you may."

David jumped up and ran to the desk. He opened a drawer and took something out. It was, Serafina saw, a book, and his eyes were alight with excitement when he showed it to her. "Look, it's a book about King Arthur and his knights of the Round Table."

Serafina took the book and opened it. On the first page she read, "To my friend David," and it was signed "Dylan Tremayne." "Dylan gave you this book?"

"Yes. Ain't it fine? It was a present, and he gave me his picture too." David reached over and pulled an image from between the pages of the book. "Look at it, Mum. It looks just like him, don't it now?"

Serafina stared at the miniature painting of Dylan Tremayne, and, as always, she was struck by the good looks of the man who had come to play such a vital part in her life. She studied the glossy black hair with the lock over the forehead as usual, the steady wide-spaced and deep-set eyes, and then the wedge-shaped face, the wide mouth, the mobile features. *With those beautiful eyes, he's almost too handsome to be a man.*

The thought touched her, and she remembered how only recently it had been Tremayne who had helped her to free her brother, Clive, from a charge of murder. She remembered how at first she had resented Tremayne for everything that he was, all which ran against the grain for the Viscountess of Radnor. Whereas she herself was logical, scientific, and reasonable, Dylan was fanciful, filled with imagination, and a fervent Christian, believing adamantly that miracles were not a thing of the past. She was also disturbed by the fact that although she had given up on romance long ago, she had felt the stirrings of attraction for this actor who was so different from everything that she believed.

She had tried to think of some way to curtail Dylan's influence on David, for she felt it was unhealthy — but it was very difficult. David was wild about Dylan, who spent a great deal of time with him, and Serafina was well aware that her son's affection for Tremayne was part of his latent desire for a father.

Firmly Serafina said, "David, this book isn't true. It's made up, a storybook. It's not like a dictionary where words mean certain things. It's not like a book of mathematics where two plus two is always four. It isn't even like a history book when it gives the date of a famous person's birth — those are facts."

David listened but was restless. Finally he interrupted by saying, "But, Mum, Dylan says these are stories about men who were brave and who fought for the truth. That's not bad, is it?"

"No, that's not bad, but they're not real men. If you must read stories about brave men, you need to read history."

"Dylan says there was a King Arthur once."

"Well, Dylan doesn't know any such thing. King Arthur and his knights are simply fairy tales, and you'd do well to put your mind on things that are real rather than things that are imaginary." But even as Serafina spoke, she saw the hurt in David's eyes, and her own heart smoldered. "We'll talk about it later," she said quickly. "Are you hungry?"

"Yes!"

"You're always hungry." Serafina laughed and hugged him.

"Dylan says he's going to come and see me today. Is that all right?"

"Yes, I suppose so. Come along now. Let's go see what Cook has made for us."

The dining room was always a pleasure to Serafina, and as she entered it she ran her eyes over it quickly. The table and sideboard were Elizabethan oak, solid and powerful, an immense weight of wood. The carved chairs at each end of the table had high backs and ornate armrests. The dark green curtains were pulled back now, and pictures adorned the walls. It was a gracious room and very large; the table was already laden with rich food set out on exquisite linen. Silver gleamed discreetly under chandeliers fully lit to counteract the gloom of the day.

"You're late, Daughter. You missed out on the blessing."

The speaker, Septimus Isaac Newton, at the age of sixty-two managed to look out of place in almost any setting. He was a tall, gangling man over six feet with a large head and hair that never seemed to be brushed as a result of his running his hand through it. His sharp eyes were a warm brown and held a look of fondness as he said, "David, I'm about to eat all the food."

David laughed and shook his head. "No, you won't, Grandfather. There's too much of it."

Indeed, the table was covered with sandwiches, many of them thinly sliced cucumber on brown bread. There were cream cheese sandwiches with chopped chives and smoked salmon mousse. White bread sandwiches flanked these. Smoked ham, eggs, mayonnaise with mustard and cress, and grand cheeses of all sorts complemented the meal as did scones, fresh and still warm with plenty of jams and cream, and finally cake and exquisite French pastries. Serafina led David to the chair, and James Barden, the butler, helped her into her own, then stepped back to watch the progress of the meal.

As Serafina helped David pile food onto his plate, she listened to her father, who chose mealtime to announce the scientific progress taking place in the world.

"I see," Septimus said, "that London architects are going to enlarge Buckingham Palace to give it a south wing with a ballroom a hundred and ten feet long."

"That's as it should be. The old ballroom is much too small."

The speaker was Lady Bertha Mulvane, the widow of Sir Hubert Mulvane and the sister of Septimus's wife, Alberta. She was a heavyset woman with blunt features and ate as if she had been starved.

"I'd love to go to a ball there," Aldora Lynn Newton said. She was a beautiful young girl with auburn hair flecked with gold, large well-shaped brown eyes, and a flawless complexion. An air of innocence glowed from her, though she would never be the beauty of her older sister. By some miracle of grace, she had no resentment toward Serafina.

Lady Bertha shook her head. "If you don't choose your friends with more discretion, Dora, I would be opposed to letting you go to any ball."

Aldora gave her aunt a half-frightened look, for the woman was intimidating. "I think my friends are very nice."

"You have no business letting that policeman call on you, that fellow Grant."

Indeed, Inspector Matthew Grant had made the acquaintance of the Newton family only recently. He had been the detective in charge of the case against Clive Newton. After the case was successfully solved, and the murderer turned out to be the superintendent of Scotland Yard, it had been assumed that Grant would take the superintendent's place. And Bertha Mulvane would be happy enough to receive him as Superintendent Grant.

Serafina could not help saying, "Inspector Grant was invaluable in helping get Clive out of prison."

"He did little enough. It was you and that actor fellow who did all the work solving that case."

"No, Inspector Grant's help was essential," Serafina insisted. She saw Lady Mulvane puff up and thought for an instant how much her aunt looked like an old, fat toad at times. She saw also that her aunt had taken one of the spoons and slipped it surreptitiously into her sleeve. "It's one thing to entertain the superintendent of Scotland Yard, but a mere policeman? Not at all suitable!"

Septimus said gently, "Well, Bertha, that was a political thing. Inspector Grant should have gotten the position, but politics gave it to a less worthy man."

Lady Bertha did not challenge this but devoured another sandwich. She ate, not with enjoyment, but as if she were putting food in a cabinet somewhere to be eaten at a future time.

Serafina's mother, Alberta, was an attractive woman with blonde hair and mild blue eyes. She was getting a little heavier now in her early fifties, but had no wrinkles on her smooth face. Her hands showed the rough, hard upbringing she'd had, for she came from a poor family. Septimus had not been rich when they had met, and she had pushed him into becoming a doctor and later into the research that had made him wealthy and famous. "Perhaps Bertha is right, Aldora."

"Of course I'm right!" Bertha snapped. "And you, Serafina, I'd think you'd finally gotten some common sense."

"I'm glad to hear you think so, Aunt. What brings you to this alarming conclusion?" Serafina smiled, noting that her aunt had slipped one of the silver saltshakers into the large sleeve of her coat. She well knew that Bertha Mulvane's own house was furnished with items that had somehow mysteriously disappeared from Trentwood House.

"Why, the fact that you have a suitor who's worthy of you."

"I'm not aware that I had such a suitor."

"Now don't be foolish, Serafina. Sir Alex Bolton is so handsome, and he has a title."

Serafina shook her head, picked up a cheese sandwich, and took a bite of it. "He's not calling on me. I danced with him once at a ball last week."

"But he's coming to dinner next week," Alberta said, a pleased expression on her face. "And, of course, I know that he's coming to see you."

"Oh, he'd be such a catch!" Bertha exclaimed.

Septimus looked up from his paper. "He's poor as a church mouse," he said firmly. "He lost most of his money in bad investments and gambling."

"Oh, you're wrong, Septimus," Bertha said. "He owns a great plantation in Ireland."

"I've heard he owns some forty acres of bog land, good for nothing," Septimus said, then he turned to his grandson and smiled. "David, what are you going to do today?"

"Dylan's coming. We're going to trap some rabbits. He knows how to snare them."

Bertha's face was the picture of disgust. Her neck seemed to swell, and she barely spat out the words. "I have no doubt he's a poacher." She turned and said, "I would think you might choose your son's companions more carefully, Serafina."

Serafina said calmly, "You didn't object to Dylan when he was helping me get Clive out of a murder charge."

Since Bertha had no defense for this, she left the room in a huff. David leaned over and whispered, "She stole a spoon, Mum."

"I know. Just don't pay any attention to her, David."

The driver, a small red-faced man with oversized hands, pulled his horse up, and the hansom cab stopped. Dylan leapt out and tossed the driver a shilling, which he caught adeptly.

"Why, thank you, suh. Shall I wait fer you?"

"No, I'm not sure how long I'll be."

The driver did not look like one who would attend plays, but he surprised Dylan by saying, "I seen you in a play. 'Hamlet' you wuz called. You wuz great in that play."

"Why, thank you, Asa."

"Wot are you in now?"
"At the moment nothing. I'm thinking about retiring."
"No, sir, you mustn't do that," the cabby insisted. "You'd be depriving folks of sumfing good."
Dylan laughed. "Not really." He reached into his pocket, drew out a notepad, and wrote something on it quickly. "Give this to the fellow who takes tickets at the Old Vic tonight. It'll get your whole family in to see the play."
"Thank you, sir."
Dylan nodded and turned to the door. He ascended the steps and reached out for the knocker when the door opened and David came running out. "Hello, Dylan. Let's go catch rabbits."
But Serafina appeared immediately behind David and said, "You can't go into the woods wearing those clothes. It's cold." She turned and said, "Louisa, take David and put some warm clothes on him. Be sure he wears his grey coat."
"Yes, ma'am," Louisa said, turning her eyes on Dylan. "Good morning, Mr. Tremayne," she said. She was the prettiest of the maids, parlour maids being chosen for their good looks. She had sparkling green eyes, red hair, and a complexion like rich cream.

"Well, good morning, Louisa. I don't suppose you'd want to go rabbit catching with us, yes?"

"Oh, you are a one, sir!"

"Go along, Louisa," Serafina said shortly. She did not miss the adoring look Louisa gave Dylan. Most women, she had noticed, were susceptible to his good looks, and indeed, she did have to admit that he looked fine. He was exactly six feet tall and weighed a hundred and eighty-five pounds, and as he pulled off his hat, a lock of his glossy black hair fell over his forehead. He smiled at her, showing perfect white teeth, most unusual in England in 1857, and she could understand women being attracted to him.

"I must talk with you, Dylan. Please come to the sitting room."

"Certainly."

As soon as they reached the room, Serafina closed the door, then turned to him saying, "I've said something along these lines before, but I'm concerned about the books that you're giving David and the stories you tell him."

"Why, there's sorry I am, Lady Trent. I thought there would be no harm in the stories."

"I saw the book about King Arthur and the knights of the Round Table." She shook her head, and her lips drew into a displeased line. "I must ask you to do such things no more. If you must give him a book, give them to me first before he sees them."

"Well, of course, if you say so," Dylan said. There was a puzzled light in his cornflower blue eyes. "But, after all, most English schoolboys learn about King Arthur. It's a fine work of art."

"It's all fancy and make-believe. There was no such person as King Arthur, and those perfect knights that roam around rescuing maidens in distress simply don't exist."

"Oh, I think they might, a few of them anyway."

"I'm not going to argue about this," Serafina said firmly. She had been thinking about the problem ever since she had seen the book, and now her back was straight and a slight flush tinted her cheeks. "I'm not going to have you teaching David things that are fanciful and aren't true. If you can't abide with this, Dylan, it would be better if you didn't come for another visit."

A silence fell over the two of them, and suddenly Serafina felt something like fear. She had not realized how much she had come to depend on Dylan, not only to be a companion to her son, but in the struggle to free her brother, Clive, the two had grown very close together indeed. She felt a sudden anger that she could feel so strongly for a man, and indeed she had not since she had fallen in love with Charles Trent. She started to mitigate her statement, but she could think of no way to do it. The two stood there awkwardly until David came running in with his grey coat on. "Let's go, Mr. Dylan!"

"All right, old man. Let's go indeed." Dylan smiled at the boy, putting his hand on his shoulder. "You're going to be hunting with the finest rabbit trapper in England."

Serafina watched as the two left, and something about the way David held Dylan's hand and looked up with such an expression of absolute trust moved her so that she turned away abruptly. As she ascended the stairs to her room, she thought, *I was too abrupt with Dylan. I didn't really mean it. I'll have to make it right with him.*

Albert Givins, the coachman at Trentwood, was a small Cockney. He was an expert with horses and would not permit anyone to touch one of them. He turned now to Serafina while holding the bridle of the chestnut mare and smiled. "I've got 'er all settled for you, milady, and a fine fettle she's in. You'd better be careful she doesn't give you a 'ard time."

"Thank you, Albert." Serafina patted the neck of the mare and dodged as the horse made a move at her with her head. "Don't you dare bite me, Sadie," she said.

Albert studied his mistress with admiration. She was wearing a black riding skirt, and underneath the tailored coat she wore a blue blouse. A small tricorne hat sat on her head, and the crisp breeze brought colour to her cheeks. Albert suddenly turned and said, "Ma'am, you mustn't go in the south pasture today."

"Why not, Albert? That's the quickest way to the riding path."

"I know, but the men 'ave put that new bull into the pasture, and 'e's a bad 'un! More like a bull them Spaniards fight than one we'd like to breed to our 'erd."

"I'll be careful, Albert." Serafina started to mount when she heard her name called. She turned to see David approaching, his eyes flashing, and he was shouting, "We got two rabbits in snares, Mum, and I made one of the snares myself."

As David approached, she said, "Go show them to Danny. He'll clean them for you."

She motioned toward Danny Spears, the groom, who was in front of the stable cleaning some of the gear.

As soon as David was gone, she turned and said, "I wanted to talk to you, Dylan."

"Yes. What is it then?"

Serafina saw that Dylan was expecting a lecture, and she found she was having trouble. "Walk with me along the fence." The two walked away, leaving Givins to hold the mare, and Dylan said nothing. She knew he was casting a glance at her from time to time, and finally she stopped and turned to him. "I know you think I spoke to you rudely this morning, but you must understand, Dylan. It's hard for a woman to raise a son without a husband. David misses a father, and he's put you in that role."

"He's a fine boy, him," Dylan said, his speech revealing his boyhood in Wales. "Very proud of him you must be."

"Yes, I am, and he is a good boy. But I'm concerned about his future."

"You're afraid I'll make an actor out of him or a poet or something fanciful like that, is it?"

Serafina knew that Dylan Tremayne had a quick mind. He had jumped immediately at the thought and spoken as if it had come from her own mind. "It's not that exactly," she said, "but when I was younger I had some fanciful ideas much like you do now." She hesitated then said, "I found out that fancy doesn't last, and it's not real."

"Is it people you're talking about now?"

Indeed, colour rose in her cheeks, for she had been thinking of her husband, Charles. She'd had romantic notions about him as big as the Alps, and they had all come tumbling down when she had found out what kind of a man he really was. Since that time she had been afraid to trust anything that could not be verified in a laboratory or on a sheet of paper.

"I suppose it's partly my father who taught me to trust reason and logic and things that could be weighed and measured in a laboratory."

"Well, those things are necessary, but there is beauty in the world. Look at that." Dylan waved at a skylark that was making his way across the sky above them. "What a fellow he is! I'm sure there are people who can describe the mechanics of his flight, how he does it, but, Lady Serafina, I'm more interested in the beauty of it and the songs that he sings. Listen to that."

Serafina followed the flight of the skylark and was trying to prepare an answer when she suddenly heard Danny Spears cry out, "David, get out of there!"

Serafina whirled and saw that David had gone into the pasture where the bull was kept. With one quick turn of her head, she heard the sound of hooves and turned quickly to see the red bull Albert had warned her about heading straight toward David. Her heart seemed to stop, and she cried out, "David — !"

She saw at once that there was no time. Albert was too far from the fence, and Danny was even farther. She started running, knowing it was hopeless, but she was surprised as Dylan ran as fleetly as a deer and hurdled the fence using his arm as a fulcrum. He ran straight toward the bull, ripping off his coat as he went, and when the bull was no more than ten feet away from David, he shouted and waved the coat at the huge animal. Serafina saw the bull's attention turn from David to Dylan. The bull whirled quickly, raising dust in the pasture, and made for Dylan. Dylan threw the coat at the bull, hoping, she thought, to throw it over his face, but it missed.

And then she saw the massive horns of the bull swing in an arc and, to her horror, strike Dylan in the side. He was lifted like a bag of feathers and rolled in the dirt. Serafina knew she screamed, and she ran forward and saw that David had slipped through the fence to safety. She turned back toward Dylan and watched with terrifying dread.

Serafina had never known such a sickening feeling. The bull was savaging Dylan, who was trying to fend him off, but the wicked horns swung, and she saw blood leave a red track along his left leg. "Dylan!" she cried as she ran forward but had to stop at the fence.

Suddenly Danny was running. He held a shotgun in his hand and slipped through the fence as if he were greased. The bull swung his horns again, and the blunt side caught Dylan in the head. He lay still. But when the bull lowered his head, she heard the shotgun explode. The charge caught the bull in the nose, and he bellowed as he backed off. Danny, small but bold as a lion, ran forward and let the bull have the other charge. He bellowed again, turned, and fled, his hooves like miniature thunder on the hard turf.

Serafina slipped through the gate and ran to Dylan's side. She had seen the terrible blows, and blood was seeping out of a wound on his left leg. When she held his head, she felt a knot beginning to swell.

She looked up and said, "You were wonderful, Danny!"

"I keep this shotgun to run the crows away. It was only bird shot," Danny said, his eyes wide.

"Is he all right, Mum?"

Serafina turned to see Albert Givins and Peter Grimes, the footman, coming. She called out, "Get a door and carry him to the small laboratory."

She pulled Dylan's head up and knew that the horns could have penetrated his body in other places, even if no blood showed yet. She was holding his head tightly to her breast when she heard David say, "Is . . . is he going to die, Mum?"

"No, he won't die." She sat there until the men came carrying a door, and all together they picked up the still form of Dylan Tremayne and placed him on it, then looked at Lady Trent for instructions. "We'll take him to the outside laboratory," she said.

Danny Spears swallowed. "But that's where you take the dead people to cut them up."

"There are instruments there." She turned to her son. "David, run quick to the house and get your grandfather."

"I'll get him right now!"

She walked beside the makeshift stretcher

as the four took the injured Tremayne toward the small building that her father used for autopsies, among other things. She tasted a bitterness in her spirit. *I said awful things to him and told him not to come back!* She had suddenly an overwhelming impulse to cry out to God to save Dylan, but she was out of the habit of prayer and not a word would come to her lips.

Two

If Serafina Trent, the Viscountess of Radnor, prided herself on anything, it was her calm, reasonable, and logical approach to all matters, no matter how minor. As she walked beside the wounded Tremayne, however, she found that her hands were unsteady and her mind was filled with a dread that she had never known. Glancing over her shoulders, she saw the bull at the far end of the pasture, and the thought of what the vicious animal might have done to David sickened her. Her son was her treasure on this earth, and the thought of his being savaged by the bull was more than she could bear.

She looked down. The wounded man was being borne by Albert Givins, the coachman, and Peter Grimes, the footman, with the help of two other male servants. As they walked, carefully carrying the burden toward the outside laboratory, Serafina forced herself to remain calm.

The outside laboratory was simply a rectangular, redbrick building some twenty feet by thirty-six, the walls pierced by several windows and covered by tile. It was separated from the house by a series of enormous yew trees, and Serafina moved ahead now toward the door. The men paused with their burden as she opened it and quickly turned on the gaslight. One quick look assured her that the table on which autopsies were conducted was the logical place. It was waist high and would make it easier to tend to Dylan's wounds. "Let me put something on that," she said to the men and quickly found several blankets. She made a pad out of them, working efficiently, then turned and said, "Bring him in and put him on this table."

The men moved carefully, and Serafina said, "Be as gentle as you can. He may have some broken bones."

"Yes, ma'am, so it be," Peter said. He and the other three men got a firm hold, and Peter said, "On the count of three we go. One. Two. Three."

Serafina could not help but notice that Dylan's face showed no response as he was lifted and placed on the blanket.

"That's very good."

"Wot else can we do, ma'am?" Albert asked.

She did not have time to answer, for David came running in, his face still pale and his voice unsteady. "Mum, Grandfather isn't here. He's gone to a meeting of the Royal Society in London."

She stood there uncertainly, and then Aldora came in, having followed Danny. "What is it? What's happened?" she cried.

"It's Dylan. He's been badly injured. He needs a doctor."

Aldora stared at the still form of Dylan and said, "Father's not here."

"I know. We'll have to get another doctor. Get someone to fetch Dr. Goldsmith as fast as he can."

"I'll do that, ma'am," Albert said quickly. He was a small man, having been a jockey at one time, and never lost his cockney accent. "I'll take the phaeton and the matched bays. They be the fastest."

"Hurry, Albert! Explain the situation to him and get him here as fast as you can."

"Yes, ma'am. I'll be quick as the wind."

As Albert ran through the door, Serafina turned to see David, who was staring fixedly at the still body of Dylan Tremayne. His lips were trembling, and he was so pale she feared for him. Going to him quickly, she put her arm around him and said, "You don't need to be in here."

"It's my fault."

"No, of course it's not your fault. It was an accident." Looking quickly up at Aldora, she added, "Dora, take David to the house, and don't let anybody else come here. There's no time for visiting. Oh, and tell Mrs. Fielding to get the small parlour made up into a bedroom."

Aldora blinked with surprise. "Into a bedroom?"

"Yes, get a bed in it. Get some of those chairs and couches out."

"I'll do it myself," Aldora said, but she cast an apprehensive look toward the body of the wounded man. "Is he . . . is he going to die?"

"No, of course not. Now, David, you go with Dora, and I'll come and tell you after I've treated Mr. Dylan's wounds."

"Yes, Mum."

"Is there anything else we can do, ma'am?" Peter asked.

"After I've treated him, I'll want you and the others to carry him into the house to the small parlour."

"Yes, ma'am, we'll be outside in case you need us."

"Thank you, Peter."

Serafina did not watch the men leave. Her mind was already bent on the job that was before her. Going back to Dylan, the thought came to her, *I've taken care of dead bodies on this very table, but I wish father were here.* Taking a firm grip on herself, she went back and began to examine Dylan. Blood was running down from his scalp onto the table. A gust of relief came to her lips as she saw that it was a minor cut that would require only a few stitches. A quick examination revealed that his shirt was torn, and his left side was bleeding profusely. His left trouser leg was soaked with blood, and through the rip in the cloth she could see the jagged wound left by the tip of the horn.

She moved quickly across the room, brought several instruments back on a tray, and set them down on the table. With quick, efficient movements, she cut the shirt off rather than try to unbutton it. When she pulled it from him as gently as she could, he groaned slightly as she moved him. She pressed cloth bandages against the wound in his left side, and as she did, Dylan struck out involuntarily, uttering a small cry.

Quickly she put her hand on his forehead and looked down into his eyes. "Can you hear me, Dylan?"

A long moment's pause, and then slowly

his eyes opened, and he whispered, "Yes."

"You've been badly hurt. You must lie very still."

"What's wrong . . . with my side?"

"I'm looking right now. You have a bad cut. Does it hurt when you breathe?"

Dylan took a deep breath and grimaced. "It feels like somebody . . . kicked me."

As well as she could, Serafina examined the ribs. "I don't think they're broken," she said, "but they may be cracked. You'll have to lie very still while I clean your cuts."

She worked quickly and efficiently and noticed that he had turned his head to one side and was watching her. "Is David all right?"

"Yes. He's fine. Father's not here, so I sent for Dr. Goldsmith. But I need to get these wounds cleaned up. We don't want anything to get infected."

Serafina cleansed his side with alcohol and then put a bandage on it. No matter how gently she moved, she saw him flinch as she touched his side.

"You have a cut in your head. One of the horns probably struck you there." She held up two fingers and said, "How many fingers do you see?"

"Two."

"Follow my hand with your eyes." She

moved her hand up and down and then from side to side and said with relief, "You don't have a concussion."

"How did I get out of there?"

"It was Danny. He grabbed a shotgun loaded with bird shot and drove the bull away."

"Good thing he did."

"Very good thing indeed. Now, I've got to get your trousers off."

Dylan's eyes opened wide. "What?" he gasped.

"I've got to get your trousers off. Lie still." She took the scissors and began cutting at the cuff. As she did, Dylan protested vociferously. "You can't do that!"

"This is no time for modesty, Dylan. You have a bad wound in this leg."

Dylan said nothing, and she quickly cut the trousers away and pulled them off. "That's a bad cut. It's going to need stitches."

"Can't you give me something to cover up with?"

"Don't be foolish, Dylan," she admonished him but took a large piece of cloth and handed it to him. "Here."

She began to clean the leg, and once when the towel slipped off, he grabbed at it, gasping at the pain in his ribs.

"I didn't know actors were so modest," she said with a partial smile, then looked at the cut and shook her head. "If that horn had caught you an inch or so to the right, it would have been death for you. There's a big artery that runs down the leg here. You would have bled to death before we could have gotten you here."

Dylan looked at her, and she met his eyes. "God was with me then," he said quietly.

"Yes, I think He was." Her statement surprised herself and Dylan as well, for she had never said so much about God before.

To cover her confusion, she whirled, went over to the medicine cabinet, and came back with a bottle. "This is ether," she said. "It'll put you to sleep."

He started to protest, but she shook her head. "It's going to be very painful sewing that leg up. Now lie still. You'll get sleepy and be gone almost at once. When you wake up, you'll be all treated." She put a cloth over the lower part of his face, dropped three drops onto it, and then watched carefully.

The use of ether was the greatest advancement to date in scientific medicine. It had been developed a few years earlier, and doctors no longer had to work at such a fast pace. Before the discovery of ether, when there was no such thing as putting someone to sleep, patients fought and jerked against the agony brought on by the knife to the point that a surgeon's most valuable asset was his ability to operate quickly. That had all changed with the discovery of ether. After an American surgeon, Dr. Crawford Long, operated on an etherized patient, the practice of medicine was revolutionized. Serafina watched closely, wishing someone were there to help her, but the wound was bleeding badly and needed attention immediately.

She worked deftly and quickly, for she had some experience with wounds like this, having assisted her father and watched him carefully.

As she worked, in one small corner of her mind, she thought of David and how he could have been the body on this table instead of Dylan. The thought of his death unsettled her, and she forced it out of her mind as she cleaned up the leg and began to put the stitches in.

Lady Bertha Mulvane was thrown forward as the horses came to an abrupt halt. "Henry, can't you drive more carefully?" she protested. She waited until the coachman jumped to the ground, opened the door, and lowered the step. As she got out, she began saying loudly, "I'm going to get another man if you can't do better, Henry. You jostle me around like I was a load of potatoes."

Henry Twiller was accustomed to this, and nothing changed in his face. "Yes, Lady Bertha, I'll be more careful," he said wearily.

Bertha was not through with her sermon, but she stopped suddenly when another carriage pulled up. It caught her eye, for it was one of the new expensive carriages, a Victorian, named after Queen Victoria, of course. She watched as the driver pulled the horses to a stop, and a groom came up to take them. Recognition came, and she called out loudly, "Sir Alex! Sir Alex!"

The man who turned to her was tall and well-built. Sir Alex Bolton had hair the colour of straw, and his eyes were half hooded, a pale shade of blue. He was wearing the latest fashion — tight-fitting grey trousers and a blue waistcoat.

"Good afternoon, Sir Alex."

"I'm sorry, your name escapes me. I'm very bad with names."

"I'm Lady Bertha Mulvane, the oldest sister of Mrs. Newton."

"Why, of course, I remember you, Lady Mulvane." He glanced toward the house saying, "I'm just leaving my card. I would like to call on the family if I may."

"Why, they'll be so happy to see you, Sir Alex. Come in at once."

Lady Mulvane led the way, and as soon as she stepped in, she said to Daisy, a housemaid, "Is Lady Trent at home?"

"Oh, yes, ma'am, but there's been a lot of trouble."

"I didn't ask you about that. I just simply want to know where Lady Trent is."

"She's in the small parlour, but —"

"That's enough, girl. Come along, Sir Alex. Lady Trent will be happy to see you."

"I feel like I'm intruding."

"Not at all. Come this way."

Bertha led the way down the long hallway and turned in toward the right. The door was shut, which was unusual. "This way, my dear sir."

"After you, ma'am."

Bertha gushed her thanks and then stepped inside the room, followed by Sir Alex. She paused, and for once Lady Bertha Mulvane was speechless.

She stared at the scene before her, and Sir Alex did the same.

"What in the world —" Bertha finally gasped. She was in shock, for the room was changed. The furniture had been removed, and a bed was placed beside a wall and a table beside it. What was even more shocking was the fact that a half-naked man sat on the side of the bed, and her niece, Lady Serafina Trent, was sitting beside him.

Serafina took the situation in at once. She had just prepared the bed and had asked Dylan to sit down while she checked the bandages to see if they were firm. He had put on a pair of linen drawers but wore nothing else. His chest had been tightly bandaged and his left leg as well. She had instructed him to sit there while she took his pulse and had sat down beside him to reach him more conveniently. She was amused by the shocked looks on Lady Bertha and Alex Bolton's faces and said quite calmly, "Good afternoon, Sir Alex." She knew that her aunt was desperate for her to marry into nobility, as if another title would help Lady Bertha's lineage.

Bolton was at a loss for words and could only say, "Ma'am . . ."

"I don't believe you've met my friend Mr. Dylan Tremayne. Mr. Tremayne is an actor, one of the rising stars in the world of the theatre. Mr. Tremayne, this is Sir Alex Bolton."

Bolton had no idea how to respond to the introduction. Actors were, of course, on the lowest scale in the social order — beneath the scales of most people, as a matter of fact. He finally inclined his head, and Dylan watched him, a curious smile touching his lips. "Happy it is I am to meet you, Sir Alex. How are you, Lady Bertha?"

Bertha's face turned red, and she demanded stridently, "What are you doing, Serafina?"

"Well, I was about to order tea for Mr. Tremayne. Perhaps you'd care to join us."

Bolton regained his wits. "It . . . ah, doesn't seem an opportune time, Lady Trent. Perhaps I could come another day."

"Oh, certainly. You must come back again. Will you show Sir Alex to the door, Lady Bertha?"

As the two left the room, Dylan turned and said, "Who was that fellow?"

"Oh, just a man who wants to marry me. Here, let me help you lie down." She assisted him in moving into a comfortable position and said, "I know you must be in pain. Those are terrible wounds."

"I've had worse, me."

"Here. I want you to take some of this. It'll make you sleepy, but it'll take the pain away. Dr. Goldsmith will be here soon, I'm sure."

"Why is he coming?"

"To check for other injuries." She looked down then, and a silence fell between the two of them. Finally she said, "Dylan, I'll never forget what you did. David would have been killed if . . ." Serafina paused.

"Well, we couldn't have that, could we now? The world can wag on without me, can't it? But not without David."

Serafina was caught by his words. "Why would you say that, Dylan?"

"Why, I'm nothing but a poor actor. That boy, he's going to be a very important man." He lay there for a while, and already the drug was affecting him. He spoke slowly and with some effort. "And, after all, Lady Trent, he's your son."

Serafina did not speak but saw his eyes close, and he began to breathe deeply. She struggled for a time to put away the awful and catastrophic result that might have come if Dylan had not been there, and her heart seemed to fill. At that moment she knew something about the nature of his emotional state, which she usually tried to avoid. This was not something she could put in a test tube, nor was it a matter of little concern to her. She thought of David, and his face came before her — the bright eyes, the fair hair so much like her own. She thought of his playing in the yard with

Napoleon, the enormous mastiff who guarded him like the crown jewels, and riding his horse, Patches. Despite herself, her eyes misted over. Suddenly, unable to contain herself, she reached forward and picked up Dylan's hand. She held it in both of hers and then kissed it, something she had never done in her entire life.

"Thank you, Dylan. I will never forget it," she whispered with a half sob.

As always when Inspector Matthew Grant approached Trentwood House, he felt a sense of apprehension. This feeling was otherwise unusual, for he had proven his physical courage time and again in his encounters with criminals. The word was out among the lawbreakers of London, "Don't try to bribe Grant. Stay away from him. He doesn't play games."

As he moved up the steps that led to the front door, Grant's mind went back to the first time he had come to this house. He had been in the company of Superintendent Winters. The two of them had come to interrogate Clive Newton, a suspect in the murder of a famous actress. Grant had a memory that was almost photographic. He could remember everything about that visit, but the clearest thing of all was his first sight of Aldora Newton. He did not need a painting or a daguerreotype; her features were imprinted on his mind. For one instant he stood there thinking of the woman he had come to love. He saw her auburn hair, which had a mere touch of gold, and the large, well-shaped brown eyes, the flawless complexion, and most of all, he thought of her shy, appealing manner. It was not the manner of many of the women in high society. She flushed easily, and Matthew Grant found this charming.

Shaking off his nervousness, Grant knocked firmly on the door and was greeted by Ellie Malder, the tweeny housemaid. "I suppose you've come to see Miss Aldora, Inspector."

"Yes, I have, Ellie. I don't have an appointment."

"Never you mind." Ellie smiled. She was an attractive girl of fifteen with her best feature being her large, brown eyes. "Come inside, Inspector. I'll see if Miss Aldora is available."

"Thank you."

Stepping into the foyer, Grant once again felt his apprehensions coming back. He came from a poor background and had known hardship most of his life. The ornate furniture, decorations, and paintings, and the gleaming tile floor of the foyer, somehow depressed him. Dora appeared at the top of the stairs, and he watched her as she came down quickly. She smiled for him and held out her hands, which he took. They were soft yet firm at the same time.

"I should have asked permission to come, Miss Aldora."

"Oh, don't bother about that, Matthew. I'm glad you came by. Come along. I sent Ellie to make some tea, and we'll have it in the large parlour." It was just a chance remark on Aldora's part, but somehow it struck Grant. *The large parlour,* which meant there were *two* parlours, while Grant had grown up in a home with no parlour at all. As he followed her down the hallway and turned into the room, he thought suddenly of what he had once read in a book on astronomy. The nearest star to our own solar system was Alpha Centauri — which was millions of miles away. He felt that his distance from Aldora's world was at least this far.

"Sit down, and tell me what you've been doing."

"Oh, we've had several interesting cases," Matthew said. He began talking about some of them, for it was all he had to talk about with her. She had balls, fox hunts, and other such activities. Matthew Grant focused on only one thing in his life, and that was catching criminals and seeing that they went to jail or were hanged. He did not understand how she could be interested in such things, but somehow she was. She sat there with her eyes fixed on him, and when the tea came, there was a grace in the way she set about serving him. When he had sipped his tea from a delicate china cup, he asked, "How is Mr. Tremayne doing?"

"Oh, Dylan is doing so well! It's been two weeks now since the accident with that awful animal, and he's made rapid improvements."

"That's good to hear." He smiled and asked, "How do you like having a famous actor in the house, Miss Aldora?"

Dora smiled and shook her head. "Oh, he's ever so nice. He's so polite. All the servants just love him."

"I'll bet all the female servants are in love with him," Matthew said and watched the colour mount to her cheeks.

"Yes, I suppose they are. He is handsome."

"It's a good thing that bull's horns didn't catch him in the face. An actor's good looks are his stock in trade, I suppose."

"Yes. I thought about that."

They talked for some time about the accident, and finally Dora changed the subject. "I'm so sorry you weren't named superintendent. It was so *unfair!* Everyone thought you were going to get that position."

Actually the failure to be appointed to superintendent had cut deeply into Matthew Grant. He was next in line after Superintendent Winters, and when Winters had gone, he had expected to be promoted. He could not complain to Dora nor tell the complete truth, so he said simply, "A great deal of politics was involved. The new superintendent is Edsel Fenton. He has connections in high places."

"Do you think he's an able man?"

"Oh, very able."

"Well, do you like him, Matthew?"

Dora's use of his first name made Grant glow. "Not really. He's not a likable person, but he's fair enough, I suppose."

They talked as they drank tea and nibbled small pieces of jam cake. He was interrupted, however, when suddenly the door opened and Dora's aunt Bertha came in. The heavyset woman had blunt features. She felt that it was her duty to see that the Newton family maintained its place and kept the proper behaviour.

"What's this?" Bertha said loudly, her eyes fixed on Grant. "Sitting alone in a parlour in the dark?"

"We were just having tea, Aunt Bertha. Would you care to join us?"

"I must say we would never have had a thing like this happen in my day!" Bertha drew herself up and aimed her rather prominent nose at Matthew Grant. "It shows a lack of propriety and good taste. I'm surprised at you, Inspector, but then, you come from a world that doesn't understand what good manners are."

Grant had come to his feet, as had Aldora, when Bertha had begun her tirade, and now he bowed slightly and said, "I'm sorry if I have broken any of your rules, Lady Bertha."

"They're not my rules! They're the rules of good society, but I expect you wouldn't know about that."

"Aunt Bertha," Dora said, her eyes flashing, "you mustn't say such things!"

Bertha Mulvane, however, had much more to say. She was primed to deliver a long sermon on the bad manners of the lower class — in which she placed a lowly inspector from Scotland Yard. Aldora knew her aunt very well and said hurriedly, "The inspector has come to see Mr. Tremayne.

Come along, Inspector. I'll take you to his room."

Bertha glared at Grant and got in one parting shot. "You might buy a book on social etiquette, Inspector, and learn how to behave among the better classes."

A hot reply rose to Grant's lips, but he managed to shut it off. "I'll run out immediately, as soon as I leave here, and buy some books that will improve my behaviour."

Dora whispered as she led him down the hall, aware that Bertha was watching them go, "Don't pay any attention to her, Matthew. She's just an old grump!"

The small parlour that had been made into a bedroom for Dylan Tremayne was brightly illuminated by the sunlight that streamed in through the big windows on one wall. Dylan was sitting across a small table from David, and as he watched the small boy, he was fascinated, as he always was, by the workings of David Trent's active brain. He knew that Serafina did not like that David showed more interest in matters of the imagination than in science, but it pleased Dylan. He waited, watching the sunlight touch the boy's fair hair and thinking how much it looked like Serafina's with a distinctive curl.

David's dark blue eyes were touched with just a bit of aquamarine colour, and he was sitting on the edge of his seat, studying the board in front of him. Finally he reached out and moved one checker.

"Now, boy, are you sure that's what you want to do?"

"Yes."

Dylan laughed. "Well, that was the right move. You see, I have no place to go except to let you jump me. Here you are." Dylan pushed the disc forward and thought about how adept the boy was at draughts. "You know," he said, "I think that's three games in a row you've beaten me."

"You're just letting me win, aren't you?"

"Not a bit," Dylan protested. "You beat me fair and square. You know," he said, "the Americans call this game 'checkers.' "

"Do they?"

"Yes, indeed, they do. Americans are strange people. Everybody knows it ought to be called 'draughts.' "

"You beat me twice yesterday, Dylan."

"Well, it's good for a fellow to lose once in a while, see?"

"How can it be good to lose?"

"Why, you learn things from losing, David. The Bible says it's good for a man to lose."

David stared at the big man across the table from him. He had grown very fond of Dylan in the brief time he had known him, and he demanded again, "Why would it be good to lose?"

"Because losing is a part of life. It's how we learn to do things, don't you see?"

"No, I don't understand."

"Well, the first time we played draughts, you and I, you lost. But you learnt something from losing. You learnt something in that game. Every time you lose, you ask yourself, *Now why did I lose? What can I do next time to see that I don't?*" Dylan paused and looked David in the eye. "Let me ask you a question, David. Would you rather go to a party or a funeral?"

"I've never really been to a funeral, but I think I'd rather go to a party."

"Ah," Dylan said and sat back in his chair. His glossy black hair needed trimming, and a lock of it fell down over his forehead. His cornflower blue eyes were wide-spaced and deep-set, and his wide mouth was able to express his thoughts simply by a twist. Now he smiled and said, "The Bible says it's better to go to the house of mourning — that's the funeral — than it is to go to the house of feasting."

"I'd rather go to a feast."

"Most of us would, but you don't learn anything from partying. You learn from losing and having hard times. When I went in the Army, you think they gave me a soft bed and a maid to bring me food every day cooked especially for me? Not a bit of it, old man, not a bit! I slept on the floor, and I hate to tell you the things I had to eat. But it made a soldier out of me."

David listened intently then said, "Tell me a story, Dylan."

"Your mother doesn't like me to tell you stories, at least not the kind I know."

"I don't see why. They're fun."

Dylan was not ready to argue the point with a ten-year-old. "Now, listen to me. We're going to play a game, and you'll learn something from it."

David's eyes sparkled. "What kind of a game?"

"Come over here to this bed. Get up on it now, boy. That's the way. That's the lad!" Dylan moved to make room for David rather slowly, but he pulled his feet in, tucking them underneath his knees on the bed. "Now, I'm the captain of this ship, my name is Odysseus, and you're the crew."

"It takes more than one man to be the crew for a ship," David protested. "No ship has just a one-man crew."

"Well, you've got lots of mates there. Look," Dylan said, pointing to the empty space beside David, "there's Oscar. See him sitting right beside you? Look, he's got a black patch over his right eye. Probably lost it in a battle. His father was a blacksmith who made armor for kings. You see him now?"

Falling into the game, David laughed and said, "Yes, I see Oscar."

"Well, look on the other side of him. That's Punch. He was in prison for refusing to bow down to the king, but he escaped. He's a good sailor now."

David said, "Look, old Punch has a long scar on the side of his face."

"Now you're seeing it, you are." The two went on, David's eyes bright, and he laughed from time to time, but when his mother came in, he suddenly looked guilty.

"What are you doing in that bed, David?"

"It's not a bed, Mum, it's a warship. Dylan's the captain, and I'm the crew. This is Punch, and this is Oscar, and that's Jarrell sitting over there. Come on, Mum, get on the bed. You can be part of the crew."

"I most certainly will not." Serafina gave Dylan a sharp look. "More fanciful games, Captain?"

"Just a bit, but I'm doing it this way to

teach David about great literature."

"It doesn't look like any literature to me. I don't see a book."

"Oh, we remember things we act out much longer than things we read in a book."

Serafina shook her head, displeasure on her face. "You're not well enough for such antics as that, Dylan."

"Oh, I'm fine. Now, if you'll help, Lady Trent, we can give David a lesson he'll never forget."

Despite herself, Serafina was intrigued by the behaviour of Dylan Tremayne. He was like no man she had ever known before. When they had first met, she had been displeased by his fanciful thoughts and his belief in the supernatural, especially in religion. But she couldn't resist a sudden surge of gratitude, knowing that David's desire for a father was, in part, being fulfilled by the black-haired actor.

"All right, I'll play. What part of the crew am I?"

"Oh, you're not part of the crew," Tremayne said. "Sit over there in that chair, ma'am."

Serafina went over and sat down and said, "Now what?"

"I'm Captain Odysseus, the great Greek soldier. David here is Marvin the Spike. He is a rough fellow."

"And what am I then?" Serafina asked.

"You, my dear lady, are one of the beautiful Sirens who lure seamen to their deaths." Dylan's eyes were sparkling, and he used his hands to gesture as he said, "When a ship goes by the Island of the Sirens, these beautiful women come out, and they begin to sing. The sailors, of course, are lonely men. They've been at sea forever, it seems, without seeing a woman. When they hear the beautiful voices of the Sirens, and when they see the beauty of their faces and forms, they are entranced."

"And what happens then?"

"Why, the sailors steer the ship toward the Sirens to get closer, so they can see their faces and hear their voices better, but they're so entranced they don't see the rocks. And the ship, inevitably, crashes into the rocks, and the sailors always die."

"What does this have to do with literature?" Serafina demanded.

"Why, it's from *The Odyssey,* ma'am. Don't you remember?"

"I never read it."

"Well, every schoolboy and every student at Oxford and Cambridge has read it. You see, David, I'm a Greek king. Odysseus is my name. A very clever fellow I am, and I am also a very curious man. I want to see and hear new things. So, when my ship gets close to the Sirens and we begin to hear their voices, I know the story of many men who have died because of those beautiful women. So, I want to hear a Siren and see her face, but I don't want to die along with my crew. How can I do both, hear the Sirens and yet not die?"

"I don't know," David said.

"Do you know, Lady Trent?"

"I'm not interested in such things."

"Well, you should be. It's great literature. Here's what happened. Tie me to the mast, Spike."

"With what?"

"Pretend you've got a rope. Tie me tightly to the mast."

David immediately began going through the motions, and Dylan asked, "Am I tied so tight I can't break lose?"

"Yes, Captain."

"Good. Then I want you to take wax and put it in your ears and in the ears of every crew member."

David began actively moving around the bed. "Here's for you, Punch. Get your ears full of it. Here's for you, Oscar, and you, James." He went through the list of imaginary crew then said, "Now what, Captain?"

"You sail close but stay away from the rocks."

"What about you?"

"You put wax in your ears, boy, and then, in effect, the whole crew will be deaf, but I'll be able to hear."

"Yes, sir." David pretended to put wax in his ears.

"Now, everybody's deaf who's sailing by the Sirens except me." He turned and smiled at Serafina. "Why don't you sing something, Siren?"

"Sing what?"

"Oh, anything. The Sirens' voices were so beautiful that it didn't matter what they sang."

Serafina, despite herself, entered into the game. She sang an old song that she remembered from her childhood, and when she had finished, Dylan said, "Now, Spike, you can turn me lose. We're past the Siren."

David jumped up and pretended to turn the captain lose. "Now take the wax out of your ears." Sitting there cross-legged on the bed, Dylan Tremayne said, "There, you see, I'm the only man who ever heard the Sirens sing and lived to tell about it."

"What did the Siren sound like, Dylan?" David asked.

"Dull you are, old man! I can never tell that!"

"Did you ever get back home?"

"Yes, I did."

"Is this what they teach the boys at Oxford and Cambridge?" Serafina demanded.

"Indeed, it is, and in every private school. Every schoolboy has to know *The Odyssey.*"

"I don't see what good it does. It's just a story."

"Ah, but there's more in it than you might think, Lady Serafina."

"What's in it, Dylan?" David demanded.

"Here's what's in it. You've got to take risks in life, see? Odysseus didn't have to listen to those Sirens, but he wanted to experience it."

Serafina shook her head. "He could have gone around them, couldn't he?"

"But then he would never have heard the Sirens' song. He would have missed out on a great experience. There are things you can't go around, Lady Serafina. If your life is to be complete, you have to risk all to experience them."

"Like what?" David asked, his eyes bright.

"Well, like love. Love is a wonderful thing, but it has risks."

"What kind of risks?"

"Well," turning to the boy, Dylan said,

"you know when you love someone, you run the risk of getting hurt. Sorry I am to tell you, but those you love can hurt you more than anyone else. If you don't want to get hurt, go live in a cave and don't let anybody in. You won't have much of a life, but you won't get hurt."

Serafina was fascinated at the workings of Dylan's mind. She put her gaze on her son and saw that he had that familiar expression of thinking deeply. "Would it hurt for me to love you, Dylan?"

"It might. What if I failed you?"

"You would never do that."

"I hope not, but sometimes those we love hurt us."

"But not you."

Serafina listened quietly but said nothing. She was thinking of her love for her husband and how he had failed her so terribly and hurt her almost beyond endurance. She suddenly said, "I'd rather you learn from books, David." Her voice was strict, and both David and Dylan looked at her with surprise.

"Some things can't be learnt that way," Dylan said.

At that moment Dora came in with Matthew Grant. "What are you doing sitting on the bed, David?" Dora asked.

"We're learning about things," David said. "I'm Spike, and Dylan is Captain Odysseus. We've just been on a voyage, and Mum there is the Siren."

Grant suddenly laughed, his eyes filled with humor. "I wish I could have studied *The Odyssey* that way. I learnt by getting my knuckles rapped by the schoolmaster."

Serafina asked, "How are you, Inspector?"

"Very well, and you?"

"We're all very well."

"And how's your patient?"

"He doesn't pay attention to the doctors. Dr. Goldsmith gave him a strict diet and a list of things not to do."

"I hate lists of things."

"He can walk with a cane now."

"Is that Dr. Goldsmith's idea?" Grant inquired.

"No," Dylan said, "it's Dr. Serafina Trent's idea. She won't let me pick up a toothpick," he complained.

They talked for a while, and Serafina finally asked, "What about Superintendent Winters? I see he escaped the noose."

"Yes, ma'am, deported for life. I've been to see him. He's a broken man." He turned and said, "Dylan, when will you be able to go back to work?"

"Oh, soon enough, I suppose."

"What will you be doing? A new play?"

"I've been asked to play the lead in an eighteenth century Restoration drama. It has the title *The Unfaithful Wife.* Isn't that terrible?"

"Is it a good part for you?" Grant asked.

Dylan shook his head. "I don't like Restoration dramas."

"What is a 'Restoration drama'?" Serafina asked curiously.

"Well, when Cromwell came to power during the Commonwealth, the theatres were all closed. But when Charles II was restored to the throne, that era is called 'the Restoration.' The theatres reopened, for Charles was a wicked man indeed, very sensual, and the plays are . . . sensual to say the least. I just don't feel comfortable playing a man without morals."

"I don't understand." Serafina shook her head. "It's only a play. You've played other roles of people who weren't really you."

"I suppose that's true, but I'm not certain I can do it as a Christian."

"Are there many Christians in the acting field, Dylan?" Grant asked curiously.

"Very few. It's a hard life, and I'm afraid there is much immorality that goes on."

The door opened then, and the tweeny maid Ellie came in. "A note just came for you, Miss Aldora."

"Thank you, Ellie."

Taking the note, she read it quickly and said, "It's from Gervase Hayden." She looked at the two men and said, "She's a good friend of mine. Her uncle is Edward Hayden, the Earl of Darby."

"I'm afraid I don't know the gentleman," Grant said. "I wouldn't be likely to unless he's committed a crime."

"Oh, he would never do that," Dora protested then read the rest of the note. "Her uncle is giving a ball for her, and she wants me to come, and you too, Serafina."

"I don't like balls."

"But you have to! Our families are so close." Indeed, the families were close. Their properties adjoined, and Edward Hayden was the godfather of Dora. "You're invited too, Dylan."

"Me? I don't know that family."

"Gervase knows you though. She saw you in *Romeo and Juliet.* I'm afraid she's developed a tremendous admiration for you." She laughed aloud. "She's very passionate. Quite pretty too. The ball will be in two weeks. Do you think you'll be able to dance by then, Dylan?"

Serafina said, "He'd dance now if I wasn't watching him every minute, so he'll be able to dance by then. But," she said, staring directly at Dylan, "I'll have to keep you from straining that leg."

Matthew felt strangely out of place and got up, saying, "I must go. I have work to do."

"I'll show you to the door," Dora said. The two left the room, and when they reached the front door, she stepped outside. "I wish you could go to the ball. I'd invite you if I could, Inspector, but it's not my place."

"I'm not an aristocrat, Dora. I don't fit in."

She saw the unhappiness in Grant's eyes. "At least you can invite me to something. Next Friday there's a performance at the Imperial Theatre," she said. "Melody Fords will be singing. I'd like very much to go."

A sudden desire sprang up in Grant. "I'd love to take you, but what if Lady Mulvane or your parents object?"

"Oh, Aunt is going to object to anything I do, but my parents will let us go, I think."

"Then I'd like it very much. Is it formal?"

"I'm afraid so," she said with a smile. "I'll look forward to it, Matthew."

"Good day, Miss Aldora. It's been a pleasure." Turning, Matthew Grant left the house, and his thoughts were disturbed. /

must be losing my mind — falling in love with Aldora. Her family would never accept a policeman into their ranks. He walked toward the carriage then smiled. *But at least we'll get to hear some fiddles playing at that musical.*

Three

Septimus Newton had no use for most public officials, although he was a medical examiner, often called on by police and Scotland Yard to help identify any clues that might come from a dead body. He spent a large portion of his life in his laboratories, and at the present moment, as the sun streamed in through the window of his outdoor quarters, he paused from his task — the dissection of a tiny shrew captured in his garden — and absentmindedly reached behind him for a cucumber sandwich. He bit off half of the small sandwich, chewed thoughtfully, then turned. Picking up a pen, he dipped it in ink and made a notation in his notebook.

Just as Septimus finished making his note, the door opened, and his wife entered. Alberta was wearing a simple, modest pearl-grey dress with delicate white lace. It was edged with green around the neckline and at her wrists. Her cheeks were bright, for the wind outside had brought colour to them, and as she stepped closer and saw what her husband was doing, she said, "Septimus, you can't do that!"

"Do what, my dear?"

"You can't mess about cutting up those animals and eating at the same time. It's not genteel."

"Isn't it?" Septimus looked surprised. He cast a look at the remains of the small shrew and then at the platter of cucumber sandwiches. "A man must eat, you know."

"But not while you're doing that nasty business!" Alberta exclaimed. "Come now and wash your hands."

Obediently Septimus got up and allowed his wife to lead him to a table where she filled a basin with water out of a pitcher and watched as he soaped his hands and dried them off. "Now, is it all right if I finish my sandwiches?"

Alberta shook her head. "Septimus, I don't know why in the world you have to eat out here. We have a perfectly good dining room, or Cook would be glad to fix you something in the kitchen."

"But, my dear, I would have to quit work to do that." Septimus put his arm around Alberta and gave her a hug. His wild hair gave him a startled look, and he leaned over and kissed her cheek. He whispered, "But I'll try to do better in the future. All right, Wife?"

"Oh, you'll never change," Alberta sighed. She leaned against him, for she knew very few women in her station received such attention from their husbands. Septimus might forget most things, but he usually remembered to speak well and compliment her. "That's a new dress, isn't it?"

"It was new two years ago."

"Oh, I suppose I've seen it before."

"Not over fifty times I would think. Septimus, I want to talk with you."

"Why, certainly. Come and sit down over here. Have some of my sandwiches."

"No, I don't want any." The two sat down, and Alberta said, "What do you think of Inspector Matthew Grant?"

"Why, he seems like a jolly good chap. Fine member of the police force I'm told."

"I don't mean professionally. I mean what do you think about this attention he's showing to Aldora?"

"Why, I hadn't thought about it."

"I think you should. After all, Aldora is going to have to marry very soon."

"Why must she marry?"

"Oh, don't be obtuse, Septimus! You know

that's the only life for a woman in this society." Indeed, this was true enough. Women who could not manage to capture a husband usually became awkward guests in the house of a relative, not a desirable fate.

Septimus took another bite of his sandwich and said, "How do you think Dora feels?"

"Oh, it's hard to tell about that girl. She likes everyone, of course, but he's not a fit suitor for her."

Septimus was an astute man in science, but sometimes he lagged behind in other areas. He suddenly straightened up and a frown creased his brow. "Has Bertha been talking to you?"

"Well, yes, she has. She says that we must forbid Dora to see Mr. Grant again."

"Bertha doesn't have enough to do. She has no life of her own, so she tries to run ours."

Alberta looked at her husband with surprise. Very rarely did he ever speak a word of criticism about anyone, and he had shown a remarkable restraint toward Bertha Mulvane. "But I suppose Bertha is right. She would be marrying beneath her station."

"Well, I married above my station, and we turned out all right." Septimus grinned and pinched Alberta's arm. "You know, I hate messing around with our children's lives. It's much safer to do my experiments and autopsies. After all" — Septimus paused and amusement danced in his eyes — "dead people don't have any problems. What about Alex Bolton, this fellow that's calling on Serafina?"

"We don't know very much about him. He seems very taken with her."

"Well, I doubt she'll have him. She hasn't shown any interest in a man since Charles died."

"She's a young woman. She'll marry again, but I'm not sure Sir Alex is the proper man for her." She sighed and shook her head sadly. "It's so hard getting girls settled."

"Well, Serafina's not exactly a girl. After all, she is almost thirty, and she's been married."

"She's very smart in scientific matters, but I'm not sure she does well in other areas."

Alberta's observation seemed to bring a silence over the room. Each of them was thinking of Charles Trent, Serafina's husband, now dead for three years. He had seemed a likely enough choice, and Serafina had been happy and filled with joy before the marriage, as young girls should be. But both her parents had noticed that early in the marriage she had changed, and each of them had suspected that Charles was not a good husband.

"Well, we'll have to wait and see, I suppose," Septimus sighed. "Where is Serafina?"

"She's gone to town with David. She's taking him by the tailor to get him fitted for some new clothes. He's growing very fast." She rose and said, "I've got to get back to the house. You're going to have to go to the tailor too."

"Why should I do that?"

"You don't have a thing to wear to the ball at Silverthorn."

Septimus had risen, and now he stood there, an awkward figure indeed, and shook his head. "I'd rather be dissecting a body than go to a thing like that. I hate balls!"

"We have to go. It wouldn't be right not to, and you'll have to have a new suit."

"I've got a suit."

"You don't have a thing fit to wear to the ball. Your clothes are terrible. We're going tomorrow to the tailor."

"Henry David Thoreau said, 'Beware of all enterprises that require new clothes.' " Septimus spread both hands out in a gesture of despair, "And after all, Thoreau is never wrong."

As the carriage made its way through the busy streets, Serafina peered out through the yellowish fog. Just why London fog was that colour no one had ever been able to ascertain, but always during the fall a great yellowness cloaked London, and lamps were lit even during the day. Sometimes this fog spread out until it extended miles from the heart of the city, and complaints were often made that the fog caused pain in the lungs and uneasy sensations in the head. Serafina had been to London a few times when the fog — which was called "a London peculiar" — was so thick you could take a person by the hand and not be able to see his face, and some people had literally lost their way and drowned in the Thames.

"Mum, why does London smell so bad?"

Serafina turned to David, who was sitting beside her in the carriage. "Well, big cities almost always smell bad. We're fortunate that we can live a little ways out of London. There's nothing, I suppose, that can be done for the way the place smells."

"If I lived in London, I'd want to make it better."

Serafina smiled and reached over to squeeze David's shoulder. "I'm sure many people would like that, but you have to put up with some difficult things if you live in London."

The carriage finally drew to a halt, and Albert Givins leapt down from his seat and came at once to open the door. "Bad day for a visit to London, Lady Trent. Can't even see the sun, ma'am," he complained.

"It is worse today, isn't it, Albert? Nevertheless, we'll have to put up with it."

"I'll wait right here while you take Master David to go get fitted."

"Here, Albert, get yourself something good to eat from one of the street peddlers." She handed him a coin and smiled. "We may be quite awhile."

"Thank you, ma'am. A kidney pie would go down pretty good."

Leaving the carriage, Serafina led David down the street. After the relative silence of Trentwood, the noise of the London streets was almost deafening. The carriages and many horses were part of the problem. The sound of horses' hooves clacking over the cobblestones and of wheels grinding along struck her ears. The click of women's pattens with wooden soles on the sidewalk, the bells of the salesmen, and the cries of street peddlers selling items such as dolls, eels, pins, rat poison, and a hundred other things added to the noise. Children swarmed the streets. They were poor, often called "Street Arabs," and they begged Serafina for money.

"It's noisy, ain't it, Mum?" David said.

"Yes, it is. I'm not sure all this is good for your ears. Come along now."

"Mum, I'm hungry."

"Well, let's get you something." She stopped beside a peddler and bought a kidney pie from a thin man with a stovepipe hat askew on his head and a soiled apron around his waist. When David finished eating, they bought sweetmeat candy and a piece of candied fruit. "You're going to get fat," she said, smiling down at the boy, "if you keep on eating like that."

"I don't care. It's so good!"

"Well, come on. We've got to get your clothes fitted." She led him toward the sign and was barely able to make it out through the fog: Jonas Tyler — Tailor.

"That took a long time, Mum," David complained as they emerged from the tailor shop. "I don't like to be fitted."

"It's necessary, David," Serafina said.

They passed by several shops and then noticed a poster that advertised a play. Serafina saw Dylan's name on it, and she pointed it out. "Look, Mr. Dylan's going to be in a play."

"Can I go see him, Mum? I've never seen a play."

"I don't think this would be exactly the right one for you to see." Serafina remembered Dylan saying that it had such immoral features that he was reluctant to act in it. As they made their way along the crowded streets, Serafina was surprised that Dylan had agreed to be in the play. He was goverened by such strong moral rules, and she determined to go see it.

They were approaching the carriage when David said, "Listen, I hear singing."

Indeed, Serafina heard it too. She looked ahead through the fog and saw a small crowd gathered around a few people standing with their backs to a building. "Those are church people, David. Sometimes they preach in the streets."

"Not in a church?"

"I'm not sure why they do it, but yes, that's correct."

"Look, there's Mr. Dylan!"

Serafina looked closely at the small group singing and saw Dylan Tremayne. Curiosity got the best of her, and when David said, "Let's get closer," she agreed.

The singing was lusty, and the group sang enthusiastically if not always on key. She could hear Dylan's clear voice rising slightly above the rest, and she listened carefully to the words of the tune:

All hail the power of Jesus' name!
Let angels prostrate fall;
Bring forth the royal diadem,
And crown Him Lord of all.

Ye chosen seed of Israel's race,
Ye ransomed from the fall,
Hail Him who saves you by His grace,
And crown Him Lord of all.

Let every kindred, every tribe
On this terrestrial ball,
To Him all majesty ascribe,
And crown Him Lord of all.

O that with yonder sacred throng
We at His feet may fall,
Join in the everlasting song,
And crown Him Lord of all.

Looking around after the singers had finished, Serafina saw that the crowd was mostly drawn from the poor people of London. A few middle-class observers were standing on the outer ring, but she saw none of whom society would call "quality people."

No high-class folks in this group.

She looked carefully at the two men standing next to Dylan. One was called Yago the Gyp, a lean, dark-complected man — a gypsy really, with a gold ring in his right ear. He was also, she knew, a former safecracker. The other man was Lorenzo Pike. Pike was a huge, burly man with florid, blunt features and a pair of bright, merry blue eyes. Both men, who were plainly dressed, had been helpful in protecting David during the affair of Clive's trial.

Lorenzo Pike stepped forward and lifted his loud, powerful voice. "Well, beloved, we are here to give honour to Jesus, the King of Kings. He shed His blood on the cross of Cavalry so that an ex-thief and criminal such as myself might be saved and have a place in a heavenly mansion. Glory to God and the Lamb forever!"

Lorenzo preached plainly and obviously enjoyed his own sermon. Serafina listened and was puzzled. She did not understand the religion of Dylan and his fellows. She knew they were Methodists — the bottom of the ecclesiastical ladder in England. They were called "enthusiasts," and the Anglican leaders made light of them, accusing them of all sorts of misbehaviour.

Finally the sermon ended with a rousing

prayer by Lorenzo, and as soon as the amen was said, Serafina saw Dylan come straight toward her. "Well, Lady Trent, it's good to see you."

"Hello, Dylan."

"Hello, Mr. Dylan," David said. "I could hear you singing above all the rest."

"Could you now? Well, I sounded like an old crow today, me. Bit of a cold."

"No, you were the best of all," David said stoutly.

Serafina was thinking of what had taken place and said, "Dylan, I don't understand this. Do you think it would help anybody to be at a service like this?"

"Well, Lady Trent, it's a service for those who probably wouldn't attend any church, and I'd like to think proclaiming the Gospel to the poor is what Jesus did best."

"I suppose that's so."

"We saw your name on a building, Mr. Dylan," David piped up.

"Yes, we did." Serafina nodded. "I see you've decided to be in that play you were worried about after all."

"No, ma'am, not at all. I declined, but the bills were already up."

Serafina was not too surprised. "I somehow felt you'd do that, but it'll be quite a sacrifice financially, won't it?"

"Well, if you are having my opinion, God feeds the sparrows, so He can feed one poor out-of-work actor, don't you think?"

"Yes, I'm sure that's true."

"I did have to make a few cuts. I had to leave my rooms, and I'm staying with Matthew now."

"Matthew Grant?"

"Yes, the inspector himself. He heard about my problem and was kind enough to invite me. There is a kind fellow, he is!"

"Well, I could tell the man had a good heart."

Dylan hesitated then said, "You know, he's very sad that he's not invited to attend the ball."

Serafina looked troubled. "I didn't know he was one for such things."

"Well, he looked forward to dancing with your sister, but I'm sure that's impossible. After all, he's merely a policeman, but of course, I'm merely an actor and I'm invited."

Serafina made her mind up instantly. "I'll invite him. He'll be my guest."

"Do you think that some people might object?"

Serafina well knew that "some people" would be Lady Bertha. "It will be all right," she said. "How shall I get in touch with him? You know his address, of course."

"I'll be glad to deliver the invitation in person, Lady Trent, and a happy man he'll be."

"Very well, you and the inspector must come to our house early. We'll all go together in our carriage."

"There's kind you are now! Well, I'll go tell the inspector the good news. Come, I'll see you back to your carriage."

As Dylan turned to lead them to the carriage, Serafina was thinking, *This is going to cause difficulty. Bertha will be angry. But Grant was very kind to us during trouble, and it's little enough to do for him.*

Four

Banks of dark, glowering clouds had threatened rain all morning, billowing fuliginous shapes like enormous spectres. The family had watched the skies anxiously, dreading a deluge. By one o'clock they were all ready to leave for the ball, though the threat of rain was even more severe than before. The clouds were rolling in from the north, and finally Septimus Newton said, "There's nothing we can do about the rain, and I'd just as soon call the whole thing off."

"Now don't be foolish, Septimus," Alberta said. "We've got to go."

"Do we have enough umbrellas to go around?" Bertha asked. She had practically invited herself to the ball and had spent the morning harassing all of the servants of Trentwood in her preemptory fashion.

"What good does a parasol do?" Septimus said. "Look at that thing! What possible use could it be in a downpour?"

He gestured at the parasol in his wife's hands, a flimsy thing made to match her dress. It was small, frilled, and embroidered with joined ivory and wood sticks, designed primarily to protect a lady's complexion. The one that Bertha carried was ogee-shaped, and neither these two, nor any of the rest, were of any use in rain.

Bertha's face was twisted with anger as she said loudly, "I think it's a disgrace that we're taking that actor and the policeman to the ball."

"I don't think that matters, Bertha," Alberta said, struggling to open the parasol. "The earl said to bring them, and it would be most rude not to pay heed to his words."

Septimus had listened to Bertha all morning long, it seemed. He had taken refuge in his laboratory on the second floor, and now that it was time to leave for the ball at Lord Darby's, he spoke in a strained manner. "Come along. The world was drowned by water once, and we may be drowned on the way, but at least let's make a start." He led his wife and sister-in-law out of the house, handed them up in the carriage, and then got in and sat down, calling out, "All right, Givins, let's get this thing over with." He settled back as if he were embarking on a journey of a thousand miles, even though

Silverthorn, the ancestral home of Lord Darby, was only twelve miles away.

"Blasted nuisance," he muttered under his breath. "Whoever thought up such things as this ought to be made to eat his own head!" With this dire statement he slumped in the corner and began, as usual, carrying on some complicated mathematical problem in his head, ignoring the jabbering of his wife and the complaints of Bertha Mulvane as the carriage moved forward under the darkening sky.

"Do you think my dress is all right, Serafina?"

Dora had joined Serafina in her room as they prepared for the ball. She turned around, and Serafina studied her dress, which was of a bright green satin hue trimmed with glittering black jet and black velvet ribbons. Three black feathers were arranged in Dora's hair and held in place by a diamond hairpin.

"It looks very well indeed. I'm sure Inspector Grant will like it at least."

Aldora flushed slightly. "I'm not wearing it just for him," she said defiantly. "But one must wear something to a ball."

Serafina laughed. "It would be quite shocking if one wore nothing to a ball."

"Serafina, what a terrible thing to say!" She giggled. "What a funny sight that would be!"

At that instant David came running in, his mouth twisted with displeasure. "Mum, I want to go with you."

Serafina knelt down to his level. She took his hands and held them tightly. "You're too young for such things, David."

"You could hide me in your carriage. No one would see me."

Serafina laughed, reached out, and hugged him. "I'm afraid that wouldn't answer, but remember you're going to have great fun with Danny. When it stops raining you can ride Patches, and the two of you can go try to find another bird's egg to add to your collection."

David brightened up. "That will be fun." But then he shook his head. "What about when it gets dark?"

"We already talked about that. Ellie is going to read to you after supper, and you can play games with her until bedtime. You know how much fun you have with Ellie."

"I'd rather go with you."

"And I'd rather stay here with you, but grown-ups have to do things they don't want to do."

"Look, Serafina," Dora cried. She was

standing at the large window looking down. "Matthew and Dylan are here."

"Well, we mustn't keep them waiting." Serafina gathered David into a hug and kissed his cheek. "You go along now."

"When will you be back?"

"We plan to stay over just tonight. We'll be back sometime tomorrow. I'll see you then."

"Good-bye, Mum. You have a good time." David turned and ran off in search of the groom, who was his chief playmate.

"I suppose we'd better go," Serafina said. "Come along."

The two left the room and went downstairs. They reached the first floor and moved into the foyer just as the door was opened by Louisa Toft, Serafina's maid. "Oh, it's you, Mr. Dylan," Louisa said. The beautiful young woman of twenty-three was absolutely stricken with Dylan Tremayne. Serafina noted the adoring look in her maid's eyes and started to rebuke her but then gave up. All women seemed to look on Dylan in that fashion. She wondered, not for the first time, how much he was able to resist the obvious advances that some of them made.

"Hello, Dylan," she said and stepped forward.

"A good day to you." Dylan smiled. He was wearing an outfit that Serafina had never seen before — a blue velvet frock coat, a white linen shirt, a complicated black cravat with a small diamond stud, black breeches pressed into a nice crease, and dark glossy boots. His dark hair was groomed beautifully, and his handsome face was sharply delineated by the gaslight. He smiled and said, "We're going to get wet, I think."

"I hope not," Aldora said. "How are you, Inspector Grant?"

Grant wore a pearl-grey suit with a modish, short waistcoat and shawl collar, and his pointed standing collar was decorated with a simple cravat. He also wore black shiny boots. "How are you, Miss Aldora? And you, Lady Trent?"

"Oh, I'm so excited," Dora said. Her eyes were glowing, and she looked exceptionally pretty as she smiled at the two men. "I do hope it stops raining."

"The others have already left," Serafina said, "but there's no hurry. We have plenty of time."

They left the house, and the ladies were handed into the carriage, seated so they could face forward. The men, as custom demanded, sat with their backs to the driver. The covered coach was one Dylan had never seen before, and after Serafina told the driver to begin their journey, he said, "This is new, isn't it?"

"Yes, Father just bought it. It's called a vis-à-vis."

Dylan ran his hand over the smooth walnut door that made up the body and settled back in the softness of the brown leather seat. "This is the way to travel." He smiled.

"Are you ready for the ball, Miss Aldora?" Grant asked.

"Oh, yes, it's going to be so much fun. Do you like balls, Inspector?"

"To tell the truth, I've never been to one."

Grant's simple answer startled the two women. Balls were a part of their lives, and to think here was a man who had spent over thirty years on planet earth without ever having attended one seemed very strange to them indeed. Serafina studied Grant without appearing to do so. He was an intensely masculine man with thick silver hair, which she knew was prematurely grey. He had unusual hazel eyes, and there was a strength about him that most men would envy. He was not a man of many words, and Serafina admired him for that. She spoke up then saying, "Well, we will average out. I've been to far too many."

"You don't like balls?" Grant asked, turning to face her.

"I think they're a frightful bore and a waste of time."

Dylan laughed. "There's a pessimist you are. That sounds like a description of being in jail."

"What a terrible thing to say!" Dora giggled. "But you've never been in jail."

"Oh, yes I have. I was arrested once down in Cornwall."

"What was the charge?" Matthew asked.

"Assault and battery, and tearing up a saloon."

"Were you guilty?" Serafina smiled despite herself.

"Mostly I was, but it wasn't my fault. I was provoked. The man spoke evil of Wales, and it was my duty to correct him."

As they rode through the falling rain, Serafina found herself as fascinated by Dylan as she had been from the beginning. In all honesty her initial impression had been quite negative, but she had learnt that underneath his deceptively handsome features worked a quick and agile mind. He had been places and done things that she had never heard of, and now she sensed some of that quick mind as he asked, "What about the family of Lord Darby? I know nothing about them."

Serafina shrugged. "Our families are very close. As a matter of fact, Lord Darby is Aldora's godfather."

"That's right. He is." Dora nodded. "He never fails to send me a present on my birthday."

"I suppose it's a very large place?" Grant asked.

"Oh yes," Serafina said, nodding, "larger than Trentwood. The house is enormous. It must have twenty bedrooms."

"Well, devil fly off!" Dylan exclaimed. "That would be like operating an inn."

Dora was shocked. "What an awful thing to say, Mr. Dylan!"

"Well, it is a bit ostentatious." Serafina shrugged. "They have, I would guess, some twenty-five servants in all."

"What's the earl like?" Grant asked.

"He's very nice. He's fifty-five years old now, a rather tall man, very lean, and quite good looking. He's rather dignified, but he unbends mostly with his wife and his niece, Gervase."

"And his wife is so nice. Her name is Heather," Dora said. "She's younger than Lord Darby, and you know they have a true romance. She told me about it one time.

Her husband is a wonderful singer, and he would come and sing love songs under her balcony."

"They're a very happy couple. It makes me believe that happy marriages can take place." Serafina spoke almost without thinking and then suddenly felt the eyes of the other occupants on her. She flushed slightly and closed her lips, determined to say no more along this line. Her own marriage was something about which she seldom spoke.

"Do they have children?" Dylan asked, feeling her discomfort.

"No, and that's the one sad thing about them," Serafina answered. "Both of them wanted a large family, but it never happened. Lady Heather had several miscarriages. One child lived but only two days. They don't talk about children anymore. You would never know how sad it makes them unless you are around them a great deal."

"What about the rest of the family?" Dylan asked.

"Well, the earl has two brothers. One of them is Rupert Hayden. He's five years younger than Lord Darby. He's the businessman of the family," Dora said.

"Business is about all he cares for," Serafina said. "He never married, and he spends his life taking care of the estate."

"The earl's other brother is named Arthur Hayden," Dora said. "It always makes me sad to think about him."

"Why sad?" Matthew asked. "Is he ill?"

"No, but he's so different from the other men in the family. The most graphic example I know of a man's who's out of his place."

"That's interesting you should say that, Dora," Dylan said. "You know the Bible says that 'as a bird that wandereth from her nest, so is a man that wandereth from his place.' Kind of a sad verse."

"Well, Arthur Hayden is a sad man," Serafina said. "He's forty-five now, and he's never done anything to bring any public disgrace on the family. He's a good painter. He wanted to study in France and Italy, but Rupert persuaded the earl to put a stop to that. Arthur is not a man of business, and his failure to please his brother has caused him to drink too much. And this, of course, is a great sadness to Gervase, his daughter."

"Gervase saw you in *Romeo and Juliet,* Dylan," Dora said, smiling, "and she's the one who insisted that you come tonight. So, you'll have to be very nice to her."

"I'm always nice to ladies. Is she cross-eyed or ugly in any way?"

"Don't be foolish!" Serafina said sharply. "She's a very beautiful young girl. Very spirited and has a quick wit. She's also a dedicated Christian. Sings at the church all the time and visits the sick and the elderly. It's just sad to see her father waste his life."

"I'm sure it also grieves his mother, Lady Leona Hayden, greatly. She was the second wife of Lord Darby's father, Leslie, and she lives at Silverthorn, though she's a widow and an invalid of sorts. Her mind doesn't work very well anymore. She becomes confused." Serafina paused and looked out at the rain. "Of course, Edward, Rupert, and Leah are not Lady Leona's children. They're the children of her husband's first wife, Edith Carrington. Leah's son, Bramwell St. John, lives at Silverthorn too. Everyone calls him St. John."

"Yes, Sinjin," Dora said, emphasizing the characteristically British pronunciation.

"You know, the Americans find that quite interesting," Dylan said, "how St. John could become a thing like Sinjin, but it's his name. He can call himself anything he wants. What sort of chap is he?"

"He's about your height, lean, and a very good athlete when he chooses. He's had some problems though," Serafina said hesitantly.

"It's so sad." Dora shook her head. "He went to Oxford and fell into the sins of young men."

"What are the sins of young men, Miss Aldora?" Dylan asked, humor dancing in his eyes. "I've never been able to get them straight. Would you care to go into that a little bit further?"

"You are awful, Dylan! Now, I'm not going to talk about the sins of young men. I suspect you know far more about them than I do."

"I expect you're right." Matthew grinned. He nudged Dylan with his elbow. "I'll explain it all to you when we're alone, Dylan."

"Well, it sounds like a typical English family," Dylan said, "with some heroes and some villains."

"Oh, there are no villains in the Hayden family. Just some sadness," Serafina said. "But I suppose you're right. All families have this sort of thing."

As the carriage bounced over the road, Serafina sat back and listened to Dora speak to Matthew, drawing out of him some of his experiences in Scotland Yard. She studied the face of Dylan, wondering what really went on, wondering how she had ever become so involved in the life of an actor. It disturbed her sometimes, for she knew that her interest in him was more than casual. Still she thought of how he had risked his life — nearly given it, in fact — to save David, and she knew she would never forget that as long as she lived.

"You look very well, my love."

Edward Hayden came to stand behind his wife, who was sitting at her dressing table. He put his hands on her shoulders, and she reached up and covered them with her own. "Thank you, dear. I think it was very sweet of you to give this ball for Gervase, but you spoil her terribly."

"I know I do, but I can't help it. She's been like a daughter to us, hasn't she?"

When Heather did not answer, Edward understood he had touched on the one subject that could bring sadness into his wife's fine eyes — their lack of children. Quickly he started to speak again, but she spoke first.

"I've been a failure to you, Edward."

"Don't say that." He leaned over and, stooping down, kissed her cheek. "You're enough for any man."

"We should have adopted a son, but I was so certain that God had promised us a son of our own." This had been disturbing to

Heather. She was an exemplary Christian, and she had told everyone that God had promised to give her and Edward a son. When only one child had lived, and that one for only two days, she had since suffered in thinking she had misread the will of God.

"God's ways are hard to understand. Any of us can mistake our way," Edward said. He straightened up and shrugged slightly. "We always have St. John."

"I suppose so." Heather's response was slow and rather grudging. The thought of her nephew, Bramwell, as a son was not pleasing to her.

"I suppose we'd better go down. Our guests from Trentwood will be arriving soon."

"Yes, I'll be ready in just a moment."

Bramwell St. John knocked on his mother's door, and at the sound of her voice he opened it and stepped inside. He was wearing a brown coat with dark green trousers, and his snowy white shirt set off his olive complexion. He was a handsome young man of twenty-eight, and as he stepped inside, there was some sort of dissatisfaction in his face. "Well, you look very nice, Mother. Another ball for us, eh?"

"You look very nice, St. John, but before we go down, I have something to tell you."

"It sounds like a sermon coming up."

"Not a sermon, but just a warning. You've got to be more careful or you'll lose Edward's respect."

"I don't think I ever had his respect."

"You could have had," Leah said quickly. "They have no son of their own, and they would have welcomed you as one if you had learnt to behave."

"It doesn't matter." St. John shrugged his trim shoulders. "When my uncle dies, Rupert will be master of all, and he has no use for me nor ever has. We'll be poor relations around here. I don't much fancy that."

Leah St. John was taller than most women with very dark hair and dark eyes to match, almost black, indeed. She had thin lips, high cheekbones, and a rather sour disposition, the result of a stormy marriage. Her husband, Roger, had been a soldier, and Leah had loved him almost unreasonably. She was a proud woman, conscious of her aristocratic heritage. She looked at the young man before her, thinking how she had struggled to encourage him, but there was a streak of rebelliousness in him that she recognized as coming perhaps from her, perhaps from her dead husband.

"Things change, St. John. Edward doesn't love Rupert. They're not very close brothers. I know he hates to think of Rupert being head of this family. He knows how cold and unfeeling he is." She came forward and reached up to put her hand on his cheek. "If you would only learn to please your uncle, he might name you as his heir."

"That's not very likely."

"Well, consider that Rupert might die."

St. John suddenly smiled. There was something unpleasant about this smile, however. He could be charming enough when he chose, but there was a sardonic streak in him that went against the grain for many people. "Wouldn't it be convenient if a bolt of lightning would strike down both Rupert and Arthur, then he'd have no choice but to make me his heir."

"That's no way to talk, St. John!"

"Well, it would take something that startling to get my uncle to accept me as his heir. Poor Arthur is unfit to be head of the family. Edward loves him, but he knows him too well."

St. John suddenly laughed, put his arm around his mother, and hugged her. "I have it! You know how Uncle Edward dotes on Gervase. I'll marry her, and he'll make me his heir to please her. You know how she's his favourite."

"St. John, she's your cousin!"

"What does that matter? She's adopted, so she's no kin to me." Suddenly he shrugged and stepped back from his mother. "I'm going to warn Gervase about that actor that Lady Trent is bringing."

"I think that might not be out of place. She's foolish over him, and you know what a foolish young girl can do."

"Certainly. They're not like steady young men such as I am, right?" He laughed, turned, and left the room.

Gervase's maid was putting the finishing touches on her mistress. Gervase had beautiful hair, golden and long, and now done up in a most attractive fashion. She had green eyes and a fine figure. She felt a touch on her leg and looked down at the large cat. "Jeremiah, what do you want?"

"I think he wants to be let out," the maid said. Della Munson knew her mistress very well. "I don't know why you like that cat. All he does is fight and bring you dead things."

"They're presents. He thinks they please me." Leaning over, Gervase stroked the blunt, scarred head of Jeremiah and said, "You love me, don't you, Jerry?"

A knock suddenly sounded, and she called, "Come in. Oh, hello, St. John. My, you look nice. Is that a new suit?"

"Yes, I've run up another bill with my tailor. Uncle Edward won't like that. You look very nice."

"Thank you, St. John. You can go now, Della. You've done very well."

"Yes, ma'am."

As soon as the girl left, St. John came over and put his hand on her head. "I think I'll mess your hair up. That bloody actor won't look at you then."

"Don't you dare!" She stood to face him, having to look up, for she was not a tall woman. "He's such a handsome man, St. John."

"Of course he is. That's what actors are: good-looking, shallow people with no brains and no morals."

"Oh, you're wrong about that! He's very smart. He helped get Aldora's brother Clive free when he was accused of murder. Now you be nice to him."

"Oh, I'm always nice, and I'll be especially nice to the policeman. What's his name?"

"Inspector Matthew Grant. I think he's in love with Aldora."

St. John grinned. "Well, that won't help him. I've decided to marry Aldora myself."

He laughed as she stared at him. "The Viscountess of Radnor can afford to support one penniless and useless husband of a beloved sister, don't you think?"

"Don't be mean, St. John. You have so many gifts. Why don't you finish school and make something out of yourself like Clive? He'll be an excellent barrister one day."

"Too much trouble."

"You'd better be careful. I heard Uncle Rupert telling Edward that he ought to make you go to work."

"Oh, he sings that sad song all the time. He despises me, but then he despises most people, doesn't he? Come along. Let's go down and prepare to meet the guests."

They walked downstairs together, and he whispered, "There, they're coming in right now."

Indeed, Lord Darby and his wife Heather were standing together, greeting the newcomers. He smiled at Serafina saying, "Lady Serafina, your family arrived in good form a short time ago. They'll be joining us later." He turned then and said, "And here's the dear girl. I claim a godfather's right to a kiss."

He leaned over and kissed Dora on the cheek, and she said, "I've missed you, Uncle."

"And I missed you."

Serafina said, "Let me introduce your guests. Mr. Dylan Tremayne and Inspector Matthew Grant. This is our dear friend Lord Darby and his wife, Lady Heather, and this is Miss Gervase Hayden and Mr. Bramwell St. John."

After the brief introduction, Serafina said, "I told you, Lord Darby, about how these two gentlemen were such a help in getting Clive freed."

"Yes, I was very pleased to hear that, and we're very happy to have you for the ball."

Heather smiled. "Your rooms are ready. I'm sure you want to go freshen up before dinner."

"Crinshaw," Lord Darby said, turning to a cadaverous-looking man, "will you show our guests to their rooms?"

Matthew and Dylan followed the butler upstairs. He led them down the hall, then opened two doors. "This will be your room, Inspector, and right across the hall will be yours, sir."

"Thank you very much." Matthew waited until the butler left and then walked in and looked around. "What a room!" he murmured. "I feel like a blasted impostor. This is not my kind of life."

"Nonsense," Dylan said. "Carpe diem!

Seize the day, man! Enjoy the food and dance with Dora."

"I feel out of place. Everyone will be wondering what a grubby policeman is doing here."

"It's nobody's business to go poking their old noses into! Think of it like this: you're twice as intelligent as anybody you'll meet here. Just do what I do."

The workings of Dylan's mind always intrigued Grant. "What are you going to do?"

"What I always do." Dylan smiled. "Let's think of this as a play. I'm expected to be the empty-headed, egocentric actor who's moving above his station. What does that matter? Let's just enjoy the food and the ball."

"Well, that's fine for you, but I'm no actor."

"We're all actors, Matthew, yes? All of us are playing roles all the time, pretending to be something we're not." He walked around the room gesturing as if he were on a stage. "Shakespeare hit it right on the head in *As You Like It.* He said:

All the world's a stage,
And all the men and women merely players:

They have their exits and their entrances;
And one man in his time plays many parts.

Matthew laughed. "A fine bunch of hypocrites you make us out to be!"

"Not at all, Matthew. I'm only tormenting you. I can play a role like that, but you're Matthew Grant, an inspector with Scotland Yard. Don't try to be anything else, and Dora will be very proud of you."

"I hope so," Matthew said gloomily. "I'm not accustomed to this sort of thing with rich people."

"Don't worry about it. Rich people are only poor people with money, you see?"

"Yes, but money makes a difference."

FIVE

Lady Bertha Mulvane would never admit to it, but she had one serious problem — she was totally and completely colour-blind. This resulted in a very strange and often almost frightening combination of colours in her attire. She was never willing to admit, however, that others could see something that she herself could not.

The dress she wore to the ball was a particularly leprous grey, and the shawl around her neck was purple — not just a mild purple but a blazing, screaming, shouting purple that clashed with everything else she had on. No one had ever come directly out and confronted Lady Bertha with the truth, for it would have been dangerous saying such a thing to one who believed herself perfectly normal, capable, and even superior in every way. She was dominating now the small group that had gathered prior to going into the ballroom, saying to Lord Darby in stentorian tones, "I must apologize for my family, Lord Darby, and to you, too, Lady Darby. I want you to understand that it was not any of my doings to invite that awful actor fellow and that policeman to the ball."

Edward Hayden, the Earl of Darby, was accustomed to the antics and blindness of Lady Mulvane. He was perfectly aware that she had no legal right whatsoever to call herself Lady Mulvane, but it made the old woman happy. "That's quite all right, Lady Mulvane," he said. "They'll be interesting enough, I'm sure."

"Yes, indeed!" St. John, who was standing back slightly from his uncle and aunt, said, "We're all aware, Lady Mulvane, of the help that these two gave to Lady Trent in the matter of her brother, Clive."

"It's one thing," Bertha sniffed, "to be involved with the frightful people on stage and even worse the criminals that the inspector is forced to deal with, but to bring them into a proper society shows a lack of feeling."

"Well, Gervase was quite taken with Mr. Tremayne when she saw him in a play. She doesn't ask for much, and it was the least I could do. And, of course, when Lady Trent invited the inspector, that was enough to tell us that they would be perfectly acceptable guests."

They looked up to see the two men in question approaching them, and Edward said, "You two are all settled, I take it?"

"Yes, Lord Darby, we are," Dylan said pleasantly. "Very gracious of you to allow us to come. Not many men of your station would welcome a lowly actor and policeman to a ball." As soon as he said this, Dylan saw every eye go to Lady Mulvane, and she made an expression as if she had just swallowed a toad. Her face turned almost as purple as her dress, and Gervase, who was part of the group, said, "Did you choke on something, Lady Mulvane?"

Lord Darby changed the subject and asked Dylan what had happened to the superintendent of Scotland Yard who had been convicted of the murder for which Clive had been accused. "He's being deported to Australia for life," Dylan said. "Sorry for him, I am. I've been to see him several times."

Rupert, who had been standing off to one side watching the scene carefully, spoke up. "Well, it's regrettable to see justice not done. He should have been hanged, of course."

Dylan shook his head. "I feel sorry for the

man. His life is ruined."

Rupert snorted. "He should have been hanged. He would have been if he had been a working man."

Gervase was looking up at Dylan, and she asked, "What do you say to a man who's faced such ruin?"

Dylan shrugged. "To someone who's lost everything there's only one comfort, and that is the Lord Jesus Christ."

The remark seemed to cast a net of silence around the group. Serafina was amused. She herself was accustomed to Dylan's outspoken religious beliefs, but she saw that Darby and his wife and the others were rather stunned by it. "You'll have to get used to Mr. Tremayne's brand of religion. He's quite outspoken about it. I expect he'll wind up as a Methodist street preacher one day."

St. John was standing beside his mother, and he suddenly changed the subject. "You might have a case to solve here, Lady Trent."

"Whatever do you mean, Mr. St. John?" Serafina asked. "And don't take my reputation as a detective too seriously. Inspector Grant here is the one who is adept at catching criminals. I was just lucky in one or two cases."

"What sort of case would be in a setting like this?" Dylan asked with surprise.

"Why, you probably haven't heard about it," St. John said, "but Lord Darby was fired upon by someone. The bullet narrowly missed him."

"Is that true, Sir Edward?" Serafina asked, turning to face him. "I never heard about it."

"Oh, there was nothing to it. I was out in the woods, and there were other hunters there. You know how far a rifle bullet can carry. It could have been half a mile away. He missed a shot, missed all the trees, missed me, too, by a goodly margin."

"Not all that goodly," St. John argued. "The bullet came within a few feet of your head."

Darby simply laughed. "It was just a hunter in the woods," he said. "Shall we go in?"

The party entered the glittering ballroom where chandeliers hung from the ceiling, their crystal facets winking in the barest movement of air. Lights burned from the gas brackets on the walls. Diamonds sparkled from the throats and arms and hair of the women, and reflected light glanced off the polished tables and on silver and in glass. Already there were many people there, and the musicians who were ensconced at one end were playing a sprightly tune.

Gervase at once went to Dylan and said, "You'll discover that I have very few social graces, Mr. Tremayne. I've always thought it rather evil that a woman has to wait until the man asks her to dance. Therefore, would you dance with me?"

"I totally agree with you. Men and women are equal in all respects."

"I hope you remember that, Dylan," Lady Trent said sarcastically. "There have been times when I have felt you were not quite so sure of that dictum."

"Nonsense. I'm always on the woman's side. It will be a pleasure to dance with you, Miss Gervase."

As they went to the floor and began to dance the waltz, she said, "You're a better dancer than I am."

"Part of the stock of actor's tricks that I've been forced to develop, but you are a beautiful dancer. You've probably had more practice than I have."

"I doubt that. But I do want to tell you how much I enjoyed your performance in *Romeo and Juliet.* I thought your Mercutio was magnificent."

"Words I love to hear! Do you go to the theatre much?"

"As often I can. Uncle Edward spoils me greatly, I fear, and my father assists him as well as he can."

"I haven't met your father, have I?"

Dylan did not miss the fact that his question threw Gervase into a brief silence. It was as if she were searching for an answer, and finally she said, "He will probably be a little late. He wasn't feeling too well tonight."

"I'll be happy to meet him."

"Well, he doesn't like parties or balls."

"Is he much like Mr. Rupert?"

"Oh, no, not at all! They have the same father but different mothers. Lord Leslie's first wife was a very gentle woman. Rupert seems to have none of that gentleness."

"You apparently don't care for your Uncle Rupert."

"Oh, let's not talk about that. Change the subject."

"Very well. Your dress is beautiful, Miss Hayden, and you dance divinely."

"There! Let's have a lot more of that. You may lie to me all you please about my ability as a dancer and my beauty. Actors are known for such things. I refuse to believe a word you say, but it's pleasant to hear."

Across the room, Leah St. John had come to stand beside Edward and Heather. They watched the dancers, commenting on various individuals, and finally Leah said,

"Edward, do you think it's wise to let Gervase have her way?"

"About what, Sister?"

"I understand that it was she who asked the actor, Mr. Tremayne, to come, or rather she asked you if she could do such a thing and you said yes."

"He seems like a fine enough chap, and Gervase has a lot of sense. Besides, he adds a little colour to the ball, don't you think?"

"Gervase has very good sense, Leah," Heather said with a smile. "She's not likely to fall in love with an actor."

After a brief silence Leah turned to face the pair. "I wish her father had more of that."

"Well, Arthur's sensitive," Edward said reluctantly and with some sadness, "and I suppose he'll never change."

Rupert had joined their group, and he said now, "No, he never will change. It's a pity. Men should change."

Edward laughed and turned to face Rupert. "You're a fine one to talk, Rupert. When was the last time you changed? I believe it was when you were fifteen and decided not to be a lawyer."

Rupert straightened up, and a frown scored his features. "I trust you're not saying I'm like Arthur."

"No, you're a practical man and Arthur isn't."

Heather at once defended Arthur, for she was fond of him. "He's got a sweet spirit. I always liked him. Now, enough gossip about family. Let's enjoy the ball."

Across the room Grant was chatting with Dora when St. John suddenly appeared. He had obviously been drinking, and Grant, being highly attuned to such things, noticed it immediately.

"I'm afraid you're going to have to give up your pursuit of Aldora, Inspector."

Grant blinked. It was improper of the man to say such a thing. "I'm sure I don't know what you mean," he said stiffly.

"I've decided to become her suitor," St. John said and grinned loosely.

"Don't be silly," Dora said. "You know that could never happen."

"But it would solve all my problems. Plenty of money in your family to support a trifling beggar like me." He turned to Grant and said, "Are you enjoying the ball?"

"Not really my sort of thing, Mr. St. John."

"No, catching criminals would be much more exciting, I'm sure. You and your actor friend are in the same boat as I am."

"I don't know what to make of that,"

Grant said, studying the younger man carefully.

St. John smiled, pleased to have offended Grant. "We're not quite the ticket, as they say. Come along, Aldora. Time you had a dance with a really excellent partner."

Matthew Grant watched as the pair moved off and felt a glow of anger. He did not like Bramwell St. John, and he muttered under his breath, "A good caning would help him, and I'd like to be the one to administer it!"

The evening had worn on, and finally Leah St. John moved over and began to speak to Alberta. The two had known each other well for years, and Alberta commented on Leah's son. "You have such a handsome son. St. John's one of the best-looking young men I know."

"Yes, he's fine-looking, but I worry about his future."

Surprise washed across Alberta Newton's face. "Why would you worry about his future?"

"He has no profession."

"But he's young. Many men older than St. John are late in finding their calling."

Leah chewed her lower lip, and for an instant, pain scored her face. "If something happened to Edward, Rupert would be the head of this family."

"Yes, I understand he has been designated as such by Edward."

"If Edward died and Rupert were the head of this family, Bramwell and I would be set out in the street without a dime."

"Oh, surely not! Rupert would never do a thing like that."

"You don't know him, Alberta. He's a cold, heartless man, and he begrudges us every bite we eat."

Alberta was shocked. She had never heard such a thing mentioned, although she had known Leah to be an unhappy woman, and now she said gently, "Edward is a strong, healthy man. He'll live for many years. Now, come and let's get some refreshments."

Serafina had been watching the two women speak as she stood far back into the crowd when she looked up and saw Lord Darby making his way toward her. As he stood before her smiling, she was reminded of what a fine, handsome, strong man he was.

"I've been watching Dylan dance with a most attractive woman," Serafina said.

"Ah, your friend Tremayne is an attractive fellow himself. The ladies can't keep their eyes off of him."

"Oh, he looks well enough."

"Come now, Serafina, you know he's probably the best-looking man in England. Women turn around to watch him on the street. I've observed that much in this single evening."

Serafina knew that Lord Darby was right, and it troubled her. "Yes, but it's not his good looks I admire. I owe him a lot. Have you heard how he was injured saving David?"

"Just a little. I'd like to hear the rest of the story." He listened intently as Serafina related how David had wandered into the pasture with the wild, dangerous bull, and how Dylan had rescued him, risking his own life.

"He is a stout fellow. There's more to him than Rupert thinks."

"What does Rupert say?"

"Oh, you know Rupert. He's all pounds and shillings and pence. If he can't put a price on it, he's not interested. He thinks Tremayne is a shallow actor."

"He's much more than that," Serafina said sharply, and then she made herself smile. "Are you going to ask me to dance?"

"I shall indeed."

The two danced the next dance, and when it ended they left the floor and moved to where Dylan was waiting. "Lord Darby, I must protest. You're a much better dancer than I am."

"You shouldn't be on that bad leg so much, Dylan," Serafina said crossly.

"Well, the poor fellow can't help it. The women are practically lined up to dance with him." Edward smiled.

"Perhaps if you'll dance with me, Lady Trent, that will warn some of them off."

Serafina said, "I'm not sure of that, but we'll try it." They nodded to Lord Darby and moved back to the dance floor, but before they left, Edward said, "Oh, do you ride, Tremayne?"

"Yes, sir, but not as well as you, I'm sure."

"Join me tomorrow. We'll ride over the estate. I'll show you some fine animals and some fine farming."

"I'd be most happy, Lord Darby."

As they merged into the dance, Dylan said, "He's a fine man. I can tell."

"He is fine, and his wife is too. They're the happiest couple that I know."

"More than your parents?"

"Oh, perhaps not, but my parents have something to make them happy."

"And what's that?"

"A wonderful daughter like me."

Dylan smiled, his white teeth flashing against his tanned skin. "That is something to be proud of. I congratulate you for bringing sunshine and roses and never giving your parents an anxious moment."

The evening was almost over, and Gervase came to Dylan, who was at the refreshment table talking to Irene Tillerman, a fine-looking society woman. He had danced with her twice already and had found she was quite the "toothsome wench," as he had heard put before.

"Come along, Dylan," Gervase said, "I want you to meet my father."

Irene stared at her coldly. "We're about to dance."

"Well, you can dance later. I want Mr. Tremayne to meet my father."

Dylan said, "We'll have our dance later, Miss Irene. I wouldn't miss it."

He followed Gervase across the room, and she introduced her father. Arthur Hayden was not tall and seemed almost fragile. He had delicate features, fine blond hair, and unusual green eyes. He smiled when he was introduced to Dylan.

"My daughter has told me you are a wonderful actor. I'm sorry I missed you. What are you in right now?"

"At the moment I'm unemployed and enjoying it thoroughly. Sponging off of good people like the Newtons."

"Well, I'm sponging off of the Haydens, so I suppose we have a lot in common." The two men laughed aloud.

"I would very much like to see some of your paintings, sir."

Arthur was pleased at this. "I'd be happy to show you my little efforts tomorrow morning if you would."

"You may count on it."

They were suddenly interrupted when Bramwell came lurching toward them. He obviously was in the last stages of intoxication and apparently had decided to become obnoxious. He glared at Dylan and said, "Well, Actor, are you still here?"

"Still here, Mr. St. John," Dylan said, eyeing the man carefully. He had not offended St. John in any way that he knew of, but there was a belligerence in the younger man's eyes.

"You ought to stop using the Newtons for your personal gain."

Gervase said, "St. John, that's no way to speak to a guest!"

"I'll speak to him any way I please! I'll even give him a cuff, and he can challenge me to a duel." He made a wild swing that missed Dylan's face by a foot. Leah suddenly was there.

"Come, Bramwell, it's time for you to leave." St. John grew quiet at her touch, glared at Dylan one more time, then was led off.

Gervase expelled the breath she was holding. "I'm glad you didn't take offense. He's an unhappy man."

"He has no prospects," Arthur said. "He's like me, a parasite."

"Don't talk like that, Father."

But Arthur Hayden had been drinking heavily himself. His eyes were red-rimmed, and his speech was slurred. "I should have left this place years ago, Gervase, and made a life for myself and for you, but I was afraid."

Gervase took her father by the arm. "Come along, Father. The party is over."

Serafina had joined the group just as St. John had been led away. She turned to Dylan. "I'm glad you didn't take offense. I feel sorry for the young man. He has a hard way to go. It's never pleasant when you're a dependent."

"How would you know that, Lady Trent? You've never been a dependent."

"No, but I've seen it in others."

"This isn't a very happy household, is it? I can see unhappiness in the face of St. John's mother, and as for Rupert, nobody as harsh as he is happy."

"You're very quick, Dylan."

"Well, Gervase seems to be quite happy."

"Yes, I think she is. She's a sweet young woman."

Glancing up, Serafina saw Irene Tillerman headed straight for them. "Watch out for Irene. She's ruined two men already."

"I doubt she'd want me, an unemployed actor."

"Don't let her get her claws into you. You're rather weak where women are concerned."

"Now who has given me that reputation? As for this whole ball, I'd rather be at home playing draughts with David."

"So would I," Serafina said. "It would be much more pleasant."

Six

"Have you ever ridden to the hounds, Mr. Tremayne?"

Dylan had joined the guests out near the stables. He had been invited to take part in the fox hunt, but now a dubious look crossed his face. His ears were filled with the yapping of some forty dogs kept in check by Rupert, and he shook his head, "No, sir, I have ridden but never chasing a fox."

"An exciting sport, sir. Very exciting." Lord Edward's eyes were bright, and he touched the tall top hat that all the hunters wore, men and women. "I love to hunt the partridge in September and pheasants in October, but when November rolls around I'm ready to mount my favourite steed and make a dash across the fields after the sly foxes."

Dylan rubbed his chin hesitantly. "I'm afraid I've got too much of the peasant in me, Lord Darby. When I hunted as a boy with my father, it was always something to eat, a rabbit or even a wild pig, but never a fox."

Lord Darby found this amusing. "Really? I'm not interested in catching the fox. It's just the chase. As a matter of fact, hunting foxes wasn't a sport at all for many years. Foxes were regarded as vermin who destroyed livestock, and a bounty was put on their heads in Elizabethan days. But the deer became scarce and trees were felled for fuel and there weren't enough deer to hunt. So, the aristocracy decided to hunt foxes instead." He glanced over the crowd with a look of satisfaction. "Foxes are fast as well as tricky. We've had to breed new hounds to track them for sport."

"It seems quite exciting," Dylan said. "I don't quite understand how it works."

"Oh, it's simple enough. Early in the morning we send people out to block the holes in the hunt area. That's to stop them from returning to their dens. They're nocturnal animals, you understand. Then the next step is what we're doing right now. All of the sportsmen, plus the hounds, are gathered together to meet under the supervision of the master. That's me in this case. The next thing is to locate a fox. Usually someone will find one hidden in a thicket, and the hounds are sent in to flush him out into the open. Then we'll all call out, 'Tally ho!' And off we go."

"Sounds like jolly good fun."

"Well, the idea is simply to gallop across country and have a good time. It's a little dangerous. The horses have to jump fences and streams. People have been seriously hurt, but you can't live in a cave and be small."

"What happens when you catch the fox?"

"Oh, the hounds kill him. They customarily devour him except for his tail, which we call his brush, and his mask, which is his head and the paws. They're awarded as trophies." Rupert approached and said, "The dogs are getting nervous, Edward. Are you about ready?"

"Is everyone here, Rupert?"

"All except St. John. He got drunk last night and probably has a hangover. He and Arthur, I think, got drunk together. I think you ought to crack down on both of them. They need to show more respect for the family."

Edward suddenly frowned and turned to face Rupert. "I know they're weak, both of them, Rupert, but I think it would be a good thing if you showed a little more compassion to your brother and your nephew."

Rupert frowned, and the scowl marred his face. "They get the compassion they deserve."

Rupert turned away, and Gervase and Serafina arrived, Serafina riding a pretty little high-bred chestnut mare and Gervase a bay mare of about the same size. Gervase glanced at Dylan and moved her horse closer.

"Are you ready for the hunt, Dylan?" She was, indeed, a pretty thing. Her colour was heightened, and her back was fine and straight. She sat on her horse with unconscious grace. Her dress was a blue habit with white cuffs and lapels, and in some ingenious way, she had drawn her hair up under a dashing tricorne with a tight curl of oyster feathers.

"I don't know if I belong in this particular activity." Dylan smiled. "I'll probably fall off."

"You wouldn't be the first one," Serafina said. "Just hang on."

Edward nudged his horse closer and began speaking to Serafina. "I understand you are being courted by Sir Alex Bolton."

"Oh, yes, he's going through all his potential wives in alphabetical order to find what suits his taste. It's not serious."

Edward drew closer still. He put his hand out and touched her arm with affection. "I wish you would marry, Serafina. You're young enough to have more children."

Dylan was watching the earl's face and saw sadness in it. It came to Dylan that the nobleman was grieving over his own childless condition. He moved away so that he would not hear the rest of the conversation. If he had remained, he would have heard Lord Darby say, "What about Tremayne?"

"Well, what about him?"

"Well, I saw how you were jealous of the attention Irene Tillerman paid to him at the ball. You had a proprietary air."

"Nonsense! He can take care of himself with women like that. I think it's disgraceful the way women pursue him."

"Even you?"

"Certainly not me! He's been good to David. He saved his life, as I've told you."

"Well, Serafina, marriages have been made on worse grounds than that."

"Don't be silly, Sir Edward. I'm not interested in anything like that."

"Well then . . . let's begin."

The hounds located a fox almost immediately, and the action began at once. Serafina stayed beside Edward while Dylan fell back, and Gervase rode beside him. It was an exciting chase, sure enough. Dylan was not used to such a spirited horse, and it was all he could do to keep his seat. Finally he slowed down, and Gervase slowed with him. "Do you like this sort of thing, Gervase?"

"Oh, I love riding. I don't need a fox to make it worth my while. I come out almost every day for a nice ride." She looked at him and said, "I've decided I like you very much, Tremayne."

Dylan was taken off guard by her frankness. He turned and asked with some alarm, "You're not falling in love with me, are you?"

"Not a bit of it, but you're fun to be with."

"I'm glad you find me fun, but you need to find a nice earl and marry him."

"It would be boring, Dylan. All the earls I've known have been boring."

Dylan thought about that and then turned to face her, admiring the colour in her cheeks and her bright eyes. "What about Lady Trent's former husband?"

Gervase was silent, and the excitement seemed to fade. "He was . . . frightening to me."

"You were afraid of him?"

"Oh, he never threatened me or anything like that, but there was a dark side to him. I don't think anyone's ever found out what went on in their marriage, but Serafina was very unhappy."

"Yes, I've heard a little about that. Well, forget that." A shout interrupted their talk.

"Here we go. Stay up with me if you can!"

Edward and Serafina led the pack, and they reached a fence. It was not a particularly high fence, and Serafina moved her weight forward to make the jump easier for the horse. She was slightly ahead of Sir Edward, but she heard a muffled cry. She turned around to see that his saddle had slipped, and he was falling. "Sir Edward!" she called out and pulled her horse up beside him, afraid someone would jump the fence and land on him now that his horse had wandered away, stripped of his saddle. Once Serafina saw that the other riders were stopping, she jumped off her horse and ran to him.

Sir Edward was lying on his face, and carefully she rolled him over. He had a terrible bruise on his head; part of the fence, evidently, had struck him on the neck and raked down across his shoulders, tearing his clothing. His eyes were closed, and she took his pulse.

"Is he all right? Is he hurt?" Dismounted riders came crowding around, and Serafina said, "He's unconscious, but his pulse is strong. I don't think he's badly hurt, but we need to get him back to the house and have my father look at him."

"I'll go get a wagon," one of the younger men said and kicked his horse into a dead run.

The hunters all crowded around, and Serafina, still holding his head, said, "Please don't crowd so close."

Dylan, however, knelt down on the other side. "What happened?"

"His saddle slipped, I think."

Gervase joined them and asked, "Is there anything we can do?"

"No, my father will have to look at him." She held the man's head tenderly. "Someone go warn Heather, but be calm. He's not badly hurt."

Lord Darby was placed on his bed in his room, and Septimus examined him carefully. He looked up with some irritation at the crowd and shooed them out as if they were chickens. "Everyone out," he said. "Lord Edward is going to be all right."

Dylan asked, "Do you think he has a concussion?"

"No, I don't think so. Look, he's waking up. See his eyes?"

Serafina moved to the other side of the bed, and Dylan and Gervase stayed down at the foot.

"Can you hear me, Lord Darby?" Septimus asked loudly.

Lord Darby moved his head and winced. He reached up, and his eyes opened. He looked confused and said, "I . . . had an accident."

"Yes, your saddle gave way when you went over the fence. You took quite a fall," Serafina said. She came over and took his hand, putting her own on his head. "But you're all right now."

"I'll stay with him for a while," Septimus said. "The rest of you go away, please. He needs the rest."

Serafina left the room and stood there for a moment thinking. Something troubled her, and she said, "Excuse me, Dylan, I have an errand to run."

"Of course, Lady Trent."

Gervase looked after her. "Where is she going?"

"I never know what that woman's going to do next."

Serafina left the house and went to the stables. She hailed one of the stablehands and said, "Did you bring Lord Darby's saddle back?"

"Yes, ma'am, it's over there. The horse wasn't hurt badly."

"I'm glad to hear that." Serafina walked over and took one look at the girth. Her eyes narrowed, and she took a deep breath.

The girth had been cut halfway through, and the other part was ragged where it had not been able to bear the weight of the rider. "Someone cut this on purpose," Serafina murmured aloud. "Someone tried to kill Lord Darby."

Slowly she turned and picked up the saddle. It was very light. She carried it away and put it in the carriage that she arrived in. She put it in the baggage section, and then a grim tension came to her mouth as she turned back toward the house.

The guests had all departed by the next day, except Serafina, Matthew, and Dylan. Serafina joined Heather in Edward's room and inspected the bandage on his neck and the blue bruise on the side of his head. She waited until Heather left, then motioned Inspector Grant over.

"Edward," she said, "I have some alarming news."

Edward stared at her. "What sort of news?"

"The fall you had wasn't an accident."

"Why, of course it was. The saddle slipped."

"I found your saddle. The girth was cut in two places. There was just enough of it left intact that it wouldn't part until a strain was put on it. When you went over the fence, your weight came down and the saddle came off."

"Oh, I say," Matthew Grant exclaimed. "That's bad."

"I can't believe it. It was an accident," Edward insisted.

Serafina started to argue, but she saw that it would be useless. "Be very careful. This is two times that attempts have been made on your life."

"Oh, you and Heather worry too much, dear. You be off now. I'll be riding over to see you in the next week or so."

They left, and Crinshaw, the butler, came to stand beside Lord Darby's bedside. "You look tired, sir. Let me bring you your drink." He was a tall, gaunt man with a gentle manner. He had been with the Haydens for fifteen years and was always aware of the earl's well-being.

"No, not now, Crinshaw. I'm fine. Just bring it to me tonight at the usual time."

"You need to rest, sir, and your wine always makes you rest."

It was Crinshaw's duty to bring Lord Darby a special drink at bedtime. Only the two of them knew the formula that had been passed down from Edward's father. It was composed of a rare and expensive wine mixed with several strong spices.

"I'll be fine, Charles. I think I can sleep now."

"Very good, sir."

He moved out of the room and descended to the kitchen where he was questioned at once by the housekeeper, Mrs. Swifton. "How is he, Mr. Crinshaw?"

"Not well, if you ask me." He sat down and she poured him a cup of tea and one for herself. He sipped at it and shook his head. "Lady Trent says that the master's fall was no accident. The girth of his saddle was cut."

"Do you tell me that?" Mrs. Swifton exclaimed. "Who would do such a thing?"

"The man who shot at him last month." Crinshaw nodded. "I hope Lady Trent will use her gifts as a detective to find out who's behind all this."

The two sat at the table, old friends, and finally he got up. "Keep your eyes open, Mrs. Swifton. There's some evil in all this, and I fear we're not done with it yet!"

■ ■ ■ ■

Dylan saw that Serafina was worried. Matthew had left them to ride in the carriage, and the two of them were on horses borrowed from Sir Edward's stable. "You're worried about Lord Darby, yes?" Dylan said.

"That was no accident, Dylan."

Dylan did not answer, but he cast a curious glance at her. "It doesn't sound like it."

They had not ridden far when they passed a field. Suddenly some dozen ravens rose into the sky. Dylan watched the huge black forms rise and muttered, "My grandmother would have called that an omen."

"Would she? She believed in things like that?"

"Oh, yes, we all did. Ravens are sinister birds. Mr. Edgar Allen Poe, the American, has written a rather marvelous poem called 'The Raven.' A rather disturbing poem. You must read it sometime."

"I don't believe in things such as that."

"My grandmother did." He hesitated then said, "She was alone one day, and suddenly her husband appeared to her. He was working in the mines, and she didn't know what he was doing home. She started to speak, and suddenly he wasn't there."

"What do you mean he wasn't there?"

"I mean he just disappeared. Two hours later the manager of the mine came and told her that her husband had been killed in a cave-in."

Serafina turned to stare at Dylan. "She really believed that she'd seen the spirit of her husband?"

"Yes. The Methodists call that a *visitation.*"

The two rode on silently, and finally she said, "Dylan, do you know what a collective noun is?"

"No, I've never heard of it."

"It's the name that identifies a group. All animals have such names. A herd of cows, a flock of sheep, a pack of wolves."

"And that's a collective noun?"

"Yes, and you know what a group of ravens is called?"

"No, I don't."

"A conspiracy," she said. "A conspiracy of ravens is what we've just seen."

Dylan suddenly felt a chill. He looked up at the ravens: dark, ugly birds, scoring the air with their harsh cries. "I hate those birds," he muttered. He turned, his eyes fixed on her. "Do you think it means something, Lady Serafina?"

"I don't believe in premonitions," she said

almost violently. “It was an accident.”

Dylan said nothing, but the two of them watched as the ravens circled the sky uttering harsh, guttural cries. He saw Serafina watch as they planted their black imprints against the November sky, and he knew, despite what she said, that Lady Serafina Trent did believe in premonitions.

Seven

Father Francis Xavier moved about the small greenhouse, pleased with the vivid greens, reds, and blues. He liked the colours so much because they contrasted violently with the grim, grey world of Brixton Prison for Women. Father Xavier served as a volunteer chaplain in the prison. He was unpaid and was content with the small amounts given to him by the Catholic Church. He had managed to create — inside the prison confines of concrete, steel, and misery — a small world of his own, a little cosmos that burgeoned with fragrant flowers and shimmering colour.

Father Xavier suddenly smiled as he thought of his battles with the warden, James Hailey, who had no fear either of God or man. When Father Xavier requested permission to create the greenhouse, Hailey grunted and scowled. "You're here to save the miserable souls of these women, Father, not to grow petunias." He nevertheless gave grudging permission to the priest.

The small priest was not built on a heroic scale. He was short, rotund, with a baby face that did not show his age. He smiled often, despite the miserable world that he moved in, and had a vibrant spirit within his aging body. Now as he moved among the fragile flowers, savoring their fragrance and delighting in the rich dignity of their colours, he paused before his pride and joy — a graceful, long-stemmed crimson rose. He plucked off a dead leaf and added a pinch of fertilizer from a paper bag. He stood back to admire the elegant flower.

Suddenly he heard his name being called, and he turned to face Warden Hailey, who had stepped inside the small greenhouse. Inmates and guards alike called Hailey the Great Stone Face, and he had a violent temper that he struggled to control. He was a short man, no more than five feet seven, but his huge shoulders and limbs and deep chest gave him the appearance of a wrestler. People tended to move out of his way when he entered a room.

"Good morning, Warden."

"Morning," Hailey grunted. His face was set in a perpetual scowl, and he said without preamble, "You know Old Meg?"

"Margaret Anderson. Yes, of course."

"Well, she's dying. Better get down there," he said, a rare grin creasing his meaty lips, "and offer up a few prayers that will get her into heaven. Not that there is a heaven," he added finally. The warden seemed to take delight in mocking the priest's faith. For several years now he had tried his best to shake the chaplain's calm but without success. Now he took out a handkerchief, blew his nose, examined the result, then shrugged and replaced the handkerchief in his pocket. "Poor woman's got the notion that there's pie up there in that sky. She thinks she's going to sit around plucking on a harp for the rest of eternity." He laughed shortly and without humor. "Well, Chaplain, you'd better hurry. She's not going to last long." He turned but then suddenly wheeled and stared at the priest with something like animosity in his eyes. "Of course, you can pray all you want. It won't make any difference. There ain't nothing out there. When we die we're gone — just like dumb animals."

Father Xavier had no chance to reply, for the warden disappeared out the door slamming it behind him. He thought for a moment of how he might answer the chaplain but finally gave up. He left the greenhouse and made his way through the labyrinthine passageways of the prison, barred at intervals by steel doors. He greeted every guard by name as he did the inmates whom he passed. When he reached the door marked Hospital, he stepped inside, where he was greeted by a small man with sunken cheeks and moody eyes.

"You come to see Old Meg, I expect."

"Yes, Dr. Zambrinski."

"Well, you'd better speed it up. She's almost gone."

Quickly the priest moved into the ward and saw the woman lying under a thin white sheet. He hurried toward her, leaned over, and studied her face. He thought for a moment she was already gone, but then her eyelids fluttered slightly and opened, revealing watery eyes staring vacantly from her emaciated face. Her lips were dry as leaves as she whispered in a tone barely audible, "Father — ?"

"Yes, Margaret, it's me. Would you like to confess?"

The dying woman nodded slowly and began to gasp out her sins. Father Xavier was not easily shocked, but the catalog of wrongs and iniquities of all sorts and fashions that the woman had stored up in her memory was monumental. He listened without speaking, and finally her voice faded and her eyes closed.

"I'm going to pray for you, my sister."

"Wait." Meg's eyes opened, and she said in a husky voice, "One more . . . sin, Father."

The priest leaned forward, for her voice grew fainter. He caught every word, and as the old, dying woman spoke, Xavier's eyes opened wide, and his lips parted with an expression of amazement. The voice droned on until finally it faded, and her eyes shut. There was a grimness about it, and Xavier stood by her side, whispering consolations and giving the last rites. It was thirty minutes later that the thin breast of Margaret Anderson suddenly rose then fell with the finality of death.

For many moments Father Xavier stood there beside the woman, studying her face. His mind was reeling with what he had heard, and he knew that though Margaret Anderson had gone to meet her Maker, the effects of her life were still in force. *It's like throwing a pebble,* he thought, *into a still pond. The circles spread out farther and farther until they reach the shore.* He folded the woman's hands, then turned slowly and walked between the two rows of beds. Dr. Zambrinski looked up from another woman he was treating. "Is she gone, Father?"

"Yes, she is."

"Well, I'm sorry, but she was no pleasure to herself. Probably glad to be out of this world. We'll arrange for the funeral to be held this afternoon."

"Thank you, Doctor."

Moving slowly with a strange expression in his eyes, the small priest made his way back to the warden's office. He was permitted to go in by an orderly, and Warden Hailey looked up. "She dead?" he demanded.

"Yes, she's gone."

Hailey shrugged his beefy shoulders. Death was no stranger within the walls of Brixton Prison. "Well, it's all over for her. Too bad." He leaned back in his chair and stared at the priest. "You've been a long time. I suppose the woman had a lot to confess — drunkenness, foul language, adultery?"

The mind of the priest went back, and he seemed to hear the woman's thin, frail voice as she spoke her last confession to him.

"It was more than that, Warden, more terrible than that."

EIGHT

Edward Hayden was standing at one of the tall windows in the drawing room staring out at the dead world. November of '57 was scheduled to be one of the coldest on record, and now the dead, grey tint of the grass, the trees stripped of their leaves and holding their naked arms toward the skies, seemed to cast a pall on the earl. Quickly he walked over to the large fireplace, turned his back to it, and put his hands behind him, locking his fingers together. He gave a quick glance at his wife, who was sitting at a Louis Quatorze desk writing a letter.

He kept his eyes on her, thinking how she had kept her attractiveness even through her later years, and his mind went back to the time when he had first seen her. It had been at her coming-out, and he had first seen her bowing to the Queen in a graceful curtsey. She had turned, and her eyes had met his, and although Edward Hayden, Earl of Darby, had courted other women in his youth, somehow he had known at that instant that this was the woman for him. A smile touched his lips, turning the corners up, and the thought came to him, *I was a romantic young devil. I certainly was.* He did not regret it, however, and now he stood before the fire, the silence of the room broken by the crackling of the logs in the fireplace and the regular beat of the huge grandfather clock on the east wall.

Growing uncomfortably warm, Edward moved across the room and sat down in a chair that seemed altogether too fragile for his weight. He despised the new fashion in furniture, for portly crinolined ladies and well-upholstered gentlemen had to lower their weight carefully on the spindly chairs and impossibly elegant settees. He glanced around the walls, which were padded and gilded, and the ceiling, which was broken up by rococo garlands and elaborate dust-catching friezes. The room was crowded, as were all Victorian drawing rooms and parlours. Wallpaper covered some of the walls, and the carpets were thick and rather dowdy. Paintings adorned the walls, and everywhere the room seemed crowded.

"I wonder why we have to have all this . . . this stuff."

Heather looked up at her husband with surprise. "What stuff?" she asked.

"Look at this room. You can hardly walk through it without running into something."

"It's fashion, dear."

"Fashion be hanged. It's bloody nonsense, that's what it is."

Heather stared at her husband. He very rarely swore, but she had noticed that since the ball and the fall from his horse, he had been short-tempered. "It is a bit busy, isn't it, Edward?"

"Oh, it's all right. I'm just in a bad temper. You must excuse me, my dear."

Heather got up from the desk and walked around. She moved behind him and laid her hand lightly on the side of his face that was bruised in the fall. "Are you still having your headaches?"

"Not bad."

"That means you are. I think we'd better have Dr. Goldsmith out to have a look at you."

"No, I've seen enough doctors." Edward reached up, covered her hand with his, holding it close to his face. "You're the medicine I need. Nothing like a beautiful woman to cheer a fellow up and drive his headaches and all of his problems away."

Heather kept her hand on his smooth

cheek and rested her other on his shoulder. She stood there for a moment, thinking what a good man and fine husband he was. Very few men during the reign of Victoria wanted large families. The Queen herself, and Prince Albert, had produced practically a troop, nine in all. This was especially true of their peerage. Men such as the Earl of Darby wanted a son to pass Silverthorn and his title to. She thought over the years that he had never once rebuked her or even hinted that he was unhappy. Heather knew that Edward loved her deeply, and her failure to produce a son was the sorrow of her life.

A slight knock came at the door, and Heather called out, "Come in."

Charles Crinshaw stepped inside. "There's someone to see you, sir."

"Someone? What do you mean someone? Who is it?"

"Well, sir," Crinshaw said, then hesitated for a moment before ending his sentence, "it's a priest. His name is Father Francis Xavier."

Surprise washed across Edward's face. "A priest. What in the world could he want?"

"He didn't say, sir, except that he needs very urgently to see you."

"Well, I suppose we'll have to see him.

Ask him to come in, Crinshaw."

"Certainly, sir."

As soon as the door closed behind the butler, Heather moved away and stood facing her husband. "What in the world could a priest be doing coming to see us? Surely he doesn't think we're Catholic."

"No, I wouldn't think so. Perhaps he's looking for money. Some charitable cause . . ."

This was not an unusual occurrence in the lives of Edward and Heather. They gave generously, and people knew it was easy to get money for the right cause from the pair.

The door opened again, and Crinshaw stepped in and murmured, "Father Francis Xavier, Lord Darby."

"Well, come in, sir," Edward said. He turned to face the priest, studying the short, roly-poly figure and unlined face. He was a good judge of character and saw that the priest was older than his face appeared. His hands were the key. They had brown liver spots and showed other signs of age.

"I'm so sorry to call without requesting permission, Lord Darby."

"That's quite all right, Father. Come in and sit down."

The priest had been unsure of his welcome, but the graciousness of Lord Darby, and the smile on the face of the woman beside him, was encouraging. "I will try to be as brief as possible." He took his seat, and Edward and Heather sat down opposite him.

"What is it I can do for you? Is it a donation you're seeking?" Edward asked, trying to be helpful.

"Oh, no, indeed!" A flush touched Father Xavier's face. "Nothing like that. It's something personal, sir, about yourself and Lady Darby."

Puzzled expressions crossed the faces of Edward and Heather, who exchanged quick glances. "Well, sir," Edward said, "just speak right out."

"Please don't think me impertinent, Lord Darby and Lady Darby, but I have one question to ask of you. It may be that my coming is inappropriate."

"Ask anything you please, Father," Heather said.

"May I ask then, Lady Darby, if you were in the City Hospital on May the twenty-fourth in the year of 1839?"

Heather blinked and shot a quick glance at Edward. "Yes," she said, and her voice was unsteady. "We were there on that exact date."

"Why does this interest you, sir?" Edward

asked. "Surely it can have nothing to do with you."

"Only indirectly, sir."

"I can't imagine why you asked that question," Edward said. He knew that Heather did not like to be reminded of that time in their lives, nor did he, and his words were bitten off in a rather short fashion.

"I know the question sounds impertinent, but let me explain. I am the chaplain at Brixton Prison for Women. I have been there for some time, and just yesterday I received a call to go to the bedside of a woman named Margaret Anderson. She was simply called Old Meg by the inmates and guards. I suppose you've never heard of her?"

"Why, no, I don't know as I've ever heard the name. Have you, Heather?"

"No, I haven't."

Speaking very carefully, Father Xavier said, "Old Meg was in City Hospital the same that you were, on May the twenty-fourth of the year that I mentioned. I know that you had a child on the twenty-third."

"Yes, we did, but he did not live," Heather whispered.

The priest did not miss the look of sorrow in the woman's eyes. He was adept at reading faces, and for all his bland, innocent appearance he had a sharp, penetrating mind. "You may not know, then, that Margaret Anderson had a child on that day, the same day your son was born."

"I don't remember anything about that. It was a rather painful birth."

"Where are you headed with this, Father, if I may ask?" Edward demanded. His eyes were narrowed, and he could not think of any reason why this man had come to his home. He was a man of authority, accustomed to dealing with others, and the priest seemed innocent enough, but he could not be sure.

"Let me be brief," Xavier said quickly. He saw that his words had shocked the two, and he knew that what he had yet to say would be even more traumatic for them. "Old Meg made her dying confession to me yesterday. She told me about her child who was born, and she was very much aware that you were down the hall from her. Everyone knew that Lady Darby was in the hospital and that she had borne a son." For a moment he hesitated and then knew there was no easy way to break the news to these two. "Here is what she told me. She told me that her child died, and in the night . . ." He hesitated and cleared his throat. "In the night she brought her dead child to your room. She said that you were asleep, and your son was in a crib next to you. She put her dead infant in your crib. You were apparently sleeping very soundly. She dressed her dead infant in the garments that your son wore, picked up your baby, and took him back to her room."

The silence was almost palpable. The faces of both Edward and Heather were absolutely pale. Heather was unable to speak, and Edward finally said in a strained voice, "And you're telling me, Father, it was our child she took?"

"That's exactly what I'm saying, Lord Darby. I wanted to be very sure about this, so I went to the City Hospital. They were reluctant to talk to me at first, but the general administrator finally gave me access to the records." He looked up, and his eyes held the two. "Only one child died on May twenty-fourth. That child was listed as Trevor Hayden."

Suddenly Heather turned and grasped Edward by the arm. "It's true! God was telling me the truth!"

Her words confused the priest, and he said, "I don't understand. What truth was it that God told you, if I may ask?"

"Before our son was born, God began to speak to me, and He told me that our son would be a blessing to us and to many others. So when he died, or when we thought he died, it was a terrible blow that shook my faith. I haven't sought God since then, not as I should."

Xavier saw that the anguish in the woman's face was not intermingled with joy.

"Perhaps this is God's way of bringing you back to Himself."

"I've never forgotten it," Edward said. "When my wife was expecting, we committed that child to God. She told me many times that God had promised her he would be a blessing to many."

"I've wondered all these years how I could have missed God's will so badly."

"Where is the child she bore?" Edward asked, his mind working quickly.

"That's the problem, Lord Darby." A wrinkle appeared on the priest's brow, and he said, "The boy disappeared when he was only thirteen years old. Old Meg was a prostitute. Life must have been hellish for the boy. She told me that she was unable to find him. She thinks he's in London, but she's not sure of it."

"But surely she had a family. Perhaps the boy went to one of them."

"No, she had no family, sadly enough. She told me so when she first came to the prison, and she never wrote letters — if she could write — and she certainly never received any."

The three talked for some time about the possibilities, and Edward and his wife wrung every word from the priest about Meg and the baby, who was now a young man of eighteen. Finally the priest said, "It may be that you can't find the boy. Meg certainly couldn't, although she probably didn't look very hard."

"If he's alive, we'll find him, and we thank you for coming."

The priest got to his feet, fished in his pocket, and handed the earl a small paper. "There's my name. You can find me at Brixton Prison almost anytime. Please get in touch with me if I can help."

"We will indeed do that. We owe you a debt of gratitude."

"I hesitated about coming, but the Lord seemed to tell me that it was the thing to do. I'll be praying that you find your son."

The two made their farewells to the priest, and as soon as the door closed, Heather turned, and her face was alive in a way that Edward had not seen for years. "He's alive! Our son is alive! I knew that it was God speaking. I just didn't have faith."

"We mustn't get too ahead of ourselves

here. We may not be able to find the child."

"Yes, we will. God is in this, Edward."

"Yes, He is." Now Edward's eyes glowed with a fire that Heather had seen only rarely. "If our son is alive, I'll find him!"

Nine

The sun had hidden itself for most of the day and even now made a decrescent shape in the grey December sky. Morning had brought a whirling snowstorm that caught London and the surrounding counties off guard. As Serafina stood looking out the window, she marveled at the beauty of fresh snow, which had sculptured the entire landscape into an enormous filigree — ornamental works of incandescent brightness.

It makes the world look so clean and innocent and pure. The thought came to her, and she smiled at her own flight of imagination. "That was like something Dylan would say," she murmured aloud. Her eyes admired the estate and the diaphanous workmanship of the snow. All was delicate, and the elaborate iron fence looked like a fragile piece of fine lace. Nothing was sharp or elongated now. Every shape was rounded, and it made the world a softer, even a kinder place — or at least the notion struck her for the moment. Shifting her glance, she watched as Dylan and David played in the foot-deep snow. The faint sound of their voices drifted toward her, and the sight of David's face — the joy and the smile and the brightness of his eyes — pleased her. As for Dylan, he was like a large boy. She watched as he lay flat on his back and moved his arms from his hips to over his head. *Making snow angels. Now David will have to make one too.* Indeed, the boy did imitate the man, and finally Dylan reached out, picked up David, and tossed him lightly into the air. She could hear her son's delighted squeal, and it pleased her.

"Serafina, you're going to have to do something about that man."

Caught off guard, Serafina turned and saw her aunt Bertha standing immediately behind her. Bertha's hands were clenched tightly as she stared out the window, and a frown scored her face, making twin furrows between her eyebrows. Her mouth, Serafina noted, was like a steel trap. There was little kindness in it, and she realized how hard she had to work at keeping her aunt pleased.

"What are you talking about, Aunt Bertha?"

"What am I talking about? I'm talking about that . . . that actor out there. Look at him, a grown man playing in the snow!" Her voice was acid, dripping dislike, and she shook her head shortly, her eyes narrowing as she watched the pair. "I'm disappointed in you, Serafina."

"Are you? I'm sorry to hear that, Aunt."

"Doesn't it bother you to have your son, the future Viscount of Radnor and peer of the realm, wallowing in the snow with a disreputable man like that?"

"Why would you say Dylan is disreputable?" Serafina was indeed curious. She could not understand her aunt's animosity. Somehow she knew her aunt had suffered something in life to give her such a bitter cast, and it was obvious that she was unable to form a pleasing relationship with anyone.

"You know what actors are like."

"I suppose they're like all other people. Some are good and some are bad."

"It's not good for David to associate with such a person. You know their reputations. They're an immoral bunch, all of them."

Serafina sought for an answer, and finally she said quietly, "David gets lonely. I know what that's like."

Serafina's strange remark caught Bertha. She stared at the younger woman, and for a moment it seemed as if she would soften. Indeed, her lips relaxed, but they quickly tightened once again.

"You're a grown woman and able to take care of yourself, but you're putting David at the power of that man, and you know what he's like. I'm surprised at you. You ought to be more careful."

"Are you forgetting that Dylan saved David's life?"

"Then you should have given him a reward."

"Given him money?"

"Yes. Pay him off."

"I couldn't do that. He wouldn't take it in the first place."

Bertha sniffed and then shook her head like a terrier shaking an animal it had just caught. "Oh, he'd take it all right! He's after your money."

"He's never asked for anything."

"He's waiting for the big ticket. That's what he's doing. Don't you see that?"

"What are you talking about, Aunt Bertha?"

"Why, he's bewitched you, Serafina. He's going to make you fall in love with him or at least fall into some sort of feeling, and he's making himself indispensable. Now he's got a hold on you because he saved David's life. Mark my words. He plans to marry you."

"That's ridiculous!"

"Wiser women than you have fallen prey to a young, good-looking man," Bertha warned. "I wish you would warn him off the place."

"I can't do that." Serafina's words were soft, but there was a steel edge to them that Bertha Mulvane had learnt to identify. And when the Viscountess Trent said something in that tone, the conversation was over.

Bertha shook her head with disgust and turned, making her parting shot bitter and cynical. "You'll find out one of these days what sort of man he is. I only hope you don't disgrace the family before then."

Serafina watched her aunt go, wondering again at the resentfulness of the woman. She was well aware, as were other members of the household, that Bertha took things — spoons, jewellery from time to time, and somehow, in a way that Serafina could not figure out, even some of the furniture — from Trentwood House. There had never been enough damage done to cause Serafina to confront Bertha, and even now she felt both anger and pity for the woman. *She has to be the most unhappy person in the world. She's so bitter.*

Serafina turned back and watched as her son and Dylan continued to play in the snow, and a smile touched the corner of her lips.

"Faster! Faster, Dylan!"

Dylan had found a sled in the barn and had rigged it so that David could ride on it. Now he was pulling it forward with all the speed he could muster. "Wait, David, and you will see something!" he cried out. He had pulled the sled up a steep incline and now glanced back at the house, which was clothed in the pristine whiteness of the morning's snowfall. His glance went to David, whose cheeks were red and eyes were dancing with pleasure. "We'll see what kind of a lad you are in just a moment."

Reaching the top of the crest, Dylan stopped and breathed deeply for a moment. His injuries from the encounter he'd had with the bull were practically gone, only a twinge in his side now and then. Matthew Grant had said, "It's a good thing that your side got beat up instead of your face. You wouldn't be much good as an actor if you were all scarred up."

Indeed, that was true enough, but now Dylan was thankful that he had regained practically all of his strength.

"Are we going to slide down that hill, Dylan?"

"Indeed, we are."

Dylan shoved the sled to the very brink. "Do you have the nerve to go down?"

"Yes!" David cried. "I can do it!"

"You must be cautious. What if you hurt yourself? Your mother would have my head." Dylan joined David on the sled, shoved off, and the sled moved forward. It picked up momentum, and he heard David yelling with joy. When they got to the foot of the hill, Dylan turned the sled sideways so that it tipped over.

David rolled over several times in the snow, and Dylan also was on the ground with him. "Is it fun, boy, you're having?"

"Yes!" David exclaimed. "I can do it by myself."

"You could hurt yourself."

"I'm not afraid."

"All right then. By yourself it is." The two made their way back to the top of the hill, and this time when David got on the sled, Dylan gave him a gentle shove. He watched as the sled started down the hill, wondering if he had done the right thing, but it turned out well. David got to the foot of the hill without turning over and immediately called, "Do it again, Dylan! Do it again!"

Dylan marched down the hill and said, "No, that's enough for now. We've got to go back to the house."

"Why? I want to sled some more."

"We're going to make snow cream."

"Snow cream?" David demanded, looking up at Dylan. "What's snow cream?"

"It's a secret formula only we Welshmen know. Come along now."

The two tramped back to the house, David's shorter legs going deep into the snow. Dylan suddenly reached down, grabbed him, and put him astride his shoulders. "Now, you ride there," he said.

When they reached the house, Serafina was standing at the open door. "I was watching you out the window on that sled. You fell. David could have been hurt."

Dylan reached up, plucked David off his shoulders, and set him down. His face was ruddy with the exercise, and he wore no cap, so his black hair contrasted almost violently with the whiteness of the snow. There was a masculinity, a strength about the man Serafina had been drawn to, and now, as always, he had the ability to make her seem small and fragile. This was something she did not like, for she prefered to think herself the equal of any man. Her common sense and rational approach told her this was not so, that many men would be physically stronger. But now she grew argumentative as she often did.

"It's dangerous. When you rolled over, he could have hurt himself."

"If a boy can't take a little bump like that, let him put skirts around his knees."

"I'm all right, Mum," David cried out. "We're going to make snow cream."

"Snow cream? What's that?"

"It's something I specialize in." Dylan grinned at her. "We have to go to the kitchen."

"Well, you can't track all that snow in. Go around to the back door."

"Right, you!"

As they arrived in the kitchen, David was full of talk. He was excited and repeated the things he and Dylan had done. Once again it made Serafina realize how hungry the boy was for companionship. There were no small boys his age in the immediate vicinity, no one for David to play with. None of the servants had boys his age, and she knew he grew lonely, so she made a resolve to spend more time with him. She realized at once, however, that Dylan Tremayne added something to David's life that was not her gift to give.

"Let's make snow cream!"

"You don't even know what it is."

"It sounds good though."

Nessa Douglas joined them, and Dylan said, "I need a few things from you, Cook."

"What would you need from me?"

"We're going to make snow cream," David announced. "You ever make that, Nessa?"

"I don't even know what it is."

"Well, if you are a good girl, I'll give you some of it." Dylan reached out and pinched the cook on the shoulder. Serafina saw her face flush and wondered again at the power Dylan Tremayne had to please women. Cook was thirty-three years old and happily married, but still Dylan's attention pleased her. "Well, tell me what it is, and I'll tell you how you can get along without it."

"It would be unlikely, not while the mistress of Trentwood is here."

"Give him what he wants, Nessa, or there'll never be any peace," Serafina said.

Dylan said, "There now. There's not much I want. Just my own way. Now, I'll have some cream, thick as you've got it, some sugar, and some vanilla."

Serafina and David watched as Nessa brought out the ingredients. "Now, I need a big bowl, the biggest you've got."

"This will have to do," Nessa said, handing him a large, deep bowl.

"That'll be just fine." Dylan mixed the sugar, cream, and vanilla and tasted it. "A little more vanilla, I think." He added a few more drops of vanilla, beat it, and then said, "Now, we need three big spoons and three small bowls." When Cook gave him a large bowl, he grinned at Serafina. "Now come outside and you'll have your first bite of snow cream."

They donned their coats and went outside. Going down the steps, Dylan said, "We need to find a nice smooth spot where nobody's walked."

"What about over there?" Serafina said, pointing to part of the lawn that was as smooth as the floor in the house.

"Just right. Come along."

"Here now, David, you hold this bowl while I do the mixing."

David grasped the bowl by the edges, his enormous eyes watching Dylan as he began to scoop snow into it. He would scoop some, mix it with the ingredients in the bottom, and continue until finally it was done. "Now then, let's have the bowls."

Serafina held the bowls out as Dylan filled them. "Let's have the spoons now, ma'am." Each of them took a spoon, and Dylan tasted the mixture. "Just right. See if you like it, David."

David took a heaping spoonful and stuck it in his mouth. His eyes opened wide. "It's cold," he said.

"Hurts your teeth a little bit, but you'll freeze them up. How does it taste?"

"It's good!"

"Why, this is delicious, Dylan! I've never heard of it before!" Serafina exclaimed.

"My grandmother Bronwyn taught me this when I was just a boy about David's age or even younger. She was a fine woman, she was. Fair and beautiful she was, in my sight anyway."

David finished his bowl and demanded more.

"Couldn't we go in the house?" Serafina asked.

"No, it wouldn't do. Snow cream melts when you take it into a house. I'll tell you what, though. We'll make some more up, and we'll put the bowl in the snow out here. That'll keep it just about right, and it'll get even better with a little aging."

At that moment James Barden, the butler, came to the back door and called, "Lady Trent, you have a visitor."

"Who is it, Barden?"

"It's Lord Darby and his wife."

"Lord Darby? Tell them I'll be right in.

Put them in the small parlour. Come on, David. We need to get you cleaned up."

"I'll just make some more snow cream and put it in the snow. Cover it up so that no varmints can get at it. We'll have some more after a while, right, David?"

"Yes!"

Serafina went inside, took off her coat, and went at once into the small parlour. She was greeted by Lord Darby and Lady Heather, and she smiled warmly in return. "It's so good to see you. I'm so glad you've come for a visit."

"Well, it's more than just a visit," Lord Darby said. "I understand your friend Dylan Tremayne is here."

"Yes, he's been playing with David all morning."

"He plays with David?" Heather said with some surprise. "You never told us that."

Serafina could not help but smile. "He's like a boy himself, a big boy, to be sure. He gets down on the floor and plays with David as if they were the same age."

"That's wonderful, Serafina," Edward Darby said. "We'd like to see him, if possible."

Serafina was curious. She turned and went to the door. "Louisa, would you fix some tea, please. For four. And tell Mr. Tremayne he's wanted in the parlour."

"Yes, ma'am."

Turning back inside, she sat down and studied them furtively. They were both upset for some reason, and she saw a tension in their faces she could not understand.

They waited until Dylan arrived, and Edward stood at once and shook hands with him. Dylan was a little surprised. He bowed to Lady Heather and greeted them both.

"We have something to tell you, Serafina." He hesitated for a moment then glanced at Heather and seemed to gain strength. "We were visited by a Catholic priest, Father Francis Xavier . . ."

Serafina listened as Darby told the story of the priest's visit. She saw then that there was hope in the countenance of both of them that had been missing before.

Serafina marveled at the story. She glanced at Dylan and saw that he was staring at the pair intently.

"What have you done about this so far, Lord Darby?"

"I've gone to the hospital and checked the records — which are scarce. Then I've gone to the police. They have looked into the matter."

"What did they say?" Dylan asked abruptly.

"They said there was no hope, that it was eighteen years ago, and they could do nothing."

"Perhaps if you talked to Matthew Grant, he could help."

"It was Grant we talked to," Heather said suddenly. "He was very sympathetic, but he offered no hope at all."

A silence fell over the room, and then Heather spoke up, her face alight. "You solved a murder, a case the police couldn't solve. Will you help us, Serafina?"

Serafina felt suddenly uncomfortable. "I'm not really a detective. I'm more of a scientist."

"We have no one else to go to," Edward Darby said. "I beg you to help us."

"That woman, from what you told me, came from the very worst part of London. I don't know that world. That's where whoever searches for him will have to go."

"I know it's not your world, but Mr. Tremayne knows it very well," Edward said, glancing at Dylan.

"As a matter of fact, I do. I was brought up in it, for the most part, when I was just a lad. I'm not very proud of some of the things I did there."

"But you know the world," Edward insisted. "I know you turned down a very lucrative role because of moral reasons, and I honour you for that. Now, I want to hire you to find our son."

Dylan did not hesitate. "I am not a detective any more than Lady Trent is, but I will do the very best I can. However, I would not want a salary to do this."

"That would not be right," Edward said. "We want you to throw yourself into the search. It takes money for things like this. I want you to take a fee, and you must have money, I assume, to carry out the search."

Serafina interrupted, "Would you excuse us for a moment? I need to speak to Mr. Tremayne alone."

"Certainly," Heather said.

Serafina moved outside, and Dylan followed her. As soon as the door was closed, she turned to him. "I have a great affection for this couple, Dylan. I don't want to raise any false hopes."

"Are you going to try to help them?"

"Yes, but I can't do it alone. If we could do this together, I would be very grateful."

"I'll do my very best, Lady Serafina. We'll trust the good Lord, and He'll help us."

Serafina never knew exactly what to say when Dylan brought the Lord into his conversation. He always spoke quite easily of God, of the Lord, of the Saviour, as if he were speaking of an intimate friend. She cleared her throat and could not think of a proper answer, so she nodded. "Let's go talk to them."

They went back into the parlour, and Serafina declared, "We will do the very best we can."

"Oh, I'm so relieved!" Heather cried. She came forward and embraced Serafina. "I know that you'll be able to help us."

Edward smiled and went forward to pat Serafina's shoulder, then turned and shook hands with Dylan. "Thank you, sir. I feel that we're in good hands." He reached into his pocket and took out a thick envelope, saying, "This is not your salary, Dylan, but I know that in cases like this you may have to bribe some people, pay for information. When you need more, come to me."

The two left, and as soon as they were gone, Serafina turned and said, "I don't know where to start, Dylan. I solved our last case by breaking a code in a book, but this isn't something in a book. It's different. What do we do first?"

There was no hesitation in Dylan's answer. "We're going to the prison. Margaret Anderson must have spoken to someone, an inmate or one of the guards."

"How will you get the warden to let us

question him? He's probably a hard man in a job like that."

Dylan smiled crookedly. It brought a dimple to the left side of his cheek that she had noticed before. "I'm relying on my charm, my wit, and my handsome features."

Serafina could not help but smile. She asked, "What if that doesn't work?"

"Then" — Dylan held up the cash — "we bribe the warden!"

Ten

"That's Brixton Prison, Lady Serafina. And a mournful sight it be too."

Dylan had drawn the carriage up to a line of horses tied to hitching posts and rails. The prison itself rose out of the cold earth, grey and bleak and colourless.

"What a terrible-looking place, Dylan!"

"That it is. It's better than the hulks though."

"The hulks?"

Dylan wrapped the reins around the iron rail in front of him and nodded. "The prisons are so crowded they have to use old ships for prisons, those which are unsafe for the sea. There's quite a few of them down at Woolwich. They're wet, dark, and verminous things. I heard as how the Defiance houses five hundred inmates on three decks. They all sleep in hammocks so tightly packed that they touch."

"What a terrible thing! I think I'd rather die."

"I'm of your way of thinking." Dylan stepped out of the carriage, walked around, and tied the horses to the rail. He then came to hand Serafina down, and they started toward the front entrance. "A good friend of mine went to the prison at Pentonville. That's the one I'd want to stay clear of. Charlie told me that the inmates are forbidden to speak to anybody else at all times. The cells are seven feet by thirteen feet, and all they have is a washbasin, a stool, and a table. That's bad enough, but even their names are taken from them. They are called only by numbers."

A shiver touched Serafina. "How frightful! They must die like flies in such a place," she whispered.

"Well, many of them do. Come along now. I've heard that Brixton is better than most."

The two advanced to where two guards were standing with muskets. One of them stepped forward and asked brusquely, "Why are you here, sir?"

"We need to see the warden."

"I'll take you." The guard, a tall, bulky man, turned to another slighter man, an albino with pale eyes and hair so blond it seemed white. "I'll take them to see the warden. You keep close watch."

"Don't I always?"

The burly guard led them into the prison without speaking. They were somewhat shocked when they stepped inside. At least fifty women sat in chairs along the walls. A high and lofty ceiling rose over them, and three other tiers of what appeared to be walkways were lined with more women in chairs. All the women wore loose, claret-brown gowns, blue-checked aprons, neckerchiefs, and small, close-fitting, white linen caps.

"What are they doing, Guard?" Serafina asked.

"Why, they're sewing, ma'am. That's what all the inmates do here."

"What are they sewing?" Dylan asked curiously. Something about the large number of women all sitting without saying a word, their hands busy at their task, was somewhat frightening to him.

"Well, sir, they make flannel underwear and stitching stays. Then, of course, some of them do the washing and ironing contracted by the prison. You could buy some of their shirts at Moses and Sons."

As they continued toward the door at the far end, Serafina noticed that none of the women looked at them. Perhaps it was forbidden. The quiet was eerie and unhealthy to her. "How many prisoners are there in this institution?"

"Seven hundred, ma'am." He turned at the door and shrugged his beefy shoulders. "Female patients don't bear imprisonment as well as male prisoners, but they're treated fairly well here. They've got a nursery for babies born to prisoners while they're in Brixton."

The guard took a key from his belt, unlocked a steel door, and shoved it open. "Come along," he said. "I'll take you to the warden."

A long, narrow hall, dark and full of shadows, lay before them. The two walked behind the guard until finally he came to a door. He knocked on it, and a deep voice from within said, "Come in."

Opening the door, the guard waved the pair in. "Warden Hailey, these people need to see you."

"All right, Mr. Simmons, you may go. Come in, you two."

As Serafina stepped into the room, she was surprised at how cheerful it was. Here in the very bowels of a cold, grim prison was a warm, cheerful office. A fireplace burned, sending a myriad of sparks upward through the chimney. A sofa was on one side of the room with a wardrobe on the other, and the warden sat at a large mahogany desk. The short, stocky man with deep-set grey eyes spoke with a harsh voice that grated on the nerves. "What is it you want?" he demanded after Dylan gave him their names.

"Warden, we've come to try to find out something about one of your prisoners who died recently."

"Why would you be curious about that? Are you family?"

"No, sir," Dylan said, "we're not. Perhaps I'd better explain." He quickly saw that the warden was unsympathetic, and when he had finished telling Father Xavier's story about Lord Darby and his wife, the warden shrugged. "I know nothing about all that. The woman is dead. You can't talk to her."

"Oh, I realize that, sir, but if we could just talk to some of the women that knew her, I think we'd be able to find traces of the boy."

"We have no time for that. The women are all busy. Write me a letter. I'll consider it."

"I have a better idea than that," Dylan said. "I'll give you a token of our appreciation, and you can give us written permission to talk to any inmate we want." Dylan drew the money out of his pocket and began counting it. The warden suddenly came to his feet, anger flashing from his pale eyes. "Or," Dylan said before the warden could speak, "you can refuse, and we'll go back to the Earl of Darby, and he'll use all his power and influence to remove you from your position."

A dead silence filled the room, and both Dylan and Serafina expected to be driven from the office. But suddenly the warden laughed. "Let's have the bribe," he said.

"That's a wise decision." Dylan handed the money to the warden, who took it carelessly, shoving it in his shirt pocket, then sat down and began scribbling on a piece of paper.

"This will be sufficient. I don't know who the woman's cell mates were. I've been here fourteen years. Hundreds or maybe even thousands of women have passed through here." He handed the paper to Dylan then sat back down in his chair. "Father Xavier isn't here today. He was called away by his church to do something or other." He cocked his head to one side and said, "The old woman was daft. Some of the guards called her Crazy Meg."

"It's the only lead we have, Warden. We appreciate your cooperation."

"Cooperation." The warden sniffed and

patted the money in his pocket. "I'm always willing to cooperate when there's a good reason, and money's always a good reason. Here, I'll assign one of the guards to you. He'll show you the ropes." Going to the door, he opened it and shouted, "Smith, come here. I need you!"

The guard, Fred Smith, was a slight man of below average height. His uniform fit him neatly, and he seemed to be an intelligent sort. He had a neatly trimmed beard and a pair of steel-rimmed eyeglasses through which he peered at them owlishly.

"Come along, please," he said after he looked at the warden's instruction. "We can't have you roaming around the prison, but I'll put you in a room, and I'll go get any inmate you want."

"We don't know which ones we want. Can you find us one who was a cell mate of the woman?"

"Ay, I can do that. Come along."

The two were taken to a small, cheerless room with a table and four chairs. Smith left and soon returned with one of the inmates, saying, "This is Alice Rimes. She knew Meg a little."

Smith left, and Serafina said, "We're trying to find out something about the woman who died called Meg."

"Meg? Wot you want to know about 'er?" She was a tall, skinny woman, and her eyes were hard as flint. After Serafina finished, she snorted. "I don't know nuffin' about Meg, where she come from. Don't reckon she had any people. She was quiet as the grave."

When Serafina saw that the woman could tell them nothing, she knocked on the door, and Smith took her away. He soon returned saying, "I can think of one woman Meg talked to at all. Her name's Mary Cotsworth."

"What's she here for, Mr. Smith?"

"For killing her child and her husband. A grim, bloody business it was. She's crazy now. I doubt you'll get any sense out of her. Have a seat, and I'll bring her back to the room."

Smith opened the door, and a woman with iron-grey hair stepped inside. "This is Mary Cotsworth," Smith said. "She shared a cell with Meg for a while."

Mary was a massive woman, big in every respect, tall, and looked as strong as any man. "Wot's it you want wif me?" she asked in a cracked voice that sounded as if it had been long out of commission.

"We'd like to know anything you can tell

us about Meg."

But it became obvious that she knew nothing of value about Meg Anderson. She stared at them with suspicion, and finally Serafina knocked on the door, and Smith took her away, saying, "I'll bring another inmate right off."

Smith indeed brought four women, none of whom knew anything of value about the dead woman. Finally he brought another inmate, saying, "This is Catherine Foss. She was Meg's cell mate for the last four years."

The woman was undersized and her face was deeply seamed. She was hardened by the blows dealt to her in life, and now she stared at the two grimly.

"Just sit down, Catherine," Serafina said quickly. "Thank you, Mr. Smith."

"I'll be right outside. You be nice now, Catherine, you hear me?"

The old woman cursed him soundly and then threw herself in a chair. "Wot do you want wif me?"

"You knew Margaret Anderson?"

"Old Meg? Yes, I knowed her. We was friends."

"We're trying to find out something about her."

"Well, she's dead. You know that, don't you?"

"Oh yes, we know that," Serafina said. "We need to trace a member of her family, a son."

Catherine's eyes went from one to another. She had a mouth like a steel trap, and there was no womanly quality about her to soften the hardness. "Wot do I get out of it?"

"You do know something, then."

"Maybe I does, but I ain't giving it away."

"We'll give you some money."

"Give me some gin."

"I'll get some," Dylan said and moved toward the door with Serafina close behind.

When they were out of Catherine's hearing, Serafina asked, "Where are you going to get gin?"

"Bound to be some drinking going on. You talk to Catherine. I'll be right back."

Dylan left the room, and they heard his voice speaking to Smith outside. The old woman stared at Serafina and sneered. "Well, how do you like it here in Brixton? You like to be cooped up here like a dirty animal?"

"I'm sorry you're here, Catherine."

"No, you ain't. Why would you feel sorry for me?"

For Serafina it was like talking to another species. Catherine Foss had descended so far down the scale that, if the reports Smith gave were true, she had crossed some border from which she could never return. Serafina had no idea what to say to her, so she sat there silently. It was not long before Dylan entered again, and he had a bottle in his hand. He held it up and said, "Your gin, Catherine."

"Give it to me!"

"You take a little of it, and then we'll talk."

The old woman seized the bottle, removed the cork, and drank three swallows. Dylan reached out and took the bottle from her.

"That's good stuff. I'll have to have more than that. I wants money too."

"I'll give you twenty pounds if you tell us what you know," Serafina said quickly.

The woman's eyes gleamed and she snapped, "All right. I shared a cell with Meg for a long time. She was my friend. She didn't 'ave no other friends. She didn't talk much. She died, I think, when she come in 'ere. It 'its some that way. They can't take it. Give me another drink."

The conversation went on, and Catherine would demand a drink every few moments. Finally her voice was slurred, and when she asked for a drink, Dylan shook his head. "I'll give you this and another bottle just like it and twenty pounds, but we have to know if she ever spoke of a son."

Catherine's eyes were glazed with drink, and she looked at the bottle longingly. "Yus, she talked 'bout her boy. She 'adn't seed him for a long time."

"He never came to visit?"

"Not ever."

"Where did they live?"

"She lived wif a man named Durkins in Seven Dials."

"Did you ever see him?"

"No. She said the boy run off when he was young or maybe someone stole 'im. That's all I know. Now gimme the gin."

Dylan handed her the bottle and gave her the money. The two got up to leave, and Catherine said, "Where's the other bottle?"

"I'll get it for you."

They stepped outside, and he said, "Mr. Smith, I'll need another bottle of gin."

"It's against the rules."

"I imagine that rule gets broken. Here's five bob. Buy a bottle and give it to the old woman. Use the rest any way you please. We'll say nothing."

Without a word Smith took the money and nodded.

The two left the prison, and when they got to the carriage they had not spoken a word. Finally Serafina burst out, "What a horrible place! Better to be dead than in a place like that!"

"You're right about that." He handed her into the carriage, walked around, and untied the team. "Well, we have a place to look. You'd better let me do the looking, Lady Serafina."

"No, I want to go with you."

Dylan shook his head, a stubborn light in his eyes. "Seven Dials is a rough place. They'd cut your throat for that ring on your finger."

Serafina turned to him. "I've been there, remember? We went there when we were helping Clive. I'm going, Dylan. Let's not argue about it."

"There is a stubborn woman, you are! All right. We'll have to get you some old clothes."

"We went in disguise before. I think I still have the clothes."

"They'll do, then. Get up!"

The horses moved forward briskly, and they sat in silence for five minutes. Suddenly Serafina said, "We've got to find him, Dylan."

"We'll do our best. I'm going to ask God to help us."

He knew this was not in Serafina's plan, and finally she responded, "I can't do that."

"Someday you will."

"What makes you think so?"

"Blind faith. That's what it is. Sometimes you have to believe God and not facts."

"That's not logical. That's not reasonable."

"Finding God isn't a matter of logic, my lady. It takes more than that."

Serafina cut him off at once. "Pray all you want to, Dylan, but we've got to find that boy. Lord Darby and his wife are good people."

"You don't know what that boy will be like. He could be a murderer by this time. A few years in Seven Dials will make a beast out of any man — or any woman."

David greeted them at the door to Trentwood House and peppered them both with questions.

Serafina hugged him then said, "Have you been a good boy, David?"

"No, ma'am."

Suddenly Serafina laughed. "Well, you're honest about it. I suppose I'll hear all about your misbehaviour."

"Dylan, come on. I want you to tell me a story."

"I don't think I can do that, David."

"Why not?"

"Well —" Dylan looked over at Serafina. "Your mother doesn't like the stories I tell."

"Oh, tell him whatever stories you want. He'll forget them once he gets older."

"No, I won't. I remember every story Dylan tells me."

Serafina frowned then laughed. "All right. Tell him some of your wild, romantic stories, Dylan."

Actually Serafina was beginning to enjoy Dylan's stories, especially those about historical characters, such as Robin Hood or King John and his crusade to the Holy Land, or those about animals or birds that he had learnt in Wales.

The three went to the playroom, and Serafina sat down and watched as David pulled at Dylan's arm. "Tell me a good one."

"All my stories are good, son. Haven't you noticed?"

"Well, make it a long one."

"Well, it'll be as long as it needs to be. Once there was a religious festival. This was a long time ago in the days when Robin Hood was still in Sherwood Forest or maybe even when King Arthur sat at the Round Table with his knights. In any case, everybody was going to bring an offering to the Lord. There was a suspicion that when the best gift was made every year, the bell in the tower would toll."

"Why did it do that?"

"Why, it showed that God was pleased with a certain offering, but it had to be a very good offering."

"Were there rich people there?"

"Oh, many of them, and they started bringing their gifts to the altar. One very wealthy man brought a load of silver that took two men to carry in. Another brought gold coins stacked in heavy piles. One by one they put their gifts on the altar, and everyone listened for the bells — but none rang."

Dylan saw the small boy was engrossed in the story, then glanced across at Serafina, who was also listening, so he continued.

"There was a man who had come to the festival. He was a poor man. He traveled around the country, and he only had one gift: he could juggle. Did you ever see anybody juggle?"

"No, I haven't."

"Why, look at this, then." Dylan went over and picked up three balls. He began to toss them in the air and said, "There, this is juggling."

"Will you teach me to do that, Dylan?"

"If you are a good boy, I may do that."

"What did the juggler have to bring?"

"He didn't have anything, and he was very sad, David. He watched other people bringing their gifts, and he had not even a single coin. Well, the festival was about over. Everyone had brought their gifts, and the bell had not rung. There was talk going around, with people saying things like, 'We haven't pleased God. We just didn't bring enough money.' People were filing out, and then just before the king left, the bell started tolling. The bishop cried out and whirled around. 'Somebody's given God an offering greater than has been given by anybody here today.' They rushed back into the large room, and guess what they saw?"

"What did they see?"

"They saw the juggler juggling his balls, eight of them at a time and gazing up at the cross that represented the death and resurrection of Jesus."

David was quiet. Finally he asked, "But he didn't give any money?"

"No, but he gave all that he had, and that's what God expects of us, rich or poor, David, to give all that we have to Him."

"Have you done that, Dylan?"

"I hope so, David."

"Mum, would you give everything to Jesus?"

Serafina felt suddenly uncomfortable, and

a flush came to her cheeks. "That's just a story, David. People don't do that anymore." She glanced at Dylan and said, "Why do you make up stories like that?"

"Oh, I want to glorify the Lord, and I thought that little parable did it. It did for me. It made me want to give more to the Lord God."

David said, "That was good. Tell me another one."

Serafina rose suddenly. "I have to prepare a few things for tomorrow, Dylan. Be here early." Dylan agreed, and Serafina said good-bye before leaving the room.

Dylan watched her go and then said, "You want to learn to juggle?"

"Yes. How do you do it?"

"You do it by dropping balls a lot then picking them up and starting over. Here now, hold these two in each hand, and this one you have to hold onto with your fingers. You have to toss them in the air just right."

David began to toss the balls, and, of course, he could not juggle. "I can't learn to do that."

"Most things you don't do successfully the first time. Tell you what. Let's play a game of draughts and then we'll practice some more juggling."

"And tell me some more stories."

"Maybe even that. A boy can't hear too many good stories, I always say."

Eleven

As the feeble light of dawn illuminated the window to Serafina's right, she turned to face it. The night had been miserable. She had been unable to sleep and had gotten up sometime early in the morning and had tried to study. She had been unable to concentrate and finally had contented herself with simply lying in the bed and waiting for dawn.

When the first light touched her window, she rose from bed and dressed rapidly. After washing her face and dressing, she hurried downstairs. Going out on the front porch, she waited, and within five minutes she heard the hoofbeats of a horse coming. The sun was feebly illuminating the landscape, and she watched as Dylan drew the carriage up, a small two-place affair, and leapt to the ground. He hurried forward. "Good morning, my lady."

"Good morning, Dylan. I'm all ready."

Dylan stared at her disguise and then nodded. "I'd venture you don't wear such clothes very often."

She had donned a shapeless grey dress that hid her rather spectacular figure well enough. The shoes had once been patent leather but now were little more than scraps which she had to tie onto her feet. A ratty-looking shawl was draped around her neck, and a floppy mob cap, such as those cleaning women wore, covered her head. She saw that the corners of Dylan's lips turned upward in a smile that he tried to conceal.

Dylan, who was usually impeccable in his dress, was wearing a pair of faded, snuff-coloured trousers, baggy at the knees and too short for him, a pair of boots that were worn almost past use, a waistcoat with only one button to hold it together, and an outer jacket of some indeterminate colour. "This is the way we need to look," Dylan said. "Nobody's going to pay attention to a pair of swells like us."

"Do you think I can pass for a poor woman?"

"Just exactly right. You look like a working woman. Just don't let anybody see those soft hands. Here, get in." He helped her into the carriage and then jumped in himself. He took the lines and said to the horse,

"Get up, Methuselah."

"What a strange name for a horse!"

"Well, it's not exactly his name. He just looks pretty old like that. It reminds me of a dog I took for a while. He had one eye, no tail, and only three legs. He went by the name of Lucky."

"You made that up."

"No, I didn't. He was a lucky dog. Kept him for a long time. Just about broke my heart when he died."

"Are we ready, Dylan?"

"We're off to Seven Dials, the worst section of London. But that's where we start looking for Durkins."

The journey to the Seven Dials district took Serafina and Dylan along the banks of the Thames. The stench was overwhelming, and Serafina held her handkerchief over her nose. "Why does London have to smell so bad?" she exclaimed.

"It's the penalty for crowding enormous numbers of people into a relatively small space," Dylan said. "Think how much human waste two million people can produce every day. And a lot of that waste goes into the Thames." He warmed to his subject adding, "Human excrement is gathered by the night-soil men and sold to nursery gardens. The streets are used as a dumping ground for night soil, dead dogs, horse and cattle manure, and rotting vegetables. The rain washes some of it away, but not much."

Serafina sat silently beside Dylan, realizing that she had never given this problem more than a casual wish that "someone would do something about it." She realized how her life was shielded from much unpleasantness that the poor and middle classes could not escape.

"What are those children doing in the river?" she asked, noting that the banks of the Thames were populated with many people.

"They're mudlarks, Serafina, sometimes called toshers. They wade through the banks at low tide, filling their pockets with copper recovered from the water's edge. Look, some of them are wearing coats with oversized pockets to put their plunder in. And there — see that tosher? He's got a lantern strapped to his chest to help him see in the predawn gloom."

"Why is he carrying that long pole?"

"To test the ground. He could stumble into a quagmire and drown."

"How awful for those children. What do they expect to find?"

"Lumps of coal, old wood, scraps of rope

— anything they can get a few pence for." He gestured toward another group of children on a slight rise. They wore robes made of old blankets that gave them the look of ragged wizards. "See those children? They're pure finders."

"Pure what?"

"That means dog manure."

"What in the world for?"

"Tanners use it in curing leather. This is bad, Serafina, but there's worse. Many of the poor are sewer hunters. They slog through the flowing waste of London, and every few months the methane gas in the sewers is ignited by one of the kerosene lamps. The poor souls are incinerated twenty feet below ground in a river of raw sewage."

A sudden chill came to Serafina. "This is awful, Dylan!" she whispered.

He almost told her that the awfulness she was seeing for the first time had always been there, but he only said, "Yes, it is."

After what seemed like an eternity, Dylan pulled up in front of a house Serafina recognized.

"This is where Lorenzo and Gyp live," she said.

"That's right. Come on in."

"You think they're having a service?"

"Not likely this time of the morning." The two had attended a service in this house, which had surprised her, for both Lorenzo and Gyp were reformed criminals. They had become active and very vocal Christians, Lorenzo at least. Gyp was a silent man who said little but beat on his tambourine fiercely during moments of excitement in the services.

Even before Dylan could knock on the door, it opened, and the bulky form of Lorenzo Pike stood before them. He was a huge, burly man with florid, blunt features. His merry blue eyes almost disappeared when he smiled, as he did now. He threw his arms around Dylan, hugging him until Dylan felt his backbone give. Lorenzo exclaimed in his usual fashion, "Well, hallelujah and glory be to God and the Lamb forever! My friend Brother Dylan and — and you, Sister Trent."

"It's us all right." Dylan grinned. "Where's Gyp?"

"He's inside fixing breakfast. Come in, and we'll have it together."

"Well, we don't want to impose."

"How can one fellow believe we can impose on one another? You ought to have better theology than that, Brother Dylan.

Come in now."

They stepped inside, and the ceiling was so low that Lorenzo had to duck. The smell of fresh-cooked meat was in the air, and Gyp turned to smile at them.

"A pair of pilgrims looking for a bite to eat, my brother."

"Hello, Dylan, and you, Lady Trent." Gyp was a lean, dark-complected man, actually a gypsy. His real name was Yago, but everyone simply called him Gyp. He had a gold ring in his right ear, and his teeth were white as he smiled at them. "Sit yourselves down there, and you can start blessing the food, Lorenzo, while I finish cooking it." He laughed aloud, his dark eyes laughing too. "I always give Lorenzo a head start on the blessings, they're so long."

Indeed, Lorenzo did pray a rather long blessing, but the breakfast was worth waiting for. It consisted of porridge, bacon, deviled kidneys and sausage, plus a mountain of hot, buttered toast and cups of steaming tea. Serafina ate hungrily and praised the food. "You are a fine cook, Gyp. Come and work for me."

"Can't do that, ma'am." Gyp flashed a gleaming smile at her. "Lorenzo would starve to death without me."

As they drank tea, Serafina listened to

Dylan explain their mission. She could not help but see, even in clothes that were far gone, he still had a certain elegance about him. She was always somewhat shocked at how black and glossy his hair was, how his eyes were large and well-shaped, and his lips full and mobile.

"So," Lorenzo said, "you want to find a chap named Durkins."

"It's very important. We don't have much of a lead, but we'll pay handsomely if you'll join in the search."

"Yes," Serafina said, leaning forward, "and five sovereigns if you find him."

"What about this woman, Meg Anderson?"

"Well, as I mentioned," Dylan said, "she died in prison. All we know about her is that she had a son eighteen years ago, and she lived for a time with this man Durkins. I don't know his first name, but we heard that he was in Seven Dials. Put the word out, will you, fellows? With a nice reward for those who come up with the man."

After the two agreed, Serafina left with Dylan. "Where to next?" she asked.

"Going to the Montevado family. You remember them?"

"Yes, I do. You and I last visited them after the trial. The mother was still very sick."

"She's doing much better now. The medical care and the medicine you paid for, Lady Trent, worked miracles."

"They're beautiful children."

"Yes, they are. I worry about them sometimes. It's hard for a young girl and a young boy to grow up in a place like this."

They said little as Dylan wound his way through the labyrinthine streets, and finally they arrived at the shack that housed the Montevado family. Dylan leapt out, helped Serafina to the ground, and then the two approached the door.

"It's you!" The speaker was a young girl just at the point of becoming a woman. Callie Montevado's father had been Spanish; her mother was English. She had an olive complexion and striking eyes, almond-shaped with long lashes, the colour of lapis lazuli, a rich azure blue. She had the beginnings of a womanly figure and had already begun to carry a knife to fight off any men who would abuse her.

"How are you, Callie?"

"I'm okay," she said. "Wot you two doin' 'ere?"

"We need to talk to you and Paco."

"Mama ain't 'ere, but Paco is. Come on in."

The two entered, and once again Serafina

was shocked at the poverty the room revealed. Accustomed to the finest furniture and spacious rooms, she thought their place resembled the den of an animal.

Paco came running in from outside, and Dylan reached out and rubbed his head. "Hey, Paco, how are you, young man?"

"Did you bring anything to eat?"

"No, I thought we'd give you some money to let you and Callie go buy your own eats. All right?" He held out a florin, which Paco took at once. "All right!" he said, his black hair falling into his brown eyes. His dark complexion gave him a handsome appearance.

"We have a job for you." Serafina smiled at the two.

"Wot kind of a job?" Callie asked at once. "Does we get paid?"

"Yes, you get paid," Serafina said. She explained that they were looking for a man named Durkins, and a young man who would be about eighteen.

"Wot's 'e look like?" Callie demanded.

"We don't know about the young man, but there couldn't be too many men called Durkins in Seven Dials. And if you find him, we can find the young man. Here, here's a down payment. I believe you two are the best detectives in London." Dylan smiled.

"We'll find 'im," Paco said. "We'll ask everybody."

"That's the idea!"

" 'ow do we find you?" Callie demanded. "Where do you live now?"

Dylan said, "I'm staying with a policeman."

"I don't want no coppers," Callie said instantly.

"Yes, you do. He's a very nice man. His name is Matthew Grant." He told her how to get to Grant's place. "Leave word with the landlady if you find out anything. We'll check with you from time to time. Come now, Serafina, we have to go."

"Good-bye, Callie. Good-bye, Paco," Serafina said. The two left, and Serafina was quiet for a time as they drove away.

"What are you thinking about? You're so quiet."

"Am I a noisy woman, then?"

"No, not actually, but something's troubling you."

Serafina looked down at her hands. She had taken off the expensive rings she wore, and she had been thinking of how the worth of one ring could have worked miracles with the Montevado family. "It's so sad seeing the poor boy and girl like that."

"They're better off than some. You see the Street Arabs everywhere. They're the ones I feel sorry for."

"Street Arabs? What are they?"

"Just young boys and girls, most of them with no parents, wandering and stealing to live. Get caught sooner or later and wind up in prison. Either that or they have to go to the workhouse."

"I wish I could do something for them."

"Why, you can. You have, for those two and their mother. You've made good friends out of them, and we'll keep our eye on them."

For three days the pair donned their old clothes and searched the district. They checked every day with Gyp and Lorenzo and also with Paco and Callie. As they were walking along the street, Serafina stood back while Dylan questioned one of the costermongers who sold his wares from a small wagon. She suddenly felt a hand run over her back and startled; she turned and saw a man grinning at her.

" 'Ow about it, sweetheart, me and you? We go 'ave a little fun, right?"

"Take your hands off me!" Serafina said, her eyes flashing.

"Oh, ain't we 'oity-toity now! What makes you so special?" The speaker was a short man with gaps in his teeth. Those that were not gone were yellow, and his eyes were rheumy. He smelled strongly of alcohol.

"Go away and leave me alone."

"I'll leave you alone," he said, cursing. "Come on, girlie." He grabbed her arm, but he quickly found himself lifted in the air. Dylan had come up behind him, grabbed him by the upper arms, and simply picked him up. He set him down so hard that the man's remaining teeth jolted.

Dylan said calmly, "Okay, on your way. You're not wanted here."

When the man scurried away, Dylan turned and saw that Serafina was staring at him. He took her arm and said, "Come on. We'll check again with Callie and Paco. Maybe they found out something."

"That man put his hands on me!"

"That's the way it goes here in Seven Dials. Don't ever come here alone, Serafina."

The two made their way to the Montevado home, and Callie and Paco were waiting for them. "We've been waitin' fer ya," Callie said, her eyes bright. "We done found 'im — Durkins! That's the one you wants, innit?"

"Where is he?"

"We'll show you."

The two followed them out, and they all squeezed into the carriage. Paco asked, "Can I drive?"

"Sure you can." Dylan was holding Paco in his lap and let the boy hold the reins. "Tell them to get up."

"Get up!" Paco yelled, and Serafina said, "Dylan, that horse might run off."

"He's got all the runaway beat out of him. He's just barely got energy enough to walk."

Callie directed them. When the streets narrowed, Dylan had to navigate the carriage carefully through the clusters of people buying, selling, and begging. The cobbled streets were often marked by open gutters filled with the night's waste. The jettied houses leaned far out over the streets, some so close at the top as to block out the daylight. The wood was pitted where sections were rotten and had fallen away, and the plaster was dark with stains of old leakage and rising dampness from the stones. People stood in doorways, dark forms huddled together, faces catching the light now and then. An old man lay flat on his back, his mouth open, perhaps dead. A prostitute looked up at Dylan, her skin pasty and her hair lusterless and full of knots. She was drunk, for she sat down abruptly in the middle of the street, muttering curses. When they finally arrived at a back street, they entered an alley and found a pair of rickety steps.

"This is it," Callie said. " 'e's up there."

"How'd you find him?" Dylan asked.

"We asked everybody," Paco said, his eyes shining. " 'E's there all right. When do we get the reward?"

"Here. We'll give you an advance right now," Serafina said. She had a deep pocket in the dress, and reaching in, she pulled out two golden coins and handed them to him. "There. You be careful now. Don't let anyone see this or they might take it away from you."

"Not likely," Callie said. She pulled the knife from where she kept it hidden and said, "I'd cut 'is bloody throat if 'e tried to steal our sovereigns!"

"That's a good idea, Callie. You hang on to it. Come along, Lady Trent. You two wait here and yell loudly if you need me," Dylan said. He got out, helped Serafina down, and the two walked up the rickety steps and knocked on the door. A faint voice said, "Wot do yer want?"

"Looking for Durkins," Dylan called out.

"Well, 'e ain't 'ere."

Dylan ignored this and shoved the door

open. He stepped inside and waited for Serafina to follow him. She had almost ceased to be shocked at immense poverty, but this was worse than anything she had seen. A man lay in a bed with several empty bottles surrounding him on the floor. He was obviously ill, for his cheeks had bright red patches, and his eyes were bright with fever. "Wot do you want with me? You a rozzer?"

"No, we've come to do you a big favor, Durkins."

"Now that ain't bloody likely."

"I'm going to give you some money if you help us."

"I can't 'elp nobody."

"You remember Meg?"

Durkins stared at him with sudden interest. " 'Course I remembers Meg. What about 'er?"

"We're trying to find her son."

"Roland? Wot's 'e done now? That's a bold one, 'e is. Wot yer wants wif 'im? 'E do you a bad turn?"

"No, he hasn't done anything that I know of. You know where he is?"

"I ain't seen 'im in years, but I 'eard 'e did six months in Dartmore Prison for putting a knife in a bloke. Good thing 'e was another bad 'un, or Roland 'ud still be in Dartmore. 'E was part of Max Benbow's band. Bad ones, all of 'em. Where's this 'ere money yer talkin' about?"

Dylan reached into his pocket. The cash that the Earl of Darby had given him was coming in handy. "Tell us all you can about the boy, and I'll give you four of these." He held up the sovereigns, and Durkins's eyes were filled with instant greed.

"I'll tell you all I knows, but I ain't seen 'im in a long time."

"Was he anything like his mother? Did he look like her, I mean?" Serafina asked.

"No, 'e didn't. I 'ave to say 'e was a good-looking boy, but 'e was too crafty and shrewd. 'Eaded for trouble 'e was."

The two stood over Durkins and fired question after question until finally in despair he said, "That's all I know. Give me the cash, will ya?"

"All right." Dylan handed him the money, and Durkins snatched it as if he was afraid it would be taken from him. "Where's Meg now? I ain't 'ear 'bout 'er since she went to Brixton."

"She died, I'm afraid."

"Died, did she? Well, she was a tough one. I'll say that for 'er."

"Come along, Serafina."

The two left, and Serafina shook her head. "He'll just spend the money on drink."

"Of course he will, or on laudanum or something else. He's not long for this world. I wanted to talk to him about his soul, but he didn't seem in the mood. Maybe I'll come back."

Serafina turned. "You really think there's hope for a man who's that far gone?"

"Yes, I do."

"You have more faith than anybody I've ever seen. Come along, let's give the rest of the reward to Callie and Paco. It's more money than they've ever seen."

Mike Sullivan found pleasure in running the Green Dragon, the toughest pub in London, as smoothly as possible. And now as he looked around the smoke-filled bar, he felt a glow of satisfaction. Sullivan had been a bruising, bare-knuckle pugilist and served as his own bouncer. Mike liked nothing better than pounding a customer who refused to keep the simple rules customers were obliged to obey. There were only three rules actually: Number one, anyone who drank and had no money to pay was beaten to a pulp by Sullivan and tossed outside. Rule number two, no firearms allowed, and the man who violated this rule received rough treatment and lost his pistol. Rule number three, no squealers allowed. The underworld understood this rule and was proud that Sullivan treated such scum as they deserved.

Sullivan's head barkeep, Jake Kilrain, had come to stand beside Sullivan, saying in a hoarse whisper, "Young Roland is foolin' with Alice."

"So what?"

"She's Frenchy Doucette's woman. You know 'ow 'e is."

Sullivan glared at Kilrain. "I ain't no nursemaid, Jake."

"You know what Frenchy done to Bob Grogan for goin' after Alice."

"The rozzers never proved that it was Frenchy that done Grogan in."

Kilrain shrugged, saying only, "The Anderson kid spent time in Dartmore for sticking some bloke with a knife. 'E won't do that to Frenchy. That Frog is the best 'and with a knife I ever see!"

"I ain't takin' no kid in to raise," Sullivan said. He downed a glass filled to the top with gin and grinned. "I'd kind of like to see Frenchy and Anderson square off. We need a little entertainment." He studied Roland Anderson with interest. "He's just a baby-faced kid, but word is he can see in the dark like a cat and open any lock he pleases."

"Mebbe so, Mike, but that won't help 'im if Frenchy slices 'im with that long shiv 'e carries."

"Ain't my problem." Sullivan thought hard then shrugged. "Maybe you're right, Jake. I'll give the boy a little fatherly advice." He moved from behind the bar and made his way across the room. The air was thick with smoke and raw whiskey fumes, and the sound of crude laughter and profane language filled the room. Of course, it all smelled like money to Sullivan.

Coming to the table where three men and a woman were seated, Sullivan studied the youngest of the men, thinking, *He don't look like much, Roland don't — but looks don't mean much.*

Roland Anderson looked up at Sullivan and smiled.

"What's up, Mike?"

He was smoothly shaven, and his auburn hair was neatly trimmed. He had light blue eyes and a deep cleft in his chin. He took pride in his appearance and could have passed for a gentleman anywhere.

"Better send Alice away," Sullivan said quietly. "Frenchy is a jealous fellow."

" 'E don't own me!" Alice said. She was a cheap-looking woman with a rather curvy figure, and her voice was shrill as she added,

"I'll see anybody I please!"

Sullivan considered that he had done his best. He stared at Anderson for a long moment then wheeled and returned to the bar.

" 'E ain't my boss — and Frenchy don't own me either!" Roland said.

Hack Wilson, a skeletal man with a knife-edged face, sat across the table from Roland. "Come on, Alice, you know wot 'e'll do if 'e catches you with another bloke."

"Too right, Roland." The third man, Charlie Wait, was thickset and had dulled features. He shook his head, adding, "Hack and Sullivan are right. Get rid of Alice."

Roland drained the liquor from his glass, refilled it, then said, "Alice, did you know Bob Grogan was a pal of mine?"

"No, I didn't."

"Well, 'e did me a good turn once, 'e did." He sipped his drink, then said idly, "I always said Frenchy would pay for doin' Bob in."

Wilson snorted with disgust. "Come on, Roland, we got this job lined up. It'll be a piece of cake."

"Yeah, we'll make a bundle, Roland. I been casin' the place for two months. The old guy always goes to his club on Wednesdays, stays all night. The servants take the night off. We waltz in, take the stuff, and scram. Now we got to —"

"Look out," Wilson broke in and nodded his head toward the door. "There's Frenchy."

Roland turned to study the newcomer, aware that everyone in the bar was doing the same. "Frenchy looks pretty mad." He smiled.

"Don't fight 'im, Roland," Alice whispered. Her face had lost its colour and her hands were trembling. " 'E'll kill you — and me too!"

Doucette was a tall, thin-blade figure of a man with sharp features. He moved across the floor with an animal-like grace and pulled a long-bladed knife from under his coat with a lightning gesture.

"You make a beeg mistake, fellow!" His chin protruded sharply, and his eyes were like glowing coals.

"Why, good day to you, Doucette." Roland got to his feet and put his arm around Alice. He was smiling and seemed totally at ease. "Alice and I 'ave been talking about you. She tells me she's tired of you, that she wants a real man."

Doucette's face flamed, and he uttered a curse and moved closer to Roland, holding the knife out. "I show you what you are, boy! I cut your throat and laugh while you bleed to death!"

Roland pushed Alice to one side and faced Doucette, still smiling. "Why, I believe you're upset, Frenchy. But you 'ave to remember, you're not as young as you once were. Alice tells me you don't satisfy her. But I'll take care of that for you."

Doucette uttered a wild cry of rage and lunged toward Roland. He made a slashing movement with the blade, but Roland turned sideways so that the blade sliced through his coat sleeve and made a shallow cut across his upper arm. At the same time, he lashed out with his foot and kicked Doucette's feet out from under him. Even as Doucette was sprawling out on the floor, Roland picked up a chair and lifted it high, then brought it down with all his might on the Frenchman's head. The edge of the seat caught Doucette in the crown, cutting his scalp and knocking him unconscious.

The action had only taken a few seconds, and a cry of admiration went up from the crowd. Sullivan came to stand over Doucette, then shrugged. "Well, he ain't dead, Roland. He'll come after you if you don't finish him off."

Roland's light blue eyes were alive, and he stooped and picked up Doucette's blade. He studied the bloody face of the man, and

Alice cried out, "Go on, Roland! Do 'im in!"

Roland leaned down, but instead of slitting Doucette's throat, he rolled him so that he lay on his stomach. Roland slashed at the material of Doucette's trousers, cutting the seat out neatly. He then drove the knife into the oak floor, snapped it off at the hilt, and looked at Alice. "Why, 'e ain't worth gettin' my neck stretched, is 'e now?"

A laugh went up, and Mike laughed the loudest of all. "You should've killed him, Roland, but this is better. Every bloke in London will laugh when they hear how you turned his bare bottom up!"

Roland walked back to his table and said, "Come on, let's go to work." He kissed Alice and said, "I'll be back with a present for you, sweet'art." He moved across the room, followed by Hack and Charlie.

Hack, his voice shaded with admiration, said, "You got class — that's what you got, Roland!"

Roland appeared not to have heard. "Let's go rob this old fellow. I need a new shirt." He touched the cut in his sleeve made by Doucette's blade. "The bloody beggar ruined me best shirt!"

Serafina and Dylan had been looking for

Benbow and his gang for days before they asked Grant for help. He had stared at them. "I know that bunch. It's dangerous for you, Lady Trent. Let me go along."

"That's a good idea," Dylan had said at once. "You know where to find them?"

"I know a couple of places."

The next day they fruitlessly searched two taverns, but on the third try they were more fortunate. Before they went in, Grant said, "You'd better stay out here, Lady Trent."

"No, I'm going in with you."

"Well, all right," Grant said with a sigh.

They walked inside, and Grant saw Benbow immediately, "There he is over there. You want to talk to him?"

"Maybe you'd better soften him up, Matthew."

"Right." Matthew grinned briefly. He walked over and stood in front of a tall, lanky man who was watching him with close-set, narrow eyes. He had a deep, red scar that worked its way from his forehead to his chin, along his jawbone, and clear down over his neck. It looked like a wound that should have killed, but Benbow was very much alive.

"What you want, Grant?" he demanded.

"A little cooperation," Matthew said. "If you act right, I won't arrest you."

"You can't arrest me."
"You don't think so?"
Something about Matthew Grant's look made Benbow drop his eyes. The other men looked as frightened as he did, but none of them spoke up.
"Okay, what is it? What do you want out of me?"
"I'm looking for Roland."
A young man who had been watching the exchange slowly stepped forward. "I'm Roland." Serafina studied the man's clean-cut features through the dirt on his face. He looked familiar, but she said nothing.
"We need to talk to you."
"I ain't done nothing."
"I doubt that," Matthew said dryly. "Come along. We mean you no harm."
They stepped outside, and Matthew said, "Well, you don't need me anymore."
"No. Thank you, Matthew."
Roland was watching them guardedly.
"We'd like to talk to you, Roland."
"Go on, then, and talk."
"Maybe we'd better go somewhere we won't be disturbed. The street is not a good place to talk."
Roland nodded his head. " 'Ow about over there at the Pink Angel? Their drinks ain't bad, and I'm 'ungry."

"That'll be fine," Dylan said.

Dylan followed the young man carefully. If he turned and fled, Dylan was prepared to chase after him, although he doubted he could catch him. He looked fast indeed. They went into the Pink Angel and found a table over in the darkened corner. A slovenly woman came and took their order. Neither Dylan nor Serafina took anything, but Roland ordered a dish of fried eels and ale. As soon as the server was gone, he looked at them and said, "Wot's this all about?"

"My name is Dylan Tremayne, Roland. This is Viscountess Serafina Trent."

Roland's eyes narrowed. "Viscountess?"

"That's right. We've been asked by a friend of mine, the Earl of Darby, to find you."

"I don't know no earl. You off your rocker?"

"I want you to sit very still, Roland, and I'm going to tell you a story. Don't say anything until I get through."

"All right. As long as I get a free meal out of it, I'll listen to your chatter."

The food came almost at once, and Dylan said, "Serafina, perhaps you ought to tell this story."

"All right, Dylan." She began, "The Earl of Darby is a good friend of mine. He and his wife have no children — that is, he has no heir to leave his title and his estate to . . ."

Roland ate steadily and had to have his ale refilled twice while Serafina was carefully telling the story. Finally she ended and said, "So, I know this sounds fantastic, but I believe you are the son of Edward Hayden, the Earl of Darby."

Roland suddenly laughed harshly. "Wot's this all about? I never 'eard such a fairy tale in all my life!"

"I know it sounds that way, but let me tell you this, Roland. You look almost exactly like Edward Darby." She had realized this while she was speaking, and she studied the young man's face. She said, "You have the same cleft in your chin, the same tawny hair with a touch of red, the same light blue eyes. There's a portrait of him in his home. It was made when he was about your age. I want you to come and look at it, Roland, and to meet the earl."

Disbelief scored the young man's face, and Serafina said, "Your name is Trevor Hayden."

"I don't believe a word of it."

"What can you lose?" Dylan asked.

"I ain't no bloody lord!"

"You could be," Serafina said. "You could be Trevor Hayden, the next Earl of Darby."

Her words seemed to hang in the air, and Roland — Trevor Hayden — stared at Serafina in disbelief. He finally drank the last of the ale and shrugged his trim shoulders. "I'll 'ave a go at it. Like you say — wot can I lose?"

TWELVE

"I wonder if this rain is ever going to stop."

Edward Hayden had been standing at the window, looking at the rain falling in slanting lines across the earth. December had brought some snow, but that had faded, and now Edward drummed his fingers on the windowsill nervously and turned to say with some irritation, "I hate this kind of weather!"

"Sit down, dear. You're gong to wear yourself out," Heather said. She nodded to the chair upholstered in a design of damask roses, its wooden arms heavily carved. An antimacassar protected the back of the chair, and as Edward came over and threw himself into the chair, she said, "Try not to be agitated, dear."

"I'll try." Taking a deep breath, Edward looked around the room, contemplating the deep wine-red curtains and the muted pink of the embossed wallpaper. The proportions of the wallpaper were perfect, and he had always liked it, but now he was thinking of things other than the beauty of a room. Finally he turned and said abruptly, "Perhaps we should have told the family what's going on, Heather."

"We couldn't have done that, dear."

"Why not?"

"Because we weren't sure ourselves. We still aren't, are we?"

"I suppose you're right." He picked up a pipe, opened a humidor, and filled it with fragrant tobacco. He picked up a lucifer and struck it, remarking, "You know, when I was a boy we didn't have things like this, this match I mean. One of the few innovations I suppose I'm really in favor of."

"It makes life a little bit easier."

The two sat there, and each of them felt a reluctance to speak of the future, but finally Edward said, "If we accept this young man as our son, Heather, it's going to make a great many differences in our lives."

"Yes, it will, and in the lives of the whole family."

"It's going to be difficult telling them, but it'll have to be done." He drew on the pipe and sent a cloud of purple smoke toward the ceiling. He sat there tapping his foot nervously, then got up and walked over to the fireplace where he poked at the log with short, vicious jabs. The action sent myriads of fiery sparks like miniature stars swirling up the chimney. "This fireplace always smokes a little," he said. Suddenly he replaced the poker and moved quickly to the window. "They're here." He stood straighter, and his face had lost some of its ruddy colour. Heather rose and moved over to the window. He put his arms around her, and neither of them could speak, for the tension seemed unbearable.

As soon as Rupert came into the room, he put his eyes on Arthur and shook his head with disgust. "Do you have to get drunk every day?"

"He's not drunk," Gervase said defensively.

"Yes, he is." Rupert stared at his younger brother and shook his head. "No sense preaching at you. You've had that for years. Nothing seems to do you any good." He started to say more, but Gervase came over and put herself between Rupert and her father.

"I don't think we need to discuss this, Uncle Rupert."

She stood there protecting her father. Rupert scowled, and as he turned he muttered, "No blasted good to anybody on earth. Try to straighten up, Arthur — but then there's no point telling you that, is there?"

As soon as the door slammed, Gervase turned and went over to her father. He was sitting at the desk, staring down at it. When he did look up, she saw the misery written in his eyes. He was a smaller man than both Rupert and Edward. The three brothers had the same father, but Arthur had a different mother.

Arthur Hayden was almost frail-looking beside the bulk of both Rupert or Edward Hayden. His face was thin, and he had an esthetic look about him that artists have sometimes. He looked up now at his daughter and said, "I'm sorry, dear. I shouldn't be drinking this early in the morning."

Gervase did not answer. She moved behind his chair and put her hands on his shoulders. "Don't worry about it. Nobody's ever going to please Uncle Rupert."

Arthur suddenly rose from his chair and turned to Gervase. His whole life was a failure, it seemed to him, and now he said as much. "If I had been stronger, or if your mother had lived, life would have been much better for you, Gervase."

"I haven't had a bad life."

"Your mother made things different. I didn't have her long, but she was like the sun in the sky to me."

"I wish I could remember more about her."

"Well, you were only four when she died."

"I'm glad you made all those paintings of her, Father. I look at them every day." But Arthur Hayden knew his own limitations. The signs of dissipation were evident on him. He was like a man who had a lingering illness. He reached out and took Gervase's hand and held it for a moment. "What's going to become of you?"

"Oh, I'm going to marry an earl with all sorts of money. Then we'll travel. Remember how much fun we had on our trip to France?"

"Yes, and to Italy. That was the happiest time of my life, I think." He suddenly smiled briefly. "What about your husband? He wouldn't want to drive a broken-down father-in-law around on a trip."

"Oh, when I get a husband I'll make him happy. But you'll always be my best friend." She reached out and gave him a hug and kissed his cheek, and when she stepped back, her eyes were filled with mischief. She had a great deal of humor in her, this daughter so beloved by Arthur Hayden.

"Husbands," she said, "are like pet dogs. You're fond of them, and you see that they're fed and are comfortable. But a woman can't get overly concerned with pet dogs or with husbands. There are more important things than that." She leaned forward and put her hands on his cheeks, and with her thumbs she pushed his mouth into a smile. "There. Fathers are more important than husbands."

The two stood there, and, as always, Gervase was able to bring her father out of the gloomy pit of melancholy into which he fell. She loved him dearly, and no one was more conscious of his weakness than Arthur himself.

"I don't think you can ask Edward for money for a horse, St. John."

Looking up at his mother, St. John smiled and lifted one eyebrow in an expression of surprise. "Why, of course I can. What would one more horse mean to him?"

"We're living on his charity."

"Well, we always have, Mother. I suppose he's used to it by now."

"You know, even if he said yes, you'd have to get Rupert to agree — and he never would."

"Maybe you could talk to Edward. You're

close to him."

"As close as a brother and sister could be when we were younger, but things have changed now." Leah St. John was suddenly moved by an inner thought that brought a grimace to her thin lips. She remembered very clearly at that moment how close she and Edward had been when they were children, but after she had married, that had all changed. Edward had not approved of Roger St. John, the man she had married, and from the time of her marriage they had drifted apart. After the death of Roger, who died in bankruptcy due to his reckless gambling, Leah had little choice but to seek shelter under his roof. "Edward's been a good brother," she said, "saddled with a sister and a nephew."

"Mother, it's only a mare, and she's a beauty. I can even make money off of her, I think. I can buy her cheaply enough and then sell her for cash."

"Rupert would never agree to it." A bitterness tinged Leah's words, and she spoke the thought that was always in the back of her mind but which she had kept hidden from St. John. "You know how terrible life would be for us, Son, if Edward were to die?"

Looking up quickly, St. John nodded. "I've

had nightmares about that."

"Life would be very unpleasant." The two fell silent for a moment, and then St. John lifted his head.

"Someone's coming," he muttered. He walked over to the window, followed by his mother, and the two stared out at the carriage that approached. The wheels sent spirals of water high as it drove through the puddles, and the coachman huddled, soaked, no doubt, to the skin. "Who can that be traveling in this kind of weather, Mother?"

Looking closely, Leah said, "It's Lady Trent."

"Yes, and that actor fellow Tremayne . . . but who's that other fellow there?"

They watched as three figures got out of the carriage and moved quickly toward the shelter of the front porch. "A bad day for visiting," St. John remarked. "You know, I might persuade Lady Trent to invest in that mare. She loves horses."

"Don't ask her. It would be absolutely unthinkable to become a beggar."

St. John gave her a stare, and his lips twisted bitterly. "Well, that's what we are, isn't it — beggars?"

"Lady Trent is here," Crinshaw announced

as he stepped into the larger parlour where Lord and Lady Darby saw visitors.

"Is she alone, Crinshaw?" Edward asked quickly.

"No, sir. There are two gentlemen here. One is Mr. Tremayne, and I don't know the other gentleman."

"Show them in, Crinshaw."

Edward and Heather stood there, each of them thinking the same thought. *What if this is really our son?* Turning to Heather, Edward took her hand. "You're pale. Your hands are trembling. This is probably not what we think. I expect that other fellow is some detective Serafina and Tremayne have hired to help find our boy."

Then the door opened, and Serafina Trent entered, followed by Tremayne and the third man. Heather gasped as the young man turned his head toward her. She stared at him and suddenly felt unsteady, as if she needed to sit down.

"I'm glad to see you, Serafina," Edward said, but like his wife, his eyes were fixed on the young man with them. "You, too, Mr. Tremayne. Bad weather to be traveling."

Serafina was studying the two and saw that they were almost beyond words. "This is Mr. Roland Anderson."

"Famous name," Sir Edward said. "A

highwayman. No relation, I trust?"

"I reckon not," Roland said. His face paled, and he showed signs of nervousness. " 'E died game, 'e did. A rare plucked one 'e was."

Both Edward and Heather were staring at the young man as Serafina repeated introductions. "Roland, this is Lord Edward Hayden, Earl of Darby, and his wife, Lady Heather."

A silence fell across the room, and for a moment Heather thought it was like a picture. Nobody was moving, but they were staring at each other. Serafina said, "Perhaps we could sit down and talk."

"Yes, could I offer you tea?" Heather asked.

"That would be very nice," Serafina said. "It's cold out. Hot tea would be just the thing."

Heather rang a bell, and when one of the parlour maids entered, she said, "Fix some tea, please."

"It's already fixed, ma'am. Shall I bring it in?"

"Yes, Rosie. Please do."

Edward tore his eyes away from the young man who called himself Roland and asked, "Are you engaged in any acting, Mr. Tremayne?"

"Not at the moment, sir." He smiled and said, "I'm glad to see you've recovered from the accident you suffered the last time we were here."

"Yes, I have."

As the two men talked, Heather could not tear her gaze away from the younger man's face. She was a demonstrative woman at times, and it was all she could do to keep the shock from reflecting in her features. Suddenly she realized the young man was staring back at her, and their eyes locked. *His eyes are just like Edward's with that light blue colour.* She had no time to think any further because Rosie came in. The next few moments offered some relief as the business of getting the tea poured and served took place.

Serafina sipped her tea and then said at once, "We have told Roland the story you told us about losing your child many years ago, or so you thought. We've also told him of Father Xavier's visit and of the death of Margaret Anderson. And we told him, of course, of her confession that she exchanged her dead baby for your live child. According to Father Xavier, it was her last request that the baby she raised in total ignorance of his real parentage should be returned to his family."

During this speech everyone was staring at Roland, and it was Heather who broke the awkward silence. "Mr. Anderson, what is your feeling about all this?"

"Why, it's a bloody good fairy tale I make of it." He looked at the pair and said pugnaciously, "I ain't no bloody lord!"

Edward sat up straighter in his chair, ignoring his tea. He began to question him. "Did you have any suspicion at all that Margaret Anderson wasn't your mother?"

"Not likely. Why should I?"

"Did she ever mention your father?"

"No. She always 'ad a man, but when I asked 'er about me own dad she claimed 'e was a sailor. 'E was going to marry 'er, she told me, except 'e got 'imself killed in a fight at sea. 'E was stationed on the *Victory.* Sometimes she said 'is name was Charlie, sometimes Fred. She was an awful liar, Meg was."

Edward said, "And you ran away when you were only a boy?"

"No, I didn't run off. Not by myself. She disappeared. Took up with some man. She left me with a pair named Morgan. They treated me bad so I left 'em and went out on my own." Roland stared at Edward, and then his eyes went to Heather. "Wot do you want with me? That's wot I'd like to know."

"You're our son." Heather's voice spoke up, and there was absolute certainty in her voice. "We want you here with us."

"Wot makes you so sure?"

Heather got to her feet and said, "Come this way." She left the room, followed by the young man and Edward, with Serafina and Dylan close behind. She led them down a hallway and paused before a very large portrait. "There. These are all Haydens. Look at this one."

Roland was staring at it. "Who's that?"

"It's me," Edward said, "when I was nineteen. One year older than you."

Roland Anderson stared at the portrait, and the others watched his face for some expression. Heather said, "Look at the eyes. The same colour as yours. Your hair is the same auburn, and look at this." She pointed at the chin on the portrait of Edward and said, "All the Hayden men have this cleft in their chin — just like you do. You're a Hayden. There's no other answer."

Roland could not speak, and Serafina saw his problem. "I know this is a great shock for you, but I think you should stay here. I believe you are Trevor Hayden. All the evidence points to it."

"Yes," Dylan added quickly. "Get to know Lord Darby and his good wife. I think God is setting a door open before you. Don't close it."

They all saw indecision moving across the young man's face. "Trevor Hayden," he whispered. "That sure don't 'ave a good sound to it."

"It's your real name, I think, my boy. Will you stay?" Edward asked, and there was a pleading note in his voice.

For a moment as Heather watched the young man, she felt fear. She was totally convinced that this was the child she never got to rear, who she had thought was in a grave with a small stone marking it. She watched his face almost fiercely, and finally he spoke. "Well, I guess . . . for a while. But I still don't believe none o' this!"

Heather and Edward were both weak with relief. "I'm glad you're staying. We'll get to know each other better. Let me take you up to the room you'll be staying in."

"All right."

Edward watched as they left the room. He heaved a deep sigh of relief and pulled open a drawer. He took some bills out, and moving back over to where the two stood, he handed the banknotes to Dylan.

"That's far too much, sir!"

"No, it's not enough."

Serafina knew that Dylan was short of

money, that he was still staying with Matthew Grant for this very reason, and she was glad that it turned out this way. She said, however, "You must be careful, Lord Darby. That young man is living in a world he knows nothing about. He's had a hard life."

"Yes, like me." Dylan's face was sober as he added, "When I was his age I didn't know anything but hardship. If I had been brought into a house like this, I think I would have turned and fled."

Edward shook his head, and doubt was etched across his face.

"But I believe God's in this, Lord Darby. Just be patient with the young man."

"We'll leave now, but call on us anytime," Serafina said.

"I can't thank you enough, both of you."

The two said their good-byes to Heather when she came down the stairs, and then they left. The rain was still pouring down, and as soon as the carriage started up, Dylan said, "Here's half the money."

"No, that's yours, Dylan."

"That doesn't seem right."

Ignoring this comment, Serafina's mind went back to the scene that she had just watched play out before her eyes. "Do you think this will all work out?"

"Yes, I do."

The carriage creaked, and the mud holes caught at the wheels, throwing the two of them from one side to the other. "Most things don't work out," Serafina said.

"Sometimes they don't. Men and women make mistakes, lady. They go off ways God never intends, but God never fails."

Serafina turned, and in the darkness of the late afternoon, his face seemed to show an inner strength that always fascinated her. "I wish I believed that."

Dylan Tremayne reached over and picked up her hand, something he had never done. She felt the strength flowing through him as he said, "There's a line in *Hamlet.* The prince says, 'There are more things in heaven and earth, Horatio, than are dreamt of in your philosophy.' I'm convinced that God is at work restoring this young man from a bad life to a pair of loving parents. I think it's going to be wonderful."

Serafina could not take her eyes away from his face. His faith was so strong, and his dark eyes glowed, and once again, as she had in times past, she found herself wishing that she had the kind of faith that this man beside her had in abundance.

Thirteen

The carriage moved slowly toward Trentwood House in the driving rain, shifting its passengers almost violently as the wheels dropped into holes in the road made by the rainstorm. Looking out the window, Dylan strained his eyes and muttered, "It's almost like moving underwater. I never saw rain come down any harder than this."

Serafina was wearing a fur jacket that blocked some of the cold of the winter storm, but she still shivered almost violently as she leaned forward to look out the window. It was after seven o'clock now, she knew, and the darkness seemed almost palpable. The cold wind whipped through crevices in the carriage, and she glanced up involuntarily. "I feel sorry for Albert. He must be freezing up there in this cold rain."

"I expect so." Dylan crunched his shoulders and even as he did, he heard Albert call out in a voice muffled by the falling rain, "Almost there, Lady Trent. I see the lights of the house."

Eagerly Serafina moved the apron that covered the window, and as the carriage lurched forward, she saw a faint yellow luminescence of lamps one moment that the next was swathed and blinded by the driving rain. Five minutes later the carriage halted, and Dylan opened the door and stepped down. There was no hiding from the deluge.

"Here," he said. "Put this over your head." He pulled a blanket out that had been placed in one of the seats to use for warmth and draped it over Serafina's head. She tried to protest saying, "You'll get wet." But he ignored her, and putting his arm around her, he led her to the porch. When they got there, under the shelter of the portico, Serafina moved the blanket away from her head and called out, "Put the horses up, Albert, and come to the kitchen. We'll all have something hot to eat."

"Yes, ma'am, I'll do that."

The wind snatched away most of Givins's answer, and Serafina looked up at Dylan. "You're soaked to the skin!" she exclaimed. "Come on inside."

"I'm too wet. I'll make a puddle."

"It doesn't matter. That can be cleaned

up. Come along." When he still hesitated, she took his arm and pulled at him. He surrendered to her guidance, and the two entered the house. They were met at once by Barden, the butler, whose eyes opened wide at the sorry spectacle they presented. "Why, my lady," he exclaimed, "I didn't dream you'd be out in this weather!"

"Barden," Serafina said, "I want you to go get a set of dry clothes from Grimes." She glanced at Dylan, measuring him with her eyes. "Clive's would be far too small for you, but you and Peter are about the same size."

"Yes, ma'am, at once."

"Wait, tell the cook to fix something to eat."

"Yes, ma'am."

"And take Mr. Tremayne to Clive's room. Get a fire started in there. Where is everybody?"

"I think they've retired early, ma'am."

"Well, I'm going to change clothes. Tell Cook we want something hot and nourishing to eat."

Without another word Serafina turned and marched away, leaving a trail of water on the oak floor. The two men watched her go, and Dylan shook his head. "She'd make a fine officer of the Cold Stream Guards, wouldn't she, Barden?"

Barden did not smile often, but now he did. "Perhaps a general. She's always been that way."

"What was she like when she was a girl?"

Barden thought for a moment then shrugged. "Shorter," he said. "Come along. I'll take you to Mr. Clive's room."

"I don't want to put Clive out."

"He's away at University. It'll be fine."

Nessa Douglas, the cook of Trentwood House, had prepared a filling meal for the three of them. They had sat down to roast goose with savory stuffing, crisp brown roasted potatoes and parsnips, and pots of scalding coffee. Now they were all finishing up the plum pudding that had been fired with brandy, and Dylan looked across at Albert Givins, the coachman. He was a small Cockney with sandy hair and a pair of watchful blue eyes. "Not bad for a late snack, I'd say."

"Yes, sir. A man could grow fat on a meal like that." Givins got to his feet and bowed respectfully. "Thank you for the meal, milady. It was fine."

"You'd better go to bed and get warm," Serafina said. "I know it was miserable for you up there on that coach."

"I've 'ad worse days." The small man

smiled and turned and walked out.

"Will you be needing anything else?" Cook inquired.

"No, this is fine."

"You just sit there, drink your coffee, and I'll clean up."

"Come along, Dylan. Bring your coffee. We'll get out of Nessa's way."

Serafina rose and picked up a large mug, filling it with coffee from the pot, and Dylan did the same. She led him to the small sitting room where a fire was burning. "Sit down. Let's thaw out. I don't think I'll ever get dry and warm."

"I'm not sure I will either. It's a blessing to have warm, dry clothes."

She sat down on a short couch that she'd had Barden place in front of the fire, and she let herself down with a grateful sigh. "Sit down, Dylan."

Dylan sat and for a while the two stared at the fire in silence. The crackling of the dry wood made a pleasant noise and the cadence of a grandfather clock added its sound. Outside the rain was still pouring down, making a steady pattering on the roof.

"It's been a long day," Serafina said finally. She took a sip of her coffee and held the cup in both hands. The coziness and the warmth, the ticking of the clock and the crackling of the fire inside the house contrasted with the wild rain and the cold outside. Both of them leaned back, and finally Serafina asked, "What do you think will happen?"

"You mean to Lord Darby's family?"

"Yes. I'm hopeful that things will go well."

Dylan turned to her and smiled faintly. "Hope is wonderful, isn't it? I've been in a few periods of my life when there was very little of it, but I'm worried about that young man."

"Why are you worried?"

"Partly just the natural concern I would have for any young fellow thrown into a situation like that. It's like a fish taken out of water and flopping around with no idea what's happened to him."

"Oh, come now. It's not that bad."

"I don't think you appreciate the difficulties that Trevor Hayden — the new Trevor Hayden I'm speaking of now — is going to encounter."

"It has to go well. Edward and Heather have wanted a son for so long, and now they have one."

"They wanted a baby, my lady. A boy that they could nourish and raise up and teach. You ought to have some idea about how much a youngster has to learn about his world. Suppose suddenly you were thrown into the workhouse. It would be a hellish experience for you."

"You aren't comparing that with what Trevor's going to go through."

"It may be as bad. In the course of things he has a lot to contend with. Just think of the rest of the family. They're not going to be overjoyed to see him, I would think. Especially Rupert."

Serafina closed her eyes for a moment and thought of Rupert Hayden. "He's not a gentle man," she admitted finally.

"No, he's not, and you can bet he's not going to be happy that it will be a stranger who will be Lord Darby after Edward dies. It's like offering a dog a big fat juicy chunk of meat, and just as he clamps down on it, you pull it back. The dog's not going to be happy, nor is Rupert."

Serafina sat there for a moment and then said, "You've got this all analyzed, but it doesn't have to happen that way."

"It's not only logical that the boy would have a hard time, but I've got a bad feeling about this."

Serafina suddenly turned and stared at him. "A bad feeling? What are you talking about?"

"I can't explain how I feel these things. I know you don't believe in premonitions and things of the heart like that. You'd call them superstitions, but I've felt odd about what this all means ever since I saw those ravens. The ones you called a 'conspiracy.' "

"Why, Dylan, they were just birds — ugly birds, I suppose, but they have nothing to do with this."

"Maybe not. I hope not for that young man's sake, but I have these premonitions, as I call them, from time to time."

"They're just superstitions. Have you ever read *A Christmas Carol* by Mr. Dickens?"

"Yes. Fine story indeed."

"You remember when old Scrooge saw the ghost, or what he thought was a ghost, he refused to believe it. When the ghost of Marley asked him, 'Why don't you believe in me?' do you remember what the old man said?"

"Yes, he said it was just indigestion, something he had eaten that didn't agree with him. He said Marley was just an old piece of cold potato."

"Well, that's what I think your premonitions are, Dylan. I can't believe in them."

"I wish I didn't. They seem so real that —"

Suddenly Dylan's words were broken off,

for David had come running in through the door. They both stood up, and Serafina said, "David, what are you doing up at this hour?"

"I wasn't sleeping. I wanted to wait for you. I thought you'd come up, but you didn't."

Serafina reached out and gathered David into her arms. "I was going to come up and check on you, but we were so cold and hungry that we had to get something to eat."

"I've missed you." David's voice was muffled as he held his face against Serafina's, who held him tightly.

"Well, we're home now."

David pulled back and turned to put his eyes on Dylan. "I'm glad you came, Dylan. You can tell me a story now to make me go to sleep."

"I'm not sure about that." Dylan smiled. "Your mother thinks my stories are bad for you."

"No, Mum, they're not bad for me. I like them."

Serafina shrugged. "Oh, you win. Go on back to bed. Mr. Dylan will be there in a few minutes."

"I'll be waiting for you, Mr. Dylan," David said. His eyes were glowing with pleasure, and he turned and ran out of the room, his sleeping gown flowing out behind him.

"I suppose I may expect a sermon from you now," Dylan said, "on the auras of fairy tales and the like."

"I don't think you know how badly David misses having a father. He's very insecure."

"Yes, I know."

Surprise washed across Serafina's face as she studied the countenance of the man before her. "He's had a difficult childhood."

"Well, I'm sure you did all you could to make it pleasant."

"Yes, but he still misses having a father. I suppose any child would."

"I certainly did," Dylan said. He suddenly turned his head to one side and studied her. "Aren't you afraid that I might tell him some wild fairy tale? I know you think they're harmful."

"No, Dylan, I don't think you'd do anything to harm David on purpose, but when people get to believing fairy tales, as you call them, they think all stories end happily. And then when life hands them a hard blow, they're not prepared to take it." She held her head high and said, "You teach him nonsense, Dylan, and I'll teach him sense. Go along now."

Dylan laughed. "Very well. I'll tell him a

wild, unbelievable story of things that don't really exist. He loves them, but I'll make sure he knows that they're just stories."

Serafina watched as Dylan moved out of the room, then she went over to stand before the fire. The warmth felt good, and she held her hands out to it, thinking deeply about her son. For a time she stood there thinking about the strangeness of what they had done for Lord Darby and his wife. She had told Dylan she did not believe in his premonitions and that the conspiracy of ravens was nothing but a chance group of birds in a field. Still, some of his uneasiness had communicated itself, and finally she turned, left the room, and went upstairs.

She had no sooner closed the door when a knock came, and turning back she opened it to find her father standing there. He was in his nightshirt and a heavy green robe that must have been older than Methuselah. She could not remember a time when he had not worn it. "Did we wake you up, Father?"

"I heard the carriage come back. What happened at Edward's?" He listened closely as she told him what had happened, then he wiped his hand across his face in a washing motion and tugged at his woolly hair. Sometimes it seemed to her he was trying to lift himself off the earth by pulling upward, an amusing habit that endeared him to her. "I don't like things like this. It's all out of order."

"You do like order, Father. You always have."

"Yes. I like to move A to B to C. I like to know what we can count on. That's why I like science, I suppose, because we can count on it." He gave Serafina a strange look then said, "What would you think if I told you I've been reading the Bible?"

"Why, I'd be shocked."

"Be shocked then, but it's not like I thought it would be."

Serafina was indeed surprised. "Why not?"

"It's the character of Jesus. He's not what I expected."

"In what way?"

"Why, He's human!" Septimus opened his eyes wide and threw his hands apart. "I read about the woman they caught committing adultery. They wanted Jesus to stone her — and I thought He would. Do you know what He did instead?"

"I don't remember."

"He said, 'Let him that is without sin cast the first stone.' " Septimus shook his head, wonder in his eyes. "Nobody else would have handled that situation like that."

"You're not thinking of joining the

church?"

"It's not a matter of joining the church. It's a matter of . . . of what I'm going to do with Jesus Christ."

Serafina was so stunned that she could not think clearly. She thought, *It's just a phase. He'll never believe in God.* She suddenly thought of her own life and how she'd had it all planned out, and marrying Charles had merely been one step. But then her world had crashed when he had been discovered as a pederast, and she knew she had never recovered from that. Quickly she shoved this out of her mind and said, "Edward and Heather now have a son. May be troublesome, but if it works out, they'll have happiness beyond their wildest dreams."

She spoke as cheerfully and as firmly as she could, but her father was staring at her. "You sound doubtful, Daughter. Why is that?"

"Oh, it's just that . . . that young man is in a world absolutely foreign to him. His speech, his manners, his history are all against him. Everything is out of place there. It's as if a red Indian were picked up out of America and put in Buckingham Palace."

"I can see that you're worried about him."

"Dylan says he has a bad feeling." The words spilled out before she could stop them, and she added hurriedly, "Of course, I don't believe in that sort of thing."

"We'll have to stay close to that family. They're going to need all the encouragement they can get. Now, you'd better go to bed. I know you're exhausted." He came forward and kissed her on the cheek, a rare example of emotion, for he was not a demonstrative man. Serafina was surprised and watched him as he moved away down the hall. Then she went in and put on her own heavy nightgown and a robe, then slipped her feet into warm slippers. She wanted to give Dylan time to tell a long story, long enough for David to go to sleep anyway, so she pulled the chair up and sat in front of the fire, taking a book up and trying to read it. It was a book of science, and she found herself unable to concentrate on it. Finally she put it down, murmuring in a bad humor, "Dylan's premonitions are worrisome. Why do I have to think about them?"

For some time she sat there enjoying the warmth of the fire, and finally when she thought it was time enough for Dylan's story to end, she left the room. When she opened David's door and stepped inside, she expected to hear Dylan's voice but there was nothing.

She stopped abruptly when she neared the bed. Dylan, fully dressed, was lying on the bed, and he had his arm around David, who was snuggling close to him. David was clinging to Dylan, holding on to his shirt, and Dylan's free hand was resting lightly on David's crisp fair hair. Both of them were sleeping soundly, and for that one moment Serafina felt strangely that this was the right thing to happen. She hesitated, then turned and walked to her own room. She realized that as different as she and Dylan Tremayne were, she put a trust in him that she put in no other human being as far as her son David was concerned.

Fourteen

As he stared at the flames that rose in the fireplace in long leaping tongues of yellow and red, Edward wished that he could simply stand there soaking up the warmth of the fire, but he knew that would not be possible. Ever since he awoke, he had been bracing himself for the scene he knew was certain to come, and now he turned and faced Heather, who was sitting at her dressing table nervously adjusting her hair. "I suppose we'd better get the family together and break the news to them," he said.

Heather put the brush down with an abrupt motion, and as she faced her husband, she read him well. "You dread it, don't you, dear?"

"It's not going to be very pleasant, I don't think."

"I'm sure they'll understand."

Edward smiled despite himself. "You would think that Judas Iscariot would understand. Because you're so gentle yourself, you think others will be, too, but it must be done." He walked abruptly to the door of the large, ornate bedroom and entered the sitting room that adjoined it. He found Crinshaw, the butler, waiting for him, and he said at once, "Crinshaw, I want you to go to all the family and ask them to meet us in the large parlour."

"Yes, sir, I'll go at once."

As soon as Crinshaw left, Heather came out and said, "Perhaps it would be better, Edward, if Trevor didn't come to this meeting — at least not at the beginning. Perhaps I can take him some breakfast in his room?"

"I know what you're thinking. If something harsh is said, you wouldn't want him to hear it."

Heather nodded and said, "Let me go talk to him first. You gather the family." She then came over and leaned against him. He put his arms around her and held her in a protective fashion.

"It's going to be all right, Heather. I know it will be. It may be difficult for a time, but I'm convinced that God has given us this blessing."

Staring at his reflection in the mirror, Roland noted that there was a determination and even a stubbornness to his mouth. He suddenly laughed with an abruptness that startled him. "Well, what 'ave you got yerself into now? Trevor Hayden, are you? Lord Trevor Hayden? Not bloody likely!" His eyes fell on the cleft in his chin, and he remembered what Heather Hayden had said, that all of the Hayden men had this characteristic. "That don't mean nothing," he muttered and turned away from the mirror. He was exactly six feet tall and lean but with a strong, athletic figure. He wore borrowed clothes — a pair of dark grey trousers, a pair of black boots that came just below his knee, and a colourful waistcoat. Now he went over and put on his own long overcoat, for despite the blaze in the fireplace, he felt chilly in the room.

He began to pace back and forth, his mind casting first in one direction then another. He was a young man who liked to know exactly where he was and how to handle himself — but ever since they had told him that he was not who he had always thought he was but another person altogether, he was beset by a sense of uncertainty.

A soft knock at the door sounded, and Trevor attempted to hide all uncertainty from his features. "Well, come in," he said loudly. He waited until the door opened, and Lady Heather Hayden entered.

"Good morning, Trevor."

"Good morning. I don't rightly know if I can answer to that name or not. It's a bit odd to wake up with a new name."

Heather smiled gently. She came over and stood close to him looking up. "I know it's difficult, but I think it would be best. We can't use two names, so if you'll just try to adjust yourself to Trevor, it would please me very much. I've had my maid Rachel bring you up some breakfast."

Instantly Trevor's face changed. "Ain't we gonna 'ave breakfast all together?"

"No, not this morning." Heather's voice was almost unsteady, and she said, "I thought you wouldn't mind if I joined you."

"All right with me." Trevor shrugged.

A small red-haired maid came in carrying a tray. At a gesture from Heather, she put it on a table, saying, "Will there be anything else, ma'am?"

"No, that's fine, Rachel."

As soon as the maid left, she said, "Here, you sit down and have a good breakfast."

"I ain't very 'ungry, you know."

"Well, try to eat something. I had the cook fix you up something very special."

Reluctantly Trevor sat down at the table. She lifted the silver cover from the tray and smiled nervously, "I hope you like your eggs scrambled. I wasn't sure, so I thought it would be safe, and these sausages are fresh. We just made them last week." She continued to speak, pouring his tea and asking finally, "Would you have anything in your tea?"

"I reckon a little sugar would be good."

Suddenly Trevor began to eat. He ate almost as if he were afraid someone would take it away from him. Heather sat down beside him and poured herself a cup of tea. He became self-conscious, knowing that his manners were not what she was accustomed to. "I don't reckon as 'ow you cooked this, did you?"

"As a matter of fact, I didn't, but I do often cook. I love to cook, as a matter of fact, but I'm afraid our cook, Annie, is much better at it than I am."

Biting into a piece of fresh toast, Trevor ate hurriedly, and finally he shoved the plate back and said, "I don't reckon as 'ow I can stay here. I don't even know 'ow to eat proper. You sees wot kind of manners I got. And I can't even talk proper!"

"Oh, those are small things, Trevor. You can learn to fit in here. Your father and I will help."

"Aw, you could try — but I'm one of the

roughs, ma'am. I . . . just don't fit in a place like this."

"But you will! I can't tell you how happy it's made my husband and me to have you in the house and to welcome you into the family."

Trevor stirred restlessly and asked abruptly, "Who else is in the family? I don't even know if I've got brothers or sisters."

"No brother. No sisters. You're all we have."

Somehow the sentence, plain as it was, seemed pathetic to the young man as he sat there watching her. "Well, who does live 'ere in the 'ouse, then?" Tremayne and Lady Trent had told him most of what he needed to know about the family, but Trevor wanted to hear more about them.

"We're actually a small family. My husband's brother Rupert Hayden is a little younger than my husband. He runs the estate. His other brother, Arthur, is even younger. His mother, Lady Leona, has not been feeling well lately. I'm sure you will like Arthur, though he has . . . troubles."

"Wot sort of troubles?"

"Well, you'll find out, I'm sure. He . . . drinks a little bit more than is good for him."

Suddenly Trevor laughed, changing his whole expression. "So do I. Anybody else?"

"Well, Arthur has a daughter, Gervase. She's eighteen, and you will like her. Everybody does, I think. My husband has tried to spoil her, but she's the sweetest young woman I've ever known. Then aside from that there's my brother's sister, Leah St. John. She has a son whose name is Bramwell, but everyone calls him St. John."

"Wot's he do?"

For a moment, Heather seemed unable to answer, but finally she said, "Well, nothing really."

Suddenly the light blue eyes of Trevor were filled with amusement. "Now that's wot I likes! You reckon I can do the same thing?"

"Oh, I'm sure you'd be bored to death. Now I want to hear about all your life, if you feel ready to talk about it."

"You won't like it, ma'am."

"It's been hard, I know. Lady Trent told me a little about your difficulties."

Trevor shrugged and gave her a few mundane details, and after a while she rose and said, "I'm going downstairs, Trevor. My husband has been meeting with the rest of the family."

"Breakin' the good news as 'ow they got to split the family silver with a prodigal son, eh?"

Heather realized this young man had a quick mind. "Something like that," she said reluctantly.

"Reckon they won't all fall over themselves with joy 'earing about me."

"Why'd you say that?"

"Why, I knowed an old man once named Jenkins who 'ad four sons. 'E 'ad a 'ouse and some money. One of the sons 'ad run off to sea when 'e was thirteen and signed on as a cabin boy. Years later 'e come 'ome missing an arm. Lost it fighting under Nelson, don't you see? Wot do you think 'e found when 'e got 'ome?"

"Why, I would think his family would be proud of him serving his country like that."

"Not bloody likely! 'E was another 'and in the pot, don't you see? I reckon it'll be the same with your 'usband's brothers and 'is nephew."

"No, they couldn't be that cruel."

Trevor started to speak, then he realized that he was as alien to this woman as if he had come from another planet. He knew the cruelties of the world well and had hardened himself against them, but this woman, he saw, had a gentleness that was almost shocking to him. He thought suddenly, *It won't take 'er long to find out that not everybody is as nice as she is.*

■ ■ ■ ■

Gervase was standing behind her father, watching as he laid the paint on the canvas. It was a picture of Silverthorn almost buried under snow. Nearly everything was white except the leaden sky. The only splashes of colour were a man and a woman walking along a road that was as white as alabaster. He wore a bright green coat and the woman wore a red one. They were holding hands, and somehow, Arthur had caught the happiness of the two.

"That's very good, Papa," Gervase said softly as she studied the painting. "I don't know how you do it!"

"Do what?"

"Why, how you catch the happiness of those two people with such a simple scene. They're just two people that not many would notice. But I knew as soon as I looked at the painting that they loved each other."

"It's your mother and me," Arthur said, his voice barely above a whisper.

"I think I knew that. You have a great gift, Papa."

"Do you think so, Gervase?" Arthur turned, held his brush lightly, and shook his head. "I can't tell about myself anymore. I don't know whether my work is good or not. I used to be sure," he said. "When I was young I thought I was going to be another Gainesboro or Turner."

"You will be yet."

They suddenly heard footsteps, a slight knock, and then the door opened to reveal Crinshaw, who said, "The master has asked me to invite you into the larger parlour, Mr. Arthur — and you, also, Miss Gervase."

"What for?"

"I couldn't say, sir."

"Very well." Arthur wiped his hands on a rag and tossed it aside. "A little bit unusual," he muttered. "I wonder what's going on?"

"I suppose we'll find out. Come along." Gervase took his arm, and the two left the room. As soon as they arrived in the larger parlour, they found St. John and his mother, Leah, already there.

Edward was there also, and he turned to Crinshaw saying, "Did you find Mr. Rupert?"

"Yes, sir, he is on his way."

"What's going on, Uncle Edward?" St. John asked, his eyes alert. Leah was sitting down on a low couch and said, "Is there a problem?"

"Let's just wait until Heather and Rupert

get here before we begin."

"That sounds rather sinister," Gervase said, her green eyes sparkling. Even as she spoke, there was a spirited air about her, and she was studying her uncle Edward carefully. She was a favourite of his, she well knew, and so did everyone else, but there was a seriousness about him now, and she knew she must not break his mood.

Heather entered from the east door, and at almost the same instant, Rupert came through the main door on the north side of the room. Heather came at once to stand beside Edward, and Rupert glanced around the room, a hooded look in his eyes. "What's this meeting about, Edward?"

"Will Lady Leona be joining us?" Edward asked.

"Grandmother is not feeling well today," Gervase answered somewhat uncomfortably, for Lady Leona's bouts of confusion troubled her.

"Very well," Edward said. "I wish everyone would sit down. There's something Heather and I have to tell you, and it will probably come as a shock to you."

St. John stared at his uncle and said impulsively, "I'm not sure that sounds like a happy beginning."

"I don't mean to show unhappiness, for

I'm not. As a matter of fact, Heather and I think it's rather good news."

"Well, hurry it up, will you, Edward? Some of us have work to do around here, even if others don't." No one could escape the contemptuous look that Rupert gave to both St. John and Arthur.

"There's been a rather startling development in our family. A short time ago we had a visit from a Catholic priest, a Father Xavier . . ."

Everyone listened carefully, for Lord Darby was not a man to waste words. When he said, ". . . so the priest got the dying confession of this woman who said — and prepare yourself for a surprise — her baby, which she had the day before our son, Trevor, was born, died. She confessed to the priest." Here Darby passed a hand over his forehead and then swallowed hard. "She confessed that she had exchanged her dead child for our son."

"What?" Rupert exclaimed and suddenly came to his feet. "Why, that's errant hogwash!"

"Don't be too quick to say that," Heather said quickly. "We've had it checked very carefully. Lady Trent and Mr. Tremayne have looked into it very thoroughly. It was they who located the young man. He knew nothing at all about this."

"It's some kind of a rogue's game, that's what it is!" Rupert exclaimed. "We've got to have the police look into this person, whoever he is."

"We've already done that, Rupert," Edward said somewhat coldly. "We've looked into it in every way we could possibly think of. But there's one proof that I don't think anyone can deny."

"Well, what's that?" Gervase asked.

"His appearance. He's the exact image of the Hayden men, even to this cleft in the chin. He has it and the widow's peak, the same colour hair, the same eyes."

Heather added at once, "He didn't believe it himself at first, but we showed him the portrait of Edward when he was the same age, and Trevor couldn't believe it."

"So his name is Trevor. I bet that wasn't his name when they dug him up."

"It's his name now, Rupert," Edward said firmly.

"I don't believe a single bloody word of it!" Rupert exclaimed angrily.

Leah had said nothing, but now she raised her voice, and there was a strange expression on her face. "You can't mean to claim this man as your son, Edward? You'd pass your title and estate to him?"

"Yes, we would. Heather and I have found the son we've always wanted. I've told every one of you at one time or another how Heather felt that God had made a promise over that child. We thought he died, and we couldn't understand God's workings, but now" — Edward's voice grew suddenly warm, and his eyes were bright with anticipation — "God has given us the son we've always wanted."

"But, sir, you must know things like this happen." St. John spoke up. "It's like the shell game."

Leah said, "Just a minute, St. John." She stood. "I'd like to see this man, Edward."

"Yes, that's why I've called you here. If you'll wait, I'll go get him." He left the room at once, and Rupert began to protest. "Heather, you surely have better judgment than this."

"I would think Edward would have better judgment," Leah said, "but he's wanted a son so badly that he'll grab at any straw."

"We'd better wait, hadn't we?" Arthur said mildly. "Until, at least, we see the young man and hear the evidence."

"I think that's exactly right, Papa." Gervase went over and stood before Heather. "You believe this, Aunt Heather?"

"Yes, I believe it with all my heart."

"Well, I can't wait to see your son. If he's anything like you and Uncle Edward, he'll be a fine man."

Nervously Heather said, "You mustn't expect too much. He's led a terrible life. He was thrown out onto the streets when he was very young, and he's had to make his own way." She continued to speak, trying to prepare them for what they would see, but it was obvious that Rupert, St. John, and Leah were angry to the bone, and her heart faltered as she considered what the young man would have to face.

Trevor looked up and said, "Come in." The door opened, and the man who called himself his father was there. At that moment Trevor looked like a very wary wild animal seeking a way out of a trap. " 'Ave you told 'em?"

"Yes."

"I don't expect there were loud cheers."

Edward managed a smile. "I didn't expect any."

"You're more of a realist, sir, than Lady 'Eather."

"I expect that's right. Nobody likes to have a windfall snatched out of his hand, do they now?"

"No, they don't."

"This won't be easy, my boy. I know it won't, but it's really up to you." Edward took a step closer and stared at the features of the young man so much like his own. "You're my son, but we missed out on so much. You'll be as frustrated and even afraid here in my world as I would be if I had to make my way in yours. You can walk away from it if you like, but I think you're a Hayden, and Heather and I will do whatever we can for you. But even so, if you can't accept us as your parents, I think I would understand."

Trevor had been on the very verge of leaving, but something about the frankness of the older man standing before him caught his attention. He had learnt to read faces as a matter of self-preservation, and he saw honesty in the face of the man before him. "Well, sir, I don't feel like yer son, but I'll stay. If I can't do it, we'll soon find out, I guess. I'm either yer son or I ain't, and I'd like to find out."

"That's all that we ask. Come along, then." Edward stopped and turned back to Trevor. "It won't be a very pleasant atmosphere, as you say."

Trevor smiled, saying, "Reckon I'm pretty well used to unpleasant atmospheres."

Sir Edward turned again and left the

room, and Trevor accompanied him. As they passed down the hallway, the young man's eyes went to the portraits of the Haydens, including one of this man who walked determinedly beside him. They were all men of wealth and education, and Trevor was totally aware of the difference between himself and these people. A sudden memory flickered into his mind of a time when he had been caught in an alley, and a man called Simon Finch had been assaulting a twelve-year-old girl. Trevor had usually not entered into other men's quarrels, but at the sight of the girl's terrified face, he screamed, "Get away from 'er, Finch!" He remembered how Finch had turned, pulling a knife, and he had felt the fiery bite of it on his arm. The fight had been short, and Trevor could not help but think how foreign a thing like this would be to Lord Darby or any of the Haydens.

Edward turned to stand beside a door, and Trevor saw the uncertainty in the older man's face. *Why, this is as 'ard for 'im as it is for me!* The thought startled him, and when Edward said, "Come in, Trevor," he shrugged and stepped inside.

Edward's glance went at once to Lady Heather who was smiling at him and biting her lip nervously. He nodded to her, then said in a determined voice, "This is Trevor Hayden. Trevor, I've explained the circumstances of your birth, but now, as I have told my family, you are my son, and I'm asking them to accept you. This is my brother Rupert."

As soon as Trevor saw the man staring at him, he recognized a carnivore. He knew cruelty when he saw it, and he saw nothing soft or easy or gentle in Rupert Hayden. The man did not speak, and Trevor shrugged slightly. "I'm glad to know you, Mr. Rupert."

"And this is my sister, Leah St. John, and her son, Bramwell."

Trevor turned to face the pair squarely. He knew little about them. He could make nothing of the woman's expression, but the young man Bramwell was staring at him with frank distaste and said, "So you think you are a Hayden?"

"So my father tells me."

St. John's face reddened, for he had been bested by a guttersnipe. "We'll see about that, won't we?" he said.

Edward saw that Trevor was aware of the antagonism in the pair and said quickly, "This is my other brother, Arthur, and his daughter, Gervase."

"I am very happy to see you, my boy."

At once Trevor saw that there was a gentleness in Arthur Hayden. He had not the strength of Edward nor the hardness of Rupert. He was so different from Edward that Trevor couldn't imagine them being brothers.

"I'm happy to meet you, Cousin." The young woman named Gervase was frank, and there was an honesty in her eyes as well as a curiosity. "I welcome you to the family. I've always wanted another cousin, and now I have one." The warmth of the young woman was like a clear sky after the storm that he had seen in Rupert's face.

Heather suddenly came over to stand beside Trevor. Her voice was gentle, as usual, but there was a fullness to it as she said, "It's like going back in time, isn't it, Edward? When I was seventeen years old, I was taken to a garden party by my parents. I was so shy I just wanted to sink into the earth. Then I looked up, and I saw a young man talking to a very pretty girl. She was my cousin Helen, who was so very accomplished and so beautiful that when I stood beside her, I felt like a witch." She suddenly smiled at her husband. "And then this young man — who was none other than Edward Hayden — left my cousin and came over and asked me to dance. That was the first time I ever saw Edward." She turned now to face Trevor, and her voice was unsteady as she said, "And now I see him again exactly as he was that day."

Trevor was shocked at the woman's emotion and could not help but believe that she was totally convinced he was her son. He looked at Edward and saw him struggling for control, and he saw that the rest of the people in the room were waiting for him to speak. Trevor straightened up and spoke directly. "Sir Edward and Lady Heather, I don't know if you knows wot you are doing. I don't know if I'm your son or not, but I 'ave to warn you, you're taking a big chance claiming a bloke like me straight out of Seven Dials as your proper son."

Heather came forward, held out her hand, and the young man from Seven Dials, who had known nothing but hardness in his life, could only smile at her. "We'll prove that you're our son. You're a Hayden, and that's all there is to it," Heather said warmly.

Gervase let her glance fall on Leah St. John, and there was no mistaking the animosity that appeared on her features. The same was true of St. John, and more than these two, the expression of Rupert Hayden spoke a deadly hatred toward the young man who was now in line to become the master of the estate and the next Lord of Darby.

Fifteen

"But surely, Edward, you must see the . . . impropriety . . . of what you're doing with this young man!"

Rupert Hayden had come early in the morning to confront Edward with obvious anger and bitterness in his face. He stood before Edward, his bulky, strong body rigid. Only by an effort did he keep himself from shouting. He had slept little since discovering that an unknown nobody was to be the next Earl of Darby. It was an office that was to have fallen to him, and now his eyes glowed with anger as he continued. "You don't know anything about this young man, and even if you did, consider who he is, what he is, what he's been."

"He's had an unfortunate life, Rupert, but with care and guidance and a little compassion we can make him into what he should be." Edward had been expecting Rupert's visit. He could understand the big man's bitterness. Rupert had always been resentful that he had not been the older son, but he had managed to keep it hidden — for the most part. Now as Edward studied Rupert, he saw that there was an anger that went beyond anything he had expected. "Give the boy a chance, Rupert," he pleaded.

"It's folly, that's what it is, folly! From what I can understand, this man has grown up in the worst part of London. He's consorted with thieves and robbers, criminals of all sorts. He has been to prison. You can't get that out of a man. As the twig is bent, so the tree will grow."

"If he's a Hayden, he has good blood in him, and I'm convinced that he is. Just look at the pictures of our father and our grandfather. How much he looks like them!"

The argument went on for some time, with Rupert growing angrier and more bitter and Edward trying harder and harder to pacify Rupert. Finally he said, "I know you had expected to gain the title at my death. And that was my intention. I never made any secret of it. But you know how these things work. The oldest son is the legitimate heir, and I intend to pour myself into making Trevor the kind of man we'll be proud of. But I guarantee you'll be provided for at my death."

Rupert ground his teeth together, and his voice dripped with fury. "All my life I've given to you in service, Edward, and now you shove me out and put that outsider in my place!" He whirled and stormed out the door before Edward could answer.

Edward frowned. The interview had left him shaken. He was not a man who enjoyed controversy, and he well understood that Rupert had, indeed, dedicated his life to Silverthorn. He knew every inch of the grounds, every laborer. He kept the books so that Edward was never troubled with the details of administering a large estate. *I know what he's going through, and I wish I could do something about it.* He sat there thinking, trying to find a way to pacify Rupert. Finally, with a sigh, he left the room and went out to the small sitting parlour where he found Heather sitting at a window. He sat down beside her and said abruptly, "I've just had a rather unpleasant time with Rupert."

Heather looked up, her eyes compassionate. "I know it's hard on him. He's been a good manager of the estate."

"Yes, but that's not what he wants."

"I understand. He expected to get the title, but now that can never be. I know it will be unpleasant for you."

The two sat there talking, and Edward found himself growing calmer. He looked out the window and saw Gervase playing with the huge Great Dane she had raised from a puppy.

He opened the window and called out, "Gervase, come in here for a moment, will you? But leave that monster of a dog outside."

"Yes, Uncle Edward."

Edward turned and shut the window. Moments later Gervase came in. Her cheeks were red with the cold and with exercise, and her dark eyes were dancing. "I love wintertime. I hope it snows some more."

"Well, I don't. Nasty stuff to get through." He studied Gervase and could not help but smile. "You and that dog make a pair. I think he's as big as you are."

"Not quite."

"You're going to spoil him."

Gervase came over and reached up to straighten Edward's cravat. "You're a fine one to talk, Edward Hayden. You've spoiled me to the bone ever since I was a child."

Heather suddenly laughed. "He certainly has. I don't think there's ever a thing she wanted that you haven't gotten her, Edward."

Indeed, this was true. Edward and

Heather had both become almost inordinately fond of Gervase. She had been only four when Arthur had returned to live at Silverthorn. He was mourning the death of his wife, and Edward and Heather had practically raised her. Edward, especially, was as fond of her as a man will grow fond of a young girl. He had taken pride in her intelligence, her wit, her strength, and Heather had once said, "You couldn't have loved a child of your own more than you love Gervase." Now as he studied her, he admired her beauty.

"I want you to do me a favor, Gervase."

"Why, of course. What is it?"

For a moment Lord Darby hesitated, and then he said, "How do you think Trevor is doing?"

"Bad!"

Edward was shocked at her bluntness. "Bad? Why do you say that? He's only been here a few days."

"He's afraid, Uncle Edward."

Edward blinked with surprise. "Afraid? I don't see that. He seems to be finding his way."

"No, he's not," Gervase said firmly. "He's smart, Uncle, and he knows that some people in this family don't accept him — never will accept him."

"They'll come around."

Gervase gave her uncle an odd look. "You always think the best of people. That's good — and it's bad."

"What do you mean by that?"

"I think it's wonderful how you can accept almost anyone, but people impose upon you."

"Well, you certainly do!" he said with a chuckle. "I've just been a big toy for you ever since you were a child. Anyway, I want you to spend some time with Trevor. You're the same age. You ought to have a lot in common."

Gervase suddenly laughed. She had a marvelous laugh, free and clear, and her whole face lit up. "Uncle Edward, you're so smart — and so dense. What in the world do Trevor and I have in common besides our age? We might as well be from different countries or even different planets."

Edward opened his mouth but found he had nothing to say to that. "I'm worried about him, Gervase. I know he's lonely, and it's difficult for him. Heather and I are doing all we can, but I think you could do a lot to make him feel more at home."

"Why, of course I will, Uncle Edward. I'll take him riding."

"Fine! He needs to learn horses. By the

time the hunt comes around, I hope that he'll be able to join us."

"I'm not sure that Trevor will find fox hunting his favourite thing."

"Why not?"

"Because fox hunting was not part of his world. I think you have to grow up with such a foolish sport to appreciate it!" She laughed again, turned, and seemed to bounce from the room.

Edward could not help smiling. "She brings sunshine into this house. She always has. I hope she can help Trevor."

Trevor approached the sideboard where breakfast had been set out. For him it was shocking how the people of Silverthorn ate. He was accustomed to eating whatever was available for breakfast, usually bread with butter and some sort of jam. Meat had been scarce in his diet, at least for breakfast.

Now as he approached the sideboard, he saw that it was laden with chafing dishes filled with eggs, meats, vegetables, various baked pastries, and breads. He glanced over to the table and noted that it was covered with pots of tea, dishes of preserves, butter, fresh fruits, and sweetmeats. He watched Arthur, who was immediately in front of him, pick up the knife and cut a thin slice of ham off of the shoulder, and Trevor did the same. He was clever enough to understand that part of his training here would be nothing but pure manners. He had also discovered that a lifetime of one kind of manners is not easily thrown off. But he had learnt to take soup out of the side of the spoon, and by watching carefully and staying one step behind the others at the table, he had managed to use the proper silverware. Now he filled his plate mostly with scrambled eggs, deviled kidneys, and sausages, which he had discovered he liked very much.

He took his seat and was intensely aware of the enemies he had sitting at the table with him. He had no illusions about the three, including Rupert Hayden, who made no attempt to hide his animosity and even now was glaring at him fiercely.

He was less certain about the intensity of Leah St. John and her son, Bramwell St. John. Leah had been cold enough to him, but St. John, on the other hand, had been fairly friendly. How much of this was real and how much was an act was a matter that Trevor had yet to figure out. He glanced across the table where Arthur and his golden-haired daughter sat. Arthur, from time to time, offered a bit of conversation, and the girl, Gervase, was friendly enough.

"Trevor," Edward said, "I'm going to London tomorrow. I would like for you to go with me."

"Wot for, sir?"

"Oh, I have some business there, and we need to go to the tailor and get you some clothes made."

A stubbornness rose suddenly in Trevor. He resented being molded into something he was not, although he knew that Lord Darby and his wife wished it greatly. "I 'ave clothes already, sir."

"Oh, you need formal clothes," Gervase said quickly. "You'll be going to balls and things like that. You need quite a few things. Listen to your father. He loves new clothes."

"I don't know as I love new clothes any more than any other man," Edward protested.

"Yes, you do, Uncle Edward. You're quite given to foppish attire."

St. John suddenly laughed. "She has you there, sir. Of course, I like foppish attire myself."

Edward blinked with surprise and stared at Gervase. "I think a gentleman should wear nice clothing. I wouldn't call such things foppish attire."

"I was only teasing, Uncle. Perhaps I'd

better go along with you so that you'll get a woman's side of the matter." She winked at Trevor and asked, "Don't you think that would be a good idea, Cousin Trevor?"

Trevor never knew how to answer this young woman. He did like her spirit though. "That would be fine with me."

"No, this is a matter between me and my son. You'll have to arrange other activities for yourself."

The breakfast continued, and Trevor was intensely aware of the looks that he got from his mother. He still had trouble thinking of her as his mother. He had discovered that knowing the truth was one thing, but accepting it was another thing altogether. He had gone over and over in his mind the strange circumstances of his life and wondered at the ease with which Lord Darby and Lady Heather had accepted him. He had found out quickly enough from Lady Trent and Dylan Tremayne that the pair had lost their child, but he could not see that he could take the place of that longing. In his mind there was no separating the rearing of a child from young adulthood, but that was not so with these two. They accepted him wholeheartedly, and he felt the burden of becoming what they wanted, even when he had no heart for it. His life had been bad enough, but it had been his. Now he was forced to think differently, speak differently, act differently, eat differently. Everything was different, and the strain was taking its toll on him.

After breakfast he went up to his room and sat there for a time staring out the window. It was a cold day outside. Christmas was coming, but Christmas had never been a big day in his own life. He could remember only a few small gifts and had usually celebrated it by getting drunk with the rowdy group he ran with.

Finally growing bored with the room, he left, and as he was going down the stairs, on the landing he met Rosie, the pretty maid he had noticed earlier. She had a very good figure and beautiful auburn hair as well as a smooth complexion. As they passed, she said, "Pardon me, sir."

"Wot's yer 'urry?"

Rosie looked up, and her eyes widened. They were beautiful hazel eyes, and Trevor smiled at her. "You're a pretty girl, Rosie. I don't know as I've ever seen a prettier one."

"Please, sir, you mustn't say those things!"

"Why not? They're true enough." He suddenly reached for her and kissed her before she could move.

"Oh, sir, you shouldn't do that!"

"Why, Rosie, I thought you liked me." He held her closely and noticed that she made little attempt to get away from him.

Suddenly a voice said, "Are you busy, Cousin?"

Caught off guard, Trevor turned and saw that Gervase had walked up the stairs and now stood smiling at him, mischief in her eyes.

Rosie pulled away at once and fled up the stairs. Her face was flushed, and she was visibly upset.

Trevor glared at Gervase. She was wearing a riding costume, he noticed, but he was angry and embarrassed for some reason.

"Been doing a little snoopin' are you?"

"Not at all."

"Yes, you were. Go on, tell me I was out of line. That I wasn't behavin' right."

"All right. You were out of line."

Trevor grew irritated. "She wasn't puttin' up no fight."

"Trevor, she couldn't put up a fight."

"If she didn't like me, she could."

"She doesn't like you."

"Why'd she let me kiss 'er then?"

Gervase shrugged, and her voice was easy and natural. "She didn't have any choice. That's the way it is with pretty young maids. When the young master of the house forces himself on them, what are they going to do? Are they going to scream and slap his face?"

"That's wot she ought to do."

"Then she'd be put out of the house without a character reference. She'd have a hard time finding another job, and you don't realize how hard it is on an attractive woman who's a servant in a big house like this. They're at the mercy of the owners. How could they complain? Some of them get with child, and then they are simply pushed out of the house, perhaps with nothing."

"Well, that ain't right."

"That's the way it is though, and that's why you need to be careful. They don't have many friends, young girls like Rosie."

Trevor stopped, gnawing his lower lip. Gervase could see his mind working quickly. Finally he shrugged, "I didn't know all 'at."

"Well, of course you didn't, but you know now, and I'm sure you'll keep it in mind. Come along."

"Come along where?"

"I'm going to take you for a ride."

"You mean in the carriage?"

"No, silly. On a horse. Have you ever ridden?"

"Never been on a 'orse in my life and don't want to."

She suddenly reached out and took his arm. "Yes, you do. It'll be fun. Come on. Go put your heavy coat on. It's cold out, and then we'll introduce you to a horse."

Trevor was of a mind to refuse, but he found himself warming to the young woman's outgoing warmth. "All right." He went back to his room, got his coat, and the two stepped outside. They were at once confronted by the huge dog that Trevor had noted before. The Great Dane advanced, his eyes on Trevor.

"Wot's 'e coming at me like that for?" Trevor demanded nervously.

"He just needs to be introduced. Here, Jason. You be nice." She stooped over and put her hand on the dog's head. "This is Master Trevor Hayden. He's a good friend of mine, so you be nice to him, you hear?" She looked up and smiled. "Now put your hand out and let him smell it."

" 'E might bite it off."

"Nonsense! Don't move quickly. He's careful who he makes friends with. If you don't, he might think you want to harm me, and then I couldn't answer for him."

Trevor laughed. "Some bodyguard you got." He put his hand out, ready to draw it back at the first sight of fangs, but the big dog smelled it carefully.

"Now, pat him on the head."

Trevor did so, still moving carefully.

"Now, kneel down beside him and put your arm around him and call him a sweet name."

"I ain't calling no dog no sweet name." He knelt down nevertheless and put his arm around the big dog. " 'E's a monster, 'e is! You 'ad 'im long?"

"Since he was a puppy."

"Why'd you name 'im Jason?"

The two stood up, and Jason seemed pacified as they walked toward the stable. "When I got him my father had been reading me stories from Greek myths, and in one that I loved there was a character called Jason. Have you ever heard the story of Jason and the Argonauts?"

"No, I ain't 'eard many stories."

"It's about a young man who had to go on a quest to recover the Golden Fleece."

"The Golden Fleece? Wot was that?"

"Oh, it was a golden ram that saved some people. He was sacrificed to the gods, and his fleece was hung up."

"Wot did Jason 'ave to do with it?"

"He was a hero. He had been robbed of his kingdom by a wicked uncle, and now he had been sent off to get the Golden Fleece and bring it back. Many heroes had gone looking for it, and all of them had died because a monstrous dragon guarded it."

"There ain't no such things as dragons."

"Of course not. It's just a story, but it was so much fun."

"Well, did 'e get the bloody fleece or not?"

"He got there, and a woman named Medea helped him. She cast a spell on the dragon, and Jason stole the fleece and came home."

"Wot happened to the woman?"

"Well, they got married."

"And lived 'appily ever after?"

"Well, actually not. I never liked the ending of that story. Medea was an evil woman really. She actually killed three of her own children."

"I wouldn't like a story like that. I like 'appy endings."

"So do I, so I wouldn't let Papa tell me the ending. But it was exciting how Jason was so heroic and brave and strong." She laughed, and he was amazed at how free she was. "You're like Jason, Trevor."

"Me a 'ero? Not likely!"

"Well, I mean he had to go looking for something that was almost impossible to get, and that's what you're doing."

"I don't know wot you mean by that."

"I mean it would be as easy to get the

Golden Fleece as it is for you to become a gentleman, to fit yourself into Uncle Edward's idea of what his son ought to be." Her words caught at Trevor, and he felt the truth of them.

"I can't never do it," he said bitterly. "You 'ave to start when you're a baby to be a lord."

He said no more, and neither did she urge him on, for they had reached the stables. Tim Moorhaven, the groom, came out. "Tim, we're going for a ride. Saddle Juliet for me."

"Yes, and you, sir?"

Trevor wasn't used to being called sir, and Gervase said, "You have a choice. You can have an older, steadier horse. We've got one called Oscar. It's like riding in a rocking chair."

"Wot else is 'ere?"

"Well, you can have a better horse, but he will have some spirit. You might fall off."

"I'll 'ave 'at one," Trevor said instantly, challenged by her words.

She laughed and said, "Saddle Prince for Master Trevor."

"I don't know, miss. He's quite lively if the gentleman ain't rode much."

"Saddle the bloody 'orse," Trevor said.

The two stood there, and Trevor watched

carefully as the horses were being prepared. He was aware that Gervase was studying him. "Why do you want to take a chance on falling?"

He turned to her and laughed. "I didn't want you to think I was afraid of a bleeding 'orse."

"I wouldn't think that."

"Why not?"

"I just don't think you'd be afraid of most things."

"No? Well, wot do you think I'm afraid of?" he challenged her.

"Like all the rest of us, Trevor, you're afraid of things you don't know and things you don't understand. I'm that way myself."

He hardly knew what to make of her speech, and finally Moorhaven brought the horses out. He helped Gervase on and then said, "Sir, you get on from this side."

Trevor glared at him. "I don't see wot difference it makes."

"It makes a difference to the horse, sir. They don't like things they're not used to."

Trevor clumsily got on, and he felt very high off the ground. He turned and looked at Gervase who was smiling at him. "Wot do I do now?"

"Don't fall off."

"Wot if I do?"

"Well, get back on then. Come on."

He said, "I don't know a bloody thing about 'orses."

"Just touch him with your heels, and he'll start walking, but keep a good hold on those reins. Sometimes they get the bit in their teeth and pull the reins right out of your hands."

The horses proceeded at a walk, and Trevor was enjoying it. He had often seen gentlemen on horseback and admired the way they handled them. Finally he said, " 'Ow 'bout we go faster?"

"Of course, but the faster you go, the more likely you are to fall off."

He touched Prince with his heels, and the animal at once responded by bursting into a canter. He bounced up and down on the saddle but managed to hang on. He looked over at Gervase, who had pulled up even with him, and saw how easily she rode. "Let's go faster," he said.

"Better not, Trevor."

"Come on." He kicked Prince with his heels, and the horse shot forward. To his shock he found it was exciting and that he wasn't afraid at all. He did well enough until they came to a tree fallen across the path. Prince rose in the air, and Trevor rose with him, of course. When he came down he felt a jar, and the next thing he knew he was turning a flip. He hit the ground flat on his back.

He lay there for a moment and found it difficult to breathe. He was aware then that Gervase had come quickly and was standing over him. "Are you all right?" she asked, leaning over. Her voice was anxious, and she put her hand on his chest.

"Of course I'm all right." He got up and grinned at her. "That was fun, right 'nough, but I reckon I need some lessons."

"Why, you're doing fine, Trevor. The main thing is not to be afraid, and you're not. Here, let me catch Prince for you."

The ride continued after she retrieved the horse, and when they finally went back, Tim was waiting for them. "Was your ride all right, Miss Gervase?"

"It was fine."

"And you, sir, did you like your ride?"

"The 'orse is smarter than me, I'm afraid, Tim."

"No, sir, you'll learn. You surely will."

As Trevor and Gervase walked back toward the house, they passed behind a copse of trees, and suddenly he reached out and grabbed her, holding her tight facing him. "You ain't no parlour maid wot 'as to give in to a bloke."

"No, I'm not," Gervase said. She did not struggle, and she was watching him carefully.

"Wot if I kiss you?"

"Why, I'd fight you."

"You'd lose."

"I suppose so, but one of the things you'd soon learn is don't kiss a woman who doesn't want to be kissed."

"You don't like me then?"

"That's not it. I like you very much, Trevor, and I'd like to help you become what Uncle Edward and Aunt Heather want you to be."

"You like me, but you don't want me to kiss you. Maybe it's because we're cousins."

"We're not really."

He dropped his arms. "Wot do you mean?"

"I'm not Arthur Hayden's real daughter. My mother was Rachel Reis. She was married to Ramon Reis, a captain of the Spanish Navy, but he was killed. My father met her, fell in love with her, and married her. He adopted me legally."

"Wot about yer ma?"

"She died when I was only four. So, you see, I'm only your cousin legally. You're really more of a Hayden than I am."

Her words confused Trevor. "Well, I didn't

know that." He felt uncomfortable, for there was something about this girl that was honest and forthright. He had seen pretty girls before but none more beautiful than this one. Finally he said, "Well, since we ain't really cousins, maybe I'll get that kiss sometime."

"I'll tell you what," Gervase said, her eyes dancing. "You stay on Prince at a dead run through the woods, and I'll give you a kiss." She laughed then and said, "Come on."

"Where to now?"

"My father's painting my portrait. I'll sit for him, and you can watch."

Sixteen

Dylan got up from the bed where he had been lying flat on his back, holding a book and reading it with considerable discomfort. Tossing the book on the solitary chair in the small room, he took two steps over to the window and stared out. The view was practically nonexistent. All he could see was the shabby building next door and a flock of sparrows fighting over some sort of food in the snow below the window. The world was white, but Dylan could see little of it. The view depressed him, and turning away, he went to the chair and sat on it with discouragement. He had left Matthew Grant's rooms feeling that he was an imposition. Money was short, and he had only a few guineas left from the fee that Lord Darby had given him. His financial future looked bleak indeed.

Shifting his weight on the chair, he looked down and saw a bright-eyed mouse had suddenly appeared from under the bed. He smiled and said softly, “Well, here you are again for a handout, I suppose.” Getting up, he went over to the meal table, took a bit of bread from under a pewter cover, and tossed it toward the mouse. He watched as she reached down with delicate paws, turned it around and around, and began to nibble. “A beautiful creature you are,” he said. “God made everything beautiful in its time.”

He sat there watching the mouse only for a few seconds, and then a loud rapping at his door brought his attention around.

“You don’t have to break it down, do you?” he muttered.

Getting up, he wondered who could be visiting him, because only Matthew knew where he was staying. He opened the door and found a woman standing there. She smiled broadly, “I found you, Dylan. You can’t hide from a determined woman.”

Dylan returned the woman’s smile. He had always liked Bess Cauthen. They had been in several plays together, and in the time before he had become a Christian, they had been somewhat more than friends. “Come in, Bess, to my palatial quarters,” he said. He stepped back, and his eyes ran over her. She had flaming red hair, broad lips tinted with some sort of cosmetic, and dark blue eyes. Her figure was good, although she was a little heavier than he had remembered her. She was wearing a green coat, and somehow she looked older.

"Well, you've come down in the world, my boy," Bess said.

"Yes, I've lost my fortune, Bess, you'll be sorry to hear. You'll not be interested in me anymore, poor beggar that I am."

"Well, you don't have to be poor anymore." Bess took a step closer to him, and he could smell the aroma of her perfume, the same she always wore, which smelled like gardenia blossoms.

"What does that mean, Bess?"

"Oh, I'm not offering to keep you. You're not suited for that, but Knowles is looking for you. He wants you to take that part in *All for Love.*"

Instantly Dylan shook his head and shrugged his shoulders. "Well, you've made a trip for nothing, Bess. I'm not taking that role."

"You're a fool, Dylan! Knowles is the best producer in New York, and that play is going to be a hit. It's going to make us both famous."

"Not me, Bess. I'm out."

For a second Bess stood looking at Dylan.

She reached up and tapped her full lower lip with a forefinger and finally shook her head with something like disgust. "I know what it is. You're too holy to be in a play like that."

"Don't put it like that, Bess. It's just that I don't agree with the values of that play."

"It's about men and women in love. You believe in that, don't you? I seem to remember you knew a little along those lines when we were together."

A faint colour tinged Dylan Tremayne's cheeks. He knew she had bested him here, for they had been lovers at one time. Since he had given his life to Christ, he was struggling to find his way out of all that, and all he could say now was, "I just don't want to be in a play that makes sex such a mechanical thing."

Bess stared at him in disbelief. "Dylan, it's only a play! It doesn't mean you're like the people in the play."

"I know, but it could lead some people in the audience in the wrong direction. I just can't do it."

Bess moved closer and put her arms around his neck. She pressed herself against him, and he was intensely aware of the warmth of her body and also of his own desires. Pulling his head down, Bess kissed him on the lips. She let herself linger there, and Dylan could think of no way to avoid this scene. Pulling away would seem rude, and they had been close at one time.

"I miss you, Dylan. We could have a good life together."

Dylan sought rapidly in his mind for a reply, but he could not think of a single word to say. He was actually relieved when another knock came at the door. "Excuse me, Bess," he said.

"You expecting company?"

"Nobody knows I'm here. How did you find me?"

"I went to that friend of yours in Scotland Yard, Inspector Grant. He told me where you were living."

"That's probably Grant now." Opening the door, indeed Dylan did find Matthew Grant standing there. He was bundled up in a heavy coat, and his cheeks were red with the cold. "Come in, Grant. I believe you know Miss Cauthen."

"Yes, how are you, Miss Cauthen?"

"I'm fine, Inspector. Have you come to arrest Dylan?"

"No, not at all. He's a good friend of mine."

"Well, he needs good friends," the actress snapped, shaking her head with disgust. "I brought him the best news an actor could want. George Knowles is the biggest producer in New York, and he's offered the leading role in a new play to Dylan. He'll be starring with me. The fool is turning him down. Try to get him to be sensible, would you, Inspector?"

Grant suddenly smiled. "I haven't had much success in making Mr. Tremayne follow sensible ways. He had good quarters at my place, but instead he prefers to come to this rat hole, so you see how much influence I have."

Bess turned and put her hand on Dylan's chest. She said firmly, "I'll be expecting you. I'll tell Knowles you're thinking about it. It'll give you a little time, but you've got to do it, Dylan."

Without another word she turned and left the room. Grant watched her go, and then his eyes came back and fastened on Dylan. "Beautiful woman," he said. "What's this about a part in a play?"

"Oh, it's a play that I don't care to have anything to do with."

Grant stared at him. He was well aware that Dylan had little money, and he said now, "Come on. Let's go get something to eat."

Glad to get out of the confines of the

small, dingy room, Dylan grabbed his coat and pulled on his hat, and the two left. They went to a restaurant only two blocks away, ordered, and Grant said, "Now, tell me all about this play."

"Oh, it's a play about marital infidelity, but the problem is it glorifies that very thing. It makes a mockery of marriage, and I'm not going to have anything to do with it."

Grant was fascinated by Dylan. They had become close when they worked together to find a way out of the gallows for Serafina Trent's brother, Clive. Now as he ate, he tried to think of some way to help the man in front of him. He had a real affection for Dylan, and finally he said, "Well, it looks as though a Christian would have a hard time in the theatrical world. Many of the few plays I've seen have been pretty raw."

"You're right, Matthew. I just can't do it."

"Well, you'll have to find another profession. Maybe you can become a full-time detective with Lady Trent."

Dylan smiled, but he shook his head. "I'm afraid not. There's not enough crime going on that she's interested in."

"Well, in any case you're moving back in with me. You can't stay in that horror of a room."

"It's not so bad."

"It's terrible! Look, I never use that spare bedroom anyhow, and I'm gone most of the time. Don't be a fool, Dylan. Pride is the sin that got Lucifer thrown out of heaven, you know."

Dylan was forced to agree, and Grant added, "I have an invitation for you. Did you know Clive Newton has come home from Oxford?"

"No, I hadn't heard."

"Well, we're invited to dinner at Trentwood tomorrow to welcome him home."

"How did you know about that?"

"Oh, Lady Trent thought you were still living with me, and she sent word by one of her servants. And, of course, you are living with me from now on. Get your things together. We're moving you back in."

Dylan smiled. "You're a good fellow, Matthew."

"Somebody's got to keep an eye on you. Come along. Let's get you moved. We'll leave about three tomorrow. Lady Trent says David wants you there early."

At the mention of David, Dylan smiled. "He's a fine boy."

"You're getting pretty close to him, aren't you?"

"I think he's lonely."

"He has everything, but he's lonely."

"He misses having a father, I think."

The two returned to Dylan's room, gathered up his meager belongings, and moved them out. As they were carrying them out to the carriage, Grant turned and said, "That actress — Bess. You two were pretty close at one time?"

Once again colour rose in Dylan Tremayne's cheeks. He hated it when he blushed. "Well, no more."

They reached the carriage and loaded his effects in it, and when they got inside, Grant said, "You're a strange fellow, Dylan. Most men would find it hard to say no to that woman."

"She's in another world, Matthew. I was there once, but I'm glad to be out of it. Let's get me settled, and then you can tell me how you're going to get rid of all the crime in London."

Daisy White, Alberta's maid at Trentwood House, opened the door and found a gentleman standing there. "Yes, sir?" she said.

"My name is Alex Bolton." The man handed her a card. "Would you please let the family know that I am here."

"Oh, yes, sir. Come in out of the cold." She waited until Bolton was inside, then took his coat and hung it up with his hat. "If you'll wait right here, sir, I'll let the family know that you've come. Terrible weather, sir."

"Yes, it is." Bolton shivered slightly, for it was freezing cold outside. "I've come early, but I wasn't certain of getting here at all if this storm gets any worse."

"Yes, sir. It's a bad snowstorm all right. I'll be right back."

Daisy walked down the hall and turned into the larger parlour. She found Alberta, Clive, his sister Dora, and Lady Bertha Mulvane there. "Sir Alex Bolton is here." At once Lady Bertha exclaimed, "Good, he's here early! Show him in, Daisy."

"Yes, ma'am."

As soon as the maid left, Bertha gave a triumphant glance toward Lady Alberta. "You see, my dear, it's working out just as I said. He'll be quite a catch for Serafina. He has everything a gentleman should have."

"Is he rich?" Clive asked, grinning.

"Don't be foolish! It's Sir Alex Bolton. Of course he has money."

Clive wanted to remind Bertha that not all of the aristocracy had money. It was not uncommon for women who had inherited money from a tradesman husband to marry an impoverished nobleman simply for the sake of a title. On the other hand, men with titles but no money often found wealthy women to marry. "Have you informed Serafina how fortunate she is?"

Bertha gave Clive a disgusted look. "I wish you'd be quiet, Clive. They haven't taught you anything at Oxford."

The door opened then, and Daisy led Alex Bolton in. "Sir Alex Bolton," she announced and then left the room.

Clive went forward at once and said, "We haven't met, Sir Alex. I'm Clive Newton."

"I've heard so much about you," Sir Alex said with a smoothness that came from a lifetime of breeding. Part of his charm came from his flawless manners. He was in his mid-thirties but looked younger. His tapered face gave him the look, more or less, of a fox, but he had well-set, deep eyes that enhanced his handsome appearance. "I must apologize for coming early, but the storm is getting so bad that I was afraid I wouldn't get here at all."

"Oh, that's quite all right," Lady Bertha said. "Won't you sit down? Tell us what you've been doing, Sir Alex."

Alberta said, "Take a seat by the fire and thaw out."

"Thank you, Mrs. Newton. I think the snow is over a foot deep now and coming down worse than ever."

"Well," Dora said, "we might get snowed in. Wouldn't that be fun?"

Alex Bolton turned his charm on the young woman. "It would be, indeed, a pleasure."

Clive stood there listening as Bolton smoothly answered their questions. For some reason he was skeptical about Sir Alex Bolton. There was no reason he should be so — except he had heard from one of his friends that Bolton's financial problems had become rather critical. As always, when a man came courting his sister, Clive was very much aware that women were quite the prey for handsome, smooth noblemen such as Sir Alex Bolton. There was something too smooth, too polished about the man. There was no roughness in him at all, and Clive liked to see a little of that.

Sir Alex turned to Clive, and his eyes narrowed. "I read about your misfortune to be arrested recently, Mr. Newton. It must have been a trying thing."

"Oh, no, it was a piece of cake," Clive said breezily, determined to show Sir Alex that anyone could pretend to be smooth. But it had not been just a piece of cake. The threat of being hanged had frightened Clive, as it would any reasonable man. He still had nightmares at times, thinking of how closely he had come to paying the ultimate penalty. "I had good detectives, my sister and Mr. Dylan Tremayne. Also Inspector Grant of Scotland Yard. With a trio like that, there was really never any danger."

"Now, that's not so, Clive," Alberta said. She looked across the room at her son and shook her head. "We were all scared to death, and I'm thankful for Inspector Grant and for your sister and Mr. Tremayne."

"I'm not quite sure of Mr. Tremayne's identity. Is he a private detective?"

"No, he's an actor. You must have seen him. He was in *Hamlet* not long ago down at the Old Vic."

"I don't believe I saw it, but how can an actor be a detective?"

"He's a very witty fellow. Sharp as a razor," Clive said instantly. "But I don't want to talk about my troubles. I know you've come to see Lady Trent. So I will rescue you. If you will come with me, I will take you to her."

Bolton stood to his feet, his face alert. "Well, if you will excuse me, I believe I will go with Mr. Newton."

The two left the room, and Clive led Bolton down a hallway that took them to the front door. "We'll have to put on our coats."

"Are we going outside?" Bolton asked with surprise.

"Yes, my father and my sister often work in a small laboratory adjacent to the house. The way this snow is coming down, I think we'd better bundle up."

"Indeed, I think you're right. I've never seen snow come down so hard."

The two men put on coats and hats and left by the front door. The snow was coming down in flakes as big as shillings, and the sun was weak and dim in the storm. Clive, however, said, "I've always liked the snow."

"I don't. It's messy and inconvenient, but I'll give you this, it has a certain beauty."

As the two men walked along, Clive asked, "Do you live in London, Sir Alex?"

"Just outside. I like the country fairly well myself, although my family does have a town house in the city. I stay there quite often."

Clive listened as Sir Alex talked about his activities. The two men waded through the snow, which was indeed a foot deep now, until Clive gestured toward a rectangular building. "That's my father's laboratory. My sister often assists him."

"What do they do out here?"

"My father is a medical examiner for the police."

"I didn't know that."

"Oh, yes, they call on him to help with crimes from time to time."

"But does Lady Trent indulge in this kind of work?"

"She loves it. Come along. She'll be glad to show you and tell you about their activities."

Clive opened the door and stood back as Sir Alex went in. Sir Alex had taken only two steps inside when the door closed behind him, but he didn't hear it. There in the middle of the room, underneath bright gaslights, was a table. Dr. Septimus Newton was on one side and Viscountess Serafina Trent on the other. They both were wearing white jackets, and even as Alex Bolton stood there, Serafina's hand moved. She had a scalpel in it, and she was making a Y-shaped cut in the chest of a corpse, an elderly woman, who lay naked on the table.

"I brought Sir Alex to see you. He's interested in your work, Serafina. Father."

For a moment Serafina did not look up but finished the cut and then brought the scalpel down the middle of the body, stopping at the pubic area. She looked up then and said, "Well, Sir Alex, you're a little early for dinner."

Alex Bolton had a rather delicate stomach. He stared at the gaping cavity that had been exposed by Lady Trent's scalpel and tried to speak, but he found his throat was so full that it seemed to be closed.

Serafina was studying him with something like a slight smile. "My father and I have an interesting case, a murder victim, we think. We're checking the body for poison. You can watch if you'd like, and I'll explain what we're doing."

Sir Alex Bolton was at a loss for words, but now he was afraid he was going to lose more than his speech. He gurgled something that sounded quite unlike human speech, then turned and shoved past Clive, opening the door and plunging into the storm.

Clive moved and closed the door. He was laughing, and his eyes were sparkling with devilment. "I don't think Sir Alex is interested in dead ladies."

"Clive, you did that on purpose," Serafina reprimanded. She was not angry, however, and her own eyes were sparkling.

"Well, if he has matrimony with you on his mind, my dear sister, he'd better get accustomed to bodies being cut up."

Serafina laughed, saying, "You're a devil, Clive. Go find him and make sure he's all right. We'll be finished here shortly."

"Cut away, Sister. Father. Call on me if you need any help."

Septimus laughed. "A lot of help you would be. Go off with you now."

As Clive left, Septimus regarded his older daughter with interest. "I don't mess around with your life much, Serafina, but are you interested in that gentleman?"

"Oh, I don't know. Lady Bertha is."

"But it won't be Lady Bertha he wants to marry."

"He may not want to marry me either after what Clive has put him through." She laughed fully and freely. "It's awful of me to laugh, but did you see the look on his face when he saw what we were doing?"

"You may have frightened him off."

"Well, if a little thing like a corpse frightens him off, he's not for me anyhow." She turned to the body. "Let's hurry so we can be ready for dinner. Dylan's coming early to spend some time with David."

"I don't think we can make it through this storm, sir."

Matthew Grant stuck his head out the window of the carriage and was almost blinded by the snow that was coming down in myriads of flakes. The backs of the horses were covered with it, and as he glanced up, he saw the face of the driver was pale. "It's not far, Driver. The Trentwood House isn't more than a quarter of a mile. You can't turn back now."

Pulling back inside the carriage, Grant said, "I've never seen it snow this hard."

"It's cold too. It must be well below freezing."

"Somebody," Grant said moodily, "ought to invent some way to heat carriages."

"I don't see how that could ever be. You couldn't put a stove in one of these. You'd burn the whole thing up."

The two men had left Grant's room and hired the carriage, even though the snow had been falling intermittently all day. The countryside was rounded, and when the sun did shine, it glittered like hills covered with diamonds. But the falling flakes were so thick now that it was almost impossible to see more than a few feet ahead.

Finally the driver called out, " 'Ere we are, sir." The words sounded bitter, and the driver glared at Grant as he stepped out into the storm.

"Thanks for the ride," Grant said, handing the driver the fare with a generous tip. "Come along, Dylan."

The two men made their way to the front

door with some difficulty. The snow was at least a foot and a half deep now and unbroken. As soon as they knocked on the door, it opened, and they were met by Dora and David. David cried out, "Mr. Dylan, you're here!"

Dylan caught the boy, who had come hurdling at him, picked him up, and tossed him high in the air. "You can't come out in this snow."

Dora said, "Come in, David." She turned and said, "How are you, Inspector?"

"I'm fine, Miss Aldora."

Dylan saw something pass between the two, and not for the first time he wondered if they were in love. Grant would not be the pick of most aristocratic families to be the husband of a younger daughter. But Dylan saw that Dora was very glad to see him, and she said, "Come inside. I know you're freezing."

Once they were inside, the servants took their coats and hats, and David, who had been talking nonstop, said, "Come on. I want to show you my dormouse. He'll let you pet him."

"Oh, that's for me!"

Dora watched as David hauled Dylan off, tugging at him. "Dinner will be at six," she called after them and saw that David paid no attention. Turning to Matthew, she said, "They're great friends. Come along. We'll go to the small sitting room. There's a fire there. You can thaw out."

"I could use it. It's bitter outside. The driver nearly rebelled on us, it's so bad."

She led him to the sitting room, which was not large but elegant, with a Sheraton table and chairs in gleaming wood and a Bokhara rug, which Grant suspected would cost what he made in a year.

Dora said, "Here, pull your chair up in front of the fireplace. I love a fire in the winter, don't you?"

"Yes, I do."

Grant held his hands out to the fire, but his eyes were on Dora. He lost his heart to her almost the moment he first looked at her. Now as the fire crackled and snapped in the fireplace, he studied her as she spoke. The gold highlights in her auburn hair reflected the yellow flames of the fire. Her widow's peak added to the beauty of her face, but Grant especially adored her large brown eyes and the two dimples that appeared when she smiled or laughed.

But it was not just her physical beauty that attracted Grant. There was a spirit in the young woman that he found refreshing. In his work as a policeman he saw the worst of men and women, and there was a goodness and a purity and a sweetness in Aldora Newton that drew Inspector Matthew Grant like a magnet draws a steel filing.

"Tell me more about your cases," she said.

"Why would you be interested in police work?"

"I think it's fascinating."

He laughed and said, "It's pretty grim and often boring work." He hesitated and then said, "I know you're responsible for our invitation. Lady Bertha would never ask a mere inspector."

"Not at all," Dora said, and the two dimples appeared as she smiled. "David wanted Dylan, and I wanted you."

Her words warmed Matthew Grant. *"I wanted you."* How good that sounded to him! He didn't know the distance from earth to the nearest star, but he knew the distance from a police inspector to the daughter of the entitled was immense. "Who else will be here?" he asked.

"Just the family and Sir Alex Bolton."

"Who is he?"

Dora explained, "He's interested in Serafina."

"Is she interested in him?"

"Who can tell about her? My sister never seems interested in anyone."

"What about Dylan? She's interested in him."

"Oh, he fascinates her. They're so different. He's all romance, and she's all facts and scientific things. But she sees David loves him."

They were suddenly interrupted when the door opened, and Lady Bertha came charging in, her face flush with anger. "In my day we didn't do things like this, Aldora!"

"Things like what, Aunt?"

"A gentleman and a young woman did not hide themselves in a room, sitting in the dark."

Clive had come in behind his aunt and walked around her into the room.

Grant said, "Lady Mulvane, it's good to see you again."

Bertha was not through, however. She glared at Grant and said, "I should think you would be aware that your behaviour is not at all appropriate."

"I'm truly sorry, Lady Bertha. I intended no harm."

"I was the one that brought the inspector in here. He was freezing, and I wanted to thaw him out."

Clive interrupted and addressed Grant, "Come along. I want you to meet Alex Bolton. He had the shock of his life a little while ago."

Dora giggled. "I think you're absolutely frightful, Clive. You shouldn't have done such a thing."

"What you did was not illegal, I trust, Clive?" Grant joked. He liked the young man very much and had been inordinately pleased when Clive had been freed from the terrible predicament he was in.

"Well, all I did was take him to see my sister and my father. He walked in on them while they were cutting up a corpse. I think that discouraged him a little bit." Clive's eyes were dancing, and he could not contain the laughter. "It was quite a surprise. I doubt if our guest will be able to eat much dinner."

"I'm ashamed of you, Clive. Now, it's time to go in to dinner," Lady Bertha announced. She put herself between Aldora and Grant, and Grant knew it was more than a symbolic action. She was absolutely determined that no member of the Newton family would have anything to do with a mere inspector of Scotland Yard.

Louisa Toft, Serafina's maid, was a talkative young woman with an insatiable curiosity. She was a beauty with red hair and green eyes, and she had been trying for some time to get Serafina to tell her about her sister and the policeman. Serafina understood that the household servants were all fascinated by the lives of the family, but she had refused adamantly to say anything about the relationship of her sister and Inspector Grant.

"And that Sir Alex Bolton, my, he ain't half a treat, is he?"

Serafina smiled, for she knew this was her invitation to tell Louisa her feelings about the man. "I'm not going to give you any details on my love life or my sister's love life, but as soon as something changes, you'll be the first."

"Oh, ma'am, I didn't mean —"

Serafina looked up and saw fear in the maid's eyes. "Oh, come, Louisa, I am only teasing. There's nothing between me and Sir Alex. I can't speak for my sister; there may be something there."

Rising from her chair, she checked her dress and her hair then left the room. She went up to David's schoolroom and found Dylan and her son on the floor playing with David's toy soldiers, of which he had a multitude. "Mum, I'm the Duke of Wellington, and Dylan's Napoleon, and I'm winning."

Serafina was pleased, as she always was

when David had a good time. "Well, all right, but the battle is over, young man. Go on and let Louisa get you cleaned up for dinner."

"Yes, Mum."

Dylan got up from the floor where he had been sitting, dusted himself off, and grinned. "Do you suppose Louisa would clean me up too?"

"No, that would be unseemly." She smiled. "Come along. We'll be late for dinner." She turned to go and then changed her mind. Turning to him, she said, "Thank you so much, Dylan, for showing such an interest in David. He talks about you all the time."

"Well, I talk about him a great deal too. Maybe you could hire me to be his butler or his man, just as Louisa is your maid."

Serafina laughed. "Oh, he'd love that. A full-time playmate." She hesitated then said, "You're not living with Inspector Grant."

"Well, I am now. I had a room, but it was pretty bad. So he came and forced me to go back. He's a good fellow to look out for me."

Serafina wanted to say something about his finances. She knew that he was not a rich man, actually was rather poor, but she couldn't think of a way to do it. "Come along," she said. "You'll have to meet our guest, Sir Alex Bolton."

The two left the room, and when they went into the smaller of the two dining rooms, Dylan was introduced. "Sir Alex Bolton, may I present Dylan Tremayne. Mr. Tremayne, Sir Alex Bolton. I don't believe you've met."

"No, we haven't met, but I've heard a great deal about you, sir," Sir Alex said. His smile came easily, and he added, "I don't go to the theatre all that much, but I would like to see you perform. Are you in something now?"

"No, I'm an unemployed actor."

"Oh," Alex said, and with that he expressed his entire attitude toward unemployed actors.

"Come along. I'm starved," Septimus said.

Lady Bertha took it on herself to seat people. Septimus was at one end of the table, and Alberta was at the other. On one side of the table, to Septimus's left, were David, Serafina, Grant, and Dora. Across the table Sir Alex Bolton sat at Septimus's right, beside him Clive, then Dylan and Lady Bertha. Behind Dylan and Clive a fireplace heated the room, and one of the maids fitted a fire screen behind the two men to keep the sparks from setting them on fire.

The meal started off with a thin soup followed by fish, a veal cutlet, a roast fowl, and some game. There was also a turbot of lobster in Dutch sauces and a portion of red mullet with cardinal sauce. The frying dishes, as they were called, followed — lamb cutlets, peas, then a roast saddle of mutton flavored with French and English mustard. As the meal went on, the talk went along with it. Serafina, sitting next to Grant, said quietly so the others could not hear, "I understand Dylan's moved back in with you."

"Yes." He hesitated then said, "He's a poor man like me, even worse. I do have my salary. When he's not acting, he's not making any money."

"I wish I could do something to help him."

Grant suddenly smiled and said, "You're the second lady who's wanted to help him."

"Oh, how is that?"

"There was an actress there, a very attractive woman. She brought Dylan word that some producer wants him to star in a new play, but he turned it down."

"Why did he do that?"

"Oh, it's a rather immoral play."

"Well, I honour him for it."

Grant shook his head. "I wish he had another profession."

Sir Alex Bolton, sitting across from her,

did not catch these words. He suddenly spoke up loudly enough to catch her attention. "I'm interested in your detective career, Lady Trent."

"Oh, there's nothing to that."

"Oh, yes there is," Septimus said. "Sir Alex, you wouldn't believe how Mr. Dylan and Serafina worked together on Clive's case, along with Inspector Grant, of course."

"And you haven't heard about their newest bit of detective work."

"What is that?" Sir Alex asked.

"They found the lost son of Lord Darby. Tell him about it, Serafina."

Serafina did not want to talk. "It wasn't much, really. You tell them, Dylan."

Dylan shrugged and told the story, and when he was finished, Sir Alex said, "I was under the impression that you were an actor. It seems you're a detective as well."

"Well, that's not going too well." Suddenly he grinned at David. "David's going to hire me as a full-time playmate, aren't you, David?"

"Yes!"

The meal ended with two ices, cherry water and pineapple cream, and there was wine, sherry, and Madeira. Finally Sir Alex asked Dylan about his experience in the rougher side of London. "I understand you came up the hard way."

"Indeed I did, but it's not a pleasant subject."

"Indeed not," Bertha said. "We can find better things to talk about."

When the dinner was finally over, the party was dismissed to the parlour, where Dora played the harpsichord and sang beautifully. She said, "Clive, come and join me."

"No, Dylan's the best singer."

Serafina said, "Honour us with a song, Dylan."

Dylan walked over to stand beside Dora, and the two sang a beautiful duet.

"He has a beautiful voice, doesn't he, Sir Alex?" Serafina asked.

"Well, he's an actor. I suppose that's required."

Shortly after the song ended, Serafina told David it was time to go to bed.

"Come with me, Dylan. Tell me a story."

"That I will."

They left, and Serafina said, "I'll go along and be sure that they don't stay up until midnight. He loves Dylan's stories."

As they went up the stairs, she said, "Dylan, I want to help you."

"Help me?"

"Yes, I know you're short of funds. I have

plenty of money, and you've been so kind to David."

"We're friends, Serafina. I couldn't take money for that. There's no such thing as a hired friend, is there? But I thank you."

"Grant told me about the offer you refused."

"It's not for me."

"What are you going to do? Most plays aren't for you."

"Serve God."

Serafina gave him an odd look. "I wish my life were that simple."

"I think it is." He asked suddenly, "Have you heard from Lord Darby?"

"Yes. I got a letter today."

"How is Trevor doing?"

"Edward's worried about him."

"No wonder. He has a hard task."

They went to the business of getting David in bed, and as Dylan started some fanciful story, Serafina went downstairs. She was greeted at the foot of the stairs by Clive. "I'm arranging bedrooms. We'll put Matthew and Dylan next to each other. Come along, Matthew. I'll show you your room."

"Good night, my lady."

"Good night, Inspector."

Serafina turned to Bolton, and to her surprise he came and took her hand, saying, "I suppose you know that I've fallen in love with you."

Serafina stared at him, shocked at his abrupt statement. He put his arms around her and would have kissed her, but she said, "Please don't, Sir Alex."

"Don't you care for me at all?"

"I'm not sure about remarriage. I'm not sure I will ever remarry."

"I think you will. I'm a stubborn fellow."

"Well, I'm a stubborn woman."

Sir Alex Bolton kissed her hand. "We'll see then," he said, smiling, "which of us is the most stubborn."

Seventeen

Trevor studied himself in the mirror mounted on the wall and reflected, "Well, if I ain't become a toff now." He turned around and tried to get a glimpse of what he looked like from the back and then walked over to the fire. He was wearing one of the outfits his father had bought him on their trip to the city. It consisted of black britches pressed with a knife crease, a white linen shirt, a complicated black cravat with a small diamond stud, a velvet frock coat, and gleaming black boots that came up well over his calf. For some reason the trip to the city had not been what he had expected.

He moved to the window, watching the snow fall lightly now, and saw that the hills were blanketed and the trees had lost their sharp outlines of winter. Each branch now was topped with glistening white snow. He touched the texture of the velvet coat and thought about the trip. It had been strange at first, and he had been ill at ease, but on the way to town his father had told him stories of the Hayden family and some of the details of his own life. To Trevor's relief he had not inquired into what sort of life Trevor had known. It was, Trevor knew, obvious that his father wanted his past erased as quickly as possible, and, as always, when he thought on these things, it seemed impossible for him to ever become the kind of man that his parents expected him to be.

Sitting down in a chair, he went over the trip, thinking how well the two of them had gotten along. They had gone to his father's club, where Trevor was welcomed as a member. They had eaten a fine meal and then had gone shopping. It had taken all day, so they had stayed the night. They had come home in snow so deep the horses had difficulty making their way.

A sudden thought occurred to him, and he stood up, reached deep into his inner pocket, and pulled out a leather wallet, also a gift. His father had handed him the wallet and said with some embarrassment, "You'll be needing some cash from time to time, Trevor. I don't want you to have to come to me every time you need a shilling." He took the money out now and counted it again. Four tenners, four fivers, and twenty quid in one-pound notes. It was more money than he'd ever had, and he thought of how his father's glance had grown warm as he had made the gift. He recalled also his rather awkward thanks, but his father had simply patted him on the shoulder and said, "You're a Hayden now. You'll be needing money from time to time. Always feel free to come to me, Son."

At that moment Trevor remembered he had promised his father that he would show his mother his new suit. He left the room at once and asked the maid about Lady Darby's whereabouts.

"She's in the small parlour with Lady Leona, sir."

He made his way to the parlour, and when he entered he found his mother and Lady Leona sewing beside the fire. His mother looked up and smiled. "Well, aren't you the handsome thing!"

Leona was evidently having one of her better days. Her eyes were bright, and she smiled at Trevor. "Yes, he is. He reminds me so much of the first time you brought Edward to see me."

"I remember that. It was after the ball at the Hopes'."

"Yes."

"He brought me home; the rain was so bad."

"I never thought you'd get him, Heather." Leona laughed, and her eyes sparkled. "There were so many young ladies out to catch Edward, and, of course, the mamas would have given their right arms to have their daughters marry Lord Darby, but somehow you managed to capture his heart. I never thought you'd be able to get him for a husband."

"I didn't think so either." Heather smiled. She stood up and came over to stand beside Trevor. She touched his arm almost hesitantly. "And there'll be many young ladies and their mamas after this one, too, Leona."

Trevor had no idea about how to carry on a conversation with two titled ladies, but he sat down in front of the fire on a chair and told them about his trip to London with his father. He made it as splendid a story as he could, for he saw his mother was glowing as he spoke of how he and his father had gotten along.

Trevor had almost forgotten the older woman when suddenly he heard her say, "I must go. Leslie will be home soon."

Trevor got to his feet as the old woman rose and left the room. He noticed her eyes were dull, and as soon as she left, he asked,

"Who is Leslie?"

"He was your grandfather. He married twice. You can see the genealogy. I'll show it to you later. Leslie married Edith Carrington in 1800. They had three children — Edward, Rupert, and Leah — but Edith died, and a few years later Leslie married Leona. Her name was Leona Moore. She was Edith's cousin. He had known her for a long time, and, of course, their only child was Arthur."

"But why does she say she's going to see Leslie?"

The question seemed to disturb his mother, he saw. "Well, her mind is not really clear. You'll have to be very patient with her. Sometimes her mind is sharp, but other times it's not. She may call you Leslie or even Edward. When she's in these spells, she gets confused."

"That's so sad, Mother."

Heather was touched. This was the first time he had called her Mother, and she felt a warm glow as she looked at the young man. "Well, you must pay some attention to her, smile at her, and talk to her. She lives in the past most of the time." Then, as if anxious to get away from that subject, she said, "Now, sit down and tell me more about your trip to London."

He had already told her almost everything, but he managed to find a few more tidbits. Finally, he pulled the billfold out and said, "Look, Father gave me this wallet and all this money. I 'ated to take it."

Her eyes went moist for a moment. "He's such a generous man. I know it's embarrassing to take things, but sometimes it's more blessed to receive than it is to give."

Trevor suddenly laughed. "That's sort of backward from what I've heard."

"I know, but there's an art in receiving things gracefully, and I hope you'll let us spoil you a little bit, Son. We have lots of time to make up for."

In that instant Trevor felt a warm affection for this woman. He had known no mother except Meg, who had been no mother at all. And the women he had met had been crude, for the most part, and greedy. There was a gentleness and a goodness in this woman that his quick mind seized upon, and because he knew it pleased her, he said, "I'll do my best to be a good son to you, Mother."

While Heather and Trevor were having a pleasant meeting, Edward was having a very difficult one in his study. He had been reading when Rupert had come in with Leah.

At once he saw that he was in for an unpleasant time, for both of them had dissatisfaction and even anger written on their features.

"We've got to talk to you," Rupert said abruptly. His face was red, and his lips were drawn together in a tight line. "This nonsense with the boy has got to stop."

Leah spoke at once, not so harshly as Rupert, but forcefully. "I think Rupert is right, Edward. You're making a terrible mistake by accepting this boy and giving him everything."

Edward put the book down and for a moment searched his mind, trying to find a way to make peace. Even as he struggled for such an answer, he knew there was none. He had never deceived himself about Rupert. The man was hungry for power, and it saddened Edward to realize that his death was the thing Rupert had been waiting for all these years. That would signal that Rupert would become the Earl of Darby and would rule Silverthorn. He glanced at Leah, and if he hoped to see more gentleness in her, he was disappointed. He knew she was a strong-willed woman also, and that she lived for her son, Bramwell. Edward had already done much for Bramwell, indeed had spoiled him, but Leah had high ambitions for her son. He could not blame her for this, but yet still he knew they would never be pacified with a choice that, in any way, cut them out of the estate and the title.

"I promise you," he said carefully, "that you will be well taken care of. We have time to mold Trevor to make a good, honest man out of him, and I have it written in my will that you two, and Arthur, of course, will be provided for. When I die, you will continue, Rupert, in your same way. You will be the manager of Silverthorn just as you are now, and I've expressed my gratitude at how well you have run the place."

"That's not enough, Edward. It's not fair. It's not just! I've worked all my life, and now this boy wanders in and reaps the harvest."

Edward said carefully, "We must work together on this, Rupert and Leah. The boy's had a terrible life. He needs you both, and I'm asking both of you to support him."

He had little hope that his words would find lodging and good ground, and for the next twenty minutes, he listened, never losing his temper. But at the same time he was grieved and saddened by their demands for more. When they finally left, he knew that there would be no easy way to settle this problem. In spite of all the joy he had known in finding Trevor, he knew the young man was driving a wedge between him and his brother and sister, but there was no other way.

St. John had stepped into the small dining room and was headed for the adjoining kitchen when he bumped into his mother and Rupert. He took one look at their faces and demanded, "What's the matter?"

"It's Edward. We've been talking to him about Trevor."

"I could have told you you'd be wasting your breath." St. John shrugged. He looked at them and then shook his head firmly. "You won't change his mind. He and Aunt Heather are besotted with the creature. We may as well make the best of it."

Rupert was furious. His voice lifted in anger. "It would be better if Edward died," he spat out and then walked away, shoving the door open.

"He shouldn't say things like that," Leah said.

"No, he shouldn't. He's wrong about Uncle Edward dying. Things would be worse, not better."

"What do you mean, Son?"

"Well, don't forget. If my uncle died, that guttersnipe would be our lord and master."

His lip curled, and bitterness touched his eyes and turned the corners of his mouth down. "How much consideration, Mother, do you think we'd get from Trevor?"

Leah stared at him, and he saw that the thought had occurred to her. "We've got to do something, St. John."

"Do what? The only thing that would help us is if Edward, Rupert, and that upstart all died, which isn't likely. Even if he did, Arthur would take the title."

Silence fell between the two, and then St. John laughed. "We can always handle Arthur. He's a fool, and he would drink himself to death. All I'd have to do is marry Gervase."

"Would you do that?"

"I'd do anything to keep our place here, and so would you, wouldn't you, Mother?"

Leah stared at her son and saw written the impulses that were in her own heart on his face. "Yes, I would," she said. "We'll not speak of this now."

The two left the small dining room, and in a few moments a small girl of fifteen, the new tweeny, the youngest of the servants, peeked out from behind the kitchen door. Her name was Mary, and her eyes were wide. She was a quiet little thing, having only served for two weeks on the staff. Now there was fear in her eyes, and her lips trembled as she thought of what terrible things she had heard. Quickly she moved through the room and tried to block the scene out of her mind.

As Trevor came down the stairs, he was greeted by Gervase.

"Well, hello, Cousin."

" 'Ello, Cousin Gervase. Where are you going?"

Her eyes smiled at him. "I'm going to make snow cream. Dylan showed me how to do it."

"Wot in the world is that?"

"Come along and I'll show you."

Trevor accompanied the girl to the kitchen where she commandeered a large bowl from the cook along with sugar, cream, vanilla, and two large spoons.

He followed her out the back door, and she said, "Over there. The snow's untouched. Isn't it beautiful?"

"I never liked snow much. I nearly froze to death once."

"Oh, it can be uncomfortable, but just look how pretty it is."

He did not answer, and finally she stopped, saying, "Here, take this spoon and fill the bowl up." He obeyed with a smile, and when it was filled, she began to add the cream and the sugar and the vanilla. From time to time she would add a little bit more snow, and finally she looked at him and said, "There. Snow cream. Taste some."

Trevor got a heaping spoonful and tasted it, and his eyes opened wide. "Why, that 'as to be the best snow cream ever!"

"It is good, isn't it? Probably makes us fat as pigs."

"No, we'll both be slender, good-looking people, Gervase."

"You're not very modest." She laughed at him, and then the two ate. When they had eaten all they could hold, she said, "Now we'll fill the bowl up and make another batch, then we'll leave it out here in the snow. That'll keep it cold. When we come back we'll have some more."

He watched as she placed the bowl into the drift and said, "Wot's to stop a dog or a cat from coming along and eating it?"

"Nothing, but then we'll just make some more. Where are you going?"

"Nowheres. I just got back from London."

"I noticed your new clothes. You look nice."

"Well, I thank you. I don't know wot to do with myself though. I feel useless."

"What would you be doing if you were

back where you came from?"

Trevor's lips twisted, and he shook his head abruptly. "Nothin' you'd want to 'ear about."

"Yes, I would."

"No, you wouldn't."

"All right. Have you ever gone for a sleigh ride?"

"A sleigh ride? No, never."

"Well, it's one of my favourite things. Come along."

"Here, you take the lines."

"I don't know 'ow to drive a sleigh."

Tim had hitched a powerful horse to a sleigh, and Gervase had driven out of the yard. Trevor had held on, for she drove the horses at a fast pace. Finally she had slowed down and offered him the lines. "There's nothing to it. Dolly there knows all about it."

He smiled and took the lines from her, and indeed there was little to do. He said, "Get up, Dolly," and slapped the lines on the horse's back. She at once broke into a run, and Trevor guided her with what little skill he had around the natural obstacles in the field. From time to time there would be a jolt, and Gervase would slide up against him.

Finally he slowed the horse down to a walk and said, "Why, that was fun."

"It doesn't take much to please you, Trevor."

He turned then to examine her more closely. She had the clearest and most beautiful complexion he'd ever seen. He wanted to put his arms around her but remembered that she was not receptive to things like that.

"Why do you think I'll make a go of it as something I'm not?"

"Because you're strong, Trevor."

"You don't know that."

"I can tell. And you're going to make Uncle Edward and Aunt Heather the happiest couple in the world. For years they had no children, and now they have a son. You have it in your power to make their lives happy. And it's the best thing for you too. Don't waste it."

He suddenly pulled the horse to a halt and turned to face her. He saw her watching him and could not understand what was behind her gaze. He fully expected her to shove him away, but when he put his arm around her, she leaned against him. When he kissed her, he felt her respond. He had known women before, but this was different. There was a wild sweetness in the softness of her lips, and he knew that this woman was unlike any he had ever known.

She drew away gently, putting her hand on his chest. "That's enough. I can see you don't need any lessons in kissing. Now, take me home, Sir Trevor of Silverthorn!"

Charles Crinshaw sat talking with Mrs. Swifton, the housekeeper. The two of them had been at Silverthorn for many years and were fast friends. Actually together they served as co-captains of the house. It was unlikely that a ship would ever have two captains, but with a house and staff the size of Silverthorn's, there was too much work for one. They sat there drinking tea, and Mrs. Swifton, from time to time, jotted down thoughts for the work to be done tomorrow.

"A lot of work to be done around here. Christmas is always hard," Crinshaw said. He leaned back slightly in his chair. The day had been long. His duties had been many, as always, and he was feeling his age. "I'm tired," he confessed.

"You work too hard, Charles."

"It has to be done."

"I know," she said, "but both of us are getting older. We need to learn how to slow down."

"Well, it won't be during this Christmas season. Lord and Lady Darby want to make this a Christmas to be remembered for the young master."

"I know. They have all kinds of plans." She laughed shortly and sipped her tea. "They make decisions, and it never occurs to them that someone has to make all those things happen. But I'm not complaining. This is a good place. What do you think of the young man?"

"Well, like a fairy tale, isn't it now?" He smiled at her, and the two, for a while, discussed the phenomena that all the staff had been gossiping about.

"He seems to be a good enough young man, considering his background. But I don't know if he'll ever be able to fit himself in here," Mrs. Swifton said.

"He's got a sharp mind. I think he might." He straightened up, stretched, and said, "Well, it's time to mix Lord Darby's sleeping draught."

It was an old joke between them. "Why don't you tell me what's in it?" she begged.

"No, it's my secret. One of these days I'm going to market it and become a rich man." He winked at her and said, "I'll buy a mansion, and you can be my housekeeper."

"Get along with you now!"

He disappeared into the butler's pantry, and Mrs. Swifton closed her notebook, got up, and with a sigh, left the kitchen. Christmas was indeed little pleasure for her, for it was mostly work, work, work.

"I'm very happy about the way Gervase is paying attention to Trevor."

Heather had already gone to bed and was lying there watching Edward as he moved about the room. He had always had great trouble sleeping and usually drank the sleeping draught that Crinshaw prepared. "I think they get along very well. I'm glad too."

"She took him for a sleigh ride. Did he tell you?"

"No."

"Well, she did. Just the sort of thing she does best."

"She's a sweet girl. Some lucky man will get a prize in her."

Edward turned, and a thought crossed his mind. "What about young Worthington? He used to call quite often."

"She wasn't interested in him."

"Well, who is she interested in?"

"Oh, some young man will come along." The two talked for some time, and finally Edward glanced up at the clock. "It's ten fifteen. Crinshaw must have forgotten."

"Well, that isn't likely. He's so conscious of his duties."

"Well, he's had a lot to do. I'll go down and get the drink. I'll be right back."

"Hurry. It's very cold."

Edward left the room and went downstairs into the kitchen, which was empty. "Crinshaw?" he called. When there was no answer, he walked over to the door that led to the butler's pantry where all the special supplies were. "Crin— ," he started to call again, and then his throat seemed to close.

There on the floor was the body of Crinshaw, his face twisted in agony. At once Edward kneeled over and asked, "Crinshaw, are you all right?"

But he saw at once that the man was not all right. Edward felt a chill when he realized that the man was probably dead. The body had the awful stillness of death. Quickly Edward started calling, "Mrs. Swifton — Mrs. Swifton!" She had not gone to bed yet, and she came at once.

"What is it, sir?"

"It's — it's Crinshaw. I'm afraid he's dead."

"Impossible! We were talking just a few minutes ago."

"He's in the pantry," Edward said. "Don't go look. We'll have to have a doctor . . . and the police, I suppose."

"Don't go yourself. Send Tim and Samuel."

"Yes, I'll do that."

The two stood staring at each other, and she said, "It must have been a stroke or a bad heart."

"There was nothing wrong with his heart. He had a strong constitution. I'll go tell Tim to fetch Dr. Newton and Samuel to notify the police. Don't let anyone go into the pantry."

"Of course not." She shook her head. "I can't believe he's gone. Just a few minutes ago we were talking about Christmas, and now he's dead?"

Edward could not think of a reply and left the room without a word. He found the coachman and after breaking the news said, "Go by Dr. Newton's first. Ask him to come at once."

"Yes, sir, right away."

He watched the coachman hurry away. "Dead. Almost on Christmas. I'll miss the fellow. I truly will." He thought about how long Crinshaw had worked for him and then sadly he realized, *I hardly knew him. How sad that is!*

EIGHTEEN

Serafina had gone to bed rather early, but sleep evaded her. After tossing and turning and trying every way she knew to fall asleep, finally with a sigh of resignation, she threw the covers back and got out of bed. The room was cold, for the fire had gone down, and she shivered as she slipped into her heavy wool robe and donned socks and slippers. Going over to the fire, she added several of the rich pine knots that the servants provided. Putting them on the coals, she blew, and soon they burst into flames as the rich sap ignited. For a while she stood there feeding the fire with small lengths of wood until it made a pleasant roaring sound and sent sparks flying up the chimney.

Finally she turned and walked to her desk. Sitting down, she pulled a book forward and opened it to the part she had been reading. It was an old discourse by the Frenchman

Pascal concerning a series of experiments he had made on the equilibrium of fluids. She knew that Pascal had also been a Christian of some note, but her interest was in the man's scientific discoveries.

Outside the wind keened like an animal as it whipped around the windows, and she found herself unable to continue her study. With a sigh of disgust she closed the book, shoved it away, then for a moment just sat there. Finally she moved over to a chest against the wall, opened the bottom drawer, pulled out a book, and walked back to her desk with it. The gaslight cast its glow over the book, which was bound in red leather, and for a moment she hesitated before opening it. The book was one of a series of journals she had been keeping for years, ever since she was thirteen years old. It amused her sometimes to go back and read what her thoughts had been at a time that seemed so long ago. She was amazed at how fanciful she had been as a young girl, but her father had eliminated most of that side of her character with his insistence that she rely solely on pure science.

This journal was the latest one, and as she opened it, memories arose of Clive's murder charge and how he'd almost gone to the gallows. It had only been a few months ago, but still she had troublesome thoughts about how close her brother had come to death.

She paused suddenly, for her eyes fell on a passage that she had not read since she had written it. Leaning forward she read silently the words that she had penned:

An insufferable man named Dylan Tremayne came to the house today. He's an actor, and he had come to tell our family how to take care of Clive. He first told me that Clive needed to be put in better quarters, and that he thought the family should use its influence to do so. That was very well, but then Tremayne told me that God had told him to help my brother. How pious he is! A ranting Methodist, I suppose, or something of that sort. I never could bear religious fanatics, and apparently he is one. I will admit that he is probably the best-looking man that I've ever seen — as if that amounts to anything.

The entry broke off there, and Serafina stared at the next few lines, which brought back a memory that had not faded from her mind:

I determined to find the woman whom

Clive had spent the evening with on the night the murder was committed. It made me angry that Tremayne had told me that this was no job for a woman, and I determined to prove him wrong. I went to the Seven Dials district, got out of the carriage, and told Givins to wait. I began to ask people I met on the street but with no success whatsoever. The area was terrible, worse than anything I had ever seen. Filth was everywhere, and the odor of rotting garbage was almost more than I could bear.

I asked a big man about the woman, and he suddenly grabbed me and was pulling me away. I began to try to scream and to fight him, but he was a strong brute, and I had no success. Then suddenly Dylan Tremayne appeared. He called the man by name, told him to let go of me, and when he didn't, Tremayne struck him a tremendous blow. There was a fight, and the man drew a knife, but Tremayne drove him off. I don't think I was ever so relieved in my life. Tremayne was, I must admit, a gentleman despite his profession. He made no reference to the fact that he had warned me against this but saw me back to my carriage. I tried to thank him, but the words would not seem to come.

Serafina put her hand on the book, and the scene came swarming back in her mind. She continued to read about how Tremayne had become her mentor in one respect. He knew the underworld well, and it was he who conducted the search to find the prostitute Clive had gone to the night of the murder. She realized, *I don't know what I would have done without him.*

Somehow the journal made Serafina uncomfortable. She got up, walked over to the fire, and warmed her hands, thinking of that time. She did not want to read more, but somehow she was compelled. Going back, she sat down and read through the entries, all of them, and the story of Clive's troubles came before her. She came to one passage that caused her cheeks to flame:

I had a weak moment tonight, and I suppose Dylan saw it. He kissed me, and I didn't resist him. I must be honest. It would be the only logical thing to do. I never wanted any man to touch me again, not after the travesty that Charles had made of our marriage, but when Dylan put his arms around me and kissed me, I must confess that it made me feel — well, like a woman for the first time in many years. I did not surrender, of course, to that feeling, for it went against everything that's in my heart. Dylan apologized, and I told him that it made no difference, but it shocked me down to the bone, the feelings that I had for that man.

With a quick motion Serafina closed the journal, got up quickly, and with a guilty air about her, replaced it in the chest and shut the drawer with unnecessary force. She went back to the desk, putting all thoughts of what she had read out of her mind and began to read the work of Pascal again.

She read doggedly for fifteen minutes, then suddenly the sound of feet coming up the stairs at a rapid rate caught her attention. She turned her head to listen, then rose and moved over to the door. It was close to midnight, and everyone in the house had gone to sleep, or so she supposed. She opened the door a crack and saw that James Barden, the butler, was tapping on her parents' door with some urgency. He was dressed in a robe and wore slippers, the first time Serafina had ever seen him in anything but impeccable dress. Her parents' room was down the hall, separated by several rooms from Serafina's own, so when the door opened, she heard Barden speaking rapidly but could not make out the words. When he hurried down the stairs, she closed the door and began to throw on her clothes. *Something is wrong,* she thought and dressed hurriedly.

When she was fully dressed, she went down the hall and found her father just coming out of the door wearing a robe too large for him. His hair stood in wild array, and his eyes were wide open.

"What is it, Father?"

"It's a messenger from Silverthorn. Barden tells me the man insists on being heard. He says it's urgent. What are you doing out of bed?"

"I heard Barden coming up, and I thought something might be wrong."

"Come along. We'll go find out. It must be serious."

The two went quickly down the stairs to the foyer where they found Tim Moorhaven, the coachman for Lord Darby. He was bundled up to his eyes in heavy clothes and pulled off his hat. He was a large man with red features and always spoke in a high tenor voice, almost like a woman's, that belied his huge stature.

"What is it?" Septimus asked at once. "Is someone ill?"

"Not exactly, sir," Moorhaven mumbled. His lips were numb with the cold, and he rubbed his nose with his mittened hand. "But there's been some trouble at Silverthorn. Lord Darby sent me to fetch you and Lady Trent."

"What kind of trouble?" Serafina asked quickly.

"It's Crinshaw — Charles Crinshaw, the butler, sir. Well, he's dead."

"Dead? What happened to him?"

"I don't know, sir, but Lord Darby told me to get you to come if you could, sir. He wants you to look at the body."

"Well, of course we'll come," Septimus said.

"You can ride back with me, sir. We'll see you get back right enough."

"Very good. Serafina, would you tell Barden that I'll be leaving?"

"Yes, but I'm going with you. I'll make some arrangements with Rachel to take care of David."

"Are you sure you want to go out in this weather?"

"Yes, I'm certain. We must go — it sounds serious."

"Very well. Moorhaven, we'll be ready very quickly."

"Yes, sir."

"I can't understand it. It must have been an accident," Septimus said.

■ ■ ■ ■

As usual, Trevor remained awake later than most in the house. He was used to late hours and had tried to read a book Gervase had given him. It was a novel, and he had never read a novel before. The name of it was *Oliver Twist,* and he found himself interested in spite of his usual distrust of books. He was reading in front of the fire in his room when suddenly he realized that he was hungry. He had not eaten much supper and now he found himself ravenous. He decided to go to the kitchen and find something to munch on.

Marking his place carefully in the book with a slip of paper, he walked out the door and was surprised to see Arthur and Gervase coming toward him. He was confused for a moment and said, "Well, I didn't expect to find anyone else up."

Gervase said at once, "There's something wrong. We don't know what exactly."

"Something wrong? There ain't a fire, is there?" Trevor asked.

"No, it's not that."

"Well, I was just going down to get something to eat. Maybe I could go with you."

"Yes, come along," Arthur said. "We heard

Moorhaven driving the carriage away, and then one of the maids came and told us that there was some kind of problem. Let's see what it is."

The three were descending the stairs when they were met by Emily Swifton, the head housekeeper. "Lord Edward's in the parlour, Mr. Arthur, if that's who you are looking for."

"What's happened, Mrs. Swifton?"

"I don't rightly know, sir, but it's trouble."

Arthur moved quickly down the hall accompanied by Gervase, and Trevor tagged along behind. They went into the smaller of the two parlours where, as soon as he was inside, Trevor saw his father and Rupert, both of them looking troubled, especially the earl.

"What are you doing up?" Edward asked with surprise, looking at the three.

"We heard there was some sort of trouble, and we were worried," Arthur said. "What is it, Edward?"

"It's Crinshaw. I'm afraid he's dead."

Arthur's eyes opened wide. "Crinshaw? Whatever happened? Was there some sort of accident?"

"We don't know yet," Rupert broke in. "He's dead in the butler's pantry."

"Are you certain — well, of course you

are," Arthur caught himself. "Did it seem to be his heart?"

"How can I know? I'm no doctor," Rupert snapped. "All I know is that he's dead."

Edward said, "I sent for Dr. Newton. We need a physician to make the report. I sent for the police also."

"The police!" Gervase said with surprise. "Why would you need the police?"

"I think in the case of sudden death, it's always necessary to notify the police."

They were interrupted suddenly when Lady Leona Moore came in. Her lavender robe covered her down to her toes, and a pair of heavy black shoes peeped out from underneath the hem. "What is it?" she asked. "Is somebody ill?"

"What are you doing up, Leona?" Edward asked.

Lady Leona looked like a small bird. She bobbed her head about and moved her eyes around the room and said in a clear, distinct voice, "He's dead, isn't he? Leslie is dead."

"Now, Mother, come along. You shouldn't be up like this," Arthur said. He went over and took her, but she reached up and touched his face. "I knew it was death. A bird got into my room last week. Everyone knows that means death."

"Now, Mother, that's just superstition.

Come along." Arthur led his mother out of the room, and they could hear her protesting, "Leslie is dead. A bird got into the room . . ." until their voices faded.

"She's getting worse." Rupert shook his head. "She may have to go to Bedlam sooner or later."

"No," Gervase said strongly. "We're not putting my grandmother in that place!"

Rupert started to answer, but Edward said abruptly, "Of course we won't. We're going to take care of her. She's harmless enough. Just confused is all."

"What do we do now?" Gervase asked.

"We wait for Dr. Newton and the police."

By the time they reached Silverthorn, Serafina and her father were both numbed by the cold. The temperature was below freezing, or so she thought. When they pulled up in front of the house, a servant was waiting to open the door and help Serafina out of the carriage. As she climbed down, she had to hold on to him for a minute because her feet felt numb. "It's bad cold outside, lady," the man said. "Let me help you up the steps."

Serafina said, "Thank you," and found her lips were so numb she could hardly speak. The big man helped her up the steps, and she waited until her father had navigated the short journey. The door opened, and Edward Hayden said, "Come in, Septimus and Lady Trent." He put his hand out, and Serafina took it. "Come in. It's freezing out." He got them inside and said, "You'll need to thaw out after that cold ride, I expect. Come into my study. I'll explain what has happened."

Serafina followed with her father beside her. In the study a small fire burned, warming the room. Both of them went over to it and began to thaw out. Almost at once Septimus asked, "What's the problem, Edward?"

"It's my butler, Charles Crinshaw. I'm afraid he's dead. It came as quite a shock."

"What happened to him, do you know? Was it an accident?" Serafina asked.

"No, it wasn't an accident, I don't think. It may have been his heart. It seems to have been very sudden."

By the time they warmed up sufficiently, Edward led them through the house into the kitchen, which was occupied only by Annie Simms, the cook. On the far side was the butler's pantry where Crinshaw had kept special spices and records. It was his domain.

Edward asked, "No one has been inside

the pantry, have they, Annie?"

"No, sir, I've been watching all the time."

Serafina and her father moved forward, and Lord Edward stepped aside. "There he is, poor fellow."

Serafina let her father go first. Septimus leaned down and touched the man's throat, but they both knew that that was futile. Death was in the man's face. He had a look of surprise and agony on his features, and his eyes were wide open. Serafina caught an odor that seemed strange to her. She moved closer to her father. They examined the body as well as they could without touching it, and then both of them rose.

"Who found the body?" Septimus asked.

"I did," Edward said. "It was quite a painful thing."

"What time was it?"

"It was late, after ten. Crinshaw always brings me a drink every evening before I go to bed. It's an old habit of mine, and Crinshaw was faithful, always on time. He didn't come tonight for some time, and I thought, perhaps, he might have forgotten it — though that would have been unusual for him. Then when I got here I found him as you see him." He shook his head. "He was a good man."

"Have you notified the police?" Serafina

asked quietly.

"Yes. They should be here soon. Does it look like a heart attack to you?"

"I can't say until we're able to move him."

Serafina turned to face Edward. "Nothing must be touched until the police have made their investigation."

"Of course you're right. I hate to leave him there, but then that doesn't matter to him now, does it?"

Matthew Grant was sleeping soundly when he heard the banging on his door. He awoke at once. He grabbed a robe, slipped into it, and padded barefoot on the cold floor to the door. He opened it, prepared to have it out with whoever was disturbing his sleep, but then he blinked and said with some surprise, "Superintendent, it's you?"

Indeed it was Edsel Fenton, the recently appointed superintendent of Scotland Yard. Fenton was a short, rather overweight man of sixty-two with a reddish complexion and bulging eyes. He drank too much, which he tried without success to conceal, and loved rich food. "What is it, Superintendent?"

"There's been a death at Lord Darby's. I feel it's necessary that I go. Get your clothes on, Grant."

"Yes, sir. Come in. It's cold out."

Fenton stepped in and said with an imperious gesture, "Hurry up. I want to get there as quick as I can before anyone tampers with the scene."

"Is it a crime, sir?"

"Well, we won't know that until we investigate, will we, Grant? Hurry!" His voice was strident, as it usually was when he spoke to Grant. Grant understood well that Fenton disliked him intensely. Grant himself had been the logical choice to become Superintendent of Scotland Yard, but Fenton was a man with friends in high places, and although he had far less experience than Grant, he had been appointed. Grant was jealous of Fenton's position, and though Fenton was intelligent, there were also gaps in his abilities that Grant had spotted almost at once.

He said now, "I'll get dressed as quick as I can, sir."

The group that had gathered in the smaller parlour had fallen silent. The silence was somewhat oppressive, and finally Arthur turned to say to Trevor, "Well, how do you like your new life, Trevor? How do you feel about it?"

"Not as well as I'd like." Trevor shrugged. "I don't fit in."

Arthur smiled wryly and shook his head. "My situation exactly."

St. John was standing across the room looking out the window. When he heard this conversation, he said, "Well, it must be contagious. It's my situation also. I don't seem to fit in." He turned to see Trevor's look of surprise and laughed shortly without humor. "I suppose you've noticed that we're not always a happy family here. I don't know why you're feeling out of place, Trevor. You stepped into a good thing. You'll be the Earl of Darby someday."

Trevor felt uncomfortable around St. John. He knew the man resented him, and he had no knowledge of how to handle such things in this world. "I don't know 'ow to be an earl," he said simply.

"Why, the important thing, Trevor, is to be generous to your dependent relations!"

"Don't talk foolishness, Bramwell!" Leah said coldly.

"It's not foolishness, Mother. It's the way the world wags. Don't you agree, Uncle Arthur?"

Arthur shook his head sadly. "I hope the situation doesn't come up for a long time. Edward is a strong man. He'll live for many years, I pray."

Rupert suddenly came to the door. "The

police have come," he said. "I want you to be very careful what you say to them. Say nothing of your personal affairs."

"Why, we have nothing to hide, Rupert," Arthur said with some surprise.

Rupert's eyes were hooded, and he said in almost a whisper, "Everyone has something to hide."

NINETEEN

"Two gentlemen to see you, sir."

"Show them in, Rosie."

Septimus and Serafina had gone to the small parlour with the other family members, and Edward had moved into his study to think. When Rosie entered, he stood wearily. The death of Crinshaw had shaken him more than anything had in a long time. Charles Crinshaw was not the most genial person in the world, but he had been a faithful servant, and Edward was aware that the man had left a gap that would be difficult to fill. As the two visitors entered, he moved around his desk and stepped forward. "Greetings, gentlemen," he said. Turning to Fenton, he said, "I'm Edward Hayden."

Fenton spoke quickly, nodding his head. "Good morning, Lord Darby. I'm Superintendent Fenton. This is my assistant, Inspector Matthew Grant."

"Yes, we have met. Sorry to meet again under such terrible circumstances, Inspector. Would you gentlemen have a seat, please." He indicated the two chairs on the other side of his desk, but Fenton shook his head with an abrupt motion.

"I think we can dispense with the pleasantries, Lord Darby. If you wouldn't mind, I would like for you to tell me what has happened here."

Edward gave the superintendent a sharp look, for the policeman's manner was rougher than he expected. "I'll be glad to do so. It's my custom to have a drink prepared each night. I take it just before I go to sleep, for I sleep rather badly."

"What sort of drink is it?" Fenton asked. His voice was sharp, as were his eyes, and there was little gentility in his actions or his countenance. "What is in the drink?"

"It's a formula that I got from my father. It's been in the family a long time. It's merely a glass of wine with some added elements to promote sleep."

"What elements?"

"I really can't tell you offhand. It's written down, of course. Charles Crinshaw has prepared it for so many years."

"And you take this every night?"

"I suppose we're all creatures of habit.

Me no less than others. But, yes, every night."

"At what time, Lord Darby?"

"I'm rather attached to keeping regular hours. The usual time was ten o'clock, although that could vary a little."

Superintendent Fenton studied the man before him with an aggressiveness in his manner, which Matthew Grant had noticed before. He seemed to be putting people on trial and finding them guilty before he obtained any real facts. This had disturbed Grant from the very first, but there was nothing he could say or do about it.

"Please tell me what happened tonight, if you will, Lord Darby."

"Yes, Superintendent. I was prepared for bed, but by ten fifteen I began to wonder why Crinshaw had not brought my drink. So I told my wife that I was going to see if he was occupied or if he had forgotten."

"Was he a man to forget things?"

"Not at all, Superintendent! Crinshaw was a very regular man, indeed, in all his duties. That was why I was somewhat surprised."

"So what did you do then, sir?"

"Well, I put on my robe, and I went downstairs, and Crinshaw was not in the kitchen. Everyone else had gone to bed, so I went on to the butler's pantry, and I found him there on the floor."

"Were you certain he was dead?"

Edward moved his shoulders uncomfortably. "I've had very little to do with this sort of thing. I bent down, and he was not breathing."

"Did you check his pulse?"

"No, sir, I did not."

"And what did you do then, Lord Darby?"

"I roused my coachman, sent him at once for Dr. Newton, and I sent another servant to notify the local police. Dr. Newton has already arrived."

The questioning went on for some time with Fenton shooting questions very rapidly at Lord Darby. Finally he said, "We will need to see the body, sir."

"Of course. Nothing has been touched. I left instructions for it to be so."

"That was very wise, sir," Fenton said.

Fenton moved forward as Edward Hayden motioned with his hand. "He's in there, Superintendent."

Fenton moved inside the pantry, followed closely by Grant. He stooped down beside the body without touching it and seemed to study the face of the dead man. "What do you make of it, Grant?" he asked abruptly.

Grant was on the other side of the body. "I don't see any marks of violence." He looked over and said, "It looks as though he had prepared the drink and that he dropped it." Indeed, a large silver goblet was on the floor. "The drink is spilled, for the most part," Grant said.

"Look at his face," Fenton said. "He looks like a man in agony."

"I think that would be consistent with a bad heart, wouldn't it?" Sir Edward said. "I know little about such things, but I've heard it's a very agonizing pain."

Fenton did not answer. His eyes were running around the small room, and he saw the bottle of wine sitting on the table. He went over and asked, "Is this the wine that is used for your potion?"

"Yes, I believe it is," Edward said, leaning forward to read the label. "Yes, amontillado. That's it."

Edward stood back while the two men went over everything in the room, Grant taking copious notes. After a time, Edward said, "Gentlemen, Dr. Newton is here. I'm sure you'd like to see him."

"I certainly would." Fenton rose, and Edward asked Rosie to bring Septimus to the kitchen. When they arrived, Fenton saw two people. He started to speak, but the woman said, "Why, Inspector Grant, it's good to see you again."

Grant moved forward and bowed. "Lady Trent and Dr. Newton, it's good to see you."

Fenton's sharp eyes went from the doctor and the woman addressed as Lady Trent then back to his assistant. "You're already acquainted, I see."

"Oh, yes." Serafina nodded. "Inspector Grant was a great help to us when my brother was in need of it."

"Yes, I read the account of that. Your brother was most fortunate."

"Yes, he was."

"I'm Supt. Edsel Fenton."

Grant said at once, "I'm sorry. This is Lady Serafina Trent and her father, Dr. Septimus Newton."

"I understand you serve as a medical inspector, Doctor?" Fenton said.

"Yes, I have been active in several cases."

"And you, Lady Trent, I read the account in the paper which made you out to be quite a detective." A slight edge touched his voice, and his eyes narrowed. "I trust you're not here to play detective tonight."

"Not at all, Superintendent. I assist my father in his medical procedures."

"Oh, I see." Somehow Fenton seemed to want to make something of these words, but finally he shook his head and said, "Well, you'll need to see the body. Come this way."

Fenton had taken over completely, and he led the group to the pantry. "In there, Dr. Newton," he said.

Septimus stepped forward and looked again at the body. Serafina moved closer but merely stood there watching him as he worked. In a very brief time he stood to his feet and said, "It may have been a heart problem, Superintendent, but it's impossible to tell until we've done an autopsy."

"I see no point in an autopsy if the man died of a heart attack!" Fenton snapped.

"I cannot tell what caused his death. An autopsy is necessary if you want to be sure."

"Certainly I want to be sure," Fenton said somewhat hesitantly. "Well then, proceed."

"I can't do that here," Septimus said. He spoke mildly and looked down at the body. "We'll have to take the body back to my laboratory."

"And how long will it take?"

"The autopsy itself? It will not take too long, I would think. Getting the body there will take a little longer."

Serafina said, "The body hasn't been moved, has it?"

"No," Edward said. "I made sure that no one touched it."

Fenton seemed to be irritated by her question. He turned to Grant and asked, "Why are you standing there, Grant? Get to work."

Grant met Fenton's eyes, and for a moment the two men seemed locked in some sort of struggle, but then Grant said placidly, "Yes, sir."

"Get some servants to help move the body, and we'll need a room to be used as an office to question everyone in the house."

"My study, would that do?" Edward asked.

"Very well. Come along, Sir Edward. I'll begin with you."

The two men left, and Grant said, "Just let me take one more look, and I'll help you move the body."

"I'm sure there are servants to help with that," Serafina said quietly.

Serafina and her father watched as Grant went over the room again. He went to the door where Mrs. Swifton was standing with her back against the wall.

"You're aware that the victim took a drink to Lord Darby every night?"

"Oh, yes, sir, everyone knew that."

"Do you have any idea what he put in it?"

"No, sir, he kept it quite a secret. He wasn't a joking man, but he liked to say that one day he would bottle this potion and get rich by selling it."

"When was the last time you saw Charles Crinshaw alive?"

"He was in the kitchen having a cup of tea. It was rather late, and I bid him good night and went to bed. That must have been about nine thirty."

"Thank you," Grant said. "Would you see if you could find some strong men to help to move the body?"

"Yes, sir."

After Mrs. Swifton left, Grant went back and studied the cup. He picked it up and said, "There's still a little in this cup." He picked up the bottle of wine and said, "Would you have any way of testing the contents of this wine and what's remaining in the cup?"

"Yes, of course," Serafina said.

Grant studied the body silently, and then Samuel Franks, the footman, and Tim, the coachman, came in, and Septimus instructed them as they picked the body up and moved it out. "You'll need to put the body in a wagon, if you have such a thing," he said.

"Yes, sir, we do. I'll see to it."

Serafina moved closer to Grant. "The superintendent doesn't seem very considerate of you."

Grant turned to face her. His hazel eyes seemed to glow, and as always she was amazed by his hair. He was only thirty-one years old, and his hair was prematurely silver. "Superintendent Fenton is rather defensive."

"But why is he so harsh with you?"

"I couldn't say."

Serafina thought quickly. "It's probably because he knows that you were scheduled to be put into the position he now holds. Why weren't you?" she asked.

"The way of the world. He had connections. I'll appreciate it if you could send someone as soon as possible with the results of the autopsy and of the test on the wine."

"Of course, Inspector. As quickly as we can."

Edward had grown restless under Fenton's relentless questioning. He did not like the man and felt that for a superintendent he was unnecessarily demanding. But he answered the questions, and finally Edward sat up straighter and looked the man full in the eye. "Isn't it premature to ask all these questions, Superintendent? After all, the man may have died of a heart attack."

Fenton glared at him and said, "I'll have to be the judge of that, Lord Darby." He got to his feet. "I'll leave Inspector Grant to continue the questioning. I have a great deal of responsibility. Good day, sir."

"I'll show you to the door."

"I think I can find my way." He left quickly and found Grant. "Grant, I want you to question the family and all the servants."

"Yes, sir. What am I looking for?"

"For facts, man — facts! I don't have time to teach you how to question witnesses. Now, do your job and report to me as soon as Newton gives you a report on the cause of death."

"Yes, sir," Grant said quietly and watched as the superintendent left the room, walking quickly as if to rid himself of the place.

Dylan had spent the early morning down by the harbor at the mission where he often volunteered. He had very little money, but he usually took a few things that the men might lack. Leaving the mission, he had gone to the Montevado house and was pleased to see that Maria, the mother of Callie and Paco, looked healthier. "You're looking very well, Maria," he said.

"Yes, sir. The money that the viscountess gave us has made such a difference." She was of pure Spanish blood and had been married to Ramon Montevado. He'd been dead for five years, and Maria's beauty was worn down from her work in the sweatshops. She had become ill, and it had been through Dylan Tremayne and the viscountess that her family had received care. Now there was a glow in her cheeks. "I wish you would give 'er my thanks again, Mr. Tremayne."

"Of course I will."

She said, "I 'ave to go out for a while. Callie, you entertain Mr. Tremayne."

"Yes, Mama."

Talking with Paco, who was eight, and Callie, who was almost thirteen, was always a pleasure to Dylan. They had sharpened their wits by surviving on the streets in one of the worst districts of London, and Callie, whose real name was Calendra, was turning into a real beauty. She was on the brink of young womanhood and, within a year or even less, would be quite different from the ragamuffin Dylan had first met.

He sat down and Callie fixed tea for him, and the two children, as usual, were intensely curious about what he did. They were fascinated by Dylan, and it was Calendra who asked finally, "Why is the viscountess so good to us, giving us money?"

"Why, she's a good woman, she is."

Callie stared at him and demanded, "Are you going to marry 'er?"

"Why would you say such a thing? I'm

just a poor actor, and she's a fine lady."

Calendra said, "You'd make a good 'usband. She must be stupid if she can't see 'at."

"Oh no, she's not stupid. Not Lady Trent. She's the smartest person I've ever known."

Calendra continued her pursuit of Dylan's love life, and finally he laughed and got to his feet. "Well, throw me in the river if you can't think of more questions than any human I ever saw! It's all I can do to take care of myself, girl. Besides" — he grinned and reached out and tugged a lock of her jet black hair — "I might have a baby girl who'd grow up and pester me with foolish questions. I've got to go now."

"When you coming back?" Paco asked.

"Very soon."

"Will you bring us presents?" Paco asked with a grin.

"What kind of a present?"

"Something we'll like."

"I'll see what I can do. Good-bye now."

Leaving the Seven Dials district, he went back to Matthew's rooms. He was hungry and had stopped on the way to get a kidney pie, and he was sitting down to eat it when Matthew came in. He took one look at Dylan and said, "I hope you got two of those."

"No, I didn't. I never know when I'll see you." He studied Matthew's face and said, "What's wrong? You look upset."

"Well, it's a case. You'll be interested in it. It may concern young Trevor, that fellow you found for Lord Darby."

Dylan was prepared to take a bite of the pie, but he put it down and said, "What's happened?"

"There's been a death at Lord Darby's." He went on to describe the case and said, "You may want to go out to Trentwood if you have time. Find out if the autopsy is over and bring me word."

"I've got plenty of time, but you don't seem happy, Grant."

"I'm all right." Grant did not seem all right, however. There was a harried expression in his eyes and a hardness that had been in him the first time Dylan had met him.

"You should be the superintendent."

"Well, I'm not." There was a bitterness to Grant, and he threw himself into a chair and stared at Dylan defiantly.

"God has us in His hands, Matthew. He'll take care of you." He almost spoke of Dora, but he did not. He was sure that Grant was head over heels in love with the young woman, and as superintendent he would have been a suitable candidate for a husband, but as a mere inspector, a policeman, he would never be accepted. He got up and said, "I'll go out to Trentwood. I was planning to go out anyhow and visit David."

"Send word as soon as there is a word."

"Where will you be?"

"Probably back at Lord Darby's house."

Leaving the house, Dylan found a hansom cab and engaged the driver. On the way to Trentwood he thought about what Matthew had told him and was troubled by it for some reason. As soon as he reached the house, he paid the cabdriver, adding an extra shilling for his trouble and feeling guilty because his bank roll was small indeed.

When he went to the door, he was met by Louisa Toft, Serafina's maid.

"Why, Mr. Tremayne." She smiled, her eyes glowing. "How good to see you."

"Why, thank you, Louisa."

"Come in, sir. It's cold out."

"Yes, it is."

"Can I take your coat?"

"I need to see Dr. Newton and Lady Trent."

"Oh, sir, they're in the laboratory outside. Shall I take you there?"

"No, thank you, Louisa. I know the way."

"Is there anything else I could do for you?"

Dylan Tremayne was accustomed to women who were taken with him. Actors seemed to draw women as honey draws flies. Louisa was a beautiful young woman with rosy cheeks, clear eyes, and a pleasing form. There was something in her question, more than just a lightness, and he knew that all he had to say was one word and she would respond. But he had learnt better, and now he just simply smiled and said, "Thank you, Louisa," and turned at once and went back outside. Louisa sighed deeply and shut the door.

When he reached the lab, after trudging through the packed snow, he knocked on the door and heard a muffled reply that he could not make out. He assumed it was an invitation to enter, and he stepped inside and shut the door behind him. He took in the scene: the naked body of a man on a table, with Dr. Newton and his daughter wearing white coats and standing over him. He felt the same queasy feeling he had felt the first time he had walked in on an autopsy. That time he had fainted dead away in front of Serafina, and now he wanted nothing so much as to be gone.

Serafina saw his problem and said at once, "Dylan, why don't you go visit with David.

We'll soon be finished here. He's missed you."

"I believe I'll do that." With a quick gush of relief, Dylan turned and went back to the house. He entered and went upstairs to the old nursery, which had become a playroom for David. As he walked in, David, who was sitting on the floor amidst a jumble of toy soldiers, leapt to his feet and came over to him, his eyes flashing. "Did you come to play with me?"

"Well, for a while. I came to see your mother and your grandfather too."

"Sit down. Show me some of the battles you were in when you were a soldier."

Lowering himself to the floor, Dylan began arranging the soldiers, and David peppered him with questions, asking finally, "Did you ever kill anyone when you were a soldier?"

"I'm afraid I did, and I wish I hadn't." This was inexplicable to David, for whom death was only a vague, nebulous idea. Quickly he changed the subject, and the two began to move the soldiers around.

"Not good, is it, Father?" Serafina looked at her father and saw that he was as troubled as she was.

"Not at all. We'll have to get our results to

the police at once."

"I'll go up and tell Dylan. Perhaps he'll want to take the news back to Silverthorn. I'm worried about young Trevor," she said, stripping off the white coat and putting on her winter garb before going outside.

When she entered the house, she went upstairs at once to the playroom, and hearing voices, she paused. Through the open doors she could see David and Dylan sprawled out on the floor, Dylan on his stomach moving soldiers around and David, across from him, saying, "I won, didn't I?"

"That you did, my boy." Serafina watched as David came over and sat down across from Dylan.

"I wish you had some little boys for me to play with," he said.

"Well, I guess I am a little shy of boys."

"Don't you want any boys or girls?"

"Oh, yes, indeed!"

"Well, why don't you get married and have some then?"

Dylan smiled, and Serafina saw him reach out and tousle David's fair hair. It was something David hated when other people did it, but he did not seem to mind Dylan's touch. "Why, I just haven't found the woman God is getting ready for me."

David studied Dylan's face and then asked, "Is God making a woman just for you?"

"Oh, yes, indeed, and He's making me just for her."

David was very quiet. Serafina had seen this look on his face many times when he was mulling things over, but she was shocked when she heard him say, "Maybe God wants you to marry my mum. You could live here all the time, and when you had babies, I could have some company."

Serafina found her cheeks suddenly glowing, and she did not know what to think, but she listened hard for Dylan's answer.

"Your mother is a wonderful woman, David. Much too fine for a rough fellow like me."

"But — she could train you, couldn't she? Make you into a good husband?"

Serafina could see Dylan's face. He was smiling as he said, "The Bible says, 'Whoso findeth a wife findeth a good thing, and obtaineth favor of the Lord.' So the Lord favors married men. But your mother will probably marry an earl or a duke."

"I don't want them, Dylan. I want you."

Serafina suddenly coughed and walked into the room. She pretended to have heard nothing, but she saw that Dylan had a slight smile on his face and knew that she had heard.

"Time for your nap, David."

"No, Mum, I'm playing with Dylan."

"With Mr. Dylan."

"I'm playing with Mr. Dylan." There was the usual argument to get David off to his nap, and finally Serafina was accompanied by Dylan to David's room. Together they put him in bed, still protesting, and when they stepped outside, Serafina drew a deep breath. "David adores you, Dylan."

"Well, the feeling is mutual. I've got a fondness for the boy, me. But that may not be a good thing. I may have to leave him." Then he added as an afterthought, "And you, my lady."

Serafina was startled. Her eyes opened wide, and her lips parted slightly. "Are you — are you planning to go away?"

"No, but I may get marching orders from the Lord. I know you don't believe in such things. I'll enjoy David while I can. I've grown very fond of him, Serafina, and for —"

He evidently changed his mind and said instead, "Grant told me about the business at Lord Darby's. Is there anything new?"

"I'm afraid so. The victim was poisoned."

"Do you tell me that?"

"Yes. I was certain of it from the time we saw the body. There was a smell like bitter almonds, which is an indication of cyanide. We found the body full of it. It's murder now, Dylan. We've got to take the results of this autopsy to the superintendent and to Lord Darby. I'll send word to the superintendent, but I think I'll take it to Lord Darby myself. Would you come with me?"

"Well, of course. Grant said he'd be at Lord Darby's too. What can I do?"

"I'm worried about Trevor. He's very unhappy, and he may be suspected of the murder."

"Why should he be?"

"Well, it's obvious that Charles Crinshaw was not the intended victim. I don't think anyone had a motive, but the drink was fixed for Lord Darby. I tested the wine, Dylan, and it's deadly — laced with poison."

"That's a bad one, but why would the police suspect Trevor?"

"You're not thinking, Dylan. He would be the new Lord Darby if Edward Hayden had been killed."

"Of course. It's hard to think like that. I'll go, of course, but Trevor surely isn't the killer. He'd know that he'd be the prime suspect."

Serafina was quiet for a moment and then

shook her head. "No, he wouldn't, but the real killer probably thought of that. It has to be one of the family or one of the servants, but we need to stand by Trevor."

"I'll get ready. The poor young man doesn't need this."

Serafina studied him and then said, "Dylan, please don't pay much attention to the things David said. He's just a child. He misses his father, and he has wild thoughts sometimes."

Dylan regarded Serafina, and she felt her cheeks growing warm as she thought of the things David had said to him. "Come along," she said brusquely, "we must hurry."

Twenty

"Have you seen the papers, Grant?" Superintendent Fenton had exclaimed that morning. He had been sitting behind his desk in his office, and Grant, who had been called for, stood before him waiting. Fenton's face was crimson with anger, and his smallish eyes were glinting with what appeared to be unquenchable fury. "Look at these!" Fenton threw a newspaper down and waved his hand toward them. "They're already saying that we're incompetent! I won't have it, Grant, I tell you! We have to get action quick on this one."

Grant looked down at the paper, but he had already read the story. It had not disturbed him, for the newspapers often took Scotland Yard to task for anything less than immediate resolution. "Well, sir," he said, "it's a noble family, and the newspaper fellows have to have something to write."

"Is that all you can say?" Fenton demanded. He clenched his fist and struck the paper a blow that turned over a vase, which seemed to anger him even more. His voice trembled with rage as he said, "I'm not satisfied with the way this case is being handled. I left you in charge, and I expected some sort of solution by this time. Now what have you done?"

Snow was falling outside, and the room was cold despite a fire which blazed in the fireplace to Grant's left. He was accustomed to these fits of anger from Fenton and knew there was no way to avoid them. Grant also knew that Fenton resented and feared him. Fenton himself had been a policeman on a municipal force for five years. Before that he had been a lawyer. His had been a political appointment, and both men knew it. There was no way, Grant understood, that he would be able to satisfy Fenton, but he tried.

"I've interviewed every servant, and of course, I've spoken to each member of the family."

"And you've come up with no conclusions, but I have."

"You have, sir?"

"Yes. I think it's fairly obvious who the guilty man is."

"And who might that be, Superintendent?"

"Why, that fellow the Haydens dragged in off the streets and claimed for their son. 'Trevor' they call him now, but I've had a man do some checking, and he was a scurrilous rogue out on the street. Grew up in the middle of crime. Oh, the local policemen knew him quite well! He was always in trouble of some kind."

"He never committed murder."

The vein in Fenton's temple seemed to throb with energy, and he snapped angrily, "You presume to tell me how to run this department?"

"No, sir, of course not. I'm only saying that —"

"I know what you're saying. It's obvious, man! The poison was obviously not meant for the butler. It was meant for Lord Darby."

"I think we can agree on that, sir, but young Trevor —"

"If Lord Darby had died, Trevor Hayden would be heir to all of Darby's estate and his title as well. I'm surprised you don't see it, Grant. It's plain as the nose on your face."

"I don't think the young man would be so stupid."

"What do you mean stupid? He would

have gotten the entire estate."

"He's also the logical suspect. He's a bright young man, Superintendent. Nothing's wrong with his mind. He's had an unfortunate childhood and grew up in a terrible situation. True, he's had bad companions, but that was no fault of his own."

"He has no morality whatsoever. He couldn't have after growing up in the Seven Dials district. Now, I want you to concentrate on that fellow. Does he have an alibi?"

Grant chewed his lip and hesitated to answer for a moment, then he shook his head. "No, sir, but many of the others don't have alibis either. It was late at night. They had all gone to bed. As a matter of fact, none of the family has an alibi, nor the servants either, but it's inconceivable that a servant would have done this thing."

"All right. Trevor's your man. Get out there and find some evidence. I want to close this case in a hurry and shut these stories down, and I want it quickly. You understand me, Inspector?"

"Yes, sir, I understand you very well," Grant replied. His voice was level and even, for he had learnt that any resistance or disagreement with Fenton was useless. Turning, he left the office and headed for Silverthorn. As soon as the door had closed,

Fenton leaned back with a look of satisfaction. He smiled slightly and said, "There, Mr. Inspector Grant, let's see what you will do with this!"

Gervase had been practicing on the harpsichord, which was in the larger of the two parlours. The maids had come and gone, doing their cleaning work, but as always, as Gervase had practiced, she had put her whole heart and mind into it and had blotted out any outside influences. She was an excellent performer and took great pleasure in practice, which made her even more adept.

Finally she leaned back, flexed her fingers with satisfaction, got up, and walked over to the window. She loved the snow and watched it for a while as the flakes drifted by. Some of them seemed as big as shillings. The snow was tapering off though and was not deep on the ground. Most of it had melted off during a warm spell, but she was still hopeful that there would be a white Christmas.

Leaving the parlour, she moved to the attic room that her father had converted to a studio of sorts. It had been a dark, gloomy place, but Arthur had had two large windows put in, and now the pale sunlight illuminated the canvas he was standing before.

"How's the painting going, Papa?"

"Very well, I suppose." Arthur turned and smiled at her. He looked tired, but then he always did. He had not been drinking, Gervase noted at once. She had become an expert in detecting her father's condition. He was not a man who could handle alcohol well, but on this particular day his eyes were clear and his hands were steady. "What do you think of it?" he asked, gesturing with his brush toward the canvas.

Gervase moved closer to get a better view. It was a painting of a hunt with horses jumping over a fence, the hounds running full tilt through the woods. "I can almost hear the dogs barking." She smiled. "And look. That fellow's going to lose his seat if he's not careful. It's a beautiful painting. What are you going to do with it?"

"Put it with the rest, I suppose."

"You really ought to have a show, Father." Gervase came over and stood in front of him. She reached up and pushed a lock of hair that had fallen over his forehead to one side and said, "One day you'll have a show and be recognized."

"I doubt that seriously."

Gervase saw the troubled light in her

father's eyes. She was accustomed to this. He was basically a sad man. She knew he had been devastated by the loss of her mother, and she wondered that a man could have such a love that would last for so many years. Toward her he had been as kind and as thoughtful as he would have been if she were his blood daughter. The fact that she was no blood relation did not seem to matter to Arthur Hayden, and at that moment Gervase felt a sudden rush of affection for him.

"I know what. Let's go down to the kitchen and see if we can get a preview of what the Christmas dinner will be like."

Arthur held the brush in his hand and looked down at it for a long moment. Finally he lifted his eyes and shook his head. "I doubt if there'll be much Christmas cheer in this house, not with murder hanging over it."

"It's a terrible thing."

"Crinshaw wasn't a man to open himself up much, but he didn't deserve to die like that." He passed his hand across his face as if to wash away a memory and said, "Has that policeman been talking to you?"

"Oh, yes, he's been talking to everyone, I think. I believe he's baffled."

"I'm not surprised. I doubt if anyone will

ever know who poisoned Crinshaw."

"Well, the police are convinced that it was meant for Uncle Edward, which is the only thing that makes sense. Who would want to poison poor Charles Crinshaw?"

"Yes, it's an inevitable conclusion." He hesitated, then shook his head. "I want to work a little bit more while I have the light. You go on down and bring me up some tea later."

"Of course, Papa." Gervase left, and as she descended from the attic to the second floor, she saw Trevor coming out of his room. "Hello, Trevor," she said cheerfully.

"Hello."

Gervase saw at once that there was gloom on Trevor's face and said, "You're coming with me."

"Coming where?" Trevor asked. He was casually enough dressed, with a pair of navy blue trousers, a white shirt, and a woolen waistcoat. As Gervase noted this, she lifted her eyes to his face and once again was struck at his resemblance to Edward and to several other of the Hayden ancestors in the portrait gallery. *He has to be a Hayden,* she thought, not for the first time. *No one could deny the resemblance.*

"Come on," she said. "We're going down to scrounge something from the kitchen.

I'm sure Cook will feed us a little."

"All right," Trevor said, and the two went downstairs.

They found Annie busy preparing the evening meal, and when Gervase smiled and demanded something good, she said, "Well, I made some fairy cookies for Christmas. You can have some of those and some tea."

"Is there any coffee?" Trevor asked.

"I'll make you some, sir."

Soon the two were sitting down munching on fairy cookies, Gervase drinking tea and Trevor coffee. The cook had gone outside, and although Gervase tried to pull him out of his gloom, he did not seem to respond. Finally she asked, "What's wrong, Trevor? You seem so discouraged."

"I don't belong in this place," Trevor said gloomily. He held one of the fairy cookies in his hand, studied it, then dipped it into the coffee and bit it off. "I wish I was back in my old life."

"Well, that's a terrible thing to wish."

"It was bad enough, but sometimes I think this is worse. At least things were simple there." He gave a sardonic smile and shook his head. "All I 'ad to do was stay out of the 'ands of the police."

Impulsively Gervase reached over and covered his hand with her own. "Don't say that. That's not the way for you to live. You're a Hayden, and there are great things that you can do. You're going to learn and study, and you're going to be a fine gentleman, Trevor. One day you'll be Sir Trevor Hayden, Earl of Darby, and you'll marry a beautiful woman and have beautiful children."

Trevor suddenly laughed. He was very conscious of the warmth of her hand on his. "You do know 'ow to encourage a fellow. I think you're the brightest spot in me life, but I'm not so sure all those things will 'appen."

"It's gloomy right now because of poor Crinshaw's death, but time passes."

"I've been thinking about that, and 'as it occurred to you, Gervase, that I'm the prime suspect?"

"What are you talking about?"

"If my father 'ad died, who would get the greatest benefit?"

"Why, I hadn't thought of it."

"It would be me, of course."

"Why, nobody would think that."

"Grant thinks so, or 'e acts like it."

"No, he couldn't think that. It's — it's unthinkable."

Suddenly Trevor reached out and put his hand over Gervase's, imprisoning it. "You're a good influence on me. Perhaps my good angel. I need one. You don't know the terrible life I've led."

Gervase in turn was acutely conscious of the warmth and strength of his hand. "I'm no angel," she said, "but I know God's going to look out for you."

"You really believe that, that good always comes out on top?" Trevor demanded.

"Yes," Gervase said simply. "I do believe that."

Trevor held her hand for a moment then released it. Finally he said quietly, "I'm glad you believe that, Gervase, and I 'opes you always will."

As usual, David had put up a clamor to accompany his mother. Serafina had noticed he seemed troubled when she was out of his sight, and she was always careful now to tell him exactly where she was going and when she would be back. Now she knelt beside him, with Dylan standing behind her, and she put her arms around him. "I must go over to visit some old friends of ours who have a problem, but I'll be back this afternoon, and you and I will do something wonderful."

"What?"

Serafina laughed and hugged him. "You

think up something wonderful."

"Will you come back too, Mr. Dylan?"

"I suspect I will. You know me, old man. Always looking for a free meal."

Serafina kissed David on the cheek then stood, and as she turned to leave, Dylan came over, bent down, and put his hand out. David took it, but his eyes were troubled.

"Now, old man, I'm leaving you in charge of this whole establishment. You see to it that things are done right. You can do that, can you?"

"Oh, yes, I'll do that, Mr. Dylan, but hurry back, will you?"

"As fast as I can."

Dylan joined Serafina, and the two walked outside the house. When they were in the carriage and Givins had spoken to the horses, Serafina turned to Dylan saying, "I worry about David. He seems so insecure."

"But, after all, Serafina, he's seven years old. He lost his father. It's only natural."

"I suppose so." Serafina fell into a silence, and from time to time Dylan would turn slightly to examine her profile. He had kissed her twice, but both times it had been when she was weak and troubled. He knew that she had the power to stir him and also to awaken the sense of loneliness that lately had begun to fall upon him. He felt the urges of a lone man but always moved like the needle of a compass to a woman. And since he had known Serafina Trent, she had drawn him in a way that no other woman had. He noted the slight changes of her face as the carriage bumped along the frozen ruts — the quickening, the loosing, the small expressions coming and going. Her hair rose back from her temples and was drawn up on her head with some loose pieces cascading down her neck. He then saw a change come over her face and wondered what had entered her mind. Suddenly she turned to face him, and their eyes met.

"Why are you staring at me, Dylan?" she asked abruptly.

"I don't know. Do you mind?"

Suddenly she smiled. "I suppose not. After all, I stare at you sometimes." She showed him a glance, half-startled, and a quicker breath stirred her breast. It was actually a startled expression as if she had discovered something. Colour came to her cheeks, and quickly she turned away from him, her indrawn breath making a slight echo in the coach. She began to talk of the murder of Charles Crinshaw, and he knew that she had been disturbed by something that she saw in him . . . or else saw in herself.

The moment passed, and finally they arrived at Silverthorn. He got out of the coach and helped her down. She looked up at the driver and said, "Albert, go to the kitchen, and I'll have them fix you something hot."

"Thank you, Lady Trent."

The two of them went up the steps to the imposing structure, and looking up at it, Dylan said, "Why would anyone build a house this big? A man can only be in one room at a time."

"Pride, I suppose."

"I don't understand it. Why would a man want twenty suits when he can only wear one? Why would he want fifty horses when he can only ride one?"

Serafina suddenly laughed. "You know better than that. Your Bible talks about the pride of life. That's what builds these massive homes and makes a person buy more clothes than they need."

The door opened, and they were greeted by Rosie Mason, the parlour maid. "Come in out of the cold, Lady Trent, and you, Mr. Tremayne. Would you like to see Lord Darby?"

"Is Inspector Grant here?"

"Well, yes, ma'am. He's in Lord Darby's study. Would you like me to announce you?"

"Please, Rosie. We'll wait here."

The two stood there, and after removing his coat and hat, Dylan began to walk down the line of portraits, pausing under each one. He read an inscription aloud. "Leslie Hayden. He looks like Edward. He must be his father."

"They all have a family likeness. Have you ever noticed that in some families the children all look exactly alike, while in others they look nothing like one another?"

As they examined the portraits, Serafina commented, "Trevor can never deny his Hayden blood. His portrait would look perfectly right along with these others."

Rosie came back and said, "Inspector Grant would like to see you in the study, ma'am."

"We'll find the way, Rosie. Thank you."

The two went to the study and found Grant sitting behind a desk. A notebook was before him, and he rose at once. "Good morning, Lady Trent. How are you this morning?"

"Fine, Inspector."

"Hello, Tremayne. How's your day?"

"Oh, I'm just a leaf blown by the wind. An unemployed actor is the most useless human being on the face of the earth."

Grant laughed. "Maybe I could get you on the force as a policeman."

The idea amused Dylan. "I've been a soldier. I suppose I can break heads just as well on the police force."

"Don't be a fool. That's not what a policeman does," Grant said with a slight smile. "Sit down, both of you."

The two sat, and Grant resumed his seat. "I've interviewed everybody in this house, most of them more than once, and one conclusion I have is what you have probably decided. There are two things really. One, that Lord Darby was the intended victim, and two, the murderer has to be someone in the house."

"I think that's very likely. A stranger coming from the outside would not have access to the butler's pantry. There are so many servants. He'd be noticed instantly. It has to be someone here."

"Have the servants told you anything at all?" Dylan asked. "I mean anything that would help?"

Grant leaned back and sighed and shook his head. "It's not going to be easy. These cases never are, but I think —" Grant stopped speaking when Trevor entered the room.

"Sorry. I didn't realize you were in 'ere, Inspector Grant. 'Ello, Lady Trent and Mr. Tremayne."

After a round of greetings, Grant said, "Come in, Trevor. Sit down and join us."

"No, thank you. I'd better be goin'."

He turned to leave just as Lady Leona entered the room. She looked around, but she ignored everyone but Trevor. There was an intense look in her eyes, and she stood there for a moment perfectly still. She was wearing a simple light blue dress with a woolen shawl around her shoulders. Her hair had not been fixed, and she had a rather strange look about her. She came over to stand before Trevor, reached up, and touched his cheek.

"Good morning, Leslie."

Trevor stared at her and looked startled, as if he wanted to turn and flee. "You're looking well this morning, Leslie," she said. "Tell Cook not to hold the meal for me. I'll be a little late." She patted his cheek again, turned, and walked out.

"Why is she calling you Leslie?" Serafina asked, staring at Trevor.

"She's done that twice before. I asked Gervase about it. Leslie was 'er 'usband's name."

"Oh yes, she married Leslie after his wife Edith died."

"Poor thing," Serafina said. "She's confused, isn't she?"

"I wish she'd leave me alone. She gives me the creeps," Trevor said and shook his shoulders in a gesture of either fear or disgust.

Serafina said, "I talked to Lady Darby about it once. She says she will go for days in a perfectly normal manner and then she'll have these spells. It's been going on for quite a while, I understand. Sir Edward told me that she'd been having mental problems even before she married Leslie. But he also said that for the last two years, she's been having the spells closer together."

Trevor shook his head. "I don't like it," he said. "It makes me feel odd."

"People out of their minds often do," Dylan said. He stood up and put his hands on the young man's shoulders and smiled. "But it will come out all right. You'll see."

"I don't think so." The young man turned and walked away, and both Serafina and Dylan felt an impression. The old woman's behaviour was indeed weird, and both of them had a fear of mental instability. They watched Trevor go with concern.

"He's pretty low," Dylan observed. "Can't say I blame him much."

"Poor fellow," Grant said. "You'll have to excuse me. The superintendent will be expecting me."

After Grant left, Serafina said, "Trevor's not the killer. I'm certain of it."

Dylan suddenly gave her a quick glance. "Just a feeling you have, is it now?"

Serafina returned his glance. "I'm afraid that's all it is right now. You're the one for feelings, not me. But we can't go on feelings. I think Lord Darby is still in danger. I think we'd better watch him carefully."

"Yes, that would be the thing to do. Shall I take the first watch?"

"That would be best. We may have to press Lorenzo and Gyp into service."

Dylan shook his head doubtfully. "The killer is inside the house, Serafina. Those two are unbeatable in their way, but they'd be little use in close quarters. You and I will have to guard Lord Darby." He hesitated then added, "It won't be easy. The murderer knows more than we do about Lord Darby's movements. But the good Lord willing, we'll keep him safe."

Serafina hesitated, then said quietly, "Yes, the good Lord willing."

TWENTY-ONE

The servants had put Christmas decorations up in several rooms according to Serafina's directions. She always liked to do this for David's sake, and now as she walked through the room, she commented to the housekeeper, "You've done a beautiful job, Mrs. Fielding."

"Well, thank you, ma'am. It's a pleasure to do it for the little fellow. That's a fine son you have."

Serafina smiled at Rachel Fielding. She was almost fifty, a solid woman with black eyes and black hair — without a single white hair among them. She was a widow, and her husband, James, had been the butler before he died.

A knock sounded at the front door, and Serafina turned saying, "I'll get that. I think the maids are all upstairs cleaning." She walked to the front door and opened it to find Inspector Grant standing there. He looked nervous, and she said, "Why, come in, Inspector. We've been expecting you."

"Well, I feel a bit odd barging in on Christmas Eve and disturbing the family."

"Nonsense. We wanted you here. Let me help you with your coat."

Dylan and Serafina had asked Grant to find someone to watch over Lord Darby during Christmas — in effect, to be a bodyguard. Sergeant Sandy Kenzie had volunteered. He was a good, steady man, and there was no danger while he was on watch.

Serafina took Grant's coat and hat and hung them up on one of the hooks on the wall. "It's a beautiful day for Christmas."

"Yes, it is."

"What do you usually do on Christmas?" Serafina asked.

"Nothing much."

To Serafina this was a sad reply. She knew that Matthew Grant was a lonely man. He'd had a terrible childhood, Serafina had heard from Dora. His father had been hanged for murder, a murder which had never been proved definitively, at least not in Matthew Grant's opinion. She knew this had made him bitter, but he seemed to have mellowed lately, and she attributed this, to a great extent, to his obvious feelings for Dora.

"I'll get Dora to show you the decorations. Maybe you can help."

"I don't know much about that," Matthew said. He followed her into the kitchen where they found Dora whipping something in a large bowl as she stood among several servants, including the cook, who were working furiously.

"Matthew," she said smiling, "you're just in time. Here, you can beat this."

Matthew blinked with surprise then laughed. "I don't know anything about cooking."

"All you need is a strong right arm. You beat this until your arm drops off."

Serafina said, "You two make sure there's plenty to eat."

"There always is," Dora said. She watched Matthew as he held the bowl in one hand and then stirred the contents in with the other. "I'm making a cake," she said. "What shall it be?"

"I like all kinds of cake."

She began to talk to him about the Christmas festivities. "On Christmas Eve we all gather in the parlour and sing hymns. I don't even know if you can sing. I've never heard you."

"I sing beautifully," Matthew said, lifting one eyebrow. "Probably the most beautiful voice you ever heard."

"I'll venture you're boasting."

Matthew found himself unwinding, and the servants who watched them slyly were impressed that an inspector from Scotland Yard could be such a fine-looking man and also willing to do a menial task like cooking.

They were interrupted finally when Aunt Bertha came in through the door. "Aldora, I want —" She broke off suddenly when she saw Matthew standing there. "Oh, Inspector Grant."

"How are you this afternoon, Lady Bertha?"

"Very well, thank you." Bertha started to say something then changed her mind and said, "Aldora, will you come with me for a moment, please. It won't take long."

"Why, certainly, Aunt Bertha. Here, Matthew, you can start making the pudding."

"But I don't know how."

"Cook, show the inspector how to make pudding. I'll be right back."

As soon as they were in the hallway, Bertha said angrily, "I've warned you about letting that policeman call on you. He's not fit company for a young woman of your station."

Dora knew that Aunt Bertha was the

world's greatest snob. "And why not, Aunt Bertha? He did a great deal toward saving Clive from hanging. Don't you have any thoughts of gratitude about that?"

"Gratitude's all very well," Bertha said. Her eyes narrowed, and she stared at Dora. "You're not thinking of letting that man court you, are you?"

"I would be very honoured if he did. He's a fine man."

"He's a policeman."

"I know he's a policeman, Aunt Bertha." Dora was usually a mild-mannered young woman, but this time her aunt had overstepped a line she had drawn in her own mind. She had found that Matthew Grant was not at all what she had expected. She had supposed that a policeman from Scotland Yard would be hard and demanding, but toward her, Matthew Grant had been gentle and observed every rule of propriety. "I'll have to ask you not to interfere, Aunt Bertha."

"Why, you —" Bertha was shocked beyond measure. Dora, in her entire life, had never once challenged Lady Bertha's decisions, and now it was as if she were looking at a girl she had never seen before. Dora was standing straight and meeting her gaze.

"You will not pursue this any further, or I

will be forced to speak to my father. He's very fond of Matthew, and he would not be pleased if he knew about this conversation. We'll hear no more about it."

She turned to leave, and Bertha stood there, her face red and words boiling to her lips. "I don't know what the world's coming to! Policemen coming to spend the holidays. Actors with the run of the house! Next it will be the dustmen coming to have dinner with us." She turned and stomped off down the hall, her back rigid with anger.

In the morning, the sun, red in the east, cast a rosy gleam over the unbroken snow that covered the countryside like a blanket. The trees were all rounded off, and there were no sharp corners or edges to any of the outbuildings. The fences also were rounded with small mounds of snow, and David had woken up excited. Serafina had insisted that he have a good breakfast, and after they had finished, the maid had come in and said, "Mr. Tremayne is here, Lady Trent."

"Dylan!" David shouted and slid off his chair, running headlong from the room. Serafina laughed and followed him as quickly as she could. It was David who opened the door and stood looking up, his face excited.

"Dylan, you came!"

"Why, of course I came, old man. You don't think I'd miss Christmas, do you?" Dylan had a long package in his hands, something wrapped in paper.

"Is that a present for me?"

"David, that's not very polite."

"Why not, Mum?"

"Well, if it's a present for you, Mr. Dylan will tell you about it."

"Now don't fuss the boy around on Christmas morning. I did come bearing gifts. One for you, Lady Trent, and one for Master David Trent."

"Can I open it now?" David asked instantly.

"We have several other gifts for you, David," Serafina said. But she saw the excitement in her son's eyes and said, "Well, if you'd like, you can open your present now, David."

Dylan handed the package over to David and said, "I'm not much on wrapping."

"I don't care." David ripped the paper off, and Serafina found pleasure in the sight. They both turned to watch the boy, and finally as the last bit of paper fell to the floor, David's eyes grew large. "It's a sword," he breathed, holding it in his hands.

Indeed it was a curved saber in a sheath

decorated with silver. Dylan pulled the sword from the sheath. "There you are, Master David Trent, a genuine saber from Her Majesty's cavalry — the Royal Dragoons."

"Where'd you get it, Dylan? It's wonderful!"

"I carried it when I was in the Dragoons, old man."

"What a wonderful gift," Serafina said. "David will treasure it always, I'm sure."

David took the sword and had to use both hands to hold it. He started to swing it around, but Dylan laughed, "Wait just a minute or you'll cut somebody's head off."

"Did you ever kill anybody with this, Dylan, an enemy soldier?"

Serafina saw the smile leave Dylan's face, and he dropped his head. Ignoring the question he said, "One of these days you may serve in the cavalry yourself, then you'll have a sword already made."

"I'll keep it always," David said, his eyes shining as he looked up at Dylan. "Thank you very much for giving it to me."

"Can't think of anyone I'd rather have it." He turned then and said, "I have a gift for you, too, Serafina." He saw her look for a package and said, "It's a little different from David's. It's an invitation. They're doing

Handel's Messiah at the Music Hall this afternoon. Have you ever heard that performance?"

"Yes, I've always loved it." She realized what she had said and then tried to cover by saying, "One doesn't have to be a practicing Christian to enjoy music like that."

Dylan smiled at her. "No, but it certainly helps."

"I want to show this sword to Grandfather," David piped up.

"Well, don't run with it. That wouldn't be a very good Christmas if you impaled yourself," Dylan said, smiling.

Dora and Grant had left the kitchen and gone for a walk. They'd had a lovely breakfast, presents had been opened, and now they were walking in the snow. Dora was wearing boots, and Grant, of course, the same. They walked along the path, and Dora said, "I hate to mess up the snow. It's all perfect and smooth, and then you walk in it."

"Still beautiful though," Grant said. "I've always disliked snow. Cold weather was the enemy when I was growing up, but this is beautiful."

The two walked along, and she asked him about the case at Lord Darby's, and he told her what the situation was.

Finally they stopped at a fence and looked out in the field where a flight of black birds had swept low over the snowy ground. She turned to him and said rather breathlessly, "Matthew, I brought you out here for a very special reason."

"And what might that be, Dora?" He studied her and noticed that her smile was wide and pleasantly firm. She'd had an effect on him from the first time they had met that no other woman had ever had. She seemed to colour the world and add something to it, something like a faint charge of electricity. His darkest moments had come when he had thought it impossible that they could ever be anything more than mere acquaintances.

"I wanted to ask you for a Christmas present."

"Why, I don't know what I could give you. You're one of those women who has everything. What could I buy you?" he asked, shrugging his shoulders. "Not clothes or jewellery. Inspectors from Scotland Yard don't make that kind of money."

"No, it's not that I want. I've always had those things. It's something . . . very special." Suddenly she looked down, avoiding his eyes, and he saw that she was twisting her fingers together. She was wearing mittens, but he could see that her hands were unsteady.

"Why, you're troubled, Dora."

"I'm . . . I don't know how to say this to you . . . about what I want you to give me."

"Why, Dora, you can ask anything of me. You know that by this time."

Then Dora lifted her eyes and was still, and he was conscious of her gentle fullness. Her eyes were shadowy, and her breast softly rose and fell with her breathing. The pull of her presence served to strain Matthew Grant forward against his sense of propriety. "I'd give you the world if I had it, Dora. Just ask."

"I want . . . I want you to ask me . . ." She paused and had trouble with the words. "To marry you."

Matthew Grant could not have been more surprised than if the sun had fallen out of the sky. It was the desire of his heart to love this woman and to be with her the rest of his life, but he was a hard realist and knew that the daughters of aristocratic families did not marry policemen. For a moment he could not speak, wondering if he had heard her right, and then he saw the softness in her eyes and the tears gather there.

"Why, Dora, don't cry," he said. He

reached out and brought her forward like a man reaching for something he is afraid he might lose. He saw the faint colour stain her cheeks, and she held him with a glance. And then something whirled rashly between them, swaying them together. He kissed her, and there was a sense of a wild sweetness and an immense shock that came to him. He knew that his whole life was changed at this moment out here in the snow with this woman. He lifted his head and said with triumph in his voice, "I'll have to talk to your father."

It was almost midnight by the time Serafina and Dylan arrived home from the performance. Dylan had purchased three tickets and given one of them to Givins so that he could get in out of the cold. After the performance they had gone to a restaurant to eat before coming home. When Givins had opened the door and helped Lady Serafina out of the carriage, he had put out his hand to Dylan, who took it at once.

"Thank you, sir. It was a wonderful, wonderful thing. I never 'eard such music."

"Why, I'm glad you liked it, Albert."

The two walked up the steps, and Dylan expected Serafina to go inside at once, but she paused and turned to say, "I don't know what's wrong with me. There's probably a name for it, but I just find myself, somehow — I don't know — unsatisfied, I suppose." She turned to him, and the moon cast its skeins inside the observatory, which seemed to coat her face with silver. "I suppose I want more than science. That was always enough for me before, but it isn't now."

Dylan was standing so close he could hear the sound of her breathing. "What is it you want, I mean, as a woman?"

"I want to give David a good start in life."

"That's for him, and you're doing that. But what's for you?"

Serafina was confused, and in the silence and the closeness of that room she heard herself say something she had not intended to. "I'm envious of women who have good marriages."

"Are you now?"

"Yes. I need someone to talk to. There are people all around me. My parents have a good marriage. They can tell each other anything. I guess I need someone too."

"Someone to love?"

"I don't know about that. I had a wretched marriage. You know about that, Dylan. It scarred me deeply. I —" She was going to say something but changed her mind. "It was not a good marriage."

"Well, I know what I would do." Dylan stepped forward and put his hands on her upper arms. She felt the strength of his hands, and looking up she saw a slight smile on his face. "If you weren't the Viscountess Serafina Trent, but were just — oh, say Sara Newton, a cook maybe — I'd know what to do then."

His imagination had always intrigued Serafina. "What would you do if I were Sara Newton, cook?"

"I'd do — this." He pulled her forward and kissed her, and for a moment she resisted. And then, with hesitation, she lifted her arms and put them around his neck. At that moment, to Dylan Tremayne, it was like falling into softness, through layer and layer of softness, and the feeling of it was a goodness without shame. And then he stepped back, and he heard her let out a small sigh as she reached up and brushed her fingertips across his lips. She started to speak but found she could not, for there was thickness and a fullness in her throat, and tears burned in her eyes. Suddenly she leaned forward and put her head on his chest, and then her shoulders began to shake. She had not cried like this since she was a small child, and she was horrified at herself.

Dylan simply put his arms around her, saying nothing. He held her close and put his cheek against the top of her head and smelled the fragrance of her hair.

Finally Serafina, who had been stirred by the moment, looked at him and whispered, "Sometimes, Dylan, at times like this, I wish I were plain Sara Newton, cook." She turned then and left, and he followed her, knowing that somehow they had stepped over a line and could never be to each other what they had been all this time in the past.

Twenty-Two

Sergeant Sandy Kenzie met Matthew Grant as the inspector came through the door to the outer office. Kenzie was a small man with a spare frame and the echoes of old Scotland in his voice. He reached up, stroked his mustache nervously, and said, "How are you today, sir?"

Grant took off his coat, hung it on the hook fastened into the wall, removed his hat, and then turned to face the sergeant. "I'm fine, Sandy."

"You look tired, sir."

"Well, I could use a bit of rest. I feel like a mouse in one of those cages where they run around and around and never get anywhere."

Kenzie clicked his tongue against his teeth and said with a voice touched with sympathy, "It's not going well, sir, I take it."

"It's not going at all, I'm afraid. All we know for sure is that there was a murder done, but as far as evidence, there just really isn't any."

"I'm sure you've done your best, sir."

Grant started to go to his desk, but something about Kenzie's attitude stopped him. "What is it, Sandy? Are you upset about something?"

"Not me, no, sir. I'm vurry well, but the Superintendent, he's been in three times asking when you were going to come in and give him a report."

"I got the messages you sent, but I was waiting until there was something to report." A heaviness seemed to descend upon Grant, and he said, "I suppose he's upset."

Sandy snorted and shook his head. "Upset's not the word, sir. He's frothing at the mouth, if you don't mind my saying so."

"Well, he'll just have to froth, I suppose."

"He — he wants to see you, sir. He left word with me that as soon as you came in, you should give him his report."

"I could write it on the back of a postage stamp," Grant said bitterly. He stood still for a moment, a sturdy man of slightly above average height. His hazel eyes were usually attentive, but now his lids were drooping with fatigue. "All right. I suppose I may as well go in and get it over with."

"I'm vurry sorry you have to put up with

all this, Inspector. It's a shame. I've wished a hundred times —" Sandy broke off and said, "Well, you know what I wish. I think a great mistake was made, and the Yard will pay for it."

Grant understood very well what Kenzie meant. He himself had been bitterly disappointed when Edsel Fenton had been appointed to succeed Superintendent Winters. He had kept his disappointments to himself and determined to do no complaining, and now he tried to smile. "Well, that's the way the world wags, isn't it, Sergeant?"

"I'm afraid so."

"I'd best go see him, I suppose." Turning, he left the office, walked down the hall, and stepped inside the door marked Supt. Edsel Fenton. A sergeant sat at the desk, and as Grant came in he looked up and said, "Good afternoon, Inspector."

"I understand the superintendent wishes to see me." He saw a nervousness in the sergeant and said, "Don't worry about it, Sergeant."

"He's not in a very good humour, sir, I'm sorry to say. You can go right in. He doesn't have anybody with him."

"Thank you, Sergeant." Matthew spread his shoulders, walked toward the door, and, taking a deep breath, opened it, stepping inside. He put his eyes at once on Fenton, who was sitting at his desk, which was covered with paper. His head came up, and his eyes narrowed. "So," he snapped, "you've finally decided to come and let me know what's going on!"

"I'm sorry, Superintendent, I was hoping to find some information that would please you."

"Well, I take it you haven't!"

"No, sir, not really."

Fenton's face was flushed and he shook his head, resembling nothing so much as a bulldog. "You've been on the case for a long while now, and you haven't turned up a single solitary clue?"

"I'm afraid not, sir. We know that there was poison in the wine bottle. We know that the victim sampled it before taking some up to Lord Darby. But anyone in the house could have poisoned the wine . . . The cook did tell me that she once saw Crinshaw do something unusual."

"Do what? Be specific, Grant!"

"She saw him fix the potion and drink it off. He didn't know she saw him, and she never told him about it. But it shows potential for a pattern. Perhaps he sampled Lord Darby's potion as a habit."

"Well, that doesn't help very much, does

it?" Fenton shot a defiant look at Grant, then said loudly, "I've decided to arrest Trevor Hayden."

Grant shifted uneasily then settled back on his heels. "I think," he said distinctly, "that would be a great mistake, sir."

"Don't be a fool, Grant!" Fenton suddenly rose to his feet. He was a corpulent man, overweight, and Grant could see a vein throbbing in his forehead. Grant had often noticed that when Fenton became upset the vein did exactly that. Fenton raised his voice now until it was almost a shout. "You've made a miserable botch of the whole job, Grant!"

"I'm sorry, sir."

"You're sorry! Well, that helps a lot, doesn't it?" Fenton leaned forward and pounded the desk with his fists. He was shouting now, his voice high-pitched and almost wild. "You've got to do better than this, Grant! The papers are crucifying us! I've given you plenty of time, and you haven't done a thing!"

Grant tried to defend himself. "I'm sorry I haven't been able —"

"You haven't been able! My sentiments exactly — and that's why I'm taking you off the case. It's obviously too much for you."

"I wish you wouldn't do that, sir, and I

wish you wouldn't arrest Trevor Hayden. He's too shrewd a lad to do a thing like this, knowing he'd be the prime suspect."

"You're off the case, Grant — and that's final! I'm going to take it over myself." Fenton began to pace the floor, shouting at the top of his lungs. He reached the office wall, doubled up his fist, and struck it. Then he turned and said, "I'll get to the bottom of this! Now, if you don't watch yourself, Grant, you'll go back to being a mere policeman. I'm going to —"

Grant was watching the superintendent carefully, his mood plummeting, for he knew Fenton had been looking for such an opportunity as this. Suddenly he saw that Fenton's mouth was opening and closing rapidly, and then Fenton's eyes protruded as he gasped and clutched at his chest.

"Superintendent, are you all right?" Grant stepped forward and saw that Fenton seemed unable to breathe. He put his hand on the man's arm. "Come and sit down, sir."

"I . . . my chest. It's . . ."

Grant seized Fenton's arm and started to lead him to the chair, when suddenly Fenton let out a strange cry and his legs collapsed. He fell on the floor, still clutching his chest. "Doctor! Get a —" He could not even finish the sentence. His eyes rolled up, and his feet kicked twice, and then, alarmingly, he drew his legs up and was gasping, rapidly drawing in shallow breaths.

Grant jumped to his feet and ran to the door. "Sergeant, the superintendent is ill. Get a doctor here immediately."

"Yes, sir!"

Grant turned and dashed back into the room. He knelt down beside the superintendent and saw that the usually ruddy face of Fenton was now pale, and that he was gasping, and his lips were turning blue. Grant felt absolutely helpless and sat waiting for the doctor to come. Several times he spoke to Fenton, but Fenton never answered. And finally, Fenton gave a hoarse cry and suddenly went limp.

"Superintendent! Are you all right?"

But Superintendent Fenton was not all right. He lay in that particularly relaxed fashion that the recently dead have, and looking down at him, Grant knew the doctor could do nothing when he came.

He rose to his feet and stood looking down at the still figure. He murmured aloud, "Poor man!" He had endured a great deal of humiliation from Fenton, but despite that, Grant felt a gush of compassion for him. He murmured as he looked down at the pale face, "When you got up this morning, you had no idea you would never see the sun rise again!"

Both Serafina and Dylan had returned to Lord Darby's home. They had agreed that as unlikely as it might be, the murderer might strike again. It was always possible, and Serafina said as they sat together in the kitchen sharing a pot of tea, "I'm not happy with the way things are going."

"If you are having my opinion, it seems to me that they're not going at all," Dylan murmured. He turned the cup around in his hand, studied the contents, and then drank it off. "I don't know where to go with this. As a detective, I have nothing to buy a stamp for!"

"The police don't know either."

The two sat there sipping tea and were surprised to see Grant enter the room. He had a strange look on his face and sat down after greeting them. He said nothing, and both Serafina and Dylan watched him with some surprise. Finally Dylan rose, got a cup, and filled it for him. "That's freshly made, Matthew. Can you tell us what's been happening?"

Both of them saw that Grant was troubled — or perhaps just perplexed. He sipped the tea, put the cup down, then looked up at them. "Superintendent Fenton is dead."

"Dead!" Dylan exclaimed. "What happened?"

"It was a violent heart attack. He'd been having heart problems for some time, and he paid no attention to his doctor's orders. I was with him when it happened."

"I'm sorry to hear it. He wasn't a very pleasant man," Serafina said, "but I wouldn't wish that on anyone."

Dylan expressed somewhat the same feelings. He knew the superintendent only slightly and had not been impressed. "Well, who will be in charge?"

"I will be, at least for a while. I've been appointed acting superintendent."

"Why, devil throw smoke!" Dylan exclaimed, his face aglow with a wide smile. "You deserve it."

"I hope they'll make it permanent," Serafina said. "Surely they will this time."

On the way to the Darby estate, Matthew had been thinking about the case and about his new position. "If we don't break this case soon, I may be thrown out on my ear. The public is pretty demanding."

"Right you! If we could solve this case, I would be a happy fellow," Dylan said. He would have said more, but he paused, for

Trevor had walked into the room. He was wearing a pair of brown trousers and a waistcoat against the cold.

"I'm sorry. I didn't mean to interrupt."

"That's all right, Trevor. Come in," Serafina said. "We have some rather sad news."

Instantly Trevor looked behind him. "What's the matter now?" he demanded nervously.

Grant spoke up at once. "Superintendent Fenton died earlier today of a heart attack. I'll be in charge of the case now."

Trevor said nothing, but the three saw that he was nervous. "I suppose that I'm the prime suspect."

"Now don't be foolish, Trevor. You wouldn't be vicious enough to kill anyone," Serafina said at once.

"Nothing has been said from here about that," Dylan said quickly, "and you're a wise man. You'd realize that you'd be the prime suspect."

"Which I am," Trevor said.

"Not to me," Grant said. "I agree with Lady Trent and Dylan. Whoever did this, it wasn't you."

Trevor Hayden straightened up and looked as if a load had been removed from his back. " 'Good to 'ear you say that. I've been worried about it. I . . . I was about to get meself out of 'ere — go back to being a petty thief again."

The door opened again as Trevor was speaking, and Lady Leona came in. Matthew turned to her at once and spoke. "Good afternoon, Lady Leona."

"Inspector, are you back to ask more questions?"

"It's not Inspector now, Lady Leona," Serafina said. "Mr. Grant is now acting superintendent."

"Oh, is that important?"

"Well, it is to me." Matthew smiled slightly.

Leona stood there for a moment, and Serafina asked, "Would you like some tea?"

Lady Leona did not answer. She seemed to have fallen into some kind of mood. Her eyes were usually sharp, but at this moment they were wide and seemed glazed. She turned toward Trevor and said, "Come along, Leslie."

"My name is not Leslie," Trevor protested.

Lady Leona paid him no attention. She took his arm and said, "We have things to talk over, my dear."

Trevor cast an agonizing glance at Serafina, who stood and said, "Let me take you into the parlour. We'll have some tea there, Leona."

"You leave me alone, Edith!" Lady Leona glared almost wildly at Serafina as she bit the words off.

Serafina froze at the use of the name. Edith, she knew, was in the world Lady Leona had created where people who were long in their graves still lived. It disturbed her, and she felt a quick compassion for the older woman. "Are you feeling badly?" Serafina asked.

"What do you care, Edith? You've got what you want! You stole Leslie from me! But I had my revenge, didn't I?" She suddenly laughed, a high-pitched, unearthly sound, all the time glaring at Serafina.

"She's not herself, is she?" Grant asked quietly. "Should we get her son to care for her?" But even as he spoke, Lady Leona turned and walked out of the room.

"She seems harmless enough, but that was strange, her calling you Edith," Dylan said.

"Yes. I've talked quite a bit to Lady Heather about the family history. She knows it all, of course. It's really rather confusing in a way."

"What did she say?" Dylan asked.

"She said that Leona, as a very young girl, was in love with Leslie Hayden. Leona Moore she was then. She was a plain girl, and Leslie fell in love with a woman named

Edith Carrington, who was Leona's cousin. She told me that when Leslie married Edith, Leona had a nervous breakdown. Lady Heather said she never completely recovered, that she would have some sort of spells, she called them."

"What a sad thing," Grant murmured. "Not to get the one you love."

"Oh, she got him," Serafina said quickly. "Edith Carrington died after ten years of marriage and having the three children — Edward, Rupert, and Leah."

"And then Sir Leslie married Leona?" Grant asked.

"Yes, he did," Serafina said, "but not for five years. Leslie was distraught over the death of his wife. He and Edith were a great love match."

"And Lady Leona waited all that time and then finally married him, is it?" Dylan asked.

"Lady Heather was reluctant to speak of the match, but Leona and Leslie did marry and had Arthur."

"He's quite different from the other children, isn't he?" Dylan said.

"Yes," Serafina replied, nodding, "he is. It's a tangled affair, and I'm afraid, sooner or later, Lady Leona will become more than the family can care for here at home."

"Well, the family can handle that. They'll

just hire someone to watch over her, more or less a personal attendant," Dylan said.

"I suppose so. It's sad. She had high hopes for Arthur, but he never seemed to fulfill them. She's had a sad life."

"She seems perfectly logical and clear minded most of the time," Grant said.

"Yes, but her lapses are getting worse," Serafina said. "Lady Heather is greatly worried about her and so is Arthur."

"It's natural he would be worried about his mother."

"Well, I've got to start looking for other evidence and questioning people," Grant said. He drained the rest of his tea and got up. "But bless me. I don't know what other questions to ask."

"You'll think of something." Serafina smiled, and then the three left the kitchen, all of them feeling somewhat depressed over the state of the case.

TWENTY-THREE

Serafina was exhausted as she climbed the stairs. Each step seemed higher than usual, and she had to force herself to go on. Finally she reached the third floor, which was actually the attic that Arthur used for a studio. She and Dylan had divided the day into twelve-hour shifts, one of them always watching over Lord Darby. As she moved toward the door to the studio, she thought, *We can't keep this up. It's too difficult on both of us.*

The door of the studio was open, and she called, "Mr. Hayden —"

At once Arthur appeared. "Why, it's you, Lady Serafina. Come in, please." He led her to the heart of his studio and motioned toward a canvas on an easel. "I've been working on this for some time now. Can't quite get it right."

Serafina moved closer and saw that it was a portrait of Gervase. "Why, you deceive yourself, sir! You've caught her to the life!"

"You think so?" Arthur was pleased, and his thin face showed excitement. "It's for her birthday"

"She will be very pleased," Serafina said. "You have real talent. I always admire artists such as yourself. You do what I could never do."

Arthur's face glowed, and he waved her to a chair. They talked for a time, and finally he said, "I lost my way after my wife died. I just gave up on life — which was terribly unfair to Gervase."

"How long were you married?"

"Only three years." He suddenly turned and pointed to a portrait of a beautiful woman. "That is my wife. She had Gervase when I married her, and, of course, Gervase was easy to love. She still is."

"She's very, very devoted to you, Mr. Hayden."

"Call me Arthur, please. I think she is, and I to her." He looked at the picture on the wall, and the two stood there and looked at it. "I just gave up after she died," he said finally. "It was wrong, I know."

"I know your family must have encouraged you."

"They tried to — especially Mother — but I wouldn't listen. I was wallowing in my grief." He passed his hand over his face as if to brush away a memory. "I've been a great disappointment to my mother."

Serafina said quietly, "Your mother is not well. I'm aware of that."

"Most of the time she's fine. She goes for weeks and is cheerful and goes about her business, not that she has much business. But then her mind goes back in time, and she thinks she's living with my father again. I wonder if this sort of mental illness is common."

"It's not at all unheard of. I did a study on it once. It affects mostly older people. I know you're troubled about it."

"She's had a difficult life. All she has now is me, and all I have is Gervase." He smiled suddenly, and his smile made him look much younger, and there was a pride in his eyes and in his countenance as he said, "She's been the light of my life!"

"It's amazing how much Trevor is like his father and his grandfather," Lady Heather said. She had invited Serafina to have a late breakfast with her, and the maid had brought the food into the sitting room.

"Alike in what way, Lady Heather?" Serafina asked.

"Well, of course, I have only known two

of them — Edward and his father, Leslie. They were quite a lot alike. Both of them thoughtful, very considerate. Both were very even-tempered." She went on describing the things that Trevor had in common with the two men and finally she said, "Trevor is very much like his grandfather, Leslie Hayden."

"I understand he was terribly disturbed after his wife died."

"Oh, yes. He loved her to distraction."

"But he married Lady Leona."

"Well, not for five years." Lady Heather hesitated, picked up the tea to sip it and then put it down. Her eyes were troubled. "I was against the marriage."

"You didn't want her to marry Leslie?"

"No, I didn't."

"What did you have against the marriage?"

"Well, Leona was always a stubborn woman, and even as a girl, she was much the same. She always got what she wanted. A cousin of ours had a pony that Leona lusted after, I mean really coveted. She finally managed to get the pony, although our cousin was brokenhearted."

"She doesn't seem like that kind of woman."

"She doesn't show that side of her character, but she is very stubborn. She wanted

Leslie for years, but he fell in love with Edith."

"I understand Leslie and Edith were very happy."

"Very much in love." Lady Heather's face glowed. "I wish you could have seen them together. When Edith was in a room and Leslie would come in, Edith would just light up. And he had the same love for her. I like to think that Edward and I have some of that in us. But, of course, she died, and Leslie grieved to distraction. Edward talked about it often, how he thought that his father would die of grief."

"How did he die? I never heard."

"Of gastric fever, the doctor said. Some sort of stomach ailment. It was the same ailment that Edith had died of."

Serafina suddenly sat absolutely still, and her eyes were fixed on Lady Heather's face. She did not move for a moment, but her mind was working quickly. "Both of them died of gastric fever?"

"Yes, it was a terrible thing."

"Yes, indeed it is. What were their symptoms?"

"Oh, severe stomach pain. Leslie's skin was affected, a bad rash."

"Was there vomiting and diarrhea?"

"Yes, it was terrible. Edward can't bear to

talk about it."

"And his wife Edith had the same ailment?"

"Yes, that's strange, isn't it? You know, when Leslie was on his deathbed, he told his son that he couldn't bear to think of how Edith had suffered. He was suffering so himself, and he said, 'I know now what she went through, and I would to God I could have spared her.' "

"That's a sad, tragic story," Serafina said. Then she added, "Well, I have some things to do. I'm glad that you are pleased with Trevor."

"Yes, I am. I couldn't ask for a better son."

Serafina took her leave and went to her room. She sat down in a chair and stared at the wallpaper unseeingly. She didn't move for a long time. It was a habit she had formed whenever she was faced with a difficult problem in the laboratory or in logic. She did not move, but her mind was working rapidly, her eyes open but preoccupied with something beyond her field of vision. Finally, after a long time, she got to her feet and stood absolutely still, and her voice was strangely tense as she said, "I must do it!"

Dylan awoke immediately when the faint tapping came at his door. The moonlight was flooding in through the windows, and the grandfather clock in the room he occupied showed that it was almost three o'clock. "Who the devil could that be?" he muttered. He got up and grabbed a robe and slipped it on as he went to the door. When he opened it, he became wide awake. "Serafina, what's wrong? Is it trouble?"

"Let me in, Dylan," she whispered.

Dylan stepped back, and when she stepped in, he closed the door. "Is there trouble? Has somebody attempted to kill Sir Edward?"

"No. Get dressed, Dylan. You're going to have to help me."

"Of course."

Serafina turned her back, and he turned and threw off his robe. She heard his movements as he dressed, and then he was beside her, and she said, "Get your coat. It's still cold outside. And gloves if you have them."

"Right, you."

When Dylan had his coat, gloves, and a hat on, he followed her down the stairs. He saw that she was warmly dressed as well. He did not ask questions, and the house was totally silent. They stepped outside, and she picked up a lantern she had placed there, then led him away from the house. She was headed toward the shop where the horses were shod and the blacksmith did his work. She turned then and said, "You're a wonder, Dylan Tremayne. One man in a million would come on an errand like this without asking questions."

"I think it must be serious for you to ask such a thing."

"Yes, it is." She hesitated then said, "We're going to rob a grave, Dylan."

For some reason Dylan was not surprised. He knew that this woman had strange ways of thinking. He had seen it before. She would sit motionless mulling over a problem and then suddenly the answer would come. "I'm your man. Are you looking for bodies for you and your father to experiment on?"

"No, I'm looking for something more important than that. I don't know what you'll need to get into a casket, likely a very heavy casket."

"A crowbar would probably be best."

The two went into the blacksmith shop, and Serafina held the lantern high while Dylan searched for a crowbar. He found one without any trouble and said, "Ready. Lead me to the tomb."

She suddenly put her hand on his arm and said, "Thank you for being such a good man, Dylan. I didn't think a man alive would do a thing like this without having a fit."

"Am I a rat with green teeth?" He smiled as he spoke. "It's always interesting being with you, Serafina. Just opening up a grave might be one of the minor things that I remember about our relationship. Now, lead me to it. Do we need to saddle some horses? Is the graveyard far?"

"Not at all. It's right over there on the corner of that field."

She led him across the snow. Strips of it were still there, and the grass was stiff and dead underneath. As they moved across the ground, a huge owl sailed over, catching their eye. They saw him disappear and then suddenly drop to the earth. There was a faint scurrying, then a muted cry, and Dylan shook his head.

"There's death on the wings. I wonder what they call a bunch of owls," Serafina thought aloud.

"I don't know, but I've thought about your conspiracy of ravens very often. It seems a fitting thing tonight."

They reached the burial ground, which was bounded by a black wrought iron fence. She swung the gate open and gestured at the mausoleum. "There's where we're going." Dylan moved forward and by the moonlight was able to make out the names — Leslie Richard Hayden and then Edith Marie Hayden, beloved wife.

"Can you get us inside?"

Dylan did not answer. They found that the door was made of heavy oak and was not locked. He swung it back, and she stepped inside. It was a small mausoleum with only two caskets, one on each side. "Which one shall I open, Serafina?"

"Both of them."

She stood there watching as he inserted the wedge of the crowbar inside the top of a heavy casket. He sought for leverage then pushed down. A creaking sound echoed throughout the chamber. He reached out and swung the top back but avoided looking down.

"There you are," he said.

Serafina moved forward and bent over the casket. Dylan did not. He turned slightly to one side and kept his eyes on the open door. He was not a fearful man, but something about this gave him a queasy feeling in his stomach. He saw her put the lantern down, reach into her pocket, and get something out, but he didn't question her. She bent over the casket, and once again he turned his eyes away to avoid the sight of what she was working on. Then he heard her say,

"Very well, Dylan. Put the lid back on." Still looking away from the interior of the casket, he closed it.

"Now open the other one, please."

The other casket opened as easily as the first, and Serafina went through the same procedure. He heard her say, "Now you can close this one." He closed it quickly, and she said, "We can go now."

Relief washed through Dylan, and he walked outside and said, "What now?"

"We've got to go to the lab."

"You mean right now?"

"No, it might alarm someone if they simply found us missing in the morning. We'll go back to the house. We'll have breakfast, and then I'll make up some excuse for us to go back to Trentwood." She said, "Come along. I'll explain what I've been doing." Dylan listened carefully as she spoke, and by the time she got to the house, she turned to say, "We've got to go to the lab quickly."

"Right after breakfast," he said. "You think this will tell you something?"

"I'm a scientist. I don't make guesses. I'll give you my opinion though: it won't take long at the lab before I will know something."

■ ■ ■ ■

The gaslights were on full in the laboratory. Septimus was not there, for which Serafina was grateful. She did not want to explain what she was doing. Her father had a rather solid connection with the police, and it was well for him not to know that she and Dylan had been out robbing graves. She worked quietly, and Dylan sat on a chair watching her carefully but saying nothing. She appreciated his silence, and by the time her work was finished, the sun was high in the sky. She looked at the clock and saw that it was ten minutes till noon. She came to stand before Dylan and said, "Now we know something."

Dylan rose to his feet. "What is it, Serafina?"

"Both Leslie Hayden and his wife Edith were poisoned."

Dylan stared at her in disbelief. "You can tell that? How can you tell?"

"They were poisoned by arsenic, Dylan. Arsenic is an element, so it never breaks down. It remains in its victim's hair, fingernails, and urine. If you're examining a fresh body, you can find an inflamed stomach and probably some arsenic in the digestive tract.

The red blood cells are stored in the veins, and the body usually looks yellow and takes on the appearance of someone who has been very sick. But, of course, these bodies are too old for that. But the hair of both of them is filled with it. If we did a complete autopsy, which we may have to do, I'm sure we'll find more arsenic in the remains."

She fell silent, and Dylan said, "What are you thinking? Lady Leona Moore?"

"Certainly. There's no question about it. We know she hated Edith for marrying Leslie, and then later on, after she killed Edith and married Leslie herself, she found out she could never have his heart or his love. Those had gone to Edith, so Leona killed him as some sort of punishment."

"And how does this fit in with the death of Crinshaw?"

"I am thinking," Serafina said slowly, "of how she confuses people, and how she relives the past. You remember how she mistook me for Edith, and she thought Trevor was Leslie? I found out also that she sometimes calls Lord Darby Leslie. They look very much alike, of course, so that was natural enough. But I think we've got to move quickly. She probably did the poisoning when she was in one of her spells. She may not even remember it, not when she's in her normal state. But we've got to get back. We can't take any chances. Come along, and we must hurry!"

Twenty-Four

Lady Leona had been sitting in her favourite chair crocheting. When the knock came at the door, she lifted her head and raised her voice, saying, "Come in." She kept her eyes fixed on the door, and when Arthur stepped in, she put the crocheted piece down on the table beside her and said, "Arthur, come in. I thought you were the maid."

"No, nothing so grand as that." Arthur smiled. He came over and leaned down to kiss her on the cheek. "How do you feel today?" he inquired gently.

Leona hesitated then said, "Very well. Why do you ask?"

"Oh, it's been a hard time with all this business about Crinshaw's murder, and I worry about you." He pulled a small chair up beside her and asked, "Do you think you could handle a bit of good news?"

Leona looked at her son and smiled slightly. "That's been rare enough in this house. What is it?"

"Well, I've been thinking lately about myself. I know I haven't been the kind of son that you wanted. I know I showed great weakness when I just gave up after my wife died. That was not manly of me."

Leona reached out and touched her son's cheek. "You loved her very much, didn't you?"

"You know I did. She was my whole life, Mother, and when she went away it was like I couldn't function."

"I know well enough what that's like."

"I know," he said. "You felt the same way about Father, didn't you?"

"I loved him with all my heart. Except for you, I gave him more love than anyone else."

The two sat there silently, and finally she shook her head as if to clear it and asked, "Well, what's the good news you're talking about?"

"Ever since Crinshaw died, something has been bothering me. He died so suddenly, and whatever plans he had he'll never complete them now. I got to thinking about myself and my life and my painting. And I've made a decision."

"You're going to take up your career again?"

"Yes," he said. His voice was eager, and

his eyes were glowing with excitement. "I had no idea I had so many paintings. They're stuffed everywhere in my studio. There are over a hundred and fifty of them. Some of them are not much, just beginner's things. I've kept every painting I ever made, except those I gave away. But some of them are very good, and you know Hershel Townsend told me once that if I ever wanted to have a show, he would have it in his gallery. I've written him a letter, Mother, and told him I would like to have a show, and I know he'll be agreeable."

"Why, that's wonderful, Arthur," Leona said. She lifted her head and looked at him with something like pride in her eyes. "That would make me very happy indeed if you would come out of the shell you've been in."

"Well, I have been in a shell, haven't I? It hasn't been fair to you nor to Gervase, and she's been faithful to stay close to me. And I want to promise you this. No more heavy drinking."

"There's a good son," Leona said warmly. "Now, why don't you help me up to the attic. I'd like to see all those paintings."

"Some of them you've never seen. You think the stairs would be too much for you?"

"Not with you to help me." Leona got up

out of her chair and took Arthur's arm. The two of them left, and soon they were climbing the stairs.

He moved very slowly with his left arm around her waist and his right holding her arm, and as they ascended, he said, "I'd like very much to make you proud of me, Mother."

"I am proud of you, Arthur. I always have been."

The horse rose in the air, clearing the large log that had fallen across the riding path, but as he came down, he faltered and dug his front hooves into the ground so suddenly that Trevor was caught unprepared. He shot over the big bay's head and turned a somersault, landing flat on his back. He saw the horse looming over him and feared that he would be trampled, but the hind hooves struck not one foot from his head, and he lay there for a moment weak with relief.

"Trevor! Trevor, are you all right?"

Trevor got to his feet and saw that Gervase, whose mount had cleared the same obstacle easily, had reined up and was coming back. She came up to him, and her eyes were wide. "Are you all right, Trevor?" she asked, her voice tense.

"Oh, yes, I'm fine. Just a clumsy oaf is all."

"That was a hard fall. I've taken many like it myself."

Trevor looked ruefully at the big bay named Pilot. "Pilot," he said, "you're a bad 'orse." Then, changing his mind, he said, "No, you're not." He went up to the bay, held his hand out, and the bay nosed at it and nibbled at his fingers. "You just 'ad a bad rider." He petted the horse on the neck and said, "No more jumping for me."

"You frightened me to death," Gervase said. "When I saw you go down, I was afraid Pilot would land on top of you."

"So was I. You know, I always 'eard that your whole past flashes before you when you think you're about to die."

"Is that what happened?"

"No, I was too scared for that. All I could think of was a thousand pounds of 'orse-flesh landing on my face." He saw that she was still afraid, and he reached out and took her hand. "Don't worry. I'm fine."

"Let's walk for a while," she said.

"All right." He picked up the reins, held them by the very end, and she did the same. They began to walk down the pathway. The snow lay in thin white ribbons, but the earth beneath was exposed for the most part. The ground had thawed somewhat and gave slightly under their feet. Large trees rose in ranks on each side of the riding path, and since the sun was past the meridian now, they were beginning to cast long shadows on the ground.

"This is really a pretty place, Gervase," he said. "I've never seen anything like it."

"I'm glad you think so. I've always loved it. When my father brought me here, I was too young to know much, but I have a few faint memories of how bad things were for him and for me for a while, of course. But then Silverthorn became a wonderful place to grow up."

"What about your birth father?"

"He was a sailor. He was killed in action at sea. I don't know much else about him."

They walked along, and Trevor finally said, "I've been watching Father and Mother since I've come 'ere. They're a 'appy pair. They really love each other."

"Yes, they do, and you've made their happiness complete. I'm so thankful to God that you finally found your right place."

Trevor suddenly halted and turned to face her. She stopped also, and the two stood still for a moment. She could see the clear resemblance to Edward Hayden in his face, and as always, it gave her a strong sense of satisfaction. She said, "You know, so many things don't work out in this world, Trevor. There are so many bad endings to stories."

" 'Appy endings come mostly in books," he agreed.

"But this is like a storybook ending. Here you are, an orphan leading a terrible life, and suddenly out of nowhere, you are found and restored to a loving father and mother who thought you were dead. It's almost unbelievable."

"It is to me. I sometimes lie in bed and think that after I go to sleep, I'll wake up back in that awful 'ouse where I lived in London."

"No, you've found your place."

Suddenly he reached out and took her free hand with his. It was cold, and he said, "Your 'and is cold. You should wear gloves."

"A horsewoman can't wear gloves. She needs to feel the horse through the lines." She was watching him steadily, and suddenly she smiled at him and said, "Anyway, you're holding my hand."

"Am I?"

"Yes, you are."

"Well, that shows my poor breeding. To 'old a lady's 'and is something that gentry would never do."

"Oh, yes they would, and more than that,

I'm afraid."

He tightened his grip and said, "I want to 'ear about all of the young men that you've been interested in. Who gave you your first kiss?"

"Jonah Reardon," she said promptly. "He was thirteen, and I was twelve. He grabbed me and kissed me, and I ran home crying. I washed my mouth off until my lips were sore. I knew so little. I was afraid I'd have a baby."

Trevor suddenly laughed at her. "We learnt about life a little bit earlier than that in the Seven Dials district — most of it pretty bad."

"You're still holding my hand."

"It's from a sense of gratitude," Trevor assured her. "If it weren't for you, I think I would 'ave gone back. Father and Mother were nice, but I was afraid that I would never learn to be a gentleman." He suddenly lifted her hand and kissed it. "First time I ever kissed a lady's 'and."

Gervase said nothing for a moment, and then her voice was quiet as she said, "You do it very well, Trevor. You don't need any lessons in hand kissing."

"What about other kinds of kissing?"

Suddenly she laughed and struck him lightly in the chest with her fist. "That's enough of that now. Come along. Get on that horse. We're going back to the house." She turned, but he took hold of her arm. "I meant what I said. I couldn't have stayed 'ere if it 'adn't been for you."

"I'm glad you feel that way. Are you still worried about being accused of Crinshaw's murder?"

"Yes," he confessed. "I'm still the logical suspect."

"It will never happen. Come on now. Your life is going to be like a storybook. You're going to be cleared of all guilt, you're going to become a gentleman, and one day you'll be the Earl of Darby. You'll marry a beautiful princess and have four children, all girls."

"No, I insist on two boys and two girls."

"Very well, you will have your own way, I suppose." She laughed and said, "Aren't we foolish?"

"Yes, it feels good. Let's go. I'll try not to fall off on the way back to the stable."

After his ride Trevor went to his room, cleaned up, and changed clothes. He intended to go down to his parents' room and spend part of the afternoon with them, but as he was passing Lady Leona's quarters, the door opened, so he said, "Good afternoon, Lady Leona."

"Come in. I want to show you something."

Trevor hesitated, but she smiled and took his hand. "It's something I haven't shown anybody in a long, long time."

Reluctantly Trevor went inside the beautiful room. The walls were covered with a wallpaper such as he had never seen, with figures done in light green and contrasting darker green. The door to the right, he suspected, led to her bedroom. "What is it, Lady Leona?"

"This. You haven't thought of this in a long time, have you, Leslie?"

Her use of the name Leslie was somehow frightening. He did not correct her, but he was afraid of her mental illness. He once had been taken by a friend to Bethlehem, some called it Bedlam, where the insane people of London were kept. They were treated scurrilously, and many of the gentry laughed as if they were strange animals of some sort. Ever since that day he had been afraid of anyone who showed signs of mental problems, and he felt it especially in this room with this woman.

She went to a small Louis XIV desk and opened the drawer, and when she came back, he saw that she was behaving in a strange manner. "Look, you remember this, Leslie?"

Trevor saw that she was holding a beautiful necklace. The chain was of gold, and there was a large red stone. "It's very nice, Lady Leona."

"Oh, yes, it's very nice." She seemed to become more agitated. "You remember that you gave it to Edith, and all the time you knew that I wanted it."

"That — that wasn't me, Lady Leona."

She was almost babbling now. "You always loved Edith. You should have married me, but you married her, and it broke my heart. Oh, yes, it did!" She suddenly reached out and grabbed his sleeve. "I found a way to get my revenge after she was dead. She wanted to be buried wearing this necklace. You didn't know that, did you, Leslie? She told me many times, but when she was finally laid down, just before she was buried, I put another one around her neck, a cheap thing, and I kept this one. It took a long time, Leslie. Finally she was gone."

The old woman was talking in an incoherent manner, and Trevor was trying desperately to think of some way to escape. Suddenly she pulled at him, and he had to follow her. "Here," she said, "sit down."

"Really, Lady Leona, I need to go."

"Sit down, Leslie. You never had any time for me like you did for Edith, but I've got something that you will like." She turned to a mahogany chest, opened it, and pulled a bottle out with a glass. "Look, it's that wine that you always loved so much. This is the last bottle that's left. You always loved it, and Edith did too." She poured the glass full almost to the brim and said, "I want you to share it with me."

"I really don't care for any wine," Trevor said.

"Here, take it." She forced the glass toward him, and automatically he took it. "Now, drink it up. We'll drink to us — to me and to you, Leslie, Earl of Darby."

With resignation Trevor thought, *If I just drink this, I can get out of here.* He started to raise the glass to his lips when suddenly the door to the bedroom burst open. Lady Serafina rushed into the room, followed closely by Dylan Tremayne and Matthew Grant.

Trevor rose, and at that moment Serafina was there to take the glass out of his hand. She smelled it and held it out. "It smells of bitter almonds, Grant; almost certainly it's cyanide."

Grant smelled the wine and then he had a strange look on his face. "I don't know how to handle this. The woman's obviously not responsible."

"What's wrong?" Trevor asked. "What do

you mean cyanide? Poison?"

"Yes." Serafina turned and studied the old woman, who had grown very quiet. "We discovered that your husband, Leslie, and his first wife, Edith, were both poisoned. You did it, didn't you, Lady Leona?"

Leona had been babbling before the trio had entered, but now she had grown very still. She whispered, "She took him from me — but I had my revenge — oh, yes." Suddenly she blinked and looked around with astonishment. It was, they all realized, another one of those abrupt changes. She was staring at the glass in Serafina's hand and then turned to look at Trevor. "Trevor, you're here."

"Well, yes, you asked me in."

"Did I?"

Grant said to Serafina, "What can we do?"

"I'm not sure, but whatever happens will not be pleasant."

"It's going to be hard on Arthur."

Grant pulled his shoulders together in an irresolute manner, and his lips grew thin. He said, "Lady Leona Hayden, I'll have to arrest you for the murder of Charles Crinshaw and also under suspicion of the murder of your husband and his wife Edith."

The words fell from his lips and a sudden silence filled the room, a heavy, ominous silence. Suddenly Lady Leona said faintly, "I must — I must lie down for a moment. Could I do that, Superintendent?"

"Yes, of course. Serafina, would you help Lady Leona?"

Serafina came forward, took Leona's arm, and guided her to the door that entered the bedroom. She led the old woman to the bed, and Leona turned and sat down on it. Serafina reached down and lifted her legs and then helped her lie back on the bed.

"I loved Leslie," she said in a strange monotone, "but he didn't love me. Isn't that terrible when you love someone and they don't love you back?"

"It's very hard," Serafina murmured. "You just lie there for a moment and rest while I go have a word with Superintendent Grant."

"I loved him, and he didn't love me," Lady Leona said. Serafina stared at the woman's face. She had killed three people beyond doubt, and yet there was a pathetic quality to her. Perhaps all mentally unbalanced people have it. Without a word Serafina walked outside. The three men turned to look at her.

"It's going to be terrible for Arthur," Serafina said.

"Who's going to tell him?" Dylan asked.

"I suppose I'll have to do it," Grant

sighed. “It’s the bad part of being a policeman.”

“There’s no easy way. No matter how he hears it, or who he hears it from, it’s going to break his heart,” Serafina said. “He really loves his mother, and I think he was the only thing on this earth that she really loved — except, perhaps, for Leslie and Gervase. Poor, poor woman.”

“Will you stay here with her, you two, while I go tell Arthur, and then I’ll have to go tell Lord Darby.”

Grant turned and left without another word, and Trevor was pale. “I never ’eard of anything like this.”

“You know, I’ve seen death on the battlefield,” Dylan said. “That was bad enough, but somehow it was — I don’t know how to say it — different from the deaths of murdered people, especially those poisoned by one they trusted. I can’t imagine what’s going to happen to her.”

“Will there be a trial, you think?” Trevor asked.

“There’ll have to be some kind of legal action. The woman is guilty of murder.”

“But she’s crazy. Crazy people, they don’t know what they’re doing.”

“The law doesn’t look at it like that, I’m afraid,” Serafina said. Her mind was already working, and she said, "I'll have to get to Sir Leo Roth. He's the best barrister in England. He'll help her if she can be helped." The three stood there talking for some time in a low voice, and then Serafina said, "I'll go sit beside her until Grant gets back."

She turned and walked into the room and at once uttered a cry. Dylan rushed in and looked over her shoulder with Trevor right behind him. They saw Lady Leona Hayden not on the bed but crumpled in a small heap beside her vanity table. There was a bottle before her, a small brown bottle, and Serafina rushed over to it. She smelled it and shook her head. "Pure cyanide! It must have killed her instantly."

"Shall I put her on the bed, Serafina?"

"No, leave things just as they are," Serafina said. "Grant will need to make careful notes. She reached out and touched the woman's silvery hair. "Poor creature," she said. "She saw what was coming, I think, and couldn't bear it. I can't blame her too much." She rose and said, "I'll stay here with her."

"I'll go get Grant," Dylan said.

"I'll go with you," Trevor said quickly. "I need to be with Gervase. She's going to take this 'ard. She loved the old woman."

"Yes, go to her. Help her all you can, Trevor."

The two men left, and Serafina Trent looked back at the crumpled body. "What a waste," she murmured. "What a terrible, terrible waste!"

The shock that had gone through the house when Grant had given them the news that Lady Leona Hayden was dead and also that she was responsible for the death of Crinshaw was past description.

Though Serafina had persuaded Grant not to bring up the matter of the deaths of Leslie and Edith Hayden, Edward and Heather had taken the news about Crinshaw and Lady Leona hard, but not so hard as Arthur, of course. He had been terribly shocked at the news that his mother was dead, and even more so at the revelation that she had killed Crinshaw. His mother had been a difficult person in many ways, but he had told Serafina, "I saw this coming, but not like this. I thought she would go insane and have to be committed to Bedlam. She would have hated that."

"Yes, she would have," Serafina had replied, "but she won't have to go there now."

Trevor had spent most of his time with Gervase, and the two of them had joined to comfort Arthur as best they could. They had encouraged him to go on with his painting after the funeral of his mother, explaining that it would honour her memory if he made a success of his life.

But there was one interview that was kept secret. Grant called Rupert, Leah, and Bramwell into the study that he had been using as an office. They were shaken over the developments — the death of Leona and the revelation that she had murdered Crinshaw.

Grant let them talk, but he finally said, "I must tell you, I have not forgotten the two attempts on Lord Darby's life." He stared at Rupert and said with cold words, "I have a witness who saw you cut the girth on Lord Darby's horse — and if there is any other attempt, I will bring you into the dock. Do you understand me?"

Rupert had turned pale, and for once he was speechless. He nodded and dropped his head to stare at the floor.

"And I have another witness who will testify, Bramwell, that you took a gun and went into the fields on the day a shot came close to killing Lord Darby."

Leah protested, "He didn't do it, Superintendent!"

"You, Leah St. John, were overheard having a conversation with your son — and the two of you discussed how the deaths of Lord Darby and Rupert would please you." He waited for the two to respond, but neither of them spoke a word. "Very well. If there is even a hint of anything irregular, I will have you both brought to trial for attempted murder." He paused again, and when none of them spoke, he said harshly, "I find you beneath contempt," and left the room abruptly.

TWENTY-FIVE

It was the last day of the year, and Dylan settled in his room, looking down at the newspapers that lay before him on the table. It was ten o'clock in the morning, and he had fixed himself a breakfast and had read for a time, and now he was feeling, as he usually did on the last day of the year, a sense of frustration. He studied the papers and saw that there was nothing about the death of Lady Leona. There had been nothing in the papers, indeed, except a brief notice of her death. He smiled as he thought of how Lady Serafina Trent had managed things. He had been with her when she had called Matthew into a conference. She had set out to convince him that there would be absolutely nothing to gain in blackening the Hayden name because of one unbalanced old woman.

"What do you want me to do? The woman killed two people."

"Well, can you put the corpses on trial?" Serafina had demanded.

"Well, of course not."

"What good would it do to print all the facts? You're the superintendent."

"Acting superintendent."

"Don't you have a box full of files of unsolved cases?"

Dylan remembered that Matthew had stared at her with sudden comprehension. "You're asking me to cover this up?"

"She's dead. The man she killed is dead. He has no relatives. If it comes out she's a murderess, think what it will do to Arthur and to Gervase."

"But it's not justice."

Dylan remembered then that she had gone to Grant and put her hand on his arm and looked into his face with a gentleness he had rarely seen in her. "It would be a kindness. Isn't that better than justice?"

Dylan laughed aloud and shook his head. "This woman is dangerous. She shouldn't be allowed loose," he muttered. He thought about going out, but he really had no place to go, and finally fifteen minutes later, when a knock sounded on the door, he opened it and was surprised to see Serafina there.

"Good morning, Dylan."

"Good morning. What are you doing out

this morning?"

"I've come to kidnap you. Get your things together."

"Kidnap me? What are you talking about?"

"You're coming to the house to spend the day with David. Tonight we have our annual New Year's dinner, which will be very good, and you will be there at midnight with the rest of the family to wish everyone a happy new year."

"I wouldn't want to intrude on the family."

"Matthew is coming, and you're coming, so let there be no more discussion about it. Get whatever you need. You'll be staying overnight."

"You're a bossy woman," Dylan muttered, but was quite happy. "Let me get a couple of things, and I'm with you."

She waited until he had donned his heavy coat and put his hat on, and then they went out and got into the carriage. On the way back to the house they discussed the developments of the day.

"I have some news for you — at least I don't think you've heard it, Serafina."

"What is it?"

"Grant told me early this morning before he left that he had been appointed superintendent of Scotland Yard."

"Not just acting?"

"No. Full-fledged superintendent."

Serafina laughed in delight. "Well, that ought to make him eligible even in Aunt Bertha's eyes."

"What about you and Sir Alex Bolton?"

"He's not an honest man, Dylan. I discovered he's broke, so he's looking for a woman with money."

"Good! I hope he finds an ugly old woman with a pile of money — and that he's perfectly miserable."

Serafina laughed then said, "Oh, and tomorrow we're going over to visit Trevor and Edward. I think we need to keep a close watch on them for a while."

"I think that's a fine idea. It's all worked out, hasn't it, with Trevor? I never saw how it could, but the Lord is good to manage things."

"You really believe that," she marveled. "You look around on a world that's full of wrong and evil men being exalted and good people going down, and you can still say that it's a good world?"

"It is a good world, Serafina — at least there's good in it." He turned and smiled. "You're in it, for example, to take a lonely old bachelor out of a gloomy room and put him with a family. You know the Bible says something about that."

"You always have a Bible quotation. What does it say?"

"It says God sets a solitary in families, and that's just what you're doing with me, isn't it?"

They were lighthearted as they talked all the way to Trentwood House, and as they were mounting the steps, David came out, throwing himself at Dylan, who caught him and tossed him high in the air.

"Well, how's the old man today?"

"That's some greeting for Dylan. What about your poor old mother?"

"Mum, I get to see you all the time."

"Well, I like that!" But Serafina was laughing. "I expect you want Dylan to come and play with you."

"Yes, I got it all planned. Come on, Dylan." He grabbed Dylan's hand, and Dylan allowed himself to be towed along.

"I may not see you until supper, Dylan. He has big plans for you, I'm told."

The day had been wonderful for Dylan Tremayne. Instead of a lonely day by himself, he had been dragged around by David, playing every game the boy could think of until finally he had protested, "You're going to put me in the hospital, David. I'm an old man, you know."

But David had succeeded in wearing himself out too. He had taken a nap almost voluntarily, and then that night at the large banquet with which the Newtons celebrated, he had sat beside Dylan and eaten like a field hand. The supper had been magnificent, and afterward they had gone to the parlour where Dora had played and sung for them.

Finally midnight had come, and when the clock gave the last stroke of twelve, a shout had gone up, and everyone had gone around wishing others well. Dylan saw Matthew do something he had never thought he would see. He had simply put his arms around Dora and kissed her, ignoring Lady Bertha's glare and everything else.

After that, everyone had gone to their rooms weary and tired, but Dylan had stayed up and sat on a couch that was drawn before the fire. He was almost startled when a voice spoke. "What are you doing up, Dylan?"

Coming to his feet, Dylan said, "I just hate for this day to end."

"Well, it's 1858, Dylan. A brand-new year." She came over and sat down beside him. "We've had an eventful time. It's been a stressful year, what with Clive's arrest and now with all this trouble over at Edward's."

"But it all turned out all right."

"Yes, it did."

The two sat there for a time saying nothing, and finally Serafina, with a strange look in her eye, turned to him and said, "I'm a little bit disappointed in you, Dylan."

"About what?" Dylan asked, genuinely surprised.

"Were you watching Matthew and Dora when the new year came in?"

Dylan laughed. "Yes, I was. I didn't know Matthew had that kind of boldness in love matters. But he's bold enough where bullets and things like that are concerned."

"I was surprised you didn't give me a greeting."

Dylan was very rarely at a loss for words, but now he stared at her. "You mean —" He halted, not knowing exactly what she meant. He was very conscious of the difference between his station and that of Viscountess Serafina Trent, and he knew now at this point in his life that he had feelings for her that he had never expressed. He saw that she was watching him. She was half smiling, and there was amusement in her eyes and yet a seriousness also. "I believe I did wish you a happy new year."

"I like the way Matthew did it better.

We're good friends, aren't we, Dylan?"

"Yes, we are indeed, Serafina."

"Then I think good friends should express that friendship physically once in a while, like on New Year's Eve."

Dylan saw she was laughing at him, and he suddenly smiled. "Well, let me do it over." He reached out, took her hand, and squeezed it, pumping it up and down. "There you are, Lady Serafina. A happy new year I wish you."

Serafina stared at him. "Is that the best you can do? I thought you were romantic. I'm the one that's supposed to be cold and scientific."

Suddenly Dylan reached over and pulled her close, turning her toward him. He tightened his embrace, and when she looked up, he saw her lips were soft and receptive. He bent his head and kissed her, and at that moment he realized that this woman had something for him that no other woman had ever had. He lifted his head and said, "Happy New Year, Serafina."

"Happy New Year." Her voice was soft and gentle, and he kept his arm around her holding her close.

"You know, I've been thinking," he said. "You're not getting any younger, Serafina."

She stared at him with fire in her eyes.

"What are you talking about? I'm the same age as you are."

"Well, women age more quickly than men, you know. But I've been worried about you, so I've been working on a plan."

She saw his lips curving in a familiar smile and knew that he was teasing her. "What is this master plan of yours?" she whispered.

"I want you to make me a list."

"What sort of a list?"

"A list of all the qualities that your husband must have. You know, faithfulness, generosity, goodness. Anything that you can think of."

"It may be a very long list. My standards are high."

"Use as many sheets of paper as you need."

"And what do I do with this list of qualities that I must have in a husband?"

"Well, you give it to me."

"And what will you do with it?" she prodded.

"Why, I'll begin to teach you how you can get along without most of them."

"Why, you —" She struck him on his arm with her free hand, but he tightened his grip. "Be still, woman. I'm trying to make something of you. We Tremaynes are good at taking women and lifting them up to our station."

She suddenly began to laugh. "You're a fool, Dylan. Sometimes I think you're absolutely insane."

"That's the way it is, but I'll begin to grow on you. Just give me five or ten years, and I'll have you into shape where you'll be a fit partner for me."

She laughed then but reached up and touched his cheek. "Thank you, Dylan. I look forward to having you work on me to transform me into what I should be."

The two sat there laughing, talking, and the fire grew low, but they did not notice.

The employees of Thorndike Press hope you have enjoyed this Large Print book. All our Thorndike, Wheeler, and Kennebec Large Print titles are designed for easy reading, and all our books are made to last. Other Thorndike Press Large Print books are available at your library, through selected bookstores, or directly from us.

For information about titles, please call:

(800) 223-1244

or visit our Web site at:

http://gale.cengage.com/thorndike

To share your comments, please write:

Publisher
Thorndike Press
295 Kennedy Memorial Drive
Waterville, ME 04901

MW

MW

#1 The Mermaid in the Basement
- DC has LP

#2 The Conspiracy of Ravens

#3 Sonnet to a Dead Contessa
- BKM has LP